MY NAME IS
JOE LAVOIE

MY NAME IS JOE LAVOIE

A NOVEL

W.A. WINTER

SEVENTH
STREET
BOOKS®

Inquiries should be addressed to
Start Science Fiction
221 River Street, 9th Floor
Hoboken, New Jersey 07030
PHONE: 212-431-5455
WWW.SEVENTHSTREETBOOKS.COM

10 9 8 7 6 5 4 3 2 1

978-1-64506-053-6 (paperback)
978-1-64506-069-7 (ebook)

Printed in the United States of America

To Libby, adin

As he stepped on the drop, he remarked in a low tone, "Such is life."

PETER CAREY,
TRUE HISTORY OF THE KELLY GANG

Dead people never stop talking.

MARLON JAMES,
A BRIEF HISTORY OF SEVEN KILLINGS

THE LAVOIES, CIRCA 1991

John LaVoie, 1903–1970.

Marguerite LaVoie, 1906–1955. His wife.

Eugene LaVoie, 1924–. Their son.

Yvonne LaVoie, 1924–1924. Eugene's twin sister.

John ("Jack") LaVoie Jr., 1927–1953. Son.

Bernard LaVoie, 1928–1953. Son.

Rhonda ("Ronnie") LaVoie Harrison Adams Grant Gervais, 1931–. Daughter.

Joseph ("Joe," "Jojo") LaVoie, 1932–1991. Son.

Janine LaVoie Devitt, 1937–1963. Daughter.

Michael LaVoie, 1942–1965? Son.

Marie LaVoie, 1942–? Michael's twin sister.

EXTENDED FAMILY

Donald Harrison, 1931–1951. Ronnie's first husband.

Annamary Harrison, 1949–1949. Ronnie's daughter.

Wade Adams, 1932–? Ronnie's second husband.

Michael ("Mickey") Adams, 1954–1977. Ronnie's son.

Roswell ("Rossy") Grant, 1929–1980. Ronnie's third husband.

Bernard ("B.J."), Elaine, and Joseph Grant. Children of Ronnie and Rossy.

Armand Gervais, 1920–. Ronnie's fourth husband.

Judy Oleski LaVoie, 1926–? Bernard's ex-wife.

Robert ("Bobby") LaVoie, 1952–? Bernard and Judy's son.

Edwin ("Eddie") Devitt, 1935–. Janine's husband.

Adriana Cruz LaVoie, 1947–. Michael LaVoie's wife.

Richard and Isabel Cruz LaVoie, 1966–. Twin siblings of Adriana and Michael LaVoie.

OTHERS

Monika Bauer, 1937–? Joe LaVoie's German girlfriend.

George ("Shorty") Gorman, Jake MacDill, Clarence Coover, Jerome Briscoe. Friends of Joe LaVoie.

Arnold ("Bunny") Augustine, 1911-. Northside nightclub owner and crime boss.

Harold V. Meslow, 1919–1991. Minneapolis police detective.

Ernest ("Buddy") Follmer, 1914-. Minneapolis police officer.

William Fredriksen, 1926–1953. Minneapolis police officer.

Thomas O'Leary, 1909–1953. Ottoson County farmer.

Ferdinand Twyman, 1905–? Hiawatha County prosecutor.

Clement Bonsell, 1917–? Joe LaVoie's court-appointed attorney.

THANKSGIVING, 1991

ONE

My name is Joe LaVoie and I'm generally believed to be dead. Probably the only people who know I'm in fact alive are Meslow, the old cop, and what's left of my family. Everyone else has gone away or died themselves or forgotten, which is all right with me. That's the way it works anyway, isn't it? People pay attention as long you're making noise, as long as you're in the news, then forget about you when you're not. Don't say a word in public for thirty, forty years and everyone assumes you've passed on. Well, like I say, whatever you think, that's okay by me.

You probably have to be my age or at least the age of my little brother and sister—the twins, presuming they're still alive, which I don't—for the name to mean anything to you anyway. In 1953, if you lived in Minneapolis or really anywhere in Minnesota and the Dakotas, Iowa, and Wisconsin, the name was famous, *in*famous actually, the most infamous or notorious name there was around here then.

To us, at least at first, it was only a name, *our* name, and it was strange to see it printed in the paper and spoken out loud on radio and TV. I remember my brother Jack shouting, "Who the fuck they talking about anyway?" The three of us were listening to the news on the radio of that '49 Olds, hearing us LaVoies being talked about like the guy was talking about Al Capone or Bunny Augustine. Jack was bug-eyed, he was so mad. He hated people knowing us by our name and then not being factual in what they were saying about us. Bernard pretended he hated it too, but he really didn't—he was excited to hear his name on the radio, something he had wanted for as long as he could remember, and as long as they got his name right, the other stuff wasn't important. I still don't know how I felt about it exactly.

At any rate, that was a long time ago, and even people who are old enough to remember forget. In Minneapolis alone since then I'll bet a thousand people have been killed by gunfire. In the past few years, it's become an everyday occurrence, shop clerks and kids and innocent bystanders getting shot right and left by thugs and each other. There have even been a handful of Minneapolis cops who've been killed. I remember Jack saying a couple of days before the end how Fredriksen wasn't the first cop to get his, and then Bernard chiming in that Fredriksen wouldn't be the last either, the both of them trying to sound like what we'd done was only a piece of a much larger story, when they both knew that what we'd done was big enough to get us crushed like a trio of June bugs. Still, while our own history was about to end, objectively speaking their words were correct. In 1953, it was still big news to kill somebody in these parts, especially a cop.

There isn't a day I don't think about it myself, when I don't replay every word and deed I can drag back from that time, and when Meslow is here and on days like today, when my sister Ronnie gathers what's left of us and we go up to the graves, the thinking and replaying is even stronger. I not only think about the event itself, I think about the name—our name—and what it's meant and what's happened to us on account of it. Sometimes I lie awake the night before, instead of sleeping the usual hour or two not sleeping at all, tossing and turning until the sky starts getting pale through the curtain and then saying to hell with it and sitting up and lighting the first cigarette of another day and looking it straight in the face once more.

You might have forgotten, but I haven't. You might believe me to be dead, but I'm not—not yet—and neither is my name or my memory, which is where I've been living for the past thirty-eight years, if you really want to know.

Since I was released from prison in 1975, I have lived in three different places, each a little deeper beneath the surface than the one before.

First of all, after the Cloud, the prison then officially called the Minnesota State Reformatory at St. Cloud, I went back to the house on Longfellow Avenue in south Minneapolis, where we all grew up and where we were living, Jack and I anyway, when everything came to a head. My brother Eugene was the only one living there when I got out. Eugene had accepted Jesus Christ as his Personal Savior, was holding a legitimate job, and stayed out of trouble for more than two decades since the last time he was sent up. After the deaths and disappearances of the rest of the clan, all there was in the way of immediate family was Eugene and Ronnie. But Ronnie was having problems with husband number three and drinking more than she could handle, so, for all intents and purposes, all that was left of the LaVoies was Eugene.

People still knew who I was in 1975, and they would, every once in a while, come by the house on Longfellow and throw garbage on the lawn or torch bags of dog shit on the front steps or break a few windows. The telephone number had been changed, but you can't change or unlist a street address, and when people connected a particular address with a cop-killer, there was nothing you could do to stop them from coming around. Eugene wouldn't call the cops. Neither would I, but for different reasons. So the two of us would sit with the lights off while green apples the size and feel of golf balls slammed against the stucco walls and sometimes busted a living-room window. Eventually the attackers would stop, bored or out of apples, then scream a few threats and leave. By the sound of their voices I guessed they were too young to have known firsthand what had happened in 1953, but had heard what they knew from their parents or older relatives. For that reason I was never scared so much as infuriated by having to sit there in the dark and take that shit and then stick cardboard in the broken windows so those pissant pricks could have their fun.

There were other problems too, mostly concerning the neighbors, who said they were afraid for their children, but the worst thing about living there on Longfellow was Eugene. I hated him and wanted to kill him and might have done it if I hadn't left when I did. I would've hated Eugene even if I hadn't been convinced he betrayed us, because we all hated Eugene, had always hated him, even before he found Jesus and became something the rest of us, not even Mother, would ever be. Mother had found Jesus too, but it didn't seem to change her or make her life any less miserable, so we never considered it a very powerful force. Jesus's presence was not in and of itself enough to make the rest of us hate Eugene (though it surely contributed) because, like I said, the hatred was there before Jesus was. Granted, there's some mystery to that hatred, to where it came from. I can take a guess, but that doesn't make it less mysterious. Call it an example of Original Sin.

I'd just as soon not get into Eugene any deeper right now, not because it isn't interesting or because he isn't part of the history, but because I can only think about Eugene for so long at a time. Besides, what I was trying to focus on were the places I've been living.

So one day, after about six months at the Longfellow house with Eugene, I called Ronnie. A man answered whose voice I didn't recognize, and when Ronnie came to the phone after several minutes, sure enough, she'd been drinking. I didn't care. I said, "Ronnie, if you don't get me out of here today, I swear to Christ I'm going to kill him." Drunk as she was, she knew who I was talking about. She knew I meant it too. It was ten o'clock in the morning. By noon Ronnie and a black guy I'd never seen before had driven into town and loaded me, my chair, and a shopping bag with my stuff into Ronnie's station wagon and hauled me the hell out of there.

At that time Ronnie and her kids were living in a falling-down farmhouse west of the city, out in the sticks past Lake Minnetonka. She was still married to Rossy Grant, though Rossy had more or less moved out and Armand Gervais, the black guy in the station wagon, had more or less moved in, and little Joseph Grant, her youngest, was only a toddler. I'd always liked Rossy, who grew up in the old neighborhood, and I felt bad thinking he wasn't going to be around, but Gervais turned out to be a good guy too, once you got to know him, and he didn't seem to have the booze problem that Rossy had so maybe he'd be better for Ronnie, whose boozing at the time was almost as bad as Rossy's. The two older kids, I remember, stood and watched with eyes the size of pie plates when Ronnie wheeled me up to the house that first afternoon. They made me think of the twins, who used to stand around and watch the strange and scary comings and goings back there on Long-fellow all those years ago, never once saying a word and thinking who knew what.

Ronnie didn't want me around at first, I could tell. I was inter-rupting her and her new playmate just as they were getting to know each other. She resented having to put something over her tiger-striped underwear when she came downstairs and having to make Gervais wait while she helped me in the bathroom and having to wait until after lunch to pick up the bottle she'd quit pouring when she'd finally fallen to sleep at three or four the previous morning. Not that I cared or took any personal offense. I figured it was her house and her body, and nothing she could do at that point would be a shock to my system. I did feel bad for the kids, though—they were too young to watch their mother play around with someone who wasn't their father and get shit-faced when she wasn't fucking the new guy. Ronnie knew how I felt and resented me for it.

(Ronnie had at least one other child, Michael, presumably by second husband Wade Adams. Mickey, as he was called, was by this time in his early twenties and living out of state. I'd never met him, and Ronnie never mentioned him. A couple years later, I heard he was killed during a drug deal gone bad in St. Louis.)

She also knew that I meant what I said—that I would kill Eugene if I went back to the Longfellow house—and although she hated Eugene as much as I did, she was by that time beginning, in spite of the booze, to assume responsibility for the few of us LaVoies who were still alive. Anyway, after a month or two she got used to having me sleeping in the tiny spare bedroom off the farmhouse's kitchen and adopted the strategy of getting me as liquored up as she was before she went back upstairs to spend the afternoon with Gervais. I suppose she believed I wouldn't hear them or comprehend what they were doing or feel bad about Rossy's kids if I were drunk enough, and I suppose she was right.

For a while then everything was okay. If anyone out in the sticks of western Hiawatha County knew that the cop-killer Joe LaVoie was staying under the Grants' leaky roof, they didn't seem to care. Nobody I was ever aware of drove by to gawk or throw green apples or threaten to put a bullet between my cop-killer eyes. If they had, they probably would've been distracted by all the junk in the yard and the gorgeous blonde in the halter top and short shorts coming and going with a station wagon full of blond kids and a large black man who was definitely not the kids' father. I myself got along fine with the kids and with Gervais, and I got over the discomfort or whatever the hell it was of having my sister take care of me the way I needed, and nobody ever brought up 1953 or prison or anything else they didn't think I wanted to talk about.

Still, there was the strain I didn't recognize at first, but finally did after a few months of living in close quarters with people of the same blood and disposition.

As long as I'd been gone and as much as Ronnie had been through while I was away, I was still as much a part of her life and vice versa as ever, which is to say we were still LaVoies. I would wake up nights thinking I was back on Longfellow Avenue, not alone with Eugene like a few months earlier, but with Mother and the Old Man and Jack and Bernard and the girls and the twins. Eugene was in fact gone at that time, in prison himself, before the legitimate jobs, before Jesus, before he had the house to himself. I'd wake up hearing Mother praying or the Old Man throwing Mother's things around their bedroom. I'd imagine Jack up in his room with his little television set and paperback books, Bernard appearing for the first time in a snap-brim fedora and gangster shirt and tie, Ronnie showing Janine how to wear her sweater backside front so the buttons opened down the spine. In those dreams, one thing would lead to another and pretty soon that fat fuck Follmer would be sniffing around after the girls and Jack and Bernard and I would have our guns in the car and the whole goddamned debacle would be happening again.

Once I woke up after dreaming about my girlfriend Monika back in Nuremberg, but Shorty Gorman was in the same dream and the two of them together like that spoiled it, made me want to kill them both.

It was the booze of course and being around Ronnie who tried but couldn't help herself, not then anyway, not when she was drinking the way she was and who still, in her middle forties, had a young woman's body and was still compelled to show it to every man she came across, even her damaged brother because damaged or not he was or had been a man—it was the booze and Ronnie and what she still couldn't help at that time that made me have those dreams.

It was also Rossy Grant coming back one afternoon, slinking in the back door like a thief in his own house while Ronnie and the kids were out shopping with Gervais, telling me he watched the house with binoculars from his car parked up the road, even confessing to jacking off while watching Ronnie in her halter top through the glasses. Crying, he said he had a gun in the car but couldn't work up the nerve to kill the nigger for taking what belonged to him. Rossy was drinking even more than the rest of us, if that was possible.

Roswell Grant was born big and blond and powerful. Back in the old neighborhood he was as well-heeled and handsome a kid as we knew or could imagine. His old man had gone to college, played first-string tackle at the University of Minnesota, and now sold hardware—shelving and soda-fountain fixtures, I believe it was—to drugstores and five-and-dimes. Big and strong as he was, Rossy was too fearful a kid to play serious football and too reckless and eager to please as a young adult to hold onto the money his father supposedly gave him.

Everybody liked Rossy except his old man, who thought he was a pansy. The girls didn't care about the football or the money. They cared about Rossy's movie-star smile, broad shoulders, and gargantuan equipment, and they lined up to let him have his way with them. Ronnie was a month shy of fifteen the first time she had sex with Rossy. She'd had sex with him on a fairly regular basis ever since—through two marriages to other men, through their own stormy marriage, through three kids and a dozen affairs on both sides and everything else that had happened to them and their families. Now Rossy was afraid he'd never fuck her again.

"Talk to her, will you please?" he begged me in the dilapidated kitchen of the house that was falling down around us. "She always listened to family." Well into his forties, Rossy was still big and blond, but he no longer seemed very powerful and he needed dental work. He wasn't rich anymore either and, truth be told, probably never was—that had all been part of his lie.

I liked Rossy and wanted to help him. I wanted to—and yet I didn't. Something, maybe the booze, made me want to see Rossy suffer, miss out, be deprived of what he wanted most. Back in the old neighborhood I once walked in on Rossy fucking Ronnie on my parents' bed. They knew I was there, but it didn't matter. Their naked indifference to me was worse than the sex. The image came back to me at that moment. I sat there and watched him cry, yet I shook my head and said not one word that might give him comfort or hope. For a minute I thought he might use the gun he said he had in his car on me, then wait for the others to come back to the house and kill them, and for a minute I felt that wasn't such a bad idea. Then I thought about the kids who had nothing to do with any of this but would pay the most anyway and decided that both of us sorry bastards should get the hell out of there right then.

When Rossy finally left, I wrote Ronnie a note and called myself a taxi. It would cost a fortune for a ride all the way downtown, but when you got to go, you got to go. I had to go, so I went.

It seems odd now, almost twenty years later, to think about Ronnie and the kids, and poor Rossy too, out there in that farmhouse, and how everything has changed since then.

My life, it occurred to me the other day, can be broken down into more or less equal twenty-year parts almost like the sections of a book. The first part, not counting my three years in the Army, was spent on Longfellow Avenue, everyone alive except baby Yvonne and living together under one roof, and ran until 1953. The second was spent, most of it anyway, at the Cloud, me a convicted cop-killer considered so great a threat to society that even without a functioning lower body I was twice denied parole—hell, I was denied the so-called privilege of attending the funerals of my mother, father, and little sister. The third began, as I've related, back on Longfellow Avenue in 1975, continued for a short while at Ronnie's place in the sticks, then proceeded to these present digs, in this shitty apartment, less than a city mile from where everything began.

I sit here now, waiting for Ronnie and the kids to come for me in their van, to go up to the graves, then go to Ronnie's current home for Thanksgiving dinner. You think you'd know a place inside and out if you lived there as long as I have—what now, more than fifteen years?—but the truth is I can't describe the wallpaper in the kitchen. I'm here, most days, round the clock, day and night, but the only thing I can tell you for sure about the place is that it smells like the bacon and onions my neighbors across the hall eat three or four times a week and that the building belongs to Harold Victor Meslow, MPD retired.

Meslow, you might remember if you're old enough to remember

me and my brothers, was the cop who the papers said tracked us down after we killed Patrolman Fredriksen. R.A. Walsh, the Minneapolis police chief at that time, got most of the press during the dragnet, but it was Meslow who got the credit in the end. People probably still believe it was Meslow who gunned us down in that swamp north of the city, though in fact Meslow only held the umbrella that kept the sleet out of the eyes of the shooter, whose name was James Finnegan. Meslow doesn't like the umbrella story and probably wouldn't mind if we forgot about Jimmy Finnegan altogether.

Meslow retired from police work twenty years ago. He'd left the MPD in about 1960, when he didn't get Walsh's job when Walsh retired, and went out to some place in Colorado—Fort Collins, I think it was—where he finally secured a chief's badge. When he retired from that job he came back here and settled down to manage the real estate he'd invested in when he was a Minneapolis cop. It wasn't a lot, three or four small apartment buildings, but it gave him something to do while topping off his substantial pension. Supposedly he was still angry about the way his local law-enforcement career turned out and wanted something different to concentrate on.

He stumbled across me going into the downtown YMCA two days after I left Ronnie's farmhouse. It's hard to believe it was an accident, the two of us bumping into each other that way after all those years, but I can't explain it any other way. He looked pretty much the same as the last time I saw him, which was probably the last day of the trials, and so, I guess, did I. At any rate, we recognized each other right off the bat, and while I'd just as soon have kept going he reached out and caught one of the handles of my chair and said, "Jojo LaVoie, what's the rush?"

Nobody but family and the cops ever called me "Jojo," which one of the girls might have started calling me when we were little, and I didn't like it when the cops used it. I squinted up at him through my dark glasses—squinted up into that long, sad, wolf's face of his—and said, "Detective fuckin' Meslow."

He kind of maneuvered me off to the side, out of the way of the foot traffic there on Ninth Street, and asked me if this, meaning the Y, was the best I could do for a place to live. (He was pretty sure I wasn't there to swim or play handball.) I said it was fine, and he said what's the matter with the family, and I said the family was none of his damn business. He sighed and said, "Come on, I'll buy you a cup of coffee." I noticed he didn't call me "Jojo" a second time, so I thought what the hell, what harm would it do, he and I didn't have any business anymore, it was just the two of us private individuals, and one of us wouldn't object to a cup of coffee that he didn't have to pay for.

We went into a coffee shop around the corner and Meslow told me he'd been out West (which I'd heard already, through the grapevine) and that he'd retired and was taking it easy nowadays. I said, "Same here," and waited for him to grin at the joke, but he didn't. He didn't pay any attention to the chair either, once he'd helped maneuver my legs under the table.

Meslow had always struck me as kind of odd for a cop, not at all like that fucker Buddy Follmer, not loud and mean and predatory, not a bully and not someone who'd take advantage of his situation. (At least that was my impression.) Meslow was quieter than most cops I'd come to know, more thoughtful and maybe a little smarter, and almost always wore a disappointed expression on that long face of his. He'd apparently never gotten married and didn't socialize much with other cops either, so naturally he was known around the Courthouse, I'd heard, as the "Monk." Not that I gave a shit about any of that. And not that it made me like the guy. As my brother Jack would say, a fuckin' cop is a fuckin' cop.

Sitting there drinking coffee after all those years, Meslow asked me the obvious questions about life at the Cloud and what I planned to do now that I was out. Before I could make up something to say he said he had a place for me to live, in one of the buildings he owned, just off East Lake Street in the old neighborhood. He said he wouldn't

charge me rent. All he wanted was someone he knew on the premises—"someone to keep an eye on things," is how he put it. There were
three floors plus the basement, but there was an ancient elevator and
he had a guy who did repairs, cut the grass, and shoveled the walk in
the winter.

"Why me?" I asked him, expecting some bullshit about giving a
con a second chance, but all he said was, "Why not?" I thought, *Okay,
why not*, and although it all seemed peculiar as hell I thought about
Eugene in the house on Longfellow, Ronnie out in the sticks, and the
airless room upstairs at the Y, and figured I couldn't do much worse. If
anybody asked, I'd lie about the identity of my landlord.

What Meslow really wanted out of the arrangement was obvious
a long time ago, although nobody except the two of us seems to know
or give a shit, and it's turned out to be not such a bad deal for me.
Neither Eugene nor Ronnie has ever asked who owns the building
where I've been living the past fifteen years, and both seem happy
that I'm living independently and managing to make ends meet on
what I get every month from Hiawatha County. (The county also
sends a social worker once a week to check on my well-being and a
"health-care aide" every day to help with my physical functions.)
Meslow himself doesn't come around all that often anymore, for that
matter. He never says anything about it, of course, but I think he's
sick, maybe dying, because unless it's my imagination, his face the last
several months has been longer and grayer and sadder than usual. His
eyes have a yellow cast to them, and he coughs more than he ought to.
I wonder how I'll feel when he's gone.

In January I'll be sixty. My life is entering its fourth twenty-year
interval, and I have to acknowledge that the third as well as the second
has one way or another belonged to the son-of-a-bitch.

One night not long ago I dreamed about him. He was pawing
through the clothes in my father's closet on Longfellow. I was standing
in the back of the closet, behind the Old Man's sour-smelling suits and
trousers, and although I couldn't see Meslow's face and was too young

in the dream to know anything about him, I knew it was him. I woke up wondering if he had been a part of my life from the beginning.

Ronnie's van pulls up below my first-floor picture window and out hops her grown-up boys, B.J. and Joe. The B.J. stands for Bernard John, but nobody except my brother ever wanted to be called Bernard and nobody calls a kid Bernie nowadays so it's been B.J. from the beginning. Joe is short for Joseph Michael, my first name and the first name of my youngest brother, one of the second set of twins. Naming the boys after LaVoies was as much Rossy's idea as my sister's, Rossy always preferring the LaVoies to the Grants, saying the LaVoies, for all their problems, were more of a family than the Grants were, which I didn't fully appreciate at the time but was another reason I liked the guy. At any rate, the boys are both spitting images of their old man, big and blond and powerfully put together. The women are wild about Joe especially, Ronnie says, even though he's only seventeen. B.J., who's twenty-four and for a while dated a Vikings cheerleader, currently lives with a very attractive divorced woman in her thirties, which says something about *his* appeal.

The two of them are up the steps and in through the door I left open. I'm ready to go in my winter coat and blanket, my herringbone newsboy cap and dark glasses. After a kiss from each of them on my stubbly cheek, the boys roll me out the door and down the short ramp Meslow had built for me to the sidewalk. Ronnie's van is a dark blue Ford Astro with black M.I.A. stickers on the bumpers. Without a word, the boys lift me into an open sliding door on the passenger side. Dead weight to myself, I must be light as a feather to my nephews, who handle me the way Rossy must have handled them when they were tykes.

Ronnie sits behind the wheel, her head wrapped in a gauzy kerchief and her face all but hidden behind big round sunglasses. She turns in her seat and smiles at me, and then her own spitting image—her and Rossy's twenty-year-old daughter, Elaine—blows me a kiss from the jump seat and for one split second I'm so happy I could cry.

Gervais doesn't go to the graves. He jokes that black people don't like cemeteries, though I'm not sure it's a joke. Anyway, he has no problem with Ronnie going up there and taking the Grant kids with her, Gervais having had some family of his own die early and violent deaths and is therefore sympathetic. (I don't know the details.) Besides, today is Thanksgiving, and he doesn't want to miss the football on TV.

"Hungry?" Ronnie asks me over her shoulder as she points the van toward Cedar Avenue.

"I can wait," I tell her. The truth is, my stomach is on fire, and I don't have much of an appetite.

"You look great, Jojo," Elaine, now sitting beside me on the back seat, says, lying through her teeth. She is blonde and blue-eyed like both Rossy and her mother, with Ronnie's face and figure. Men look at Elaine the way men used to look at Ronnie, and, like Ronnie used to do, Elaine looks back. She's wearing a purple-and-gold Vikings jacket, tight faded jeans, and scuffed cowboy boots.

"Not as good as you do, kiddo," I tell her, and she shows off the LaVoie dimples.

There's not much traffic on Thanksgiving—Gervais isn't the only football fanatic planted in front of the television today. We head north on Cedar, cut through the ragged part of town people used to call Seven Corners, then get on the freeway heading toward Crystal Lake. Even in our part of the South Side, where there doesn't ever seem to be much going on except the neighborhood getting shabbier and more dangerous, I see something new every time someone takes me out. When I was a kid and had just come home after almost three years in Europe, I remember walking around town thinking what a small, drab city it was, such a plain little burg compared to Paris and London and Rome, and then coming back after almost twenty years at the Cloud and thinking it was the biggest, loudest, scariest place I'd ever seen. Now the city seems plain again, but always changing and parts of it, like I say, getting more dangerous.

Maybe that seems funny to those of you who remember us. For

a couple of months in 1953 my brothers and I were the reason people were afraid in this city. *We* were the danger, or so people thought, like we were running around looking for people to hurt, preying on law-abiding citizens the way the gangs do today. There might have been a moment here and there when each of us considered ourselves dangerous, at least when provoked, but the fact is, except for those few brief moments, no one in the world was more afraid than the three of us, two of the three of us anyway. Fredriksen and O'Leary, the two guys we killed, were never any scareder than us LaVoies, I promise you.

I can't tell you why the family graves are at Crystal Lake, way up on the North Side, where none of the LaVoies ever lived unless it was before any of us knew or could remember. Maybe it was the only cemetery space available when my mother and father first needed it, for my oldest sister, Yvonne, who died in 1924 at the age of six months, or maybe it was the only spot they could afford. It's a pretty place, full of mature oaks and evergreens and even a few of the big elm trees that survived the disease that took so many around town ten, fifteen years ago, and larger than you might expect a cemetery to be in the city. Maybe back in 1924 Crystal Lake was outside the city line, but I doubt it, because there are old houses all around it and the houses, some of them boarded up now, are city houses, not the kind you find in the suburbs. My sister Yvonne, as far as that goes, wasn't the first person buried here. Crystal Lake was already old then, almost seventy years ago, judging by the dates on a lot of the tombstones.

The Old Man used to take us up here when I was little. That was before Janine and the twins were around, but even so there were five of us kids and somewhere the Old Man would have gotten hold of a car and all of us except my mother would ride all the way up here to stand around Yvonne's grave. At first it was something I liked to do, because we never went anywhere otherwise, not that I can remember, and in those days, before the freeway, it was a long, exciting ride. The Old Man didn't own a car, but somehow, like I say, he managed to borrow or steal one somewhere, and if it wasn't too hot that day and I didn't get car sick I considered it an adventure.

The huge elms were still here in large numbers, and it was like we had passed from the city into a forest—it always seemed shady and cool. I remember Ronnie holding my hand and the two of us running up the paths between the rows of graves and headstones and picking up sticks and chasing after toads and garter snakes. I didn't pay much attention to Yvonne's grave at first, Yvonne being only a name I'd heard, and probably didn't understand that she had been my sister and Eugene's twin. I guess, as far as that goes, I wouldn't have known what a twin was in those days because I'd never had a chance to see Yvonne and Eugene together and because the second set, Michael and Marie, hadn't been born yet.

During one of those visits—it was a hot and windy summer day when I must have been about eight—I heard Jack say to Bernard, "Jesus Christ, listen to the Old Man carry on. You'd think she'd croaked this morning." The words themselves didn't mean as much to me as the way Jack said them. The words came out from between clenched teeth and sounded like sparks from a machine. For the first time since we'd been coming up here I forgot about the toads and the snakes and looked over at the Old Man and, to my surprise, saw him down on one knee, his sweaty hat in one hand, the other hand a fist pressing against his forehead, the corners of his mouth jerked down like a sad clown's, and him crying like a baby. There was a dusty gray stone about the size and shape of a brick in front of him and a little bouquet of yellow flowers lying against the stone.

"Fuckin' hypocrite," Jack muttered. "He's the one that shoulda drowned down there."

"Shit, he probably drowned her himself," Bernard said, trying to sound as angry as Jack.

Jack would have been about thirteen at the time, Bernard a year or so younger, but the anger in their voices, especially Jack's, made them seem like grownups. I was so surprised—shocked really—that I started to cry. I didn't know why I was crying, only that it had to do with the sound of my brothers' voices. Ronnie must have gone off somewhere, because I was standing there by myself, and when I looked back at the Old Man I saw that he was looking at me now and wasn't sobbing anymore.

He stared at me and said, "What the hell are *you* blubbering about?" The way he looked at me, his face red and wet and angry now too, and the words so unexpected—he hardly ever spoke to me at all—confused and embarrassed me. Jack and Bernard had gone off a ways, and all of a sudden it seemed to be just the two of us, the Old Man and me, there at Yvonne's tiny grave.

I shook my head and tried to think of something to say, but nothing came out, and by the time I thought of something he had forgotten about me and was leaning forward over Yvonne's gravestone, beginning to weep again.

"Fuckin' hypocrite," I said, but he didn't seem to hear me.

The memory of that day—of that conversation, if you can call it that, between my father and me—makes me laugh out loud. Everybody in the van turns to look at me, even Ronnie, taking her eyes off the exit ramp she's just turned on to. Elaine asks what's funny.

"I was thinking about my dad," I say. "What I said to him once."

"What?" Ronnie says, her eyes back on the road, turning onto the street that will take us into the cemetery.

"I called him a fuckin' hypocrite," I say. One of the boys laughs out loud.

"Jack said that," Ronnie says. "That's what Bernard told me."

"I said it too," I say.

"What did *he* say?" Elaine asks me, meaning her grandfather. She was too young to have known the Old Man, born a year after he dropped dead in a Met Stadium men's room, but she's heard the stories.

"Nothing," I tell her. "I'm pretty sure he didn't hear me." I laugh again, but I can tell that Elaine and the others can't appreciate what's

funny about the story. You'd have to be there, as they say. They don't
know that I was eight at the time and wouldn't have known a hypocrite from a hippopotamus.

I decide it isn't worth my breath to explain. It hardly ever is.
Besides, the Crystal Lake gate is right in front of us.

It's windy today too, and it's a cold, biting wind that pushes dead leaves
and gum wrappers across the cemetery northwest to southeast, cutting
across where we're walking. When we get out of the van, Elaine bends
over me and pulls the blanket up around my shoulders and then Ronnie
bends down and fusses with what Elaine did and then Joe takes the
handles of my chair and begins pushing me up the path, which rises
and falls depending on where you're going. I hear B.J. lighting a cigarette a few steps behind us.

Cemeteries aren't busy places on Thanksgiving. There isn't anyone
in sight except two black kids on bicycles a couple of paths over,
watching us or more precisely watching Elaine in her purple jacket and
tight jeans. Since Ronnie began bringing us up here a few years back
we've more or less fallen into a routine, where we go first to our parents'
graves, then to Yvonne's, then to Janine's, then to Jack's and Bernard's.
Because they didn't die at the same time and because we didn't own a
family plot the graves are spread out, in different parts of the cemetery.
It's a big place, Crystal Lake, though not half as big as I remember it as
a kid, so there's a fair amount of walking. There's also a lot of uneven
terrain, like I say, so paying your respects to the dead LaVoies can tire
you out even if you're only along for the ride.

This time of year most everything is blanketed by brown and
yellow leaves. At our parents' graves Ronnie pulls a whisk broom out
of her coat pocket and clears the leaves and litter off the stones. Behind
Ronnie the rest of us form a little semicircle leaning into the wind and
the tumbling leaves. No one says a word—everyone just looks down at
the identical markers.

†

MARGUERITE ANNA LA VOIE
MOTHER
1906–1955

†

JOHN MICHAEL LA VOIE
FATHER
1903–1970

The stones are polished granite rectangles set in cement more or less flush with the ground. They were ordered and paid for by Ronnie and Eugene about five years ago to replace the original markers that were supplied by the county and looked like all the other county-supplied markers at Crystal Lake. I don't know where the Old Man was or what he was doing when my mother died, only that he wasn't at home and wasn't working, and I was in prison and no one else was old enough to buy a gravestone or had the money if they were. What was left of the family was on what they called relief, and because of who we were in 1955 no one, not even Mother's fine Christian friends at the All Saints Tabernacle of the Risen Christ, was willing to provide any serious money for a LaVoie memorial. Things weren't much better when the Old Man dropped dead fifteen years later, at least as far as the money was concerned.

"I can't believe she just sat down in that park and froze to death," Elaine whispers above and behind me.

"Today I can," says Joe, shivering and making the chair shiver a little too.

For the record, Mother died on either the first or the second day of 1955, after wandering away from the county-funded nursing home where she'd been staying, not far from Powderhorn Park. Police found her body curled up in the snow under a picnic table, wearing only a housedress and mismatched carpet slippers. She had died, it was ruled, of exposure.

I still find it hard to believe the Old Man dropped dead while relieving himself at the ballpark, but that's only because the cops were looking for him at the time and no one thought it was possible that he was still in town. An inept, booze-addled, small-time hoodlum who, when he wasn't in jail or the workhouse, ran errands and did odd jobs for Bunny Augustine, kingpin of the Upper Midwest's dominant underworld organization. What he was doing and where he was staying at the time remain a mystery to this day, that is if anybody cares, which I'm sure they don't.

Ronnie says, as she always says, "Poor woman," and makes the sign of the cross, although neither she nor Mother was Catholic. I've only seen her do that at the graves.

At Yvonne's grave another thirty yards up the same path no one says a word. Yvonne drowned in a few inches of water in a basement laundry tub five months after she was born in 1924, supposedly when Mother got distracted while bathing her. None of us was around when Yvonne was alive. Only Eugene, her twin, has any firsthand connection to her at all, but Eugene, being a baby when she died, remembers nothing. And Eugene isn't present at the graves today.

I don't remember when I first understood that there had been another kid in the family—for all I know it was the day the Old Man hollered at me over Yvonne's grave. I do remember being afraid to go into the basement laundry room, not only because of the centipedes and silverfish, but because I somehow knew that Yvonne had died in that deep concrete washtub. Although Jack and Bernard used to say the Old Man drowned the baby in the tub, I never believed it. Even so, it was a terrible thing to think about, drowning down there in the dark, among the bugs and God knows what else lurked in the dank shadows, and I remember having nightmares about it once I found out.

Yvonne's marker is the brick-sized stone it's always been. Ronnie talks about replacing it like she replaced our parents' stones, but it never gets done, maybe because Yvonne has never really existed for us, was only part of a story. We can look at Eugene and try to picture what his twin sister would look like at his age, sixty-seven, but Eugene is Eugene and nobody else, no matter how hard we wish he wasn't, so that exercise isn't much use. When all's said and done, poor little Yvonne, born in March 1924 and dead a few months later, is nothing more than a faded name, another LaVoie that no one hardly remembers.

Ronnie bends down with her whisk broom and shoos the dead leaves away from the stone, which seems the least we can do under the circumstances.

Joe is pushing my chair toward Janine's grave, which is another fifty yards past Yvonne's, when I hear one of the black kids on the bicycles saying, "Who you be lookin' for, lady?"

I look over my shoulder and see the kids on the next path to our right, straddling their fat-tire bikes like a couple of cowboys on horses, in front of Elaine and B.J. The boy is speaking to Elaine and seeming to ignore B.J., which is hard to do because he is large and possibly dangerous. But Elaine is Ronnie's daughter and not afraid to speak for herself. She says, "We aren't *looking* for anyone. We know where we're going."

The other boy says, "We be your guide if you can't find a tomb you want."

Joe stops, turns toward the boys, and as he turns, turns my chair in their direction. Ronnie is behind us. Now we're all looking at the boys, who don't strike me as shy. One of them is tall and very thin, so black he's purple, the color of an eggplant, his bare head shaved so it shines. The other one is shorter but just as thin, maybe thinner, with lighter skin and a full head of curly, reddish hair. Both are wearing team jackets like Elaine's, one black and silver with a pirate on it, the other blue and silver with a five-pointed star. The tall one is wearing silver sunglasses. I'm amazed at the balls of these kids, thirteen or fourteen years old if that—no hesitation at all about stepping up and blocking the path of other people, even when the people they're blocking are older and bigger and more numerous. *Brazen* was what the newspapers called us sometimes, but we were pussycats compared to these guys.

"We don't need no guide," says B.J. "We been here before."

The other kid glances at B.J. and then says to Elaine, "You know a lot of people in these tombs, huh?"

"Just family," Elaine says.

"How many?" the first kid says.

"There are six altogether," she says.

I can't believe we're having this conversation.

The first boy squints at her. "Six," he says. "How come they not in one place?"

Elaine has finally had enough.

"Excuse us," she says and steps between the boys on their bikes. B.J., looking at first one, then the other, follows her. The boys look her over as she passes, the tall one lifting his silver shades, his eyes dropping to her tight jeans, but just stand there straddling their bikes.

"We be your guides," he says. "We know all the tombs."

Elaine and B.J. keep walking and say nothing. One path over, Joe exhales, turns the chair back in the direction of Janine's grave, and pushes me up the rise. "Fuckin' boogs," I hear him mutter. "I'm keeping an eye on those shitbirds till we're out of here."

I've had two black friends in my life—Jake MacDill in Germany and Clarence Coover at the Cloud. Jake was laid back and mellow, with an easy smile and a deep voice that made me think of black coffee. C.C., who would've been about the same age as Jake, in his middle twenties, was something else, a smart, tightly wound, corner-cutting, don't-turn-your-ofay-back-on-me kind of spade. I'm pretty sure he'd been extremely dangerous until he was shot in the spine by the owner of the liquor store he'd just robbed and cut. He'd come from a big, well-known family in St. Paul, the youngest son of a Baptist preacher, and must have been a holy terror the way people talked about him. He'd been at the Cloud since he was nineteen, sitting in his chair in

the prison's hospital wing for almost five years by the time I got there.
I was scared of him because of what people said and because he was so
different from Jake, the only other black guy I really knew until then,
and I didn't believe it when people said that *he* was scared of *me*.

Then one day when they'd wheeled us to the same table for lunch
he said, "You the boy that shot the cop, right?"

I shook my head.

He said, "You shot the other man too, that farmer you grabbed."

I wasn't talking to anybody about anything at that time and I sure
as hell wasn't about to start confessing or denying things to some shine
who'd stabbed a guy during a robbery, so I shook my head again and
kept my mouth shut.

But he looked me up and down with his yellow eyes and said,
"Well, you up for shootin' a cop, I guess you wouldn't mind shootin' a
nigger too."

I didn't know what exactly C.C. meant by that, but I was surprised
by the way he said it, and without really thinking I heard myself saying,
"I didn't shoot anybody."

He looked at me again and shook his head. "Whatever you say,
man," he said, "that's okay with me."

Several years later, just before I got my parole, Clarence said he
was scared of me way before we sat together in the canteen. He said
he figured I was criminally insane and murdered people for no good
reason, even cops. He said he'd heard that the LaVoies were crazy from
the parents on down, like those wild-ass hillbilly families in the mountains down South. I remember laughing when he said that and telling
him that maybe he wasn't too far off base, at least about the family.

At Janine's grave someone put plastic flowers in front of the big
polished stone, bright red and yellow flowers that looked phonier
than usual with the grass dead and out of color. Ronnie says that
Eddie Devitt still makes a special trip up from Kansas City to visit
Janine's grave on her birthday in September. The flowers came from
Eddie and say something both good and bad about the poor bastard,

another one of my several ex-brothers-in-law, the only one still alive and accounted for.

It's easier, now as always, to think about Eddie Devitt than it is to think about Janine. Janine is difficult to think about for a lot of reasons. She's as difficult to think about alive as dead in fact, and not just for me either, although it's maybe a little more difficult for me than for the others. I don't know.

Janine was next youngest after me, though there were five years between us, and after Janine there were only the twins. In a family with eight kids (the ninth, Yvonne, was already gone) it would have been easy for someone in Janine's spot to get lost or at least overlooked, but that wouldn't happen because Janine was what people called "exotic." While the rest of us had blond or brown hair and pale complexions, Janine's hair was dark brown, almost black, and she had what people called "olive" skin. And while our eyes were either blue or gray, Janine's eyes were as dark as her hair.

The Old Man said Janine looked like a Jew, which none of us kids had ever knowingly encountered on Longfellow Avenue but which was a serious matter, since the Old Man was convinced, at least for a while, that Bunny Augustine and his gang, mostly Northside Jews, were out to get him. Bernard once told me that the Old Man actually thought that Janine wasn't his, that her real father was in fact a Jew, maybe Bunny Augustine himself, though even when he was drunk out of his mind, the Old Man couldn't possibly have believed it, and that the Old Man had slapped Mother around for it. Ronnie said she'd heard Mother call Janine "Black Irish, from John's side," but since the Old Man always called himself French Canadian, "Black Irish" didn't make much sense to us either, though it might have helped explain to our ignorant, literal-minded satisfaction Janine's dark hair, eyes, and skin.

When she was little I don't think anybody gave Janine much thought. None of us after Ronnie—by that I mean myself, Janine, and the twins—did much to call attention to ourselves, either because we were afraid of what would happen if we were noticed or because we never thought we could get a word in edgewise. Janine wasn't as quiet as the twins, who nobody can remember saying anything for the first ten years or so of their lives, but she didn't say much for a long time—she just watched the rest of us with those big black eyes from the far end of the dinner table or from the background somewhere, sometimes smiling, most times not. I don't know if the Old Man ever called her a Jew girl to her face. I doubt if he paid her much attention at all. Besides, by the time Janine was old enough to really turn his head, the Old Man was either doing time or on the lam who knows where.

It's hard to believe, looking back like this, that Janine was somehow the cause of everything that happened in 1953. No one I'm aware of ever blamed her for what happened, and maybe what happened would have happened anyway, though I doubt it. Jack knew that Buddy Follmer had been fooling around with Ronnie. That made him mad, but it didn't make him crazy. It was Follmer fooling around with Janine— no, not even that, just the *thought* of Follmer and Janine—that set Jack off, that set the whole train of events rolling toward disaster.

But I don't want to think about that part of the story now. Suffice it to say that Janine was different from the rest of us, that she was "exotic," and that when she reached a certain age *everybody* noticed her, including her brothers.

I'm trying to stop it right here, these thoughts about Janine, but now Ronnie is standing beside me, her hand on my shoulder, thinking the same thoughts. Ronnie was six years older than Janine, but it was Ronnie who took Janine under her wing, and at least while Janine was little Ronnie was more a mother to her than Mother was.

I remember Janine following Ronnie around the house and the two of them coming home from Cianciolo's grocery on Thirty-eighth Street, Janine wearing a kerchief on her head like Ronnie, and Janine helping carry what Ronnie had bought for supper that night. Even Cianciolo's daughter, who was a year or two older, wasn't as dark and exotic-looking as Janine, and the Cianciolos were honest-to-God Italian, which made them at least as dark as the Irish and the Jews.

Anyway, wherever they went back then, it was always Janine tagging along after Ronnie and Ronnie making sure Janine got across the busy streets okay and that Janine got enough to eat. Later on, their relationship would change. Later on, the men who looked at Ronnie a certain way would look at Janine the same way, only more so, and things would never be the same. But they were sisters even in the worst of times, and I don't think either one of them ever forgot that. And when Janine was killed, Ronnie was as devastated as the rest of us.

Janine died on August 23, 1963, of multiple injuries suffered when the car she was riding in jumped a curb on Minnehaha Parkway and hit the concrete abutment of the Nicollet Avenue bridge in south Minneapolis. The car, a Corvette Stingray, belonged to her husband, but was driven by one Everett Dierking III, a forty-five-year-old husband and father of six from a prominent Minneapolis milling family, who was also killed. The car was reportedly traveling more than ninety miles per hour when it hit the bridge.

Janine was twenty-six years old when she died, which was how old Jack was when he was killed, a coincidence that was not mentioned at the funeral that Eddie Devitt, her husband at the time, arranged for her at the highfalutin Episcopal church across the street from Lake of the Isles.

Ronnie is obviously thinking what I'm thinking, because at that moment she says softly, "I never picture them the same age. Jack is always older, grown up or at least old enough to swear and stare and make people afraid. Janine—well, she's just standing there with a Band-Aid on her skinned knee and that strange, sad look on her face."

Ronnie is quiet for a while, and then says, "Oh God, Jojo, how I loved her when she was like that."

The others move off, slowly and separately, down the slope to the right in the direction of Jack and Bernard. The black boys are nowhere to be seen, and Ronnie's kids apparently believe we don't need the protection at the moment—and, besides, whether they want to admit it or not, what draws them up here to Crystal Lake, what fascinates them and makes them think about who they are and where they came from, are the graves of their gangster uncles. The kids' departure leaves Ronnie and me alone in front of Janine's grave for another few minutes.

"Are you warm enough?" she asks me. Her smoker's voice sounds raspier than usual. She's coming down with a cold, or maybe it's just where she is right now.

I nod. Yes, I'm warm enough.

"Do you think of her as much as you used to?"

Of course I do. Why wouldn't I? What's changed in the past twenty-five years that hadn't changed already and for good thirteen years before that? "Sure," I say.

"So do I," she says, but I'm not sure I believe her. Then she says, "I wonder how Eddie's doing after all this time. I wonder if it gets any easier. He calls sometimes when he's in town, but never says much about himself. I'm pretty sure he never remarried."

"Why should it get easier for him if it doesn't for us?" I say.

Ronnie has no answer for that. "Buddy Follmer—" she starts to say, but I cut her off.

"I don't want to talk about Buddy Follmer."

"Buddy brought flowers up here once," she says, ignoring me. "They were real ones too, a lot of them, expensive. Eddie ripped them to pieces and threw them in the trash."

I stare at the plastic flowers in front of Janine's stone. *You couldn't blame Eddie Devitt for the way things turned out*, I'm thinking. Well, you could and you couldn't.

"Fuck Buddy Follmer," I tell my sister. "I don't want to talk about that fat fuck anymore." I must have said it loud enough because halfway down the slope Elaine and B.J. stop and look up at us like we were talking out loud in church.

We did that a lot too, come to think of it, Ronnie and me, especially when we were very young. I remember how people, after the murders, were surprised by the fact that us LaVoies had been churchgoers, could even recite what my mother called the "sacred Scriptures" if we had to. "Jesus wept," was our favorite, of course—the shortest verse in the Bible and easily recalled when put on the spot by one of Mother's Christian friends.

Who knows why that comes to mind right now, unless it's all the crosses and praying hands and stone angels that surround us. But at one time or another all of us kids, even Jack, were more or less regulars at the Tabernacle. That was our mother's doing, as you might have guessed—the Old Man often boasting that he hadn't darkened a church's door since his wedding and that he wouldn't darken it again until his death, a promise that I'm sure was kept. We were Protestants because my mother, born an Olsson and raised on a North Dakota dairy farm, was brought up Swedish Lutheran, and because my father, who was born a Catholic in Hancock, on the Upper Peninsula of Michigan, believed in nothing but himself by the time we came along and offered no other choice. Because of the French last name people usually assumed we were Catholic, and after the murders I had a feeling that a lot of people in our mostly Protestant part of town were disappointed to find out that we weren't.

Mother began herding us over to the Tabernacle at Thirty-fifth Street and Chicago when we were toddlers, and by the time we knew what was going on, trudging off to that big, spooky barn twice on Sunday and again on Wednesday evening was a more or less constant part of our lives. I say more or less because we went only at Mother's say-so, and there were times as we got older when Mother was in no condition to order us anywhere.

We'd go to the Tabernacle three times a week for long stretches of time, six months maybe or a year, and then we wouldn't go at all for at least as long a time. Ladies from the Tabernacle would come looking for us on Sunday mornings, but instead of finding our mother in her flowered Sunday dress and little straw hat, they'd get a profane earful from the Old Man, who would tell the biddies to get the hell off his front steps and leave an honest man to his Sunday paper, while us kids hid behind the furniture and either giggled or sobbed. If the Old Man wasn't around, which was just as frequent, we'd run and hide and wait for the doorbell (if it happened to be in working order) to stop ringing.

We were marked as good little Christian boys and girls—what Mrs. Wannstedt, one of my mother's church friends, called "Sunbeams" in our neighborhood—and we were thus liable to be singled out and backed up against the wall of Cianciolo's store or wherever else one of those women might corner us and be required to recite a verse from the Scriptures. When we were little and easily intimidated, we actually managed to rattle off John 3:16 or a couple of lines of the Twenty-third Psalm ("The Lord is my shepherd"—I still can, believe it or not), but as we got older we got bolder and following Jack's lead hollered out when cornered something rude or nasty. It got to the point where only the most foolish of those foolish crones dared ask us anything, because by the time we were into our teens we were ready and willing to shout out all kinds of "verses" on demand:

"'Loose lips sink ships!' Admiral Halsey, Chapter One, Verse Two."

"'Do unto others, then head for the hills!' Harry Truman, One Will Get You Two."

"'Never piss into the wind!' Holy Moses, Fourth and Long."

I don't think any of us except Eugene actually believed in God, though for a long time some people seemed to make the mistake of assuming that because we'd been churchgoers we were dyed-in-the-wool Christians. The truth is, we were spooked by our mother's fervor, which we believed was part of a combination of factors that made her crazy, that made her no help to us when we needed it, and that finally killed her because it taught her that by dying she'd be going to a better place. Though we adopted this or that habit or artifact from her religion, we all—all but Eugene—came to hate that religion and to hate her for believing it and for letting it warp her and us too.

Eugene took to carrying a New Testament about the size of a pack of Chesterfields in his shirt pocket, and Bernard was known to pass around, probably as a joke, the little Christian "tracts" the Tabernacle bought from some publisher and made available by the carload. Ronnie and Janine both wore tiny silver crosses around their necks, but they wore those crosses while shoplifting drugstore lipsticks and movie magazines, committing adultery, and otherwise behaving unchristian-like. Janine was wearing nothing but that little cross when she died in Eddie's Stingray. By that time, though, most people didn't believe such things meant much to us at all.

Meslow the cop once told me that whatever us LaVoies called ourselves, we were Roman Catholic "in the blood." He said we were Catholics sure as we were French Canucks, at least on the Old Man's side, and as proof he pointed to what he called our obsession with death. "Catholics worship the dead, call them martyrs and saints," he said. "You're obsessed with blood and suffering, and you all can't wait to die. Your symbol is a man being tortured to death."

Meslow was raised Norwegian Lutheran, he once told me, but is no more a believer than I am. He's an old fool who thinks he can see through people's skulls and skin, that he can read people's minds and hearts. I refuse to argue with the son-of-a-bitch because that's what he wants, because I'm the last person he has to argue with—no one else, not even the few cops that are left from those years, will give him the time of day anymore. But when he accused me of being a closet Catholic, I found it impossible to keep my mouth shut. I said, "We're obsessed with death because most of us are dead." I could have added, "I myself am half-dead, motherfucker," but I didn't, knowing he would've accused me of feeling sorry for myself.

I think of that now, when I'm surrounded not just by stone angels and crosses, but by the graves of most of my family.

Is this unusual—the amount of violent death in a single family? I suppose it is, though I would guess there are thousands of black families nowadays where the survivors need the fingers of both hands to count the dead and missing. Rossy Grant used to say the LaVoies were dogged by bad luck, that we were cursed, and that anybody foolish or unlucky enough to become attached to us was cursed too. Of course, Rossy was cursed before he met us and would have probably ended up killing himself on any account—he shot himself in the back seat of the car in which he'd been living in 1980—but there are a lot of people who'd say that, as far as the LaVoies were concerned, he was right.

The LaVoies were cursed, yes, and maybe still are, but I'm pretty sure that Meslow was blowing hot air when he said it was because of the Old Man's Catholic blood.

For a long time, maybe a year or two afterward, people would come up to Crystal Lake to gawk and take pictures at my brothers' graves. Ronnie told me (I was at the Cloud by that time) that there were people who were eager to do more, to deface the stones or tear up the grass and the flowers and maybe even dig up the bodies if they had the chance. Ronnie said that my brothers being here is the reason the city started locking the cemetery gates at night, though it might have been for other reasons too, reasons having less to do with my brothers than with the general lawlessness of society and the deterioration of that Northside neighborhood.

At any rate, people would come up here and do what they felt they had to do even if it was only to stand and stare at the names and the dates on the small plain stones, some of them maybe thinking, *This is as close as I get to someone I read about on the front page of the paper for doing something I would never do, never even think of doing, something horrible and unforgivable and impossible to ignore or forget, even if they're dead now and buried and nothing but rotting bullet-riddled flesh in a couple of boxes under six feet of black dirt.* Or something like that.

As I said earlier, the LaVoies—my brothers Jack and Bernard and I—were the most infamous names around this part of the country in the fall of 1953 and for a long time afterward. I've often thought, *if people only knew how much of an accident it was, the way it all came about, if people knew how unintended everything that made us infamous was, if people knew how much we didn't intend for things to happen the way they happened.* Only Bernard ever wanted to have his name in the papers and on the news, and he sure as hell never pictured it happening the way it happened, not in a million years.

During the trials that winter and the following spring, the prosecutors called us the "criminal LaVoie family." They tried to make the juries believe that the itch to rob gas stations and stick up liquor stores and even murder policemen and hostages was as much a part of being a LaVoie as the size of our hands and feet. As a matter of fact, Ferdinand Twyman, the Hiawatha County Attorney, bent over backward to link the small stature of the LaVoie men with an "anger in the blood" that "eventually and inevitably" drove us to gun down "normal-sized" men. We couldn't help ourselves, Twyman told those jurors. Although we knew the difference between right and wrong (we'd been brought up by a God-fearing Christian mother after all), we were "driven by other, inherited forces to commit heinous, unpardonable crimes."

No one would deny there was a criminal streak in the family. The Old Man was a convicted thief, robber, and check-kiter. He had been in and out of jail for this or that offense since he was fourteen. He'd been involved, for that matter, in any number of scams and rackets that he'd never done time for, including "odd jobs" for Bunny Augustine. His oldest son, Eugene, before he accepted Jesus Christ as his Personal Savior, was a determined though not very skillful thief, had spent a year in reform school at sixteen and eighteen months at the Cloud by the time he was twenty-one. The Old Man's second and third sons, Jack and Bernard, were troublemakers as far back as anyone could remember, picking fights, breaking windows, stealing apples and tomatoes and cigarettes, and setting off false alarms at the fire box on the corner when they were still in knee pants. Jack was the instigator, the ringleader, but Bernard and, later, yours truly proved only too willing to follow him. Jack and Bernard both spent time at the juvenile detention center in Red Wing, and Bernard got to know the inside of the Cloud. I was saved from the same fate by a three-year involuntary enlistment in the Army.

Our mother was a simple and naive farm girl susceptible to fits of severe depression called "nervous breakdowns" in those days. She'd moved to Minneapolis in her late teens to attend "normal school" with the intention of becoming an elementary school teacher, but instead, in the worst decision of her life, married John LaVoie, whom she met at a Svenskarnas Dag celebration at Minnehaha Park, and resigned herself to raising their many successive children. She was eventually overwhelmed by motherhood, the family's poverty, her husband's brutality, and the criminal activities of her sons. (Her daughter Ronnie spent three months in the women's correctional facility at Shakopee for shoplifting at the Woolworth's downtown.)

Well, the Old Man might have been bad to the bone and Mother a hapless wreck, but what Jack, Bernard, and I were, through everything that happened and even when we were technically adults, was a trio of stupid kids. That's what the gawkers, vandals, and would-be bodysnatchers never understood—that the three of us were very ordinary, very confused, and very frightened cases of "arrested development." (A latter-day sociologist's term. Pardon the pun.) I don't say that for sympathy—fuck sympathy, which we don't deserve and which wouldn't do us any good now anyway—but only for the record, for whatever that's worth.

Bernard told me that the first time he and Jack held up a filling station, the two of them were sick to their stomachs afterward. They were so nervous, Bernard said, that he shit in his pants and Jack puked on his shoes, and then they both got the giggles like a couple of little girls.

"I don't even remember deciding to do it," Bernard told me. The two of us were drinking beer in his radio and TV repair shop on Thirty-third Street a few days after I got home from Germany, which would have been in late June or early July of 1953. Bernard had knocked up and married a girl from the neighborhood named Judy Oleski while I was gone. Judy had the baby, little Bobby, and Judy's old man, who was so crippled with arthritis he couldn't hold the newspaper, had turned his repair business over to Bernard, who commenced to run it into the ground. The previous spring Jack and Bernard had started stealing cars and robbing gas stations and drugstores, supposedly to help our family make ends meet.

"It was Jack's idea," Bernard said that day at his repair shop. I remember thinking, *it always is*. And I remember feeling sorry for Judy, who was sexy and strong-willed and two years older than Bernard, but would never have the kind of hold over him that Jack did. "Jack said," according to Bernard, "'There's this filling station on East Lake, just before you get to the river, and there's only an old guy around at night and it'd be like taking candy from a fuckin' baby.' That's what Jack said, out of the blue one night, the two us sitting in here with the shop closed up like we're doing now."

Bernard took a swig of his Grain Belt. There was sweat on his forehead and upper lip, and I could tell he was getting excited talking about it, remembering that first time like he might have been remembering the first time he fucked Judy.

"I'd never so much as spit on the damn sidewalk since I got out of the Cloud," he said. "For two-and-a-half years I'd kept to the straight and narrow. All I really cared about was Judy and the baby and getting us up on our feet and, you know, making something of myself. I'll admit it—I already hated the damn business. I mean, what do I care about vacuum tubes and condensers and shit like that? Old man Oleski was asking me about inventory and cash flow like he didn't have any confidence in me, and I thought, well, if I'm such a goddamn dimwit, why did he set me up here in the first place? Then I started thinking about Judy and the baby and wondering how I was going to keep everything going. One day I mentioned all this to Jack and he said, 'Well, maybe the two of us should make a couple of midnight withdrawals.'

"I didn't know what to say. I knew what he was talking about—I hadn't just fallen off the turnip truck—but, like I say, I was a married man and the father of a brand-new baby and I'd been clean as a damn hound's tooth going on three years. But then I heard myself saying,

'We're going to need some guns, aren't we?' Can you imagine that, Jojo? The first thing I said after all that time was, 'We're going to need some fucking guns.'

"Jack said, 'I already took care of that.' And he took me out to this beat-up DeSoto parked at the curb and sat me down on the front seat and opened up a towel he pulled out from under the seat and, sure enough, there were a couple of pistols—a stubby silver revolver and a mean-looking little Italian automatic. 'One for you and one for me,' Jack said and then wrapped the pieces up in the towel and stuffed the towel back under the seat. Then he grinned at me and said, 'The old bastard at that Pure Oil station sees the two of them pistolas pointing at his face and I'll give you five-to-one odds he's out cold on the floor before we can tell him it's a fuckin' stickup.'

"Jack said he'd pick me up the next night. He said to tell Judy that one of the guys from the neighborhood was going into the Army and there was a party for the guy and I might not be home till after midnight. I did and I think Judy believed me, but she hates Jack, you know, and doesn't like me hanging around with him so she put up a stink and I ended up walking out and slamming the door in her face when I heard Jack honking the horn out front. I'd had the runs all day, I was so nervous, and Jack was nervous too, I could tell, but the two of us had made up our minds to rob that filling station and neither one of us would change our minds. I'd made up my mind not to think about Judy or the baby, but that wasn't the problem I thought it was going to be, since once I got in that car and looked at Jack and knew two guns were wrapped in a towel under the seat, all I could think about was doing it.

"It was funny, Jojo," Bernard said. He was really sweating now. "I never thought about how much money there was going to be or what I would tell Judy about where I got it or anything else you might expect I'd be thinking. What I thought about was how it would look to someone standing there—Jack and me pulling up in that old DeSoto, the two of us climbing out, Jack coming around from the driver's side, me coming out of the passenger's door, the two of us walking into the station house before the old guy could even stand up from where he was sitting and grab a rag and come out to see what we wanted, a fill or an oil check or whatever the hell it might be with an ordinary customer. And then the two of us sticking out our arms with the pistols at the ends of them, Jack or me or maybe both of us together saying, 'Okay, you sorry son-of-a-bitch, open the register or we'll blow your goddamn head off!' All the way down Lake Street I was playing that picture over and over in my head, like I was sitting at the movies.

"Jack was as nervous as I'd ever seen him—I could tell by the way he was staring straight ahead while he drove, his hands practically strangling the wheel and the skin around his mouth tight like he was clenching his teeth. I think he was watching the same movie I was.

"Anyway, when we got to that Pure Oil station nothing was the way I'd imagined it. It was just after nine and there wasn't a lot of traffic down on that end of Lake Street and there weren't any other customers at the pumps. And the guy who was working there that night was not the old fart Jack had talked about—it was a kid, seventeen or eighteen he looked like, and he was out front emptying the trash can they had sitting there when we pulled in.

"Jack swore about the guy being out there in front like that, but he pulled the car in alongside a pump and when the kid came over to Jack's window and asked what we wanted, Jack said, 'My brother here has the runs and we were wondering if he could use the toilet.' The kid says, 'Sure, though I'd appreciate it if you didn't make a mess because I just cleaned up,' and the two of us get out of the car and follow him into the little house. As soon as we're inside Jack's got his gun out— he's using the automatic—and says to the kid, 'Open the goddamn register, asshole, this is a stickup!'

"He said it so fast it took me by surprise, and I had to fumble around to get the revolver out of my pocket. It happened so quick— Jack and his gun and the kid jerking open the register and Jack pushing the kid out of the way and reaching in and grabbing the bills in the drawer, then dropping the drawer on the floor and ripping the telephone cord out of the wall, leaving a ragged hole in the plaster.

"For a second I thought he might do something to the kid who was backed up against a wall next to a calendar with a half-naked girl wearing a cowboy hat on it, but all he did was look hard at the kid and say, 'Don't move or make a sound for ten fucking minutes or we'll come back and kill you.' By the look on the kid's face I would've bet he was going to stand there with his heart in his mouth until his replacement came in the next morning.

"We were in and out of that place in less than a minute, Jojo, smooth as silk. We drove across the bridge into St. Paul and left the car with the guns under the front seat in the garage of a guy Jack knew and took the Selby-Lake streetcar back across the bridge and all the way back to Longfellow. Before we got on, Jack puked in the gutter and I shit in my pants. We sat in the very back of the car, which was almost empty anyway, and when the car went past that Pure Oil station we saw the kid, honest to God, still standing in the little house. It was a good forty-five minutes later and he was still standing there against the wall, just like we left him! We both started laughing and sat there smelling like vomit and shit and giggling like kids in church. We giggled like that all the way to Longfellow and then all the way to the house.

"Ronnie and Janine were out, the twins were in bed, and Ma was talking to Jesus in her bedroom. Jack and I went up to his room and he took the money out of his pocket. There was a grand total of twenty-four dollars and sixty-seven cents.

"It was only when we stood there and looked at the money in a little pile on Jack's bed that the two of us stopped giggling, and for the first time in the past couple of hours I thought about Judy and the baby. I suddenly missed them so much I started feeling sick again and all I wanted to do was go home and get out of those dirty clothes and climb in bed with Judy. Honest to God, Jojo, I didn't give a damn about the money."

* * *

Bernard's story comes back to me now as I sit here and stare at their tombstones. In some ways I think Bernard was the saddest, sorriest one of us all, the most pathetic of our pathetic gang—not because he had a wife and child, but because he was a sweet guy before there was the wife and child, and because he was the only LaVoie who ever had a thought about the future. Bernard was the only one who cared what people thought of him, who had the desire not only to get out of the house, but to get out of the damn neighborhood, who wanted to be somebody even if he wasn't sure who.

Bernard was a snappy dresser and a fancy dancer. Bernard had somewhere, somehow learned the jitterbug, the cha-cha, and the foxtrot. And Bernard never murdered anybody.

Yes, Bernard was a liar. But I don't think he was born a liar—I think he started lying while he was pretending to be something he wasn't, and once he started he couldn't stop. Jack told me, for instance, that Bernard had stayed in the car while he went in and robbed that Pure Oil station on East Lake. Jack said that Bernard had both shit in his pants *and* puked on his shoes, and that he, Jack, except for the usual headache, hadn't been sick at all. And Jack said that Bernard took twelve dollars and fifty cents of the twenty-four dollars plus change that lay there on the bed after that job. Jack was a lot of things and most of those things weren't good, but I don't remember a single instance of Jack telling me something he didn't believe to be true. Jack wasn't a liar. Bernard was, and that made him pathetic too.

I was four years younger than Bernard and spent most of my twenty-one years up to that point believing everything he told me, at least until I was shown otherwise. I believed Bernard when he told me he won a dance contest at Bunny Augustine's North Side Club, and I believed him when he told me that one of Bunny's hostesses had not only danced with him, but sucked him off afterward, and that he had to run for his life when Bunny walked in on the two of them going at it in a men's room stall.

"Bernard can dance, but the rest of it is bullshit," Jack told me later. Jack, who was born with a clubfoot and never danced a step in his life, had to have been jealous of Bernard's nifty footwork, but he wouldn't lie about what Bernard did or didn't do. I believed Jack and felt sorry for Bernard for having to lie as much as he did.

Bernard had jug ears and was the smallest of the LaVoie men, and maybe that had something to do with the lying. Maybe that had *a lot* to do with it. Bernard stood five-foot-three—five-foot-*five* when he wore the elevators he bought through the mail, but those shoes pinched his toes so bad he couldn't stand to wear them. This was another thing I don't think people realized right away—how small we were, all three of us, no bigger than most seventh graders. After the shootout at the game farm, the papers talked about our small stature. Some of the so-called experts among the politicians and social workers and newspaper columnists speculated that it might have contributed to an "inferiority complex" that led the three young men to shoot and kill two strangers in cold blood.

As a matter of fact, Bernard's height was the only one the papers got right. The *Minneapolis Tribune* said Jack was five-four and I was five-six, shortchanging each of us by an inch, and after that everybody seemed to make the same mistake. It was the kind of factual sloppiness that drove Jack crazy, but of course Jack was dead by the time they ran those numbers in the paper and I didn't get a look at the articles until much later and by that time I didn't care. When you spend the rest of your life sitting down, you don't think about your height the way you used to.

Even so, I'm pretty sure that if the general public had seen us in the flesh, they would have been surprised and disappointed. They wouldn't have expected a gang of cold-blooded killers to be a trio of shrimps. They wouldn't expect that one of us had a clubfoot and that another one had jug ears. Maybe they wouldn't have smeared dog shit on the markers or thrown green apples at our house, not if they knew how small and pathetic the LaVoies really were. But what do I know? Maybe they would've. Maybe our size wouldn't have made any difference at all.

For several years there was nothing marking my brothers' graves. The city, apparently with Eugene's and Ronnie's blessing, took out the original stones so the vandals wouldn't know where to dig or have anything to rip out or deface. Then, not too long after I got out of the Cloud, the people who decide these things said it was okay to put markers in again if the family wanted them, and Eugene and Ronnie and I said yes, we wanted them, and Eugene and Ronnie came up with the cash to have two new ones put in. The new ones are identical to each other and sit side by side, and although they're now more than fifteen years old they still look nice, like they might have been put in much later.

The stones are plain and gray, but the granite faces are polished where the names and dates are carved in, and there's a small cross above each name.

†

JOHN MICHAEL LA VOIE JR.

1927–1953

†

BERNARD ROBERT LA VOIE

1928–1953

Bernard had been divorced for three weeks when we killed Patrolman Fredriksen, almost seven weeks when we killed Thomas O'Leary and when he and Jack were killed. This is why Judy, his wife—or rather his ex-wife—had nothing to say about where he was buried or what should be done about his gravestone. As far as anyone seems to know, neither Judy, who left town, nor Bernard's son, Bobby, who, assuming he's still alive, is now a middle-aged man with probably grown-up children of his own, has ever been up here to see his father's grave.

That might be the saddest part of all.

* * *

Ronnie's kids have stared at their uncles' graves long enough and moved off, their ears and noses red from the cold, their hands jammed in the pockets of their jeans. Elaine has taken B.J.'s arm and, looking more like husband and wife than brother and sister, they've started back up the path. Joe stands by, waiting to push my chair up the hill, while Ronnie and I look at our brothers' graves a little longer.

The black kids are here too. They reappeared on the low rise behind the graves, the cold not seeming to bother them or, if it is, not showing on their faces or the way they stand straddling their bikes. I sense Joe becoming alert, shaking off the cold. The kids don't seem to notice.

"These boys, they kill a cop," says the taller one, talking to Ronnie and me.

"Who told you that?" I say, surprised by their words.

The tall boy shrugs. "I told you, man, we be guides here. We know all that shit."

"Yeah," the other kid says. "These boys, they take a police hostage when they ripping off a bank, and when the mayor and them don't pay up, the boys shoot the police between the eyes."

Ronnie starts to say something, but I cut her off.

"That's not the way it happened."

The shorter kid looks at me. "It ain't?"

"No."

The taller kid wipes his nose with the back of his hand and says, "How do you know?"

"Because I was there," I say. "I was with them. They were my brothers, and we were a gang."

The boys take a long, hard look at me bundled up in my chair, then glance at each other like they want to see what the other one is going to say. Finally, the shorter one, looking at me in the chair again, shakes his head and says to no one special, "Huh! That be some fuckin' gang."

TWO

"**S**ome fuckin' gang."

Back at the cemetery the line made me laugh. To a pair of black kids in the city nowadays, a couple of long-dead cop-killers and an old guy in a wheelchair couldn't seem like much of a criminal organization.

The kids wouldn't have been impressed if I'd described the LaVoie brothers in our prime (if that's the word for it), with our snappy fedoras, dark shirts and jackets, and pale neckties. Jack pulling back his jacket and showing off the butt of the forty-five automatic stuck in his waistband might have made an impression, but maybe not. Probably the kids would've just laughed, not only at the spectacle of three pint-sized white guys wearing hopeless ofay getups, but at the puny armament itself, the kids accustomed to seeing today's gangsters flashing automatic pistols and military-grade assault rifles.

The hats and ties were Bernard's idea, and they might have been the only idea of Bernard's that Jack ever accepted. The two of them already had the duds when I got back from Germany, and at first I thought it was a joke.

"You look like B-movie gangsters," I said to Bernard when he showed me his stuff one day when Judy was out of the apartment. He either didn't hear me or didn't care what I thought.

Years later, after I'd moved into his building, Meslow asked me
about the getup. He told me that after the shootings, when Jack and
Bernard were dead and I was fighting for my life at Hiawatha General,
Eugene told him that the hats and ties were to make up for the shabby
way we dressed as kids. The LaVoies never had anything new, Eugene
told him. Everything we wore came from the Salvation Army or from
county relief or from the do-gooders' give-away bin at the Tabernacle.
Eugene told him that Jack for some reason was especially deprived, that
Jack was more ashamed of the way he had to dress than the rest of us, and
that Jack never forgot the neighborhood kids laughing at his patched
and too-big hand-me-downs when he was little. That was one reason,
Eugene said, that Jack had shut himself up in his room and become a
recluse who hated everyone except a few members of his family.

"Is that true?" Meslow asked me.

I said no. I said, "We wore those things because we thought they
made us look like gangsters. We thought they made us look like the
tough guys in the movies and the tough guys that hung around with
Bunny Augustine," and I believed what I said though I also had to
admit that for once in his life Eugene might have been on to something.

It was the hats of course that helped do us in—one hat anyway.
When I was scrambling to get back in the car after Jack shot Fredriksen
I accidentally knocked my hat off, and when Bernard stepped on the
gas, we took off without it. The next time I saw that hat I was hooked
up to an IV at Hiawatha General, and the next time after that I was on
trial for murder.

"Augustine's goons woulda laughed in your face," Meslow said
that day in my apartment. "They woulda said you looked like a bunch
of I-talians. Bunny and his Jewboys never dressed like that. Some
fucking gang."

"I wouldn't know," I said, tired of the discussion.

"Trust me," Meslow said. He pulled out his Pall Malls, shook one
out for each of us, and said, "You ever see Bunny in the flesh?"

I shrugged. "Bernard did, maybe," I said. Then again, maybe not.

"Bunny dressed to the nines, at least after he got established," Meslow said. "Silk suits made in Hong Kong, hats from a Jew haberdasher in New York, shoes shipped six or seven pair at a time from London, England. Bunny's top guys, smart enough to not upstage the boss, bought their suits at Hubert White downtown. Not quite in Bunny's league, but classy, top-drawer stuff, I can tell you. None of this white-tie-on-black-shirt wop shit."

Maybe that's why the black kid's line struck me funny—Meslow had used the same words ten, fifteen, almost twenty years earlier. He didn't take us seriously either, not with Jack and Bernard dead and buried and me sitting in a fucking wheelchair. Before that, though, for a month or so back in 1953—well, that was something else. Meslow and the rest of this goddamn town took us *very* seriously.

"What are you laughing at, Jojo?" Ronnie asks over her shoulder. We're back on the freeway, heading south through the gray, nearly deserted heart of the city, then heading all the way down the length of it and then west for another several miles, to a little suburban burg called Chaska, where Gervais is supposed to have been checking on the turkey during breaks in the football.

I look up at her in surprise. I didn't realize I'd been laughing out loud. "Nothing," I say. "What that kid said about us at the graves."

"Don't think about it," Ronnie says.

She assumes that what the kid said was painful, even if it made me laugh. Her response to pain was always, "Don't think about it." But I *want* to think about it. For the first time in a long while I want to think about what brought us here, about the three of us LaVoie boys and about everyone else too, about who we were and what we became, and I realize that I've been wanting to think about it all morning—maybe longer than that, maybe for a very long time.

It's easier when I've been drinking. Everything's easier, but especially thinking about the times on Longfellow and the time that began in the summer of 1953 and ended in the fall. It was only then, for those few months, that events happened one, two, three in order, the way I remember them, I mean. Before that everything is scrambled, the events, the way I remember them, coming back helter-skelter, in no particular order, or at least in no order that makes sense when I'm trying to sort them out.

At the moment, I'm stone sober. I'm a little queasy from the ride, not used to spending more than ten minutes at a time in a motorized vehicle anymore and maybe from hunger too. I don't eat much anymore, just enough to keep myself upright during daylight hours. My stomach hurts, and I'm not often hungry. If the choice comes down to a meal or a drink, I take the drink. I can't remember if I had anything for breakfast this morning.

The thought of food gets me thinking about dinnertime on Longfellow. This is way before the summer of 1953, before the time when things started lining up in order—like I say, sometimes, for whatever reason, these memories come back to me fast and furious, willy-nilly, any which way.

Right now I see the whole family, or most of it anyway, sitting around the scratched and scarred dining-room table. Jack and Bernard and I are sitting on one side, Ronnie and Janine and Donald Harrison on the other. Donald Harrison would later become Ronnie's husband, the first one, but at that time he is just a friend, a tall, skinny, redheaded kid from down the block. Eugene must be doing time at Red Wing—I don't know where else he'd be that day— and the twins are too little to sit at the table. It's my ninth or tenth birthday.

"C'mon, Ma," Bernard hollers, "we're all here. Let's eat."

Mother appears in the kitchen doorway, drying her hands on a dish cloth. She is already extremely thin, you can see the veins through the white skin on her bony arms like the blue highways on road maps, and her pale eyes are rimmed with red. She wears her graying brown hair under a blue kerchief.

"We're *not* all here, Bernard," she says softly. "We must wait for your father."

Everyone except maybe Janine, who's only five or six, and Donald Harrison, who's a guest, groans.

"Jesus, Ma," Jack says, and Mother closes her eyes the way she does when she's tired and says, "Thou shalt not take the Lord thy God's name in vain," and Jack, in a lower voice this time, says, "Jesus, God, and Mary!" sounding like a Catholic. Donald and I giggle behind our hands.

Bernard says, "I'll bet he's not coming, Ma."

But Mother, her eyes open again, whispers, like she's talking to herself, "He promised he'd be here. He said he'd be here by one o'clock for sure."

It's a Sunday, but because it's my birthday and because the Old Man promised to be here for dinner Mother didn't go to the Tabernacle this morning, staying home instead to cook a pot roast with potatoes, peas, and carrots. What with the Old Man in and out of the workhouse and the family on relief, a pot roast is a special treat and Mother skipped services to make sure things got done right. Of course, *nothing* is done right. She's burned the meat and the potatoes, and now she's letting everything get cold.

Jack pushes his chair away from the table and lights a cigarette. Mother watches through her raw-rimmed eyes, but doesn't have the will to call him on it. I see Donald glancing at his wristwatch, glancing at Ronnie who glances back, and I wish I was old enough to be angry like Jack. Jack scares me. I'm afraid he will hurt me (though he pretty much ignores us younger kids), but I'm more afraid of what will happen because of him. I'm afraid *for* him and for others who might get in his way. The cigarette is like a fuse.

We sit there for fifteen minutes, half an hour, a whole goddamn hour. Jack has smoked four or five cigarettes, one right after another, and the room is filled with cigarette smoke on top of the reek of burnt meat and potatoes. Finally, Jack stands up and leaves. Then Donald excuses himself, saying he and his family are driving to South Dakota this afternoon to visit his cousins. Bernard, who's been fidgeting since we sat down, is beside himself, caught between his desire to exit like Jack and the guilt he knows he'll feel if he leaves the table without eating Mother's dinner. Besides, Bernard is hungry. We're all hungry—it seems as though we're *always* hungry—and even cold and charred the pot roast and potatoes will be more than we've eaten at one time in a month.

I feel bad about Donald leaving because Donald is my friend and he was here because it's my birthday, or so I believe at the time. I feel bad because Jack has gone too, though I'm not sure Jack knows it's my birthday, and I feel bad because I know how awful this day has become for Mother. I wish the Old Man was dead or in prison or gone for good like Wade Adams's old man. Wade Adams's old man, another no-account drunk, went off one day and was never heard from again.

But I no sooner wish that than the Old Man appears in the kitchen doorway behind Mother. It's two o'clock on a Sunday afternoon and he's already tight, stinking of whiskey and wearing a dirty suit, which he's no doubt been wearing since the last time we saw him, which would have been sometime Friday.

He looks past Mother at Bernard and me and the girls still seated at the table and says in that loud, barroom-brawler's voice of his, "So what's the significance of this fuckin' shindig, Marguerite?"

"It's Joseph's birthday, John," Mother says. She tries to smile, but she knows what's going to happen so her smile is thin and pathetic. "I told you we were going to have a special dinner on Sunday."

The Old Man pushes past Mother and lurches into the room. His flowered necktie is stained and hanging off to one side. The fly of his baggy trousers is halfway down. I'm thinking, thank God Donald has gone home. Donald is my friend, but sometimes he tells stories about our family around the neighborhood—he does little comedy routines in which he pretends he's Mother or the Old Man—and he would get plenty of material if he could see the two of them now.

"So whose birthday didja say it was?" the Old Man hollers.

"Joseph's," Mother says. Her smile has disappeared, and her lower lip is trembling.

The Old Man drags his hand across his rheumy eyes, blinks, then makes an attempt to focus in my direction. "Joseph?" he says as though he's unfamiliar with the name. Spotting me through the fog of cigarette smoke and inebriation, he says, "Stand up, goddamn it, so I can get a look at ya!"

I push my chair away from the table and stand up. I'm trying to smile.

"Jesus H. Christ!" the Old Man bellows. "Ain't there gonna be a single fuckin' LaVoie that's taller than a goddamn fireplug?"

"John, *please*," Mother whispers, but the Old Man ignores her.

"Aahhh," the Old Man says and waves his hand in my direction.

He pulls out the chair closest to him and sits down hard where Donald had been sitting. He looks across the table and shakes his head like the sight of me disgusts him. Then he turns and looks at Ronnie sitting beside him. He reaches out and pinches her arm above the elbow and says, "And who is this lovely mademoiselle?"

Ronnie pulls her arm away, forces a tight smile, and says, "Your daughter Ronnie, Daddy." Ronnie, like Mother and the rest of us except Jack, is afraid of him. There may be times now and then when we don't wish he was dead, but there's never a time he doesn't scare us.

Now Mother is all skittery motion, fussing around in the kitchen, opening and closing drawers and cupboards, dropping utensils on the greasy linoleum, and finally bringing things out on plates and in bowls. Everything is black and cold.

I can't believe Mother is going to put that food in front of the Old Man. What does she think he's going to do when he sees it like that, looking like she pulled it out of a fire—I'm surprised he's not already on her because of the smoke and stink. Strange as it sounds, I'm all of a sudden feeling sorry for the Old Man and hating my mother, who in my eyes right now is the stupidest, sorriest person in the world.

The Old Man is a sawed-off drunken bum in a filthy suit and soiled necktie—look at the sorry son-of-a-bitch, his goddamn barn door is half open!—and all there is for him to eat is a pot roast that looks like a fucking lump of coal. I feel so sorry for him I could cry.

We all know what's going to happen—we've known for the past hour, for longer than that, for as long as any of us can remember.

The Old Man, once he's able to fix his blurry eyes on the char in front of him, yells, "What the hell is this shit?"

Mother, crying, says, "Oh, John, I'm sorry. I got distracted when I was cooking the roast."

The Old Man is on his feet, roaring and spitting and throwing the plates and bowls around the room as the rest of us duck for cover or run into the living room thinking nothing can be worse than this. But of course it can and it is, the Old Man cursing and slapping at my mother who stumbles over a chair but manages to dodge his flailing hands because he's seeing double and couldn't hit the side of a barn with a baseball bat. And then Jack appears—he's come thumping down from his room upstairs—and grabs the Old Man by the padded shoulders of his cruddy suit and yanks him off his feet, and the Old Man is falling and rolling, his head bouncing off the uncarpeted floor, and then everyone except Mother, who's begging Jack to go away, to please not hurt his father, is very quiet.

Jack, standing over the disheveled little man curled up on the floor, says, "Someday, I swear to God, I'm going to kill you."

A moment later Jack thumps back upstairs, and Bernard and I drag the Old Man into his and Mother's bedroom where we toss him face down on the bed and he immediately falls into a deep, honking sleep. A goose egg is already visible on the back of his head. Mother, snuffling, wringing her skinny hands, follows us and sits down on the wobbly chair beside the bed.

In the dining room Ronnie and Janine are on their hands and knees retrieving potatoes and carrots and peas from under the table, behind the radiator, and among the shattered dishes and glasses, putting the salvaged morsels in the two bowls that aren't broken.

When they've got most of the dinner back on the table, the four of us sit down and without saying anything begin to eat. After a while Bernard cracks a big grin and pretty soon we're all giggling, stuffing the blackened remains in our mouths and pretending it's the best birthday party ever.

Once, when I was maybe seven or eight, I heard my mother tell one of the biddies from the Tabernacle that my father kept a loaded gun under his pillow. "He says it's for when the Jews come," my mother said and began to cry.

I felt sorry for Mother, feeling bad that things were so awful they made her cry, but even more than that I was curious about both the gun and the Jews. I didn't know who Bunny Augustine was yet, and the only Jews I knew of were the Jews in the Bible stories and picture books I saw in the Tabernacle library. Those Jews had pointy beards and wore long white sheets, and while I knew they did evil things like throw stones at John the Baptist and crucify Christ, I couldn't figure out why they wanted to hurt my father. The gun was a mystery too. I'd never seen a real gun. The house either then or later was never full of guns the way the papers made it sound, like it was a fucking armory or arsenal, and even by 1953 when Jack and Bernard knew how to get their hands on guns, there were never guns stashed behind the radiators or stuffed between the cushions on the sofa. I never saw the Old Man with one.

I asked Bernard about both the gun and the Jews, and he said the Jews Mother was talking about lived up on the North Side and sometimes liked the Old Man and sometimes didn't, you never knew with Jews. As far as the gun was concerned, Bernard said he was surprised—he'd never seen the Old Man with a gun either—but the next time both Mother and the Old Man were out of the house he'd look under the Old Man's pillow.

A couple days later I asked Bernard about the gun.

"What gun?" he said.

"The gun under the Old Man's pillow," I said.

He looked at me like I was crazy. "There ain't no gun under the Old Man's pillow."

"You looked?"

"Sure, I looked. It ain't there."

I was, like I said, seven or eight at the time and didn't know yet that Bernard was a liar.

"But Mother said so."

"Mother's crazy," he said with a dismissive shrug. "She says she sees Jesus smiling at her in the dark."

A couple of days later I heard Bernard telling some of the neighborhood guys that the Old Man had a "Smith & Wesson thirty-eight caliber snub-nose revolver" under his pillow. "The Old Man mouthed off to Bunny Augustine," he said by way of explanation.

One of the boys, Rossy Grant maybe or Donald Harrison, who already knew that Bernard told lies, said, "Oh, yeah? What'd he say?"

"He called him a dirty Jew."

The other boys snickered. One of them said, "That's a load of horseshit, Bernard. If your old man called Bunny Augustine a dirty Jew, Bunny woulda killed him on the spot."

"Yeah," said one of the others, "Bunny or some other dirty Jew," and everybody laughed, including Bernard.

I mentioned the gun and the Jews to Jack. It was a hot day and Jack was sitting on the front steps paring his fingernails with the large blade of his pocketknife. Jack sort of laughed, which didn't mean he thought what I said was funny or that he was happy or anything like that—he just made the short snorting noise that might have only indicated he knew I was there. He wasn't interested in the Jews, even though I'd once heard him say he "admired" Bunny Augustine, but the mention of the gun under the Old Man's pillow did catch his attention. He said he would check it out, the gun under the pillow, and went back to paring his nails.

The next day I saw him looking for something in the kitchen. No one else was around so I worked up the nerve and asked him about the gun. He found what he was looking for—a box of safety matches—and used one to light a Lucky Strike. Though he was only twelve or thirteen at the time, Jack was already an accomplished smoker. He'd steal butts from Eugene or the Old Man or Rossy Grant, and keep them—all different brands mixed together—in a Band-Aid can in his room.

Squinting through the smoke, he looked at me and said, "Whaddya know, squirt—there *was* a gun under the Old Man's pillow."

I said, "There was?" The news and, more important, Jack's reaction made me happy.

"There *was*," Jack said. He took a deep drag on the Lucky and said in an offhand manner, "But it ain't there now."

I squinted my eyes against the smoke and said, "Where'd it go?"

Jack lowered his voice a little. "I took it," he said.

If that had been Bernard I was talking to, I wouldn't have believed it, but this was Jack and Jack said he had taken the Old Man's gun. I wasn't happy anymore. I was scared and excited. I wondered how the Old Man was going to protect himself when the Jews came after him. I wondered if Jack was afraid of the Jews too. All I could think to do, though, was ask him what he was going to do with the gun.

Jack snorted and said he was going to rob a bank. I remember I laughed, but it was the way Jack laughed—not because something was funny and certainly not because I was happy.

I never saw that gun or heard any more about it. The next time I mentioned it to Bernard he looked at me like I was a dope. "I told you," he said, "there ain't no gun under the Old Man's pillow." He laughed and said, "If there was, cripes, he'd sneeze some night when he was dreaming and blow a hole in his head." I have to admit, I thought that was pretty funny.

The next time I overheard Mother talking to one of her Tabernacle friends it had nothing to do with guns or Jews and maybe nothing to do with the Old Man. It was something else and not interesting enough for me to remember. It was just something else that made her cry.

Our house was one of the smallest on a block lined with small houses. It had two floors plus a dingy basement, was covered in ugly gray shingles, and was situated at the back of the lot so there wasn't space for either a backyard or a garage. If no one happened to be in prison, the workhouse, or reform school at the time, there were eleven adults and children living under its leaky roof.

A garage didn't matter because nobody in the family owned a car, at least not until I came home from the Army, but I wished we had a backyard so we could be less conspicuous. All we had was the long, narrow yard in front where, though there was a good-sized maple on one side of the broken private sidewalk, there was nothing to keep the neighbors from seeing us when we were outside. I was embarrassed when Mother hung our ratty socks and ragged underwear on the clothesline Monday mornings and when the boys would holler at the Old Man stumbling up the walk on his first day home from the workhouse. I felt something else, something I felt strongly but didn't understand, when first Ronnie and later Janine spread a bath towel on what small patches of grass she could find among the dirt and weeds and lay down in a candy-colored swimsuit and pretend she didn't hear the whistles and wolf calls.

Sometimes Mother would come out on the front steps and stand with her fists on her hips and holler in that reedy, high-pitched voice of hers for the boys to be quiet or she'd call the police. The boys would hush for a minute, then laugh out loud at my mother and start whistling and wolf-calling again. I'd stand beside one of the front windows with the shades pulled down and wish for Mother to go back to her bedroom and for the boys to go away so I could pull the shade away from the window a crack and stare at my sister stretched out half-naked in the sun.

We were none of us what anybody would call a happy-go-lucky bunch, but I remember thinking that Ronnie and Janine sometimes seemed awfully sad. This was strange, come to think of it, because in one respect Ronnie and Janine were the only ones who had anything approaching a normal social life. Then again, maybe it wasn't so normal, because while there were dozens of admirers, lovers, and eventually husbands, neither girl had any close or lasting friends.

Ronnie would show up once in a while with a girl or two from school, but those girls always seemed younger and less mature than Ronnie. I remember only one of them distinctly, a girl named Betty or Betsy who lived on the other side of Cedar Avenue and used to come around mostly, I'm sure, because of Jack. She had dark hair and she did something to make her eyes seem unusually large, and I remember her coming home from South High and sitting on our front steps with my sister. She had scratched "Jack LV" all over the blue cloth cover of one of her loose-leaf binderss, and I heard her asking Ronnie questions about Jack until finally Ronnie got fed up and said something like, "Oh, no, you wouldn't. Jack would slit your throat if you tried it." And Betty or Betsy, suddenly looking scared to death, ran off in tears. I don't think I ever saw her again.

It was much later when Ronnie told me that girls didn't like coming around our place. Up until that time I had never thought about our house as something you would either choose to come to or stay away from—it was always just the place where we lived and where my father and mother and my brothers and sisters and the boys who came to see Ronnie and Janine used to come to and leave again, always coming and going, like it was the Greyhound bus station. Rossy Grant and Donald Harrison and Wade Adams were around all the time. At first they were just the neighborhood guys we played kick-the-can or capture-the-flag with, and then when they reached a certain age they were there to see Ronnie and Janine and only pretended to be friends with Bernard and me. Because of his clubfoot Jack never played kick-the-can and never went to the beach, and because of his moods he didn't have any friends, boys or girls, either.

Girls, Ronnie told me, were "put off" by our house. They were scared of the Old Man when he happened to be around, uneasy about our mother emerging like a spook from her dark bedroom, and nervous about the rest of us—handsome, sullen Jack if they ever got a glimpse of him, crazy Bernard wearing a long-sleeved shirt buttoned to the neck even on hot days and whistling dance tunes he'd heard on the radio, and the silent, staring twins who people thought were either mentally retarded or deaf mutes. There was no reason to believe Ronnie's friends noticed me at all.

One girl, maybe believing she was sparing Ronnie's feelings by not mentioning other family members, told her that our house had a "peculiar" smell, like something spoiled or rotting, and that it either made her eyes water or her scalp itch, I can't remember which. Another girl told yet another girl who told Ronnie that a baby had drowned in our basement and that the house with its warped wooden floors and frayed electric cords and rooms cluttered with dirty clothes and old newspapers was a fire trap, both of which statements were true. The boys either didn't notice or were so desperate to see Ronnie and Janine that they chose to overlook the rest.

The thing about growing up in a place, no matter what other people think of it, you take it for granted. I would have liked if Ronnie had brought more girls around, because I liked to look at them and compare them to my sisters, and I liked the way a few of them looked at me when I got a little older. But I never thought it was odd that she didn't until she told me all of that years later. For that matter, I never noticed a spoiled or rotting odor in the house, though I noticed different odors in other people's houses, each one with its own, like furniture polish or bread in the oven or that hot, dry stink that came from a vacuum cleaner full of dust and dog hair. I don't think I ever thought about Yvonne drowning in the basement, though I might have dreamt about it when I was little. The boys hanging around, the noise and the clutter, everybody coming and going—all of that I never gave a second thought until I was gone and everything had changed.

I'm not sure why I thought Ronnie and Janine were so unhappy at times. Nobody except the Old Man, sometimes when he was really drunk, laughed more than Ronnie. Later on, Ronnie was famous for her laugh, which was loud and musical and what the guys seemed to think was sexy—like Betty Grable's, I remember someone saying. Janine on the other hand never laughed, or laughed so infrequently I have no recollection of it. But Janine, when she was small, seemed content. I don't remember her ever crying or looking hopeless and forlorn the way, for instance, the twins did. She seemed, if anything as she grew older, preoccupied with something, like a song the rest of us couldn't hear.

I liked watching first Ronnie and then Janine lying in the sun. They seemed like very different people in their striped or dotted or flowered swimsuits, not like my sisters but like girls from another place, even another time. I felt no sexual desire for either one, not consciously or in any way I couldn't control, but there were times when I couldn't take my eyes off them. They were like day and night, the two of them. There was Ronnie the blonde (natural at first, then even lighter, out of a bottle), fair-skinned, with a bright smile and that Betty Grable laugh. And then there was Janine, so dark that people thought she was a Jew, with dark hair and eyes and skin, the rare smile and rarer laugh, her mind seemingly fixed on something beyond us.

Both girls developed early and spectacularly, they had that in common, and both craved the male attention they began getting as adolescents. Maybe they both knew what that craving would cost them and the family, and maybe *that* made them sad.

I wouldn't have understood any of that when I spied on them in the yard all those years ago, and maybe I've got it wrong now, but there was something that broke my heart when I watched them walk out the front door with their towels and tubes of suntan lotion, pretending not to hear the whistles and the wolf calls, pretending not to mind the

weeds and the junk that littered the yard, maybe pretending they were
at some fashionable resort or on the manicured lawn of a rich family's estate. There was something so foolish about them, so open and
unprotected, their exposed skin inviting injury and hurt along with
everything else. I wanted to watch them, to see what I saw, maybe to
watch over them too, to protect them from whatever they might have
been afraid of out there.

One day, I must have been about twelve, I remember walking
home from Cianciolo's and seeing, besides Donald and Wade and
Rossy and the usual assemblage of my older sister's teenaged admirers,
Buddy Follmer staring across the front yards at Ronnie. Follmer was
the plainclothes cop who lived three houses down from us, a guy at
that time in his late twenties or early thirties, just starting to go bald
on top and already getting thick around the middle, with a broad-
beamed, sourpuss wife and two or three little kids who always seemed
to be crying. Buddy's real name (I learned later) was Ernest, and as he
got older he preferred to be called Bud instead of Buddy, and he was
the kind of guy, the kind of cop, who could be a real help to you or
could make life hell, one or the other, depending on his mood.

Even though the Old Man and Eugene were in and out of trouble
at that time, I don't remember Buddy giving the family a lot of grief.
He pushed Jack around if he caught him in the open, or said something to Bernard about the Old Man's whereabouts while passing by
the house, but he mostly ignored the rest of us. Once, when his name
came up at the table, the Old Man swore and called him a "paper-
pushin' byoo-ro-crat" who didn't have the balls to be out on the
streets with the "criminal element," which is what the Old Man called
everyone from big-time hoods like Bunny Augustine to thieving
lowlifes like himself. Bernard said he'd heard that Buddy, because
of a bad back or some such, spent most of his time behind a desk at
police headquarters, assigned to something called white-collar crime.
Meslow called him a "fucking malingerer" and testified, I believe, at
his dismissal hearing—but that came much later. Because I never saw

him wearing a uniform, it was a long time before I even thought of
Follmer as a cop.

Anyway, the day I saw him staring across the yards at Ronnie
he had stripped to his undershirt and let his suspenders droop down
around his trousers and he was washing his car, a dark blue Plymouth
sedan that had a long antenna on a rear fender but no other markings that would tell you it belonged to a cop. As I said, Buddy usually
ignored us, so I was surprised when he grinned and spoke to me when
I walked by.

"Your sister's going to get herself burned if she don't watch out,"
he said, looking back in the direction of our yard. When I didn't say
anything, he glanced at me, cocked an eyebrow, and said, "That's your
sister in that yellow two-piece, ain't it, jitterbug?"

I looked over my shoulder, not sure Buddy was talking to me.
I'd never been called a jitterbug before. For some reason, I thought it
had something to do with Negroes. I looked in the direction he was
looking. "Yeah," I said. "I guess so."

"What's her name again, your sister?" he said.

"Rhonda," I said. We never called her that, but somehow it didn't
seem right telling Follmer, who I'd never talked to before, my sister's
pet name.

He took a handkerchief out of his back pocket and wiped his face.
It was hot that day, I remember, and Buddy had worked up a sweat.

"*Rhonda,*" he said. "Oh, yeah, I remember. What is she now—
eighteen, nineteen?"

I told him what her age was—thirteen or fourteen, she might have
been then. Whatever I said, I remember thinking it was funny how far
off he could be. Anyway, when I told him what I told him he cocked
his eye at me again and said, "You pulling my leg, kid?" and when I said
no he whistled and said, "Well, well, imagine that."

Then, when I started walking away, figuring he was done with me,
he said, "Hey, jitterbug, tell that pretty sister of yours to be careful so
the sun don't give her a nasty burn."

I said I would, but of course I didn't, thinking there was something dirty in the meaning of his words and being too shy or too scared to make a joke of it.

After that, though, every time I saw Buddy Follmer he grinned at me and signaled me over with a jerk of his head and asked how I was doing. This might have been at the park or in front of Cianciolo's or outside Folwell Junior High, Buddy either alone or with someone else in the blue Plymouth pulling up at the curb and motioning me over.

Most of the time he didn't say anything about Ronnie—he just asked how I was doing and maybe playfully cuffed me upside the head. Once or twice he gave me a piece of Juicy Fruit gum, pushing a foil-wrapped stick out of the shiny yellow pack with a fat thumb. I was afraid at first, then more curious than afraid. For one thing, there was a two-way radio on the Plymouth's dashboard that made me think of Dick Tracy in the funny papers. I didn't know any other real cops at the time, and to tell you the truth, no matter what Jack said about cops in general or what the Old Man said about Follmer in particular, after a while I came to think that maybe Buddy wasn't such a bad guy. And probably because nobody else seemed to be paying much attention to me or what I was doing, I remember being flattered by his interest.

It didn't occur to me until much later that it wasn't me the son-of-a-bitch was interested in.

After Ronnie married Gervais, the two of them lived a year or two in Rossy Grant's broken-down farmhouse west of the city, then moved themselves and Ronnie's three kids by Rossy to a smaller but nicer place farther south, near the Minnesota River, in Chaska, not far from where the horse track is now.

They moved, Ronnie said, because Rossy kept coming around at all hours of the day and night, walking in on her and Gervais when they'd be sitting around in their underwear or pajamas and bringing huge, expensive-looking stuffed animals for the kids, even though Rossy hadn't held a job in years and for all anyone knew didn't have a

pot to piss in. He told Ronnie he still loved her and pretended it was
her when he was in bed with another woman and would be waiting for
her if she ever reconsidered or if Gervais left or died—or *if,* or *if.* After
a while you didn't hear what Rossy was saying, the way he went on.
Gervais, who has to be the easiest-going guy who ever shuffled across
this earth, never said a word about Rossy coming by and saying what
he said to Ronnie, often while Gervais was sitting in the same room
trying to watch a ballgame on TV. Gervais said he felt sorry for the
guy, throwing away his life the way he had. But Rossy, sorry bastard
that he'd become, was driving Ronnie nuts.

Ronnie was working on and off and at all kinds of jobs and angles
in those days. She never had a real career, though she'd taken short-
hand and typing at South before she dropped out and was organized
and efficient enough to work in someone's office. Even in the worst
of times—when, for instance, Wade Adams took off and later, when
her life with Rossy, whom she married only months after Wade disappeared, unraveled—she managed to keep up appearances. She always
dressed fashionably, maintained her va-va-voom figure, and wore her
honey-colored hair in the latest style. When she'd come visit me at the
Cloud, the other guys in the disabled ward would holler and whistle
and carry on as much as the guys did back on Longfellow, and some of
them were physically even worse off than I was. But that was Ronnie—
that's what Ronnie did to men, and even then, only half the brother I
used to be, I couldn't help but feel proud of her.

She'd been sleeping with men since she was fifteen, and only
four of them, counting Gervais, have been her husband. I don't know
who was first (I'm not sure *she'd* know), but by the time she married
Donald Harrison at the age of eighteen she'd been with nearly every
able-bodied, decent-looking male in the neighborhood. including
Gordon Givens, who owned Givens Dry Cleaners on Thirty-Eighth
Street where she worked for a couple of months, Judy Oleski's married
brother Lawrence, the upholsterer's son who lost the use of his right
arm in the war and whose name escapes me, and, yes, Buddy Follmer.

Ronnie was pregnant when she married Donald Harrison, but I couldn't tell you if the baby she gave birth to a few months later was his. All I know is that the baby, a girl they named Annamary Irene, was born with a defective heart valve and was dead a few days later and that Donald, a good guy who was crazy about Ronnie no matter whose baby it was, went off to Korea a few months after that and was killed in a firefight with the Chinese. Not long after that Ronnie married Wade Adams, another one of the neighborhood guys she'd been having sex with for years, and after Wade walked out and left her with Mickey, she married Rossy Grant.

Harrison, Adams, Grant—it was my father of all people who ticked Ronnie's first three husbands off on his fingers one day and hollered, "Jesus Christ, she's marrying the goddamn Presidents, one after the other!" The Old Man was dead when she married Gervais, which was just as well for everyone concerned and for a number of reasons starting with the color of Armand's skin.

One day Meslow said to me, "Your sister—you know she's selling it again." The old cop was angry with me, tired of my moods, and was saying things to get me riled.

"Selling what?" I said, playing dumb. I might have been drunk at the time and didn't give half a damn.

"Her ass," he said. He lit a Pall Mall without offering me one and said, "The thing is, she's getting a little old for that, don't you think? A working girl her age has to sell more for less if she sells anything at all."

I wanted one of those smokes in the worst way, but I wasn't going to ask for one, not now. I gave the right wheel a push and turned the chair toward the window.

"That dark fellow she's living with now," he said, sucking it in, then letting it out, "think he's pimping her around, or is he merely living off the gravy? Maybe he just answers the phone for her, writes down the addresses, and looks after the kids."

Ronnie told me she met Gervais at a jazz joint in South St. Paul. Gervais occasionally sat in for one of the clarinets, and one night he and Ronnie got talking at the bar between sets. She was still living with Rossy, but Rossy was gone for long stretches at a time, who knows where or doing what, and she invited Gervais home for the night. "His wife had passed the day before Christmas, she had leukemia or something horrible like that, and there was something so sad about him I just couldn't walk out of his life," she said. Gervais was already in his fifties, she figured, although with black people it was hard to tell, but anyway she said she knew by the way he talked and looked at her that he would be sweet and gentle.

And he was. Of all the men Ronnie's been with, Armand Gervais is probably the best. He was and is the kindest, most considerate of the lot—the one who after everybody had come and gone, had used Ronnie and been used by her, had made babies with her and then died or disappeared or committed suicide—he's the one who's remained.

I told Meslow he was full of shit, that he was a shit-assed crooked cop no better than Buddy Follmer (though neither one of them was a cop anymore), and Meslow, hating Follmer as much as I did, shut up, maybe a little ashamed, and let Ronnie and Gervais alone for the time being.

It was a couple of years before Ronnie brought me down to the house in Chaska, but I don't blame her for that because I was not very sociable at that time and not as happy for her as I might have been. There was an ugly meeting when she came to visit me at the apartment with one or two of the kids, and I was drunk and stunk like a skid-row bum and in front of the kids, who were not so young they wouldn't have understood, accused her of offering her ass to anyone with a dick and a twenty-dollar bill. She looked at me like I'd slapped her in the face, then pushed the kids out in the hallway, slammed the door, grabbed me by my greasy hair, and asked me just how the hell did I suppose the family would've gotten by if she hadn't.

"You stupid piece of shit!" she hissed. "After you and your brothers went off and started killing people, who do you think was keeping the twins fed? Who do you think was paying Mother's doctor bills? It sure as hell wasn't Eugene, who loved to say he was looking out for everyone, but who didn't pay enough to keep the lights on at the house, and it sure as hell wasn't the Old Man. A couple times I even had to make bail for the bastard!"

She let go of my hair and caught her breath. My head hurt and I was drunk enough so it would take me a while to sort out everything she said, but I knew even then that she'd been waiting to say it for a long time and not just to me either, but to me because there wasn't anyone else she could say it to. She almost sounded proud when she said, "I sold my ass to everyone who would pay for it, and I gave it away when it would do me some good. Either way, it was the one thing I had that I could depend on."

I didn't see her, like I say, for a year or two after that. Meslow would tell me he saw her downtown or heard something about her from an acquaintance in Vice, and while he sometimes used her to get me to talk, I'm pretty sure he was trying to do me a favor, to let me know she was still around and still all right.

Then one day Ronnie and Gervais came by the apartment with Ronnie's kids in the station wagon, and Ronnie asked if I wanted to ride up to Crystal Lake to visit the graves. I said I did—it had been a couple of years, since the week or so after I got out of the Cloud as a matter of fact—and the two of them helped me out to the car and slid me into the back seat and stowed my folded chair in back, and that was the start of what's now a tradition.

Thanksgiving, Christmas, and Easter I join Ronnie and Gervais and her now grown-up kids for dinner, someone always coming and getting me and then bringing me home again, and at least once a year—it's been Thanksgiving lately—we've gone up to the graves (usually without Armand). Ronnie and I have never since that day at my apartment exchanged an angry word, and whatever we might be thinking about each other we've kept to ourselves. We don't talk a lot, just the two of us, but then we never have. We have nothing much to say to each other really, yet at the same time there's everything a sister

and brother have in common, all the pain and anger and feelings we
don't have words for.

We are always happy to see each other.

Ronnie and Gervais's house is a tidy pink stucco affair that's maybe
half as large as that wreck of a farmhouse she lived in with Rossy, but
twice as big as the house we lived in when we were kids. It looks and
feels like a city house, as a matter of fact, though it sits on the edge of
a small country town that's becoming a suburb and there aren't any
sidewalks or alleys around it. Gervais isn't much for yard work, but the
kids pitch in and Ronnie isn't above doing a little raking herself, so all
in all the place doesn't look half bad from the outside.

Inside, the house is as clean and neat as Ronnie herself. Only
Gervais looks out of place in his rumpled cardigan and worn-out
fleece-lined slippers. When Joe and B.J. carry me, chair and all, up the
front steps and through the front door, Gervais heaves himself out of
his big La-Z-Boy in front of a newish Magnavox TV and grins. He
seems genuinely glad to see me.

Young Joe says, "Who's up, Armand?" and Gervais says, "Packers
by three," but he's grinning at me and extending that big right paw
that looks like it's stained with cordovan shoe polish and says, "What's
happenin', Jojo? You're lookin' good, man." It's been three months or
so since I've seen him. He looks old, his head covered with a salt-and-
pepper nap, but he doesn't look any older than he did a year ago and
no older than me, though he's twelve or thirteen years my senior—
seventy-two or -three, I'd guess. His hands shake a little, and his eyes
are tired-looking and watery.

In the hustle and bustle of arriving and getting coats and caps and
gloves off and put away and everybody getting this or that to drink and
Ronnie darting off into the kitchen to check on dinner I don't notice
right away another old man standing in the living room. I blink once
or twice to make sure I'm not seeing things, but I'm not. What I'm
seeing is my brother Eugene, who I haven't laid eyes on for maybe five

years. Eugene was the largest of us LaVoie men, but that's not saying much since Eugene in his prime stood no more than five-eight in his stocking feet and weighed one-hundred-fifty pounds give or take, and he seems smaller than that now. His hair, face, shirt, and trousers are all gray. He looks sick or at least sickly, but the yellow smile is vintage Eugene, making everything all at once seem a little bit younger.

"Brother Joseph," he says.

"It's a surprise!" Ronnie says, mincing back in from the kitchen on her high heels. "I called him this morning and asked if he could come."

I stare at Eugene, who's made no move to shake my hand the way Gervais did, and the only thing I can think of to say is, "Why didn't you go up to the graves?" I guess I feel an immediate need to challenge him, to put him on the defensive.

"I invited him," Ronnie says, butting in, "but he said it'd be too cold for him."

"I got a bum lung," Eugene says. "Cold air is hard on me."

"You *ever* been up there?" I ask him. All of a sudden I'm not feeling so good about things—about the day, about what we're all doing here together, us fucked-up LaVoies. "Before you got the bum lung, I mean. Or in the summer, when it's not so cold."

Eugene, not sitting down and not coming toward me, says, "Of course I have, Joe. I've been up there a dozen times."

Liar, I say to myself.

Ronnie, sensing trouble, says, "It's going to be a family reunion, Jojo. We were going to make it a surprise, but now I'll have to tell you."

I wonder what the fuck she's talking about. Who else is there? This isn't a big family anymore.

"Michael's kids are coming. With Adriana. They're in town visiting her sister, so when she called to say hello, I invited her over. She said they'd drop by after dinner."

This is a little hard for me to grasp. *Michael's kids.* They were another set of twins, a boy and a girl, like my little brother and sister, Michael and Marie, neither of whom anyone has seen for twenty-five years. Michael's wife—Ronnie called her Adriana—I've seen once, when I was living with Eugene after I got out of the Cloud. Their kids were little then, eight or nine years old, looking just like Michael the both of them, only a Mexican Michael, thanks to their mother. So what are they doing here now? Why would they want to see us after all this time? Michael—Jesus! It's hard to believe he was ever flesh and blood, all these years having been only a name, not even much of a memory.

Elaine hands me a cold can of Budweiser and a tall glass she's filled halfway. I grin at her before she heads back to the kitchen.

Only Ronnie and Eugene seem pleased about the idea of a reunion. Truth be told, I'm not sure how I feel. I guess I feel it would be a reunion if Jack and Bernard and Janine all walked in, and Michael in his uniform and Marie in whatever the hell she'd be wearing, a short waitress' dress or maybe pasties and a G-string. Mother would have to come, and I suppose the Old Man would too. I wouldn't mind seeing Donald Harrison and Rossy Grant and Eddie Devitt while we're at it. Eugene, the sorry son-of-a-bitch, and Michael's grown-up kids, who I could pass on the street and not know from Adam and Eve—they don't make a reunion.

"Okay," I say to Ronnie.

Someone maneuvers my chair around the furniture so I can get an unobstructed view of Gervais's twenty-seven-inch TV and join the conversation in front of it. Eugene sits down on the sofa and, still smiling, does his best to look comfortable, but I can tell he's thinking that this is going to be a mistake and after driving all the way down from Longfellow and having to drive all the way back again in the dark. (I didn't notice his car out front, but I wasn't paying attention. When did Eugene get a car? Maybe he took a cab.) I almost feel sorry for him. It occurs to me that I've always felt a little sorry for Eugene, even when I've wanted to kill him for what he was and what he did and the way he would always be. For no other reason than because he was Eugene.

Now it's us three old men sitting on three sides of Ronnie's glass-topped coffee table, which is covered with women's magazines and a large, blue-jacketed chamber of commerce-type picture book about Minneapolis ("City of Enterprise, Center of Excellence") and a wooden bowl half full of dry-roasted peanuts. Gervais doesn't have anything more to say now that he's greeted us and would just as soon watch the game, so Eugene evidently feels it's up to him to break the ice. He clears his throat and asks about my health.

I stare at him across the low table. The beer tastes good, and by this time I've lit a cigarette to go along with it and all of that makes me feel better. "I can't kick," I say, a cripple's joke from way back, and to my surprise Eugene catches it and grins.

"That's a good one, Joe," he says. "'Can't kick.' You were the one with the sense of humor, weren't you?"

I was? Okay.

"Yeah, well, I must have got it from the Old Man," I say.

Eugene nods. "The Old Man," he says solemnly, like he was remembering Franklin D. Roosevelt or somebody of that stature. "He did have a pretty good sense of humor, now that you mention it."

He did? Okay.

"He sure had Mother in stitches," I say, not knowing why I bother to keep the bullshit going.

Eugene looks at me, not sure anymore if I'm joking. I'm not sure either.

I turn to watch the football. The Lions have the ball, and the crowd is making a lot of noise. I've never much liked football. None of us liked football, none of us big enough to play and not get our butts kicked and jaws broken, and none of us quick or athletic enough to make up for our lack of size. Jack with his clubfoot hated football so much he once sliced open a ball he found in the street. He popped the bladder, then sliced the pebbled skin into strips and tried to feed the strips to a big stray mutt that was hanging around the neighborhood at the time.

Later, when the three of us were on the run and living out of the stolen Oldsmobile, Jack would go nuts when all he could pick up on the radio was a football game. "Goddamn it!" he hollered one time. "You'd think fuckin' football was the only thing people care about nowadays." I remember thinking, *they care about us, some of them, the cops and the newspapers anyway,* but I wasn't going to argue with Jack about it, not the way things were going. Actually, I didn't mind listening to the Minnesota games—Paul Giel and the McNamara brothers—because in those days they all seemed to come from around here, born and raised Minnesota boys. Now the players come from all over, nobody lives where they play, so why give a shit about the home team? At least in those days they were our guys.

Eugene doesn't care about the Packer–Lion game either. I can tell without looking at him that he's trying to work up the nerve or find the right words to start something the way he did when the two of us were living together almost twenty years ago. I don't want to hear it, whatever it is, so I grab the chair's wheels and push myself away from the coffee table. I hate to leave Gervais alone with Eugene, but Gervais will be all right with it, better than I'd be at any rate.

I feel sorry for Eugene, I admit it. He looks like death warmed over—that creepy smile only makes it worse—but I can't handle having to deal with him. Not today, not right now.

Everything you need in this house is on the first floor. The upstairs, where I've never been, is unfinished, Ronnie told me—her kids crash up there in sleeping bags when they're around, which apparently is an on-and-off occurrence.

Having fled the activity (such as it is) in the living room, I wheel through the connecting dining room, where the table is set and there's one of those paper-accordion thingamajigs that fold out into a 3-D turkey in the middle of the table, and past the kitchen door where Ronnie and Elaine are arguing about something while Joe looks on holding a Bud, and through the master bedroom that smells like Ronnie and has Japanese-style paintings and a big crucifix on the wall, and into the bathroom that opens on the other side of the king-size bed.

I don't have to use the facilities, I just need to be alone awhile, which is a need like any other, especially if you spend as much time by your lonesome as I do. The sight of Eugene has spooked me. So has the thought of the pending appearance of Michael's wife and kids. Ronnie calls it a reunion, like she's talking about the characters on a TV show getting together years after their show went off the air, but we're not characters on a fucking soap opera, though it sometimes seems that way, we're the real thing, people who live and then die or disappear and nobody ever sees them again. I don't want to make more of this than it is—there are families that have had it a lot worse than we have—but all I can tell you is how I feel or don't feel, since this is the only family I've known from the inside out.

You don't know the half of it, even those of you who *were* around in 1953, when people beyond Longfellow Avenue first heard about the LaVoies. One of the orderlies at St. Cloud, Jerome Briscoe his name was, when he found out I was coming to his ward, began putting together a scrapbook of newspaper clippings about the family. He went back to Fredriksen's murder and then came forward through the investigation and manhunt to the shootout at the game farm, and then forward some more through the trials and my going to prison and then followed the "saga" (his word) as it petered out over the next several years. The last clipping he had, because by that time even Briscoe had gotten bored with it, was Janine's death in that car wreck. That was in the summer of 1963, and the only reason her death made the news was the fact that Janine, whose last name was Devitt then, was known to have been a LaVoie. But Janine was killed the same day Martin Luther King, Jr., made his speech at the Lincoln Memorial so it couldn't have attracted a great deal of attention even here. And even in those days the papers wouldn't have included *all* the lurid details. (I never asked where Briscoe got the clippings. I assumed he'd somehow wangled them from the prison library.)

Anyway, Jerry kept the scrapbook on the ward and the cons spent a lot of time looking at it, especially the newcomers who thought it was interesting to have the story in front of them and one of the characters in that story two or three bunks down from theirs. Eventually, when I'd wonder about something, I'd look at it too. But—and here's my point—even with all that the newspapers in Minneapolis and St. Paul and Duluth and as far away as Des Moines and Chicago wrote about us, the coverage didn't more than scratch the surface. Not even counting the stuff that was flat-out wrong—there was plenty of that—there was so goddamn much that wasn't there that, like I say, there's no way anybody outside the family could ever know the half of it.

The papers made a big thing of the fact that we were on relief, that the Old Man was a lush and a hoodlum, that our mother was a religious fanatic with a history of nervous breakdowns, that some of us had been to reform school, juvenile detention, and prison. They said that Jack was a bitter loner, that Bernard was a heartbroken divorcee, that just back from the Army I was at loose ends and under the influence of my felonious older brothers. They made us sound like hardened desperadoes, career criminals, robbers, and killers, public enemies ("public enemas," Bernard loved to say while we were on the run), like it was something we decided to be or something that was decided for us, instead of something that we started without knowing or even imagining where it might end up. It was almost funny, the way they had it or didn't have it, and what people believed.

The official version came mostly or at least in large part from me. The Old Man and my mother were worthless to both the cops and the press—the Old Man, for instance, told Meslow it couldn't have been me, because I was still in the Navy (he didn't even get the service branch right), and my mother told one of the papers that we'd been possessed by demons that came to the house disguised as black dogs. The cops and reporters were all over Eugene and Ronnie and Janine and Bernard's ex, Judy, but Eugene was full of shit (we'd never told him anything about our comings and goings that summer), Ronnie was too shook up to talk, Janine was off in her own world, and Judy could only tell bits and pieces and then from only her angry perspective. I was the only person alive who knew what happened and why, and though I told the cops a lot—more than I should have—I never told it all. Which is why, I have no doubt, Meslow tracked me down and put me in that holding cell we've been calling an apartment—Meslow, who was supposed to know everything there was to know about us and our activities but didn't, so he could find out what had bugged him and was driving him nuts twenty years after everybody else no longer gave a shit.

I'm wandering, I know. I can't help it.

I have to laugh when I recall the expression on Meslow's face when I told him, twenty-some years later, that we were not on our way to hold up a drugstore on Twenty-seventh and Lake when Fredriksen stopped us.

"We weren't going to hold up anyone that night," I told him. "We were going to kill Buddy Follmer, but we chickened out. Jack killed Fredriksen because he didn't kill Follmer."

By the expression on that long, sad face of his you'd have thought I just told him that Jackie, not Oswald, killed J.F.K.

"Bullshit," was all he could think of to say, but he knew that it wasn't, that when I told him things like that I was telling the truth, because what would I gain by lying at that point. Maybe, for an instant, he thought I was just trying to fuck with him, to get under his skin with the mention of Buddy Follmer, who he hated as much as I did, but then he realized I was telling the truth. I remember laughing out loud, something I don't do very often, the look on Meslow's mug was so comical.

It was, at any rate, one of those things that nobody except Jack and Bernard and myself would know, and I handed it to Meslow the way you'd hand someone a cigarette—casually, without thinking much about it. There are other things I *haven't* told Meslow. Again, that's my point. You don't know the half of it. Meslow knows more than you do, but that's not everything, and pretty soon, judging by the look of him, he'll be as dead as the rest of us.

I flush the toilet and run water in the sink so Ronnie doesn't worry, but she's outside the door anyway asking if I'm all right. I say I'm fine, it just takes me a while, which she knows already from my staying with her out at Rossy's place.

I light a cigarette and toss the match trailing a tiny contrail of smoke into the toilet and see myself, I don't know why, stepping out of the Great Northern depot and onto the hot, shabby sidewalk of downtown Minneapolis in June 1953. I remember thinking, *Well, here I am again*, and wondering what I was going to do now that I was back and then thinking it wasn't at all the way I thought it was going to be, that it hadn't changed at all while I'd been gone. I remember feeling disappointed. I remember thinking I'd changed so much, that after three years first at Fort Riley, Kansas, then at Fort Dix, New Jersey, then at Armistad Barracks outside of Nuremberg, West Germany, I was a new Joe LaVoie, or at least a different one that left from this railroad station in 1950.

That was something else the papers never got into. They mentioned the military service, my tour of duty in Europe, but that was the extent of it. They never said a word about the fact that I had visited London and Paris and Amsterdam and Rome, that I'd stood at the foot of what was left of the bridge at Remagen, rode a bicycle in the Black Forest, and visited the Eagle's Nest where Hitler shacked up with Eva Braun. The reporters never knew and therefore never spoke of a G.I. named George Gorman—"Shorty" Gorman from Worcester, Massachusetts—who was the best friend I ever had, or a German girl named Monika Bauer, who was my one and only actual lover. People would have been surprised to hear about the girl, I'm sure, because there was always the hint that the LaVoie brothers weren't normal in a sexual way. But, like I say, there's a lot you never knew about us.

Bernard was supposed to pick me up at the depot, but I got held over a day-and-a-half at the discharge center in New Jersey, and when I called his apartment Judy said she didn't know where he was, and when I tried to call our house the phone was disconnected because (I learned later) the phone bill hadn't been paid for six months. I had enough cash on me for a cab, but standing there on the sidewalk in the hot summer sun looking around at everything mostly the way I remembered it, I thought maybe I should go back inside and buy a one-way ticket out of here, maybe a ticket back East and then maybe another ticket, a ship or a plane ticket, and whatever else it took to take me back to Nuremberg.

Instead, I lugged my duffel bag up Hennepin Avenue and went into a bar to get out of the sun, ordered a bottle of Grain Belt, and imagined myself walking in on Monika, watching her face go from surprise to confusion to joy when she saw me, then pulling her tight against me, smelling the vanilla scent on her neck, and feeling her full, firm body through her thin sweater and skirt. It wouldn't have happened that way—we would've had to go off somewhere, down to the park along the river or out beyond the bombed-out bicycle factory, in any case away from her parents and her sisters (who would have told her parents)—but in my mind's eye she looked up from the movie magazine she was reading and opened her mouth in surprise and then jumped up and leaped into my arms. "Oh my dear, dear Joe!" I imagined her crying in that funny little German girl way she had of speaking English. "I knew you'd come back! I *knew* it!"

Thinking about Monika like that was almost unbearable, and I can remember the hatred I felt toward my hometown and the dull men and women who lived here. At that moment I felt more removed from my family than I had when I was in Germany—at that moment they were as stupid and dull as the people walking by on Hennepin Avenue. *They* had never been to Paris or Rome—hell, they had never been to Chicago as far as I knew. They had never seen a city that had been destroyed by B-29s, they had never seen former P.O.W.s with their empty eyes and sunken cheeks, they had never seen human beings living in chicken coops and drinking rainwater they collected in empty soup cans. Everything was safe here, flat and colorless, unchanged, and unchanging. I hated the fat bartender and the two or three sons-of-bitches sitting beside me in the dark because they weren't Shorty Gorman and because they didn't acknowledge me as someone who'd been around and seen things. They didn't acknowledge me at all.

I hadn't come home from overseas the way the guys did right after the war, with their chests full of ribbons and their pictures in the hometown paper. The war with Germany and Japan was over. I was part of an occupying army, not a fighting force, and all I had to show for my three years in uniform was a Good Conduct Medal and an honorable discharge. Which probably should have been enough.

After basic training I never fired a weapon, and most of the Germans I encountered were pathetic, broken-down people. I was assigned to the famous Fourth Armored Division, but didn't spend a minute inside a tank or an armored personnel carrier. My entire two-and-a-half years in Germany were spent as a clerk-typist, first for my company's top sergeant, then for the brigade's sergeant-major. I spent most of my time sitting at a desk, typing up triplicate forms, getting them signed, then shoving one of the three pages into a bulging file cabinet. When I wasn't working, I played cards and drank beer with Shorty and a couple of other fellows who lived in my barracks.

We'd take the *Strassenbahn* into Nuremberg or Fuerth (which was smaller and dingier than Nuremberg, but right next door, like St. Paul is to Minneapolis) and hang out in one of the G.I. bars. Once in a while we'd get in a fight, but never anything serious, most of the time Shorty and myself, always the littlest guys on the corner, taking on a couple of drunken krauts or a couple of other G.I.s, blacks or hill-billies, usually coming out on top despite our deficiency in size and laughing our asses off afterward, all pumped up and full of ourselves as well as schnapps and beer.

Shorty was twenty-five or twenty-six, about six years older than I was, and he said he'd had a couple of years of college in

Massachusetts. But Shorty was like Bernard, never above stretching the truth if it suited him or if he felt like it, so one time he'd say he was a "Harvard man" and the next it was Holy Cross in his hometown or a place I'd never heard of called Tufts. He was a smart guy, though, and every once in a while he'd quote Shakespeare (or what he said was Shakespeare) or explain something about European history that he said he'd read in a book. The room we shared at Armistad Barracks was full of his books, westerns and detective paperbacks mostly, but some serious books too. He had thick biographies of Abraham Lincoln and Theodore Roosevelt and a lawyer named Clarence Darrow. The Darrow book was called *The Story of My Life*, which struck me at the time as awfully egotistical, especially since I'd never heard of the guy, but which has since come to seem like a pretty sensible title.

Shorty was a Catholic, though he'd be the first to tell you not a very good one, and one day he gave me a St. Jude's medal to wear around my neck. I'd seen medals like that on Wade Adams and the other Catholic guys in the neighborhood back home, and while I thought there was something, I don't know, weird or *foreign-looking* about guys wearing chains around their neck, I thought it was kind of cool too. I'd known Shorty for only about a month, so I had to wonder why he was giving me anything at all, but he insisted I keep it.

"Go ahead," he said with that Boston way of talking, "take it. St. Jude, you know, is the patron saint of lost causes."

I looked at the medal in my hand. It was a dull gray disk about the size of a dime. "What do you mean?" I said.

"*Lost causes,*" he said.

"I don't get it," I said. I thought he was putting me on. I'd already learned he had a sneaky sense of humor.

"Okay, fuck it," he said with a shrug. "I just got that feeling about you, is all." He stuck out his hand and said, "You don't want the fuckin' thing, give it back. It belonged to my brother Joe—the one I told you about, got killed on Guadalcanal? He was a Joe, you are a Joe. Give it back, you don't want it."

I looked at the little disk in my hand and said, "No, I want it." He might have been lying about his brother, but what if he wasn't?

Shorty grinned and said, "Just pray to God the fuckin' thing works better for you than it did for the previous owner." The two of us both thought that was funny, though I also thought it was fishy the way he could joke about a dead brother like that. Never mind how he happened to have the medal in the first place. We were a long way from Guadalcanal.

Sitting in that bar on Hennepin Avenue, I reached up and without thinking touched the spot where the medal used to hang, then remembered that I'd given it to Monika before I left Nuremberg. It was like what people do when they quit smoking—keep reaching into their shirt pocket for the pack that isn't there anymore. I reached up to touch the medal, and I thought about Monika as well as Shorty and felt good and bad at the same time. What Shorty would have called a "bittersweet feeling."

I wondered what the family might want to know about my life in Germany. There never seemed to be a lot of interest in what I was seeing and doing in the letters I'd get every once in a while from Bernard and Ronnie, but I figured they didn't know enough about Europe or military life to ask intelligent questions. Mother's letters were so full of Scripture verses, prayers, and pleas that I read my Bible that I didn't open them after a while. Sometimes Jack would scribble a sentence or two at the bottom of one of Bernard's notes, but his handwriting was so bad I couldn't make out what he said.

This will come as a surprise—it sure as hell was a surprise to me—but the best letter I ever received came from the Old Man. I'd never seen anything the Old Man had written, not a birthday card or even a grocery list, until then, so I didn't recognize the handwriting, which was large and elegant (albeit a little shaky), and when I got to the end of the two full pages front and back I started at the beginning again to make sure I understood what I'd been reading. He asked how I was doing, if the "chow" was "palatable," and how my "superiors" were treating me, then went on for almost three sides of the pages talking about Paris and Lyon and Marseilles, places he'd never been but where he said the LaVoies had distant family. He mentioned names I'd never heard of and gave me a few directions that he seemed uncertain about, but then said it was not important that I go looking for those kin because they probably wouldn't know or care who we were.

"I just thought you might like to know that the LaVoies are 'citizens of the world' and that we have 'roots' just like everybody else," he wrote near the end.

That was the only letter from home I kept, and those few words I quoted I still know by heart, like the Bible verses I could spout as a kid.

I didn't pretend that I was coming home to a hero's welcome or deserved any special treatment. I'd heard that my childhood pal Donald Harrison, who was Ronnie's husband at the time, had come home from Korea in a box, and I felt guilty not only coming home in one piece but coming home without having seen any combat. Germany was a desperate place when I was there, but aside from some drunken war vet who thought he'd settle a score, it was hardly dangerous to Americans. The donnybrooks that Shorty and I got into didn't win you any medals or get your picture in the hometown paper.

I did want to talk about Monika and show off the photos I had of her in a swimsuit, but I didn't know how that would go over with the family. I'd have to lie about her age, even to my brothers, though that wouldn't be hard when I showed them the photos. I'd also have to be careful that I didn't betray her trust by telling too much, or make my brothers think I was bragging. Jack especially was funny about girls—it had to do with his foot, I'm sure—and Bernard could be touchy too, though he was married by that time and enjoying what I assumed to be an active sex life. I would never say anything to Eugene, who I'm sure would be a virgin all his life, or to my mother or even the Old Man, who despite that letter would no doubt be impossible to discuss serious subjects with in the flesh. I'd be too embarrassed—or something—to say anything to Ronnie or Janine.

I ended up getting drunk in that joint on Hennepin, exchanged words and then blows with a loudmouthed Marine in the men's room, then ended up needing a half-dozen stitches over my right eye in the emergency room at Hiawatha General. Somehow the hospital got ahold of Bernard, and along about midnight he came downtown in the '47 Ford he'd bought when I was away and drove me to his apartment, where I slept off my bender on his couch. The next day around noon he told me all about it while Judy and the baby were down the street at the park.

"Hell of a homecoming," he said.

He didn't seem all that glad to see me, or maybe it was just that I was flopped out in his living room with blood on my face and stinking of booze while his wife was outside with his baby waiting for me to leave. He was wearing a long-sleeved white shirt and dark tie and was fiddling with a table radio trying to find some music.

"It was all I could do to talk the cops out of booking you," he said. "Good thing that jarhead wasn't any more banged up than you are."

I decided to keep Shorty and Monika and the rest of the previous three years to myself for the time being.

Despite my first impressions, I realized soon enough that a lot had changed in the family while I'd been away.

The Old Man was gone now for weeks at a time—when he wasn't in the workhouse we wouldn't know if he was running errands for Bunny Augustine or hiding from the mobster. Mother was worse than ever, sitting for days at a time in the dark back bedroom, then coming out and wandering around the neighborhood in her housecoat and carpet slippers talking, she told her friends, to either Jesus or one of the Apostles, usually John or Simon Peter.

Eugene had been "born again" at a Billy Graham rally at the state fairgrounds. Ronnie had served three months at Shakopee for shoplifting, lost Donald Harrison in Korea, and was now "seeing" several different men including, I remember hearing with a shock, our married cop neighbor, Buddy Follmer.

Janine had turned sixteen and was so beautiful to look at you wondered if she'd stepped out of a dream—men old enough to be her father were begging her to go out with them. Bernard had become a husband and a father, not to mention, thanks to his decrepit father-in-law, a businessman. Oh, yeah, and in his spare time, instead of dancing at Bunny Augustine's North Side Club, he and Jack were robbing drugstores and filling stations.

Jack had changed the least. My first day back, after he'd told me about everyone else, Bernard said, "Jack is Jack, only more. He sits in his room with his books and TV, and sometimes goes days at a time without seeing a soul or saying anything to anyone. No one's even sure he's eating."

Bernard didn't mention the drugstores and gas stations at that time. In fact, he didn't let me in on any of that stuff for several days after I returned home, I suppose, because he didn't know if he could trust me after I'd been away for so long or because Jack had told him to keep his mouth shut. Despite the trouble we'd gotten into when we were kids, I don't think it would have occurred to me on my own, without Bernard blurting it out that day in his shop. I'm not sure Jack would've ever told me.

Bernard, though, couldn't be trusted to tell the whole truth. I was curious so I decided to ask Jack myself about their criminal activity. Jack was as usual upstairs in his bedroom with the door closed and one of those daytime quiz shows on his TV. He was wearing a white T-shirt and blue jeans, and I remember thinking how pale he looked. Jack was small and wiry like the rest of us, without an ounce of fat on him, but unlike Bernard and me he avoided the sun and was never seen with his shirt off. His eyes had by that time developed dark circles around them, which gave him the look of something either hunted or haunted or maybe both.

Because Jack was killed and therefore never interrogated or put on trial for the murders of Fredriksen and O'Leary, people never knew how smart he was. A couple of the teachers he had at Folwell and South were quoted in the papers saying he was an "inquisitive kid with above-average intelligence" who would have done well in life if he'd "applied himself" or even bothered to attend class with any regularity, but I don't know if anyone paid attention to those comments. I can tell you this—Jack was far and away the smartest of the lot of us, smarter even than Ronnie, who got the best grades and lasted the longest in school.

Jack was born smart, probably inheriting his brains from the Old Man's brothers in Michigan—Robert, who we were told taught high school English, and Reynard, who was supposed to have memorized the entire Hancock, Michigan telephone directory on a bet and could work out long-division problems in his head. All I know is that Jack had a terrific memory and never forgot anything he read, which was plenty, and could answer almost any question they asked on those quiz shows. He circled spelling errors in the paperback books he read and corrected Bernard and me when we pronounced a word or name wrong. When he used bad English, which was often, I'm pretty sure he did it on purpose, to sound like the tough guy he was trying to be. It was funny, come to think of it. He didn't seem to mind Bernard telling a fib or two, but he'd fly into one of his eye-bulging rages if Bernard called something by the wrong name or placed an address in Minneapolis when it should have been in St. Paul.

Anyway, a week or so after I got back from Germany I went up to Jack's room and asked him about the robberies. It reminded me of the time thirteen or fourteen years earlier when I'd asked him about the gun that Mother said the Old Man kept under his pillow for protection against the Jews. I'd always felt like a little kid when I tried to talk to him, and it was no different now, even though I'd been in the service and lived in Europe and seen and done things he'd only read about. Since I'd been back, we'd exchanged only a word or two, though for some reason I imagined he was glad I was home.

When I went into his room, he was correcting what someone had just said on a quiz show. "It's the Cape of Good Hope that's in Africa, moron!" he shouted at a young man about his age who was standing behind a microphone on the screen. (The emcee made the same correction without the insult.)

Jack lit a cigarette with a Zippo lighter that had a fancy coat of arms on it and, turning his eyes from the television, said, "Well, whaddya say, slick? Ready to go back to Deutschland?"

"Not really," I said with a shrug.

I wondered what if anything Bernard had told Jack about Monika. I'd showed Bernard her photos, and Bernard had whistled and said something stupid like, "Well, I wouldn't shove that one out of bed for eating pretzels." I could feel myself going red, but I was proud, too, pleased that Bernard knew or could guess that he wasn't the only lady's man in the family. I assumed he would say something to Jack, but could only imagine what that might be. I would never mention Monika to Jack or show him my pictures unless he asked about her first.

"You get used to something and it's hard to give it up," I said, or something equally idiotic, knowing he didn't care about an explanation.

"What do you need?" he said, his eyes again fixed on the fuzzy gray image on the little screen. "A couple bucks to tide you over?"

I did, as a matter of fact. I'd saved almost nothing of my Army pay, but for some reason it wasn't the money that interested me when Bernard first told me about the robberies. I'm not sure what it was—the *idea* of the robberies, I guess, the idea of adventure—but it wasn't the money. That would come, but it wasn't there at the beginning.

"No," I said, cranking up my nerve. "I heard that you and Bernard were doing a little, uh, business after dark." I was trying to sound casual, like a man of the world, not like the kid I was when we'd talked about the Old Man's gun.

Jack snorted. He was still staring at the TV, though he'd reached over and turned the sound down. "Bernard call it that—'a little business after dark'?"

"Yeah, I think so," I said.

Jack didn't say anything for a while, and I was all of a sudden terrified that Bernard had told me something that nobody was supposed to know. I braced myself for the explosion. But when Jack finally said something his voice was matter of fact.

"Well, that's one way to look at it—a little business after dark. So what the fuck's it to you?"

"I don't know," I said in a hurry, relieved by his tone. But I didn't know what to say next. I was unsure of why I brought it up to him in the first place. To this day I'm not sure, though we know what they say about hindsight. For three or four days I'd been sitting around drinking beer with Bernard and walking the streets of south Minneapolis wondering what the hell I was going to do next, wondering what I was supposed to have decided about my life during the three years I was away, wondering what would happen now that I was back to square one. Shorty Gorman lent me books by Mark Twain and Jack London and Ernest Hemingway, which I read carefully and really liked, and for a while I thought I'd try to be a writer—but I didn't have the faintest idea how I would do that, and now it seemed about as likely as becoming a brain surgeon or a tennis star. (Much later, at the Cloud, I reread many of the same books, took a couple of the writing courses the prison offered over the years, and built up my vocabulary. But I never thought seriously about writing for a living.)

Jack turned off the TV. Then he went over to his dresser, a step or two away.

"What kind of weapon did the Army give you, junior?" he said.

I told him that everybody was issued an M-1 rifle, which was locked up except when we went on bivouac or pulled guard duty. He opened the top drawer of the dresser and moved aside some folded underwear and balled-up socks and held up a forty-five-caliber Colt automatic.

"This is Army-issue too, slick," he said, swinging the big blue-black pistol in my direction and pointing it at my face. He drew the hammer back with his thumb and pulled the trigger. There was a sharp metallic click.

"You're dead," he said.

The blood had drained out of my face, my throat was dry, my knees were suddenly rubber. Trying to sound like the soldier I'd been a month earlier—a man of the world—I said, "Jesus Christ, Jack." My voice was high-pitched, more like a squeak. Then, calming down, I said, "You ever fire one of those for real?"

"Not yet," he said.

I thought about the Old Man with that pistol under his pillow and thought how different the situation was now, how different Jack was from the Old Man, yet how much the excitement I felt then was similar to the excitement I felt now. It was the kind of excitement a person felt when he was both afraid and curious, when he sensed that he might be about to do something he hadn't done before or go somewhere he hadn't been.

"Where'd you get it?" I asked him.

He smiled and said, "Why? You want one?"

I didn't know how to answer. I said, "Do I need one?"

Jack snorted. "If you want to do a little business after dark you do."

I've thought about that discussion a lot over the years. I suppose Jack figured that's what I wanted when I came to his room that day—to sign up and take part in their crime wave, Jack's and Bernard's—and that's probably exactly what I wanted. I just don't remember it that way. I don't remember thinking, *I'll ask Jack if I can join them, if I can come along the next time they hold up a gas station.* As I might have said already, I don't remember anyone in my family deciding to do *anything*—to go to school or not go to school, to get involved with someone, to get married, to get pregnant, to join the Army, to rob a liquor store, to shoot a cop—we just did it. Well, that's not quite true. We did in fact decide to kill a cop, but it didn't happen the way we decided and the cop we killed was not part of a conscious decision at all.

Meslow says that's bullshit, that we like to pretend things just happen like a lightning strike out of the blue, but that most of our actions follow a will or a determination to do them. That we decide to do things, or decide to let things happen and fall in one direction or another.

"Were you in the habit of dropping in on Jack?" Meslow asked me one day at the apartment.

"No," I said. "Jack didn't want company," figuring Meslow already knew that.

"So why did you go up there that day?"

"I don't know."

"*I* know," he said. "You were bored. You were broke. You missed your girlfriend in Germany. Maybe you were jealous of Bernard, who had a job to go to during the day and a wife to fuck at night, and thought that you might get a little action for yourself. Jack was the closest thing you had to a hero. Maybe you wanted to be something to Jack."

I shook my head and said nothing, knowing that everything or nothing he said might have been true.

"You were also jealous of Bernard because of his relationship with Jack."

"Not true," I said and turned my chair away from him.

Meslow, enjoying himself, said, "Jack held a powerful attraction for you and Bernard and maybe for the girls too. You were afraid of him, but that was part of the attraction. Ronnie told me that she thought Jack was beautiful, that he was not only the smartest LaVoie, but the most beautiful too. Maybe the clubfoot had something to do with it—you felt sorry for him like you'd feel sorry for a three-legged dog. There was fear and pity and fascination all wrapped up in Jack. You didn't feel that way about your mother or father or anyone else you knew—not all those things at the same time—but you did about Jack."

"Bullshit," I muttered, and that was the end of it, at least as far as Meslow was concerned.

The truth is I don't remember *deciding* anything regarding Jack and Bernard, regarding a gun, regarding their after-hours business. If I remember anything it was the sense of simply going along with events that were already in motion. I try not to blame anyone, my father or mother or Jack or Bernard or the girls or even Buddy Follmer. I don't waste my time, though I've had plenty of time to waste, wondering what might have happened if one or two or all of us had stepped back instead of forward or turned right instead of left. It's way too late for that. What happened happened, and there's no going back except in our minds.

This much I know: nothing happened for several days after that meeting in Jack's room. I didn't walk out of there with a forty-five stuck in my jeans or with a plan for knocking over the corner pharmacy or with anything else except a vague feeling, a blurry sense, that events were somehow in motion. I'm not sure I even thought about it quite that way, in terms of events and motion, because that wasn't the way I was used to thinking.

Things happened back there on Longfellow, but I never thought of them as events that might be connected, that might be the result of events that came before them or that might cause the events that came after. As far as I was concerned, things just happened.

I spent the first couple of weeks after my discharge just hanging around. I had the feeling I was walking in deep water, in slow motion, the way you walk in a dream.

There were times, I remember, when I almost went crazy thinking about Monika. The first week or so I was home I hardly slept a wink, thinking about her and conjuring up the most incredible fantasies, and when I did sleep, I dreamt about her and sometimes about Shorty too. All the beer I was drinking sometimes helped and sometimes didn't. I kept the photos in my shirt pocket and slid them out when I was alone or thought nobody would notice. In bed at night I'd squint at the pictures under whatever light was coming in the window and drove myself into a silent frenzy until my hand finally gave me relief. If I was alone in the room I'd whisper her name, and she'd whisper my name back to me. The next day, while I was still sober, I'd write out what I'd conjured up, thinking I'd send it to her, but what I'd write was so embarrassing I could never work up the nerve to mail it and I'd tear it in pieces and flush the pieces down the toilet.

What I did send was basic, uninteresting stuff. And by the end of two weeks I was repeating myself so much I couldn't stand to send even that, so I stopped writing. The one letter I'd gotten from her—it arrived at the Longfellow address about ten days after I had—was no more interesting than mine were, which made me angry at first, then left me feeling a little less guilty about my own feeble attempts to express myself. I wrote Shorty a couple of awkward letters, but never heard back so I thought to hell with it.

I was spending most of my time with Bernard, either at his radio and television repair shop or at his apartment. At first, I only told Bernard, who sometimes at least pretended to be curious, that I had known a few women in Europe, but didn't mention any by name, so I think he assumed they were whores and didn't count for much. When I showed him the snapshots of Monika, he seemed to take me more seriously. I didn't know at the time that he and Judy were having trouble. When he talked about his life at the apartment, you'd think he was the happiest, most satisfied man on earth. He was never more specific than I was, but he did his best to make his sex life out to be a bed of roses. The way he talked in fact made me sometimes substitute images of Judy for images of Monika as I lay on my bed with my hand in my shorts.

Most of the time we talked about other things.

I told Bernard about London and Paris and Rome, about the bombed-out German cities I passed through, about Shorty Gorman and the fistfights we got into with the krauts and the hillbillies. It didn't take long, though, before I found myself repeating my Army stories to Bernard the way I was repeating my Minneapolis stories to Monika, so I shut up. Then an unexpected thing happened. The less I talked about Germany, the less I thought about it when I wasn't talking. Germany began to seem a long way off. I'd say only a month had passed before I was thinking about Judy at least as often and as vividly as I was thinking about Monika. Bernard had told me about his business with Jack and I'd had that meeting in Jack's room, and the idea of my getting involved with the two of them was taking shape in my head.

Meanwhile, it turned very hot around here about the middle of July, and I started spending time at Lake Nokomis, a popular Southside swimming beach about a mile from our house. That was Jack's idea, Jack taking me aside one day and telling me to borrow Bernard's car when he was at the shop and drive Janine and the twins to the lake.

"Some asshole says something to Janine, you shove his teeth down his throat," he said.

Janine was going off to the beach on her own or with a girlfriend and coming home at odd hours with and without her friend. Sometimes Rossy Grant or one of the other neighborhood guys would drive her home, sometimes she'd come walking up the block with her sandals in her hand, looking down at her pretty bare feet while she walked, listening to that music only she could hear.

Ronnie by that time was married and gone, and I doubt if either Mother or the Old Man knew or understood or much cared what was happening. But Jack would get worked up and wait for Janine to come home, and though I don't think he ever said a word to her, he'd raise hell with whoever might be with her. If it wasn't for his foot or whatever it was that made him so shy about his body, I'm sure he would've taken her to the beach himself and taken on every male who looked that way at Janine or said anything to her.

Janine never said a lot to either one of us. When I offered to take her to the lake in Bernard's Ford, she said that would be okay and didn't seem to care if I hung around to give her a ride home. She knew she was already a spectacular beauty, and she reveled in what she knew and as far as she was concerned the more men there were looking at her, imagining themselves with her, the better.

By the end of my first month back home I wasn't writing to or thinking very much about Monika (though she would still sometimes come to me in my dreams), and Minneapolis was at least in some ways not the same dull place I thought it was when I stepped off that train. One day, it must have been raining, I took the streetcar downtown, and, at a Nate's clothing store on Second Street, I bought a black shirt, a cream-colored necktie, and a tan sport coat. At the haberdashery two doors down I bought a snap-brim fedora. I don't remember what the outfit cost me, but I do know it took most of the money I had left.

It didn't matter. I was ready to join my brothers' gang.

THREE

W hen I check my watch I see that a half hour's passed while I've been sitting here in Ronnie's bathroom. A soft rap on the door shakes me out of my daydream, and Elaine says, "Jojo, it's time for dinner."

I clear my throat and say, "Okay, honey, be with you in a minute."

I don't know why this comes to mind right now, but it does. When I was locked up at the Cloud, especially at the beginning of my stretch, I got mash notes, love letters, even a few marriage proposals from women I'd never met or heard of, some of them from a long ways away—Arizona, Ohio, Ontario. A fifteen-year-old girl sent me a nude snapshot of herself. Another girl sent a clump of mousy brown hair tied up in a yellow ribbon. A young (I think) woman, from some place in Montana, knitted me a sweater, scarf, and afghan, and wrote that she lived for the day when she might keep me warm in the "folds of my loving embrace." At first I thought someone was playing jokes, someone from the neighborhood maybe, but then I realized the letters and gifts were for real.

Prison rules blocked that kind of mail when I was there, but that orderly I mentioned, Jerry Briscoe, the one with the clippings and scrapbook, managed to get them to me, and, like I say, I had a hard time believing what I was reading. I could understand the people who either wished me dead and burning in hell or wanted to save me through the grace of Almighty God Jesus Christ, but I could not understand why a total stranger living in Ohio or Montana would want me to have a clump of her hair or an afghan she'd knitted. "You're infamous," Jerry told me. "Your pretty face has been in the papers. Some women are suckers for bad boys and lost causes." It dawned on me then that as bad off as I was, there were people out there in even worse condition.

Turning in my chair and stretching my neck, I see my face in Ronnie's mirror. (Maybe I turned first, saw my face, remembered Jerry's comment, and the memory of those strange notes and gifts came to mind.) It hasn't been a "pretty" face for many years. My skin has not yet gone gray and sickly like Eugene's and Meslow's, but there's nothing remotely young or wholesome or particularly healthy left either. The booze shows in the venous nose and flaming cheeks, the cigarettes in the yellow teeth and maybe in the squint wrinkles around the eyes. I'm afraid I look like my old man, God help me.

Elaine is waiting when I open the door.

"You okay?" she says, bending down in front of me, and I say, "I'm fine, honey," and straightening up she lets me wheel past her and then takes the chair's handles and steers me around Ronnie's bed and out of the bedroom.

I catch a whiff of Elaine's perfume and wonder what her life is like, how much of her is Rossy and how much of her is Ronnie. She had an abortion when she was in high school, Ronnie told me, but she's not yet married. Ronnie of course had been married, widowed, and married a second time by Elaine's age if I'm not mistaken. Ronnie and Elaine would never have to send clumps of hair to crippled murderers in far-away prisons. There'd always be a man, and when that man was gone there'd be another. Elaine is by herself today, and that doesn't seem to bother anybody.

In the dining room everybody is seated or about to sit down, and Elaine and B.J. help me wriggle my chair into a spot between their two chairs. Eugene and Joe and a very pretty dark-haired girl who apparently is Joe's girlfriend and who must have arrived when I was in the bathroom are sitting on the other side of the table. Ronnie sits at the end closest to the kitchen door, Gervais at the head. Before anyone can say a word Ronnie rattles off what sounds like a Catholic blessing, and Gervais and the kids make a quick sign of the cross and mutter an even quicker amen. I wonder, not for the first time, where along the line Ronnie turned into a Catholic since only one of her husbands— Wade Adams—had been one and not much of one at that, but I'm not so curious that I want to hear the story. Maybe it was Gervais's influence, Gervais himself a professed nothing but having descended, he told me, from mixed black and Cajun people living down around New Orleans, Catholic country I'm pretty sure.

The girl's name is Heather something, and it turns out she's Joe's steady girl. She smiles across at me when Ronnie introduces us and then takes a long look when the conversation goes somewhere else. Joe has undoubtedly told her about the LaVoie brothers, and I suppose the idea of sitting across the table from a convicted killer on Thanksgiving is interesting, something she can think about later and tell the girls at the beauty college or wherever it is she'll be going on Monday. I don't blame her for that. Who wouldn't be intrigued by the idea of sharing a turkey breast and onion dressing with an infamous criminal? It's just that I'm not wild about being stared at. I'm not used to it either, because I don't spend much time with people anymore.

The girl has the decency or good sense anyway to not say anything or ask questions, maybe because Joe or Ronnie has told her it isn't something we like to dwell on during family reunions, if that's what this is. Ronnie in the meantime will fill the air with her running commentary about life in the suburbs with a jazz musician turned couch potato and as the mother of three kids (she refers to only Rossy's) who are basically good and well-meaning but who like all kids in this day and age don't appreciate all they have and everything that's been done for them.

The food is plentiful and probably good, so nobody will pay much attention.

* * *

The wild card at the table is my brother Eugene, who's eating like he hasn't eaten a decent meal in a coon's age (he probably hasn't) and when he can't eat any more will find a way to be the old Eugene again. He will recall a distant memory, something about Mother or maybe Janine and our lives together on Longfellow Avenue, and what he'll describe will be different from the way either Ronnie or I remember it.

One night, after I had gotten out of the Cloud and moved in with Eugene and we were sitting in the dark while the punks pelted the house with green apples, Eugene out of the blue said, "I think I've discovered why I've had so much difficulty all my life."

I lit a cigarette and didn't say a word, not wanting to hear, not wanting to know, knowing full well he was going to tell me anyway.

"It's because I've never been a whole human being," he said. "Half of me died with Yvonne."

Yvonne, you'll recall, was Eugene's twin sister, who drowned in our basement laundry tub. The two of them were six months old at the time, and if Eugene had made one single mention of Yvonne's death or the effect it had had on his life up till then, well, I never heard it and doubt if anyone else had either. But that was and is Eugene, who was and is the only one of us I've ever sincerely believed to have been born crazy. (My mother was crazy as long as I knew her, but I never imagined her born that way. I felt the same way about Jack.)

The fact that Eugene believed and maybe still believes he's one-half of a human being, the other half having perished in a few inches of tepid bathwater, is only one example. I could give you a couple dozen others, but what's the point? Eugene is like smoke—he's there and he isn't. You see him, you smell him, you feel him in your system, but try to grab hold of him and he isn't there. Eugene, to my knowledge, has never had a friend, never had a lover, never had anybody except us who could even testify to his presence on earth. There are records of his convictions and probations and parole. There is his employment record and Social Security number. But you'd have a hell of time finding anyone besides Ronnie and me who could speak about him as a living, breathing human being. Maybe half of him *did* die that day in the basement. Maybe more. Maybe he's existed all these years as Yvonne's fraternal ghost.

Eugene was not much more of a presence when I was a kid than she was. Everybody came and went, usually not paying any more attention than necessary to each other. I remember once telling Jake MacDill, the black guy I knew in Germany, that I'd never eaten regular meals—breakfast, lunch, and supper—until I was in basic training, and he looked at me like I was from the moon. But that's the way it was at home. We ate when we were hungry or, more likely, when there was something to eat. Nobody ever said it was bedtime. For a while Mother would get us up for school on schooldays and the Tabernacle on Sunday, but that didn't last very long. Then it was up to us. Some days we'd go to school, and some days we wouldn't. There were truant officers in those days, and they would come to the house and maybe they'd find one or two of us there or maybe not, nobody either inside or out seemed to care very much one way or the other. The Tabernacle was something else again, but after a while even my mother's Christian friends gave up on us, scared away by the Old Man or finally writing us off as beyond redemption.

I don't recollect for that matter celebrating many birthdays—I told you about one of mine—or Thanksgivings or Christmases. Sometimes there would be a charity turkey and the fixings that Mother lugged home in a shopping bag from the Tabernacle, and sometimes there would be a charity present or two on Christmas morning.

One year the Old Man pulled up in front of the house in a big Packard that I believe belonged to Bunny Augustine and strapped to the roof was the biggest Christmas tree I'd ever seen. The Old Man and another guy dragged the tree up the front walk to the house and the Old Man rang the bell like he was somebody's long-lost uncle and hollered for Mother to come to the door. When she did, the Old Man, full of himself and cheap whiskey, held the tree out in front of him and said, "Well, Marguerite, didn't I say we'd have the grandest tree on the avenue this year?"

I don't remember what Mother said, probably something about needing groceries or paying the heating bill, but whatever it was it made the Old Man go off like a bottle rocket. He shouted something I didn't understand and stomped back toward the car, letting the tree topple over into a snowbank next to the front steps. Nobody said anything more about the tree, which lay there undecorated and ignored until sometime along about Easter when all the needles had fallen off and someone, Jack I think, dragged it around back to the alley, hacked off the branches, and burned it with the trash.

Eugene is not present in any of those memories, or if he is he plays no part in them.

Why, you must be wondering, if he played such a small role in our lives, did we hate him the way I say we did? I don't know. At least I don't know why we hated him *before* he betrayed us, before the fall of 1953, when we stopped being a family and became something else. I've learned that many families have their outcast, their black sheep, and in many instances there's no one thing that person has done to deserve it. It's just a matter of who or what he is or who or what he isn't. I think in Eugene's case it was a matter of who he *wasn't*. He wasn't one of us, and who the hell can say why—he just wasn't.

About the time there was the talk about the Old Man having a pistol under his pillow, Bernard said, "Jack told me he's going to kill Eugene." We were walking either to or from Cianciolo's, and though I already had my doubts about Bernard's relationship with the truth, I remember he seemed genuinely excited about something. I asked him how come, and he said, "Because Eugene serves no useful purpose."

I might have wondered what useful purpose any of us served or was supposed to serve, the idea of serving a purpose useful or otherwise most likely never until that moment having occurred to me. Then again, I probably just asked Bernard how Jack was going to do it. Bernard said Jack was going to steal one of the neighbor's cars, drive

Eugene out into the country, make him kneel in a ditch, and plug him behind the right ear.

"That's the way Bunny does it," Bernard said. "Behind the right ear because that's the place in the brain that controls life and death."

I remember feeling a chill slide up and down my spine and maybe a little sorry for Eugene, but then a shiver of excitement too. It never occurred to me that Jack had probably not driven a car at that point in our lives, much less fired a gun. More to the point, it never really troubled me to wonder, beyond a possible brief question regarding that useful purpose, why Jack should want to kill Eugene. Jack hated Eugene so it was not surprising that Jack would want to kill him. Why exactly Jack hated Eugene I don't think I thought to ask. He just did. We all did.

Eugene was almost thirty when I returned to Minneapolis from Germany. He was living at home, holding down a full-time job at one of the grain elevators on Hiawatha Avenue, and leading as regular a life as any of us ever lived in that house on Longfellow.

Eugene was taller than the rest of us, two or three inches taller maybe, and true or not I think the rest of us imagined him looking down on us. I believe he felt (and may feel to this day) that being the first born gave him special privileges. I can't say that he lorded over us—he wasn't around that much, for one thing—it was just that he somehow made the rest of us feel worse off than we were. I remember Bernard once saying, "Maybe we're lucky Yvonne drowned, otherwise there'd be two of them," followed by Jack saying, not for the first time, "The wrong one drowned."

Jack was in many ways the negative image of Eugene, or vice versa. Jack was always there, always a presence, a physical sensation, while Eugene, again, was like smoke, not there even when he was.

When we were on the lam, Jack said that once, when he was about four, Eugene held his head under water in the bathtub for so long he couldn't talk for several days afterward, the result, Jack said, of temporary brain damage. I'd never heard of such a thing, either the incident itself or the idea of a temporary brain injury, but Jack never lied and I accepted what he said as the truth. I did say it sure as hell didn't sound like Eugene, who aside from his troublemaking outside the house was not known to be particularly aggressive, but then Jack told me (Bernard seemed to know all this) about how he and Eugene had been engaged when they were kids in a series of hit-and-run attacks on each other, one attack begetting the next the way things happened in the Old Testament. I was amazed that I'd been unaware of their warfare, but then that was the way things were in our family. You never knew if someone was on the premises or not, people always coming and going, no one on a regular schedule (except Eugene when he worked at the grain elevator), no one bothering to keep the others abreast of what he or she was doing.

At any rate, Jack and Eugene—according to Jack—would take turns launching surprise attacks on each other. Jack said that over the years Eugene had not only tried to drown him, he'd thrown scalding water at him, tried to garrote him with an automobile fan belt, sprinkled broken glass on some scrambled eggs he almost ate, and attempted to drive an ice pick into his ear when he was sleeping. Jack said he cracked Eugene over the head with one of Donald Harrison's golf clubs, tried to light him on fire when he was asleep, and almost electrocuted him by dropping an electric fan into the tub when he was taking a bath. (The plug popped out of the socket before the fan hit the water.)

Much later, Jack said, he waited for Eugene, who was wearing only his underpants, to come out of the bathroom, then drove a paring knife into his ass. Eugene let out an ear-splitting scream, whirled around, and coldcocked Jack with the wooden-handled hair brush he was holding. Eugene then dragged Jack into the bathroom, locked the door, and tried to cut off his dick with the Old Man's razor. Eugene had yanked Jack's pants down and was holding his dick in his hand when Jack managed to grab Eugene by the throat. The two of them were rolling around on the bathroom floor when Rossy Grant, who was in the back bedroom with Ronnie, kicked the door open and pulled the two of them apart. (Rossy, always the Good Samaritan, then drove Eugene to Hiawatha General to stitch up his butt.) I'd been in the Army at the time, so the fall of 1953 was the first I heard about it.

In light of all that, Jack's plan to execute Eugene on a country road came back to me and didn't seem as farfetched as it once did. It was a wonder that both of them survived as long as they did. I don't think either one ever questioned why they were at each other's throat the way they were. I don't think either one had any more reason than a dog has for trying to kill a cat. Their hatred for each other seemed to have a life of its own independent of any cause or explanation.

You would have thought, I suppose, that when Eugene was born again at the fairgrounds he might have turned away from that hatred, but Jack said he didn't. Maybe Jack wouldn't let him. Maybe Jack's hatred was strong enough for both of them and kept the warfare from ending. Jack said that before accepting Jesus Christ as his Personal Savior, Eugene was a punk and that afterward he was a punk and a hypocrite. I don't know what Eugene was saying about Jack. But, if you could take Jack at his word, which I did, they went on trying to kill each other until Jack was in fact dead.

The only explanation for my ignorance of their combat is the fact, I guess, that there was a lot I was unaware of growing up in that loony bin and that the worst of it went on when I was away. Meslow and maybe some of the newspapermen who covered the killings knew more about aspects of my family life than I did, but then they were looking in from the outside, seeing all the craziness with a trained eye, and asking specific questions about this matter or that. When I came home from the service, Eugene was working regular hours and otherwise keeping to himself. I was spending a lot of time at Bernard's, and then I joined Jack and Bernard's gang and didn't give Eugene much thought.

I remember seeing him one Sunday morning escorting Mother

up the front walk to the house after the two of them had been to the Tabernacle. Mother as usual looked pale and sick, but she wore the righteous expression she always wore after she'd been to church or to Bible study. Clutching Eugene's arm, she looked proud as well as righteous, like she finally had a man to hang on to and didn't have to depend on her lady friends, who were sympathetic to her face but made fun of her behind her back. Eugene wore his usual smug expression, like he knew something the rest of us didn't and was getting special treatment.

I suppose I should have given him the benefit of the doubt, since he'd taken Mother to the Tabernacle when the rest of us were lying around in bed or looking at the Sunday funnies, but the truth is I hated him enough at that moment I could have killed him myself.

So far this afternoon, Eugene has kept his thoughts to himself. Frail as he seems to be, he's eating like a goddamn bear, hardly pausing for breath. Only poking at my food, I glance over at him from time to time, but he doesn't look up long enough to make eye contact.

I look at Joe's girl—Heather's her name—who's eating almost nothing. I catch her staring at me across the savaged turkey and onion dressing and half-dozen beer cans that cover Ronnie's table, and, though she quickly looks somewhere else, I see for a split second the curiosity and maybe the fear and disgust that people who never knew us, who've only heard or read about us, have in their eyes when they look at me. "Face it, LaVoie," Jerry Briscoe told me at the Cloud, "when or if ever you get out of here, you're going to be a fucking freak show back on the block." And that's pretty much the way I've felt, the way I feel, though, like I said at the beginning of this ramble, there's probably not a lot of you who remember much about us or even care.

All Heather knows, I'm sure, is that I was involved in killing a man (*two* men actually) and was shot by a cop and crippled for the rest of my life. That's not the usual life story of someone sharing your Thanksgiving dinner. Heather, I'll bet, would like to ask me a question or two, would like to know more, would like to share some of the excitement and maybe even a bit of the fear and pain that a person who kills and almost gets killed in return is bound to experience. If she asked, I'd probably tell her, I'd probably give her at least an abbreviated account of the events as I remember them. I'd probably do that because she's Joe Grant's girl and maybe about to become a member of the family, or because there's something about her that interests me, that makes me want to stare back across the table at her, that forty years ago would have excited me and eventually make me lay awake at night wondering what was possible and what wasn't.

Then it dawns on me: Something about her reminds me of Janine. Though Heather's hair and eyes are dark like Janine's, there's nothing the least bit exotic about Heather's features—the two of them really wouldn't look much alike if they were sitting side by side at the table. She makes me think of Janine anyway.

I take a long swallow of lukewarm beer. Ronnie and Elaine are arguing about something, the day one or both of them saw Chris Doleman, the Minnesota Viking, at one of the malls, Eugene is filling his face like there's no tomorrow, and Gervais is craning his neck to catch the score of the football game in the living room.

I glance again at Heather, who looks away, and I wonder if any of the terrible things that happened would have happened if it hadn't been for Janine. Meslow said it would. After I told him we'd intended to kill Buddy Follmer the day we ended up shooting William Fredriksen, he said, "Well, sooner or later, you would've killed a counterman at one of the drugstores you were robbing or shot a cop who boxed you in a corner." He's probably right—once you get in the habit of using guns to take money from people, you probably use them until somebody gets hurt. Then again, armed robbery had nothing to do with shooting Fredriksen, with taking O'Leary as a hostage and eventually killing him too, or with Finnegan, the sharpshooter, killing two of us outright and putting the third in a wheelchair to die a death that's taking forever. All of that had to do with Janine.

But I'm getting ahead of myself again. If Heather asked me to tell her about the infamous LaVoie boys, I'd begin with the robberies. Ronnie, if she becomes her mother-in-law, can give her one version of the family history—her version different but at least as good as mine and surely a damn sight more reliable than Eugene's—but I'll be the only one who can tell her about the robberies. Even Meslow doesn't know everything. He couldn't, even if I told him everything he asked, which I haven't, because there are things he didn't know sufficiently to ask about and because there are things that come to me from out of the dark places in my head and heart that I had forgotten existed. That happens sometimes when I'm deep into the booze. I'll remember something someone said that I haven't thought about for thirty years. That may seem funny because, like I said, there's not a day that goes by that I don't think about those times. You have to wonder, considering everything that was said and done and asked about and described and written up in police reports and newspaper stories and court proceedings, how anything could have been overlooked, how anything could have been left unmentioned.

But things were, things are.

For instance, the first time I went along with my brothers, a hot, sticky night—July 16th, a Tuesday—in 1953. Jack came down the basement where I was lying on a Navy surplus cot listening to the radio and said, "You want in on this or not?"

I sat up and looked at him and said, "In on what? Where are we going?"

He said, "We ain't going nowhere if you don't get off your lazy ass."

I said, "I don't have a gun."

And he said, "I do."

He told me to put my shirt and tie and jacket and hat in a bag, and we'd go get Bernard. When I told him I'd just been over at Bernard's and Judy had gotten sore about something—she was always getting sore about *something*—he said, "That's Bernard's problem."

What I remember, what seems new every time I think about it, is the way Jack acted that night. He was nervous in a way I'd never seen him before. Not jittery or jumpy or anything like that—outwardly he was as calm as I'd ever seen him. He just seemed extra alert, like he was super-sensitive to everything, like he could hear and see and feel things regular people or even he himself couldn't sense in an ordinary situation. He was like something wired to go off at the slightest provocation, at the lightest touch or softest sound. Standing up, I was afraid to bump him or brush his arm. He seemed special—dangerous and unusual.

Jack had been using Wade Adams's '39 Studebaker while Wade was at National Guard camp, and the two of us used it to drive over to Bernard's. I was nervous and hot and excited, glad to finally have something to do, glad to finally have been asked by Jack to come along, glad to have a chance to make some money, but afraid too, not so much of getting hurt or hurting somebody, but of doing or saying something stupid, of showing Jack and Bernard that I hadn't grown up much at all in the Army, that I was still a kid who couldn't be trusted.

Driving the few blocks to Bernard's, I kept waiting for Jack to give me instructions, to lay out his plan, but he didn't say a word. He smoked a cigarette and stared straight ahead over the Studebaker's pointed hood and seemed so cool and yet so focused that nothing that he hadn't intended or counted on could possibly happen.

I wondered if we were going to use Wade's car on the job. That didn't seem smart for the obvious reason, but I sure as hell wasn't going to ask Jack about it. I wasn't going to ask Jack about anything. I was going to go along and do what he told me to and not say a word until I was spoken to. I remember thinking for some reason about the exercises we'd go on in Germany, when we'd bivouac in the Bavarian countryside, then split into small groups and go out on practice missions. Everybody had an assignment, and no one said a word if it wasn't required, and even though the Russians weren't more than sixty miles away on the Czech border, it all seemed to be pretend and comical. I'd fantasize about Monika or one of the officers' wives I'd

seen at the Bravo Company Christmas party and forget what I was
supposed to do.

My first job with Jack felt like pretend too, and I found myself
thinking about Judy and wondering what she was like to sleep with. I
was thinking about women most of the time since I came home, and if
it wasn't Monika it was Judy and if it wasn't Judy, God help me, it was
Janine. It was a terrible thing and I did everything I could to suppress it,
but I was no different from all the other boys on Longfellow Avenue—
the sight, scent, and thought of Janine made me weak in the knees. No
matter what I tried to remember about Monika, after a while it didn't
help. Even with her photos I could hardly recall what Monika looked
like in the flesh, much less how she would sound and smell and feel. It
was easier with Judy, who I was seeing up close and often talking to,
Judy who clearly didn't like me or want me around, but who at the same
time and for reasons I never really figured out didn't mind leaving the
bedroom door open when she changed clothes and would sometimes
catch me staring at her in one of her tight sweaters and once poured me
a cup of coffee wearing only a slip over her bra and underpants.

That first night it was Judy that I was thinking about, and I
remember wondering if I'd be thinking about women when I should
be thinking about something else and blow it all for Jack and Bernard.
I'd daydream sometimes about walking into a store and going behind
the counter and instead of taking the money out of the cash drawer, I'd
force the girl who was working there to undress. I never pictured myself
as a rapist or anyone who would lay a hand on a girl who didn't want
me to, so the fantasy always ended there, with the girl undressed or
stripped down to her underthings. Sometimes Jack would be shouting
at me, sometimes Bernard would be telling me to hurry up. Once,
either in a daydream or a nightmare, to this day I don't remember
which, Jack raised his pistol and shot me in the face.

When we got to Bernard's apartment, Bernard was waiting for
us at the curb. As much as Judy disliked me, she disliked Jack even
more. Afterward, when the papers found out she'd been married to

Bernard, they quoted her as saying that she blamed Jack for everything that had gone wrong in her marriage. Her life with Bernard and the baby was fine until Jack started coming around, then Bernard would be "different," she said. He'd be moody and cold and sometimes hostile to both her and their child. In the same interview she said I'd been part of the problem too, but that the bad times had started with Jack and it was Jack who held sway over her husband.

"Jack meant more to Bernard than me or little Bobby or my father, who put Bernard in business for himself," Judy told the papers. "I blame Jack for everything that happened, including Bernard being shot dead."

I didn't know the strength of her hatred for Jack at the time. That night I thought Bernard was standing outside waiting on the curb because it was hot upstairs and he was eager to get going. When Jack pulled up, Bernard climbed in back, closed the door, and slapped me on the shoulder. Neither he nor Jack said a word though as we drove away. Bernard carried a paper bag, and I figured he had his gangster clothes inside. Jack's duds, I assumed, were in the Studebaker's trunk or stashed somewhere for him to pick up.

We drove north to Lake Street, then turned left and headed west across Chicago, Park, and Portland, in the general direction of Lake Calhoun on the other side of the city. It was hot as hell on the street even though by that time the sun was going down and the sky in front of us was a blaze of orange and red. Lake Street was crowded as usual, with a lot of cars filled with guys like us cruising up and down past the drive-ins, car dealerships, and movie houses looking at the girls. Lake Street was where you picked up girls on the South Side, and I leaned out the window and looked them up and down as we passed like the knuckleheads in all the other cars were doing, though I didn't whistle or holler anything that might attract undue attention. There were, as far as that went, a few girls I wouldn't mind spending some time with, but there was nobody like Janine or even Judy, and, at any rate, I was with Jack and Bernard now and girls weren't part of that evening's plan.

We followed Lake Street all the way to Lake Calhoun, then took a right at the Calhoun Beach Club and followed a winding road through a neighborhood full of big, expensive-looking houses and up a hill to what Bernard told me was Cedar Lake, which I don't think, though I was born and bred in the city, I'd ever seen. We were in one of the wealthy parts of town, a part you didn't have to pass through to get somewhere else, and I might as well have been in another country, it was so new to me. I assumed that both Jack and Bernard had been there before because Jack didn't slow down at intersections to get his bearings, and Bernard, on the few occasions when he said something, sounded calm and knowledgeable. Within a few minutes we pulled into an alley and parked behind a double garage. We had passed through the fancy neighborhood and might have entered one of the suburbs, St. Louis Park or Golden Valley, because the houses and garages were smaller and newer looking than they'd been a few minutes earlier.

It was twilight by this time, but still hot as hell, and I was sweating like a pig when Bernard jumped out and opened a pair of garage doors and Jack drove the Studebaker inside. Jack and I got out then and waited for Bernard to pull the doors shut behind us. It was even hotter in the garage, which was thick with car and paint fumes, and I felt like a candle melting down to its wick as Jack opened the trunk of a dark -green Dodge that was parked in the other stall of the little structure. Nobody said a word. In the gloom it was hard to tell what Jack was doing, but then I realized he was changing his clothes. So was Bernard. Without anybody saying anything, I shook my dress-up stuff out of the bag and began changing too.

We tossed the jeans and T-shirts we'd been wearing into the trunk of the Dodge. Bernard opened the garage doors, and Jack with me sitting beside him in the front seat backed out. Bernard closed the doors and climbed in the back and the three of us drove out of the alley the way we drove in, only faster.

We hadn't been in that garage for more than three minutes, I'll bet, but it seemed like a lifetime and I don't know if it was the fresher air outside, the fancy outfits we were wearing, or the quick, efficient way Jack got us away from that garage, but whatever the cause my heart was eager and almost jumping out of my chest.

All this is preliminary stuff, I know, the little details that would put someone like Heather to sleep or set her daydreaming. It's the way I have to tell it because it includes those bits and pieces of information that I'd forgotten, that for some reason I'll never understand wash up now and again when I'm rethinking or retelling the story, and that somehow bring the whole thing, the time and the place and the people, back to life. I might try to hurry things along for Heather's sake, but it would be no use. I need those details to keep it fresh in front of my eyes.

Meslow needs those details as much as I do. One by one, in fact, we've gone over each of the jobs I took part in, even though, like I told him, the jobs had nothing to do, strictly speaking, with Fredriksen's and O'Leary's murders. "Those plates were stolen," he'll say. "A couple weeks previous your brothers would take them off a car in a parking lot downtown or somewhere in St. Paul. Then, when they'd need a car, they'd boost one in a different part of town and slap on the plates they'd lifted earlier, believing those particular plates had been forgotten by that time." Nothing new there. Auto Theft 101.

"Which they had, usually," I'll say if I feel like playing Meslow's game for a while.

He'll pour me a couple inches of the Canadian Club he'd bring me from the liquor store down the street, light me a Pall Mall, then settle down beside me, so excited to go over the stuff that his hands shook. I didn't know that Jack and Bernard were putting stolen plates on stolen cars, at least not right away. They didn't tell me, and I didn't think to ask. Then again, maybe I did. Maybe they're among the forgotten details that come floating up out of the fog.

"That first time," Meslow will say, "you were using the '47 Dodge sedan that Jack had stolen out of the Montgomery Ward lot on University. Dark green with a tan interior."

"'Forty-*eight*," I'll say for the hell of it. He pays me no attention.

"White sidewalls. A dent the size of a football on the left front fender. The plates came off a Ford parked behind a Shell station in Robbinsdale the day after the previous Christmas.

"Jack drove, you rode shotgun, Bernard sat in back behind you," he'll say. "Bernard has the guns in a sack. Jack's forty-five Army-issue Colt automatic, a nickel-plated thirty-eight Smith & Wesson revolver for him, for Bernard, and a thirty-two snub-nose Special for you. All three guns were stolen, though not by your brothers, by parties unknown, bought by Jack from a fence who operated out of a body shop in Seven Corners.

"That first time, in that '47 Dodge, the three of you hot-shit little gangsters in your two-bit I-talian gangster suits drive back into town, east on Lake Street past Lake Calhoun, across Lyndale, then south on Nicollet. There's a drugstore at Fortieth, on the east side of the street, Brennan's Rexall, that Jack's been sniffing around for a couple of days. It's open till ten on weeknights. Howard Brennan stays late and closes up, the only other person on the premises between nine-forty-five and closing time a retarded kid who sweeps the floor and hauls out the trash, plus whoever from the neighborhood might wander in for a pack of smokes or a bottle of Pepto Bismol.

"Jack drives past the store, heading south, at ten minutes to ten. He drives around the playground on the south side of Fortieth, then pulls up alongside the store, facing Nicollet. He sucks in the last of his smoke and flicks the butt out the window. Then—"

Then the guns come out of the sack and each of us takes one and Jack says to Bernard, glancing at him in the mirror, "C'mon up here and get behind the wheel. Me and Jojo are going in."

Sitting beside Jack, I can hear Bernard start to say something, then stop himself, and I can feel the blood draining out of me and my ears buzzing and my own voice coming from what seems a long way off, saying, "*Me,* Jack?"—then turning and seeing that Jack is already half out of the car with his right hand jammed in the pocket of his jacket where he's stuck the automatic. Then, also seeming to come from a long way off, there's Bernard's voice saying, "Move your ass, Jojo. You're gonna rob that fuckin' store!" and then feeling like I'm just riding along on top of my legs, my legs suddenly weak as a baby's, but following close behind Jack who's paused before pulling open the door, giving me a look, waiting for me to catch up.

At the door Jack reaches out with his left hand and grabs me by the lapel of my jacket and says, "Walk straight through to the back of the store. If the kid or anybody else is back there, show your gun and keep them there. If nobody's around, come back up to the front where I am."

And then we go in.

I feel like I'm stepping into a freezer. The store is air-conditioned, still a novelty in those days, and passing from the heat and humidity outside into that dry, frozen interior almost takes my breath away. I do exactly what Jack told me—stride down the aisle to the rear of the store, past the white-haired guy behind the counter up front and past a display of magazines where the face of Marilyn Monroe on the cover of *Life* catches my eye. The store isn't big, and I'm almost at the back where there's a door and the prescription counter, and coming out of the door just the way Jack said he might is the kid, who has a head the size of a melon and no eyebrows and you can see right away is not a hundred percent. The kid is carrying a mop in one hand and a bucket in the other, and when I yell, "Put your hands up!" he stops and looks at me without the slightest expression on his face.

I can hear Jack talking sharp to the white-haired man up in front, saying, "Open it now!" or "Hurry up, open it!" or something along those lines.

I say to the kid, "Put your goddamn hands up!" but he doesn't do anything except stand there and look at me with his blank face. I remember wondering if I was dreaming. Then I realized that I'm shivering, whether from the excitement or from the air-conditioning I don't know, and I'm going to tell the kid that if he doesn't drop the mop and pail and put his fucking hands up, I'm going to drill him when I see he's peeing in his pants. He's wearing baggy khaki trousers, and I see a dark stain spreading out from his crotch and down his right leg and a second later there's a puddle on the linoleum floor. I remember feeling sorry for the kid and thinking, *Well, he'll have to mop it up himself,* and knowing there's no way I'm going to shoot anybody, least of all an idiot boy who's pissed all over the floor where he works.

At that moment I hear Jack shouting behind me, "Hey, Buck, let's go!" and realize that I'm "Buck" and Jack has gotten whatever he got off the white-haired man up front, so I do a quick about-face and stride back up the aisle past Marilyn Monroe on the *Life* cover and past the white-haired man who without really looking I can tell has got his hands up and I'm relieved because that means Jack hasn't clubbed or shot him.

Then faster than I can give it a second thought I'm out the front door past Jack who's holding the door open for me and back in the heat and diving hat-first into the front seat of the Dodge whose door Bernard has flung open from inside. The Dodge's engine is running hot and Bernard is saying something I don't catch for the rushing noise in my ears, and then the back door flies open and Jack comes hat-first into the back seat, and Bernard behind the wheel has the car in gear and in what seems like a blink of an eye the three of us with our hats and guns and triumphant shouts are flying around the corner onto Nicollet.

Jack is down on the floor in back where he tells us to take off our hats and coats and ties and stick them down between our legs and shove the guns under the seat and try not to look like a couple of guys who just knocked over a drugstore. The heat is overwhelming even with the wind rushing in the open windows and I can imagine what Jack might feel like on the back-seat floor where, it occurs to me, he's giving anybody who happens to see us the impression that there are only two people in this car when the alarm goes out for a car with three.

I can't believe what I've been a part of, what I've done as an individual and as a member of a gang, and I'm thinking to myself it's going to take a while before it sinks in. Beside me, Bernard is laughing. He's turned on the radio, to a station playing dance music, Guy Lombardo and the Dorseys, and because Bernard is laughing, I start to laugh too. I have a tremendous urge to pee, but know that's going to have to wait.

"Bernard," says Meslow, "turns off Nicollet after a block or two and zigzags through the neighborhood until he finds a spot between two garages in an alley a block south of Lake Street near Chicago. The three of you wearing your T-shirts and jeans jump out of the car, stuff your clothes and hats and guns in a duffel bag that Jack has pulled out of the trunk and shove the duffel under some boards between the garages. Jack is holding another bag, a shopping bag with handles on it, and inside that bag is the drugstore cash, about a hundred and sixty dollars, and Jack is carrying that bag rolled up tight under his arm when he disappears between the garages heading in the direction of Lake Street. You and Bernard walk up the alley, then head toward Chicago, where you'll catch the streetcar and ride to Thirty-eighth Street, then walk the rest of the way home."

Meslow has most of it right. He's memorized our previous discussions regarding that night, though he's forgotten or I neglected to tell him about my taking a piss between those two garages, the longest and probably most absolutely necessary piss I'd ever taken in my life. I remembered, while I was standing there shaking my dick, what first Bernard and then Jack had told me about getting sick after their initial job together, and I felt good that all I had to do was pee. The lightheadedness and the shaky legs had disappeared, and I'm not sure, standing there in the thrill of our stickup and escape, I even much noticed the heat.

I can't recall anything that Bernard and I might have said to one another on the Chicago car or walking home along Thirty-eighth Street. I remember wanting to go to his apartment, to see what Judy would look like now that I was a member of the gang, though of course

Judy was and would have to be kept in the dark about our criminal activities.

Believe it or not (I know—this sounds like Bernard talking) I didn't give the money any thought at all as we made our way home, at that time not knowing how much was in Jack's shopping bag and not worrying about Jack shortchanging me out of my share. Only a few minutes earlier I had trusted Jack with my life, so I sure as hell wasn't going to worry about him running off with any money that may or may not belong to me. We hadn't talked about the money beforehand. We hadn't really talked about anything—where we were going, what we were going to do when we got there, who would be doing what—but I can't say that had been a concern of mine either. I was—at least that first time—content to go where Jack took me and do what Jack told me to do. If I felt one emotion more than any other right afterward it was just a tremendous relief that I'd been up to the job.

Bernard did not invite me in to his apartment, so we split when we reached Cedar. I was feeling the heat again (we'd walked almost a mile) and would've enjoyed a cold beer or two at either Augie's or the Blue Spruce, a couple of taverns that in 1953 sat kitty-corner from each other at Thirty-eighth and Cedar, but I thought maybe Jack would be home by that time and didn't want him to wonder where I was. I thought maybe Jack would want to go out to celebrate, or maybe he'd taken a buck-and-half out of the shopping bag and bought a six-pack of Grain Belt on the way home.

But it was after eleven when I got to the house and there was no sign of Jack either out on the steps or up in his room. Mother lay on the sofa in the living room, where she slept sometimes in the heat, and the twins were sound asleep on cushions pulled out from the two ratty easy chairs we had in the living room and set on the floor next to the sofa. I assumed that Eugene, who usually had to get up early for work, was upstairs asleep.

Too hot and excited to sleep, I went back outside and sat on the front steps with a glass of cold water from the tap. I lit a cigarette and went over the events of the evening, never quite believing it was me who'd been one of the actors. I heard myself saying softly but out loud what I said to the kid in the back of Brennan's, then watched the kid make that piss puddle on the linoleum. I saw myself striding up the aisle toward the front door, past Marilyn Monroe, past old man Brennan standing there with his hands in the air, past Jack, out the door and into the car. I could feel the heft and hardness of that revolver in my hand, thinking it was odd how natural it felt, no stranger than the feel of an ordinary claw hammer or hacksaw. I felt glad once again that I hadn't hurt the kid, knowing that I couldn't have hurt him even if I thought I had to, and felt glad most of all that I hadn't been sick afterward. I wondered how much my military training, such as it was, had played a part in my performance.

I wanted to see Jack then, not because I was worried about him or about anything else, but because I would've liked him to comment on the way I'd done my job, but Jack never showed up.

It was only after an hour or so that Janine came strolling up the street in a sleeveless blouse and white shorts, her sandals dangling from her fingertips and her eyes so fixed on something only she could see that she walked up the steps without noticing me sitting there in the dark.

"Uncle Joe!"

This time it's B.J. who's calling me, B.J. wanting me to pass something or other, the cranberries or the creamed corn, in his direction, everybody, however, looking in my direction, smiling or grinning, only Heather just staring (she's been staring for a long time), myself then coming out of what might have seemed to the rest of them to be a coma or maybe death sitting down.

Passing the corn, then the cranberries, I catch Ronnie's eye and see she's wearing an anxious look, though I can't tell if she's anxious about me or if it's something else, the impression, say, I might be making on her future daughter-in-law.

"Are you all right?" she asks, and I say, "Never better," though the truth is that night I just described back in July 1953 I was a hell of a lot better, despite the fact I had just committed a serious felony and found out something I didn't want to know about my sixteen-year-old sister.

"I wish you wouldn't dwell on things," Ronnie says, and I see her glance at Eugene, who finally seems to have finished cramming himself with Thanksgiving fixings, and I suspect what she has in mind is somehow keeping the peace in a family that hasn't known peace for its entire sorry history. Eugene looks a little green around the gills. He's smiling, but kind of glassy-eyed, like any second he's going to have to remove himself from the table and make his way to the john where he'll pay mightily for his gorging. Heather will probably think that those pathetic old LaVoies, first Uncle Joe and then Uncle Eugene, sure spend a lot of time in the toilet.

I mumble something in Ronnie's direction, but I don't want to lose that image in my mind's eye of Janine coming home that night with her sandals in her hand. It's one of those details I hadn't thought about for years, hadn't seen for a long time, hadn't mentioned to Meslow or to anybody else ever except Jack.

I told Jack the next day. About lunchtime he pulled up behind the wheel of Wade Adams's Studebaker, climbed out and looked around like there might be someone waiting for him, then spotted me in the yard, and gave me a wink as he walked up to the house with that shopping bag tucked under his arm.

With nothing better to do, I was pushing our rusty mower against a thicket of knee-high weeds up near the house's foundation, one of the few green spots in the yard, and the wink and the way he walked with that bag rolled up and held tight under his arm were all I needed to know that everything was all right. I followed him into the house and up the stairs to his room, where he closed the door and dumped the contents of the bag on the bed. I stared wide-eyed at the $158 in a messy salad of green-and-gray bills.

"Fifty's yours," he said, "take it," and I did. I took two twenties and a pair of fives, folded them carefully, and tucked them into the watch pocket of my jeans.

"Everything okay?" I asked him. I was still hoping he'd see his way clear to praising my mostly uninstructed help during the job, but all he said was, "Copacetic," and asked me what Bernard and I had done after we split up.

I told him about how we took the Chicago car to Thirty-eighth Street, then went our separate ways at Thirty-eighth and Cedar.

"See anyone?" he said. He was leaning over the bed, dividing the rest of the cash into two neat stacks.

"Janine," I said.

Jack stood up and looked at me. He shook a cigarette out of his pack and lit it, then squinted at me through the smoke. "Where was that?" he asked me.

I shrugged and said, "Out front. Walking up the street."

"What time?"

I said I wasn't sure. "About midnight maybe."

"Where was she coming from?"

I jerked my head toward the Thirty-seventh Street end of Longfellow. "From the Follmers', I think."

Jack sucked on his cigarette and stared at me. "She say anything?"

"Not really," I said. "Just hello and maybe something about how hot it was."

What she really said was, "You scared me, Jojo. Is anyone still up?"

Up close I could see that the thin blouse she was wearing wasn't buttoned right, or maybe there was a button missing. I asked where she'd been, and she said she was babysitting for the Follmers. That was odd, I thought, since I'd seen Buddy's car go past the house and around to the alley and presumably into the Follmers' garage about forty-five minutes earlier, not long after I'd come outside to sit on the steps. I knew she had been with Buddy, that she'd let him take her outside after he and his wife got home, and that she'd sneaked around the house to the garage and climbed into the back seat of his car with him. Buddy's old lady was a drinker, so she was probably already passed out in their bedroom and none the wiser. At any rate, I knew what Janine had done as surely as if she'd spelled it out for me, but there was not one goddamn thing I could think of to say to her or one goddamn thing I could or would think of to do.

In the summer of 1953 Buddy Follmer was in his late thirties, twenty pounds overweight and nearly bald, the father of three teen-aged kids as well as a little one still young enough to need a babysitter. I could not bring myself to picture Janine having relations with Buddy Follmer, much less say anything about it to her that night or to Jack the next day, though I knew damn well it had happened. I was pretty sure I could smell Buddy's aftershave on her when she passed me on the steps.

"I think she was babysitting for the Follmers," I told Jack. "I saw their car go by, and then Janine came home after that."

"Son-of-a-bitch," Jack muttered, not looking at me anymore, but looking over my shoulder, no doubt seeing in his mind's eye what I'd seen in mine.

I drove Janine and the twins to the Big Beach at Lake Nokomis that afternoon, parking Wade's Studebaker up against the curb looking down over the sand and sitting behind the wheel in the heat and watching maybe a hundred men and boys crane their necks and swivel their heads as they watched Janine walk by in her yellow two-piece swimsuit. She held hands with the twins as she walked down to the water and showed no sign of acknowledging the guys who were staring and sometimes calling out to her or whistling, though there was enough in her walk to show everyone with a pair of functioning eyes that she was aware of what the fuss was about.

Because of the twins, who were about eleven at the time, I knew she'd be left alone on the towels she spread for herself and the kids near the edge of the water and I could stay back at the car smoking cigarettes and watching her along with everybody else. I didn't want to go down to the water with her. Maybe I was afraid of what people would think, that I was a boyfriend, the two of us not looking much at all like sister and brother, and as precocious as she was with that spectacular body, no one would've mistaken us for roughly the same age. Besides, I was quite sure she neither wanted nor needed my help or companionship.

So I stayed in the parking lot and watched her and thought about her coming up the walk dangling her sandals from her fingers, the sight of her bare feet on the warm sidewalk moving me in strange ways, and wondered why at that moment what she had done that night with Buddy Follmer seemed so much more significant than what I had done at Brennan's drugstore. She'd fucked a fat, married, middle-aged cop while I'd caused a not-right-in-the-head kid to piss in his pants while my brother took money from the kid's boss. For the moment, I forgot about the fifty dollars in my watch pocket and the top-of-the-world sensation I'd felt walking down Thirty-eighth Street afterward and my desire to have Judy see me in a new and different light after having done that job.

I remember thinking then about Jack, recalling the way he looked when I'd told him about Janine coming home from the Follmers', knowing that he was having the same thoughts I was having as he sat there and stewed in the heat of his tiny room. I remember thinking too that it was different with Janine than it had been with Ronnie, because Ronnie had also fooled around with Buddy Follmer when she wasn't much older than Janine, only I couldn't decide what made it different. Maybe it was because Ronnie was fooling around with more or less everybody in our part of town in those days and that Ronnie somehow seemed more grown up at the time than Janine. I don't know. Maybe it was because Buddy himself was so much crazier about Janine than he'd been even for Ronnie, though there was no way I could have known that until later.

Anyway, there was one thing I was sure of that afternoon and that was that everything had changed or was changing or would change very soon.

* * *

In the days that followed the Brennan job I read both the morning and afternoon papers religiously, looking for mention of the robbery and investigation, comparing what the police or what the papers were supposing had happened against what I knew actually had, but during that time Jack and Bernard and I hardly exchanged a word about it.

There wasn't a hell of a lot to say about the job, since no one got hurt and there'd been no shootout or car chase, but in those days a holdup of a legitimate establishment in a respectable neighborhood made the front page and its investigation would be news. The papers said the police were looking for two, three, or possibly four Caucasian men, two of them between the ages of eighteen and thirty, about five-feet, five-inches tall and maybe 130 pounds. The three (or two, or four) of them "should be considered armed and dangerous."

The two men who entered the store, according to store owner Howard Brennan, were dressed in "the flashy sort of coat and tie favored by certain hoodlums and police characters," the *Star* said. "Neither Brennan nor an employee, Rudolf Mitterhauser, 18, the only other person in the store at the time, expressed any doubt that one or both of the robbers had been willing to shoot if their demands weren't followed to the letter." A 1947 Dodge sedan with stolen license plates, which was discovered the next day behind a duplex on the 3100 block of Columbus Avenue South, was believed to have been used for the getaway. The amount of money stolen was not disclosed, and the results of the fingerprint testing conducted on the Dodge were pending.

"We got lucky," Bernard said a couple of days later. "Otherwise we would've heard something by now. Jack and me, our fingerprints are on file, and probably yours are too, having been in the Army. Next time, Jack says, we wear gloves." But we never did. We never covered our faces either. We would have if Jack had told us to, but he didn't. So were we stupid, contemptuous of both the police and our victims, or simply didn't give a damn, knowing that our criminal careers weren't going to last long? Amazingly, for reasons that even Meslow couldn't explain, our prints—assuming they were recovered at least once—never gave us away. Our faces neither, though we were careful not to hit places in the immediate neighborhood. I'm pretty sure that one of us would have been happy to be recognized. Bernard seemed as excited about the stories in the papers as he was about the money or the jobs themselves. He especially liked the line about us being "armed and dangerous," which he seemed to think made him taller and more important than he was usually perceived. He showed me the clippings he'd saved about their earlier jobs, though for some reason, maybe the size of the take or the fact that there were more than two robbers now, none of those jobs had gotten as much attention as the latest one had. He kept the clips neatly folded and pressed flat like autumn leaves in an old green ledger book in a bottom drawer of a dusty cabinet in the back room of his shop. He'd bring them out when the shop was closed and the shades were drawn and the two of us were sitting around drinking beer before he went home for the evening. I remember thinking those half-dozen clippings in that ledger book were Bernard's most cherished possessions, maybe more important to him than even Judy and the baby, and certainly more than that crummy shop.

Sometimes, after a couple of beers, Bernard would read the clips out loud like they were poems or famous speeches or described historic events like the surrender of Japan, which I suppose is why some of the words lodged in my brain. He was dying for the papers to use our names and ages the way they talked about up and coming ballplayers or movie stars, and if there was some way they could print our photos he'd have gone to heaven without taking the trouble to die. In the ledger book there were also clippings about Bunny Augustine, the most notorious gangster between Chicago and Kansas City, and those clippings all featured photos of Bunny in interesting and flattering poses—climbing out of his Packard in front of the North Side Club, for instance, or stepping off an elevator with his lawyers at the Courthouse.

I saw Bernard staring dreamy-eyed at those grainy photos often enough to know that he'd have given anything in the world to have been in Bunny's expensive English shoes if only for as long as it took the photographer to get his shots.

The Old Man happened to be out of the workhouse and apparently not running errands for Bunny at that time, and I found myself curious as to what he might think about the Brennan job, which was close enough to home and prominently enough displayed in the *Star* for him to have noticed. He would've had no knowledge of his sons' involvement, of course, but for some reason I couldn't help but wonder what he thought.

Making sure that Jack and everybody else was out of earshot, I worked up the nerve to mention the holdup to him a couple of days later, when the two of us were sitting at the dining-room table listening to the Miller game on a portable radio he'd brought home from somewhere.

"What do I make of what?" he said louder than I might have hoped.

I'd noticed that he'd gotten hard of hearing while I was away. He cocked his head to one side like a dog when you talked to him and often asked you to repeat yourself when you said something. Bernard once said the Old Man had advanced syphilis, was going blind as well as deaf and probably crazy or crazier to boot, while Jack said the hearing loss was the result of a beating either by the cops or by a couple of Bunny's goons. I figured it was the booze, recalling that Shorty Gorman told me that *his* old man back in Worcester, Massachusetts, had drunk himself first deaf and then blind before dying of cirrhosis of the liver.

I turned down the radio as much as I dared. "That drugstore robbery over on Nicollet the other night," I said again. "Who do you think pulled that one?"

The Old Man looked at me, red-eyed and pasty-faced, over the top of a couple of bottles of Glueks. He was wearing a sleeveless undershirt. The dark hair on his chest and shoulders and poking out of his big ears had gone white while I was away, and to me at that moment he looked old and sad and sick, not at all like either an associate or an enemy of an infamous gangster.

"How the hell should I know?" he said. "Coupla kids, it sounds like."

He was soberer and maybe even saner than I'd expected, so I decided to press my luck. "A couple of kids," I repeated. "Why do you say that?"

He shrugged and belched.

"I don't know," he said in his too-loud voice. "'Cuz they ain't us. That ain't professional, the way they did it, barging in cold like that without knowing who might be inside. Suppose there was a fuckin' cop in there, looking for foot powder or something. A pro woulda had someone go in there first, look around and maybe buy something, then go back out and tell the others if the coast was clear."

He paused to listen to something that was happening at the ballpark.

"Besides," he said, "guys like Bunny and them such, they don't go around boosting drugstores. They leave that penny-ante shit to the kids."

After the shootout in the fall, the Old Man would sometimes tell the papers that he'd known all along what his middle sons had been up to, that he'd discovered guns under our mattresses and money buried in Band-Aid cans behind the house. He'd say that having gotten wise to us, he warned us in the strongest possible language about the "wages of sin and the high cost of crime." Of course, he also told the police and some of the other papers that he never had the slightest idea that his boys had embarked on that "downslope to hell."

"No, sir, I surely didn't," I remember reading in one of Briscoe's clips. "If I had, you can bet I would've whipped whatever criminal ambitions they might have had straight out of them." He blamed everybody except himself for what happened, for "this grievous tragedy," he said more than once for publication—the county, the criminal justice system, the police, the public schools, even the Tabernacle (whose door he never darkened).

"You'd think one of them experts, so-called," he was quoted as saying, "would have seen we were a family in dire need. Someone should have stepped in and lent us a hand."

Mother was oblivious to nearly everything, be it her sons' criminal activities, her daughters' promiscuous sex lives, or the larger fact that we had ceased to be a family in the normal sense of the word. Maybe we'd never been a family in the normal sense of the word. Maybe we'd always been something else, something different. But whatever we were in the summer of 1953, it surely wasn't either normal or a family.

One of our neighbors, I believe it was old man Clevinger, told the papers after the shootout that he'd lived next door to a "madhouse" that summer. He complained—and I quote, best I can remember from one of Briscoe's clippings—about "the coming and going at all hours of the day and night, the older boys slouching in and out, Jack and the one in the Army especially, never saying boo to anyone, never looking anyone in the eye. Then the parade of men and boys cruising by and calling out the dark girl's name, driving by at all hours, honking their horns, like flies after honey. The girl looked like some kind of Indian or gypsy, I'm not sure she was part of that family or just staying with them. She was always getting into someone's car and racing off. The older girl, the blonde one, would sometimes come around with men too, but I don't think she was living there at the time. Mr. LaVoie was in jail or the workhouse, I believe. As for poor Mrs. LaVoie—well, we hardly saw her at all."

Bits and pieces from that summer come back to me in dreams or nightmares or memories.

There was the afternoon when Michael the twin almost drowned, or we thought he did.

It was near the end of July, and I had driven Janine and the twins to

Lake Nokomis. Janine had gone up to the concession stand for Cokes, leaving Michael and Marie sitting on their towels near the edge of the water, and when she got back a few minutes later Michael was gone.

I was leaning against the hood of the car bullshitting with a guy I'd known at South and hadn't been paying much attention, my mind wandering back to the second drugstore job I'd done with Jack and Bernard the night before. It was a store in St. Paul's Frogtown neighborhood and everything had come off much the same as the Brennan job, only this time the store was empty because the owner was in the toilet and all Jack had to do was step behind the counter and help himself to the register while I watched the toilet door. There was only about thirty-five dollars in the drawer though, and Jack probably wanted to rough up the druggist when he came out of the can. But just then a car full of kids pulled up in front, and Bernard gave a blast on the horn of our stolen Chevy and Jack and I got the hell out of there with our penny-ante take. Fortunately, the kids were three sheets to the wind and couldn't be much help to the cops who, according to Meslow many years later, at first thought it was the kids that had cleaned out the till. Anyway, I had momentarily taken my eyes off Janine and the twins when Janine came running up the beach dragging Marie along with her.

"What's the matter?" I said when she got close, and she said, "Michael's gone."

"Gone where?"

"In the water, I guess."

I've never liked to make a fuss, never liked to be singled out and stared at, so all I did was walk down to the water as calmly as I could. It was another one of those steamy days we'd been having one after another that July, and the beach was covered with people, about half of them little boys, it seemed. I couldn't remember the color of Michael's swimming trunks. The water was hard to look at because the sun was flashing off it, and all I could see were hundreds of heads bobbing up and down on the waves. I didn't have the foggiest idea what to do. I should've asked Marie where exactly Michael had gone—Marie didn't talk much under the best of circumstances, but at least she could have pointed. Maybe there were other people—moms, kids, older men who'd been eyeballing Janine—who might have seen Michael wander off, but what the hell was I going to ask them when I couldn't even tell them what color swimsuit the kid was wearing?

I had a shirt and trousers and shoes on, so I wasn't inclined to walk into the water. I was embarrassed to admit it, but water scared me and I'd never learned to swim. I glanced back up the beach to where the car was parked and saw the guy I'd been talking to talking to Janine—Janine holding Marie's hand, but not looking too concerned about Michael—and then it occurred to me to go tell the lifeguard. He was sitting in his tall chair at the top of a ladder wearing red swimming trunks and a sailor's cap with the sides turned down and staring out across the lake through binoculars. I slogged over to the chair and hollered that my little brother was missing, and without a word he stood up and blew the whistle he had hanging around his neck and, amazingly, everything on the beach came to a stop.

In the near silence that followed, the lifeguard picked up a megaphone and hollered for everybody to get out of the water. He repeated his demand three or four times, reminding me of the drill sergeants leading calisthenics at Fort Riley, and the water was suddenly filled with people walking toward us out of the waves. The lifeguard leaned over the side of his chair and asked what my brother's name was, and when I told him he began calling Michael's name through the megaphone. Everything seemed to be happening very fast, yet at the same time everybody seemed to be moving in slow motion. I looked back toward Janine and spotted Michael standing by himself about halfway between us, holding his towel and looking back at me.

I might have told the lifeguard I saw my brother or I might not, I can't recall, but anyway I went running toward him, running in the hot sand like you run in nightmares, slipping and sliding and not getting anywhere very fast. Michael just stood there staring at me. By the time I got to him I was aware of dozens, maybe hundreds, of people staring at me, watching me, Janine and Marie and the guy from South included, no doubt thinking all kinds of things—even if they were glad for me, thinking there was something negligent or dimwitted about a grown man who couldn't keep track of his son or little brother or whoever the hell the kid was.

The only thing I could think of to do was grab Michael by the hand and jerk him up the beach and grab Janine and Marie and shove the three of them into the car without another word and get the hell out of there as quickly as possible. I promised myself I'd never go back there again.

"You said he was in the water," I said to Janine when I got my breath back.

"That's what Marie said," Janine said, angry, no doubt, about leaving the beach in such a hurry.

"Marie doesn't talk," I said, gunning the car northward on Cedar.

"She pointed," Janine said. And that, as far as I know, was the last anybody ever said about it.

Another time—this happened, if memory serves, within a week or so of the beach incident—I got in a fight with one of Donald Harrison's cousins who used to visit Donald's family from someplace in South Dakota.

Donald was dead by that time—killed in Korea—but three of his cousins would come and stay with his parents on Longfellow for a week or two in the summer. Even when Donald was alive and was my best friend in the neighborhood, I hated those cousins of his—maybe I was jealous of the attention Donald gave them, I don't know. Anyway, when Donald and Ronnie got married in the summer of 1949, we got in an ugly fight at the wedding. Jack and I worked over the three of them plus their old man pretty good behind the Tabernacle after the reception. (I don't remember where Bernard was that day.) It had started bad, two of them jumping me when I stepped outside for a smoke, but then Jack arrived and produced a sap he'd made out of a fifteen-inch length of garden hose and a half-dozen ball bearings, and even with a third cousin joining in we kicked their asses. The oldest one was out cold for several minutes, the middle one was minus his front teeth, and the youngest came away with a broken forearm and both eyes swollen shut.

I didn't see them after that, though Jack said they'd come around a couple of times when I was in the Army, and I'd forgotten about them until the summer of '53. I was lying under Wade's Studebaker in the alley trying to find an oil leak, and when I butt-crawled out, all three of those Harrison cousins were standing there, staring down at me. I didn't recognize them at first and figured they were looking for Janine, but then one of them—the youngest of the three, Dallas, who was about my age—asked if I remembered him and then I did, right away. I said something cute, like it took me awhile to recognize him with his eyes open, and then I remembered that Jack wasn't home and wished I hadn't said anything at all.

The other two, Terry and Butch their names were, hadn't changed much, but Dallas had been lifting weights or working on a road crew or something because now he had arms like King Kong and seemed to be half a head taller than I remembered him. Before I even got my fists up, he popped me square in the face. I slipped under his second punch and caught him with a good one to the Adam's apple, but then he clipped me so hard on the left ear that it sounded like a hive of yellow jackets inside my head. I must have dropped my guard because he popped me in the face again and then again and again, and my legs buckled underneath me, and I sat down hard against the right front wheel of the car.

Dallas was wearing engineer boots, and I was sure he was going to kick me in the face or ribs, but what he did while his brothers stood on either side of him and laughed like a couple of hyenas was pull his dick out and pee on me. I tried to scramble out of the way, but I couldn't stand up, and then I must have blacked out because when I opened my eyes, the three of them were gone and now it was only Michael and Marie staring down at me.

I managed to get to my feet and stagger into the house, where I washed up best I could in the kitchen. My head was still buzzing— it buzzed on and off for several years, if you can believe that—and I figured I'd never been hit so hard in my life, not even during some of those brawls Shorty Gorman and I got into in Germany.

I scraped ice off the inside of the ice box and held it against my ear until the ice melted and then sat upstairs in Jack's room with a towel wadded up against my face waiting for him to come home. It was almost suppertime when he got there. He looked at me and said, "I guess the cocksuckers found you."

I asked him how he knew that, and he said because they had come after him in the Sears Roebuck parking lot the night before. The oldest one had taken a crowbar out of their car, Jack said, but he had his forty-five on him and he grabbed the middle one by the hair and jammed the automatic's barrel in his ear and said he'd blow his fucking brains all over Lake Street if the other two didn't back off, which they did. Jack then said if he ever saw them again, he'd kill at least one and maybe all three, and they seemed to believe him, surprised as they seemed to be to see his gun.

I told Jack I wanted to kill the youngest one, Dallas, myself, but he just snorted and said forget it, they were on their way back to Sioux Falls—he'd seen them drive away from the Harrisons' a few minutes earlier—and besides, if anyone in this family was going to kill someone, it was going to be him that did the killing. I took that to mean that only he had both the guns and the guts to commit murder and, angry as I was at the time, I knew what he said was the truth. I vowed to myself, however, that I would get even with Dallas Harrison one way or the other, and later, when the three of us were on the run, I thought about tracking him down and dropping him on the spot since I was to all intents and purposes a killer myself already.

Years later, when I asked Ronnie about the Harrison cousins, she said she had no idea what happened to them, since Donald's parents had moved to California and she'd lost contact with the family. She said she wouldn't be surprised if the three of them had gotten into the same kind of trouble we had and wound up dead or crippled or in prison somewhere.

"They were just another family's heartbreak waiting to happen," she said, and that was all there was to that.

About the same time—maybe a week or two later—Bernard started acting funny, or funnier than usual. I remember going up to his apartment one hot afternoon hoping to catch Judy in one of those halter tops she wore in warm weather. When I knocked I could hear somebody moving around inside, but no one answered. I knocked again, put my ear to the door, but didn't hear anything this time, and left. Wondering if maybe I was hearing things due to my damaged ear, then thinking, *No, it was Judy* and she didn't want any company, I walked over to Bernard's shop and saw a CLOSED sign in the door. But I could see Bernard moving around in the back, so I pounded on the window. When he came to the door, I saw that he'd been crying.

He looked like hell, like he hadn't slept in a week and hadn't eaten much either. There were dark half-moons under his puffy eyes, and his stubbly cheeks looked unusually pale. His shirt was dirty and wrinkled, like he'd slept in it or tried to the past several nights.

He looked at me like I was there to collect on a bet or something. "What do you want?" was all he said.

I asked him what the hell was going on, and he said, "Nothing. Why?"

I said he looked like shit, and he sighed and said his life was over and I might as well come in and hear the whole fucking story.

Inside, the shop was like an oven, sunshine and heat streaming through the wide-open venetian blinds up front and not a window open or a fan on front or back. It wasn't a big shop—about the size of our living and dining rooms at home, I'd guess—and though it was filled with busted TV sets and radios and boxes of tubes and wires and parts I didn't know the name for, Bernard kept things pretty well organized so you could move around and find a chair to sit down on behind the counter. It was just that you couldn't breathe in there with the heat and everything closed up, so before I sat down I opened the back door for a breath of fresh air. I looked at the calendar from Magnuson's Auto Body, which had a picture of a busty woman wearing an Indian headdress and a pair of buckskin chaps on it, and noticed that the photograph of Judy and the baby that Bernard had put in a frame and set on his desk was gone.

I asked him again what was going on, and he told me that Judy had thrown him out of the apartment. I shrugged and said, "So what? Go back when she's cooled down," and he said, "No, this time she's leaving me. She wanted me out of there so she could pack."

I asked him when all this happened, and he said the day before yesterday. I said, "Well, she's still there, either that or you have a burglar," and he said, "She's probably in there fucking the landlord's son." I said I doubted it, it was too hot, and he said I didn't know Judy.

"If she could be sure I'd find out about it, she'd fuck the meter reader on top of the goddamn stove," he said, and we both laughed in spite of ourselves. I was pretty sure Bernard was exaggerating the situation, but I have to confess that thinking about Judy fucking anyone in that hot little apartment excited me.

Despite the fresh air coming in the back door, Bernard and I were sweating through our shirts. I thought, *Judy knows about Bernard and Jack and me.* She found a gun or Bernard's gangster duds, or maybe Bernard was so full of himself after a job he couldn't keep his nighttime adventures to himself, so he told her everything. I didn't really believe that's what happened, but I knew it was possible.

Before I could say anything, Bernard looked at me like he was reading my mind and said, "She hates you and Jack, says you're a bad influence on me. After our last job she was waiting up for me when

I got home and said, 'It's either me or your brothers.' I said, 'What's the matter? Why would you say that?' And she said, 'Because I don't like the way you are when you're with them. I don't like them or trust them, and I don't want them in our apartment.' I said, 'Well, give me a more concrete reason—you can't just say you don't want them around. They're my brothers.' And she said, 'They scare me, especially Jack.'"

With visions of Judy fucking someone other than Bernard at their apartment, I said, "What did she say about me?"

"She doesn't like the way you look at her."

Bernard glanced at me, then looked away. Then he gave me a sad little laugh and waved his hand, like he might have been talking about a lunatic such as our mother.

Then just like that he started crying. He rocked forward, put his face in his hands, and bawled like a baby. "Jesus Christ, Jojo," he sobbed. "What am I going to do?"

I looked at him, then looked away, not knowing what to do or say. I had never seen Bernard or Jack (or Eugene or Ronnie, for that matter) sob like he was sobbing now. I wanted a cigarette and a drink now as much as I wanted to fuck Judy. I wanted to get out of that hellhole and away from that trouble, the only bright spot I could see being the fact that apparently Bernard had not told Judy about the holdups. I didn't think, given his current state, that Bernard for once had told me anything but the truth.

I said, "I'll bet she reconsiders," just to say something, not believing it myself, and, "Maybe you should go back and see what she says." But Bernard shook his head and cried bitter tears into his dirty hands.

Judy didn't reconsider, or if she did she was too late. For all practical purposes, Bernard was gone and never coming back, and Judy and the baby would move in with her parents on Nineteenth Avenue. Bernard would keep the apartment for a while, hoping, I suppose, that she'd change her mind and return. Old man Oleski, meanwhile, let Bernard hold on to the shop, either because he was too crippled with his arthritis to take it back or because there was not enough left to take back. At any rate, Bernard and I spent the next two days and nights after our discussion sitting in his cleaned-out apartment drinking Grain Belt and cursing women. Then Jack came by, called us babies, and told us to quit crying in our fucking beer.

The next day he came by again and said if we could sober up enough, we could join him that night for a job.

FOUR

t's the doorbell that rouses me from my reverie this time, my eyes opening on Joe's girl Heather whose eyes in turn leave mine to jump toward the front door where Gervais is letting in the late arrivals. Ronnie, on her four-inch heels, prances after him, shrieking toward the newcomers, "Adriana, honey! Please come in!" then shrieking back at us, "Look, everybody, it's Adriana and Michael's kids!"

Adriana is a large, attractive, brown-skinned woman with a lot of black hair piled on top of her head. She's wearing a heavy fur coat of some kind and silver-colored shoes at least as high in the heels as Ronnie's. She's smiling at Ronnie, at Gervais, at the rest of us sitting around the dining-room table, but it's the kind of smile you smile at strangers. Behind her are a boy and a girl, hardly "kids" anymore, in their middle twenties, I would guess, both of them as brown as their mother, but not nearly as large—stocky you'd probably call them— their twin faces despite the dark complexion immediately familiar, their small noses and thin, straight mouths definitely marking them as LaVoies. Neither one of them even tries to force a smile.

Adriana Cruz grew up on the West Side of St. Paul, where there have been plenty of Mexicans for the better part of a century, but Ronnie said she's been living in Texas for twenty-five years. How Michael met her I don't know, the grownup Michael every bit as much a mystery as Michael the little boy, as much a mystery as his twin sister Marie.

I was already in my second decade at the Cloud when Michael met Adriana. Ronnie mentioned her, I believe, in a letter circa 1965, about the time Michael was going off to Vietnam. Michael had been to see me only a few days earlier, but for some reason he hadn't mentioned a girl, let alone a Mexican girl from St. Paul's West Side. Maybe there were other things on his mind, or maybe it was something else.

Michael, not Jack, was the handsomest of the LaVoie men, small but perfectly put together, a clear-eyed, teetotaling bodybuilder. In his uniform with the sergeant's stripes and gold-and-black First Cavalry patch on the shoulder, he reminded me of my days in the service—though private first class was the best I could do, I was armored and, even with all the postwar craziness, it had been a hell of a lot safer for American soldiers in Germany than it was going to be in Vietnam. Michael and I were not close. He had been to see me maybe three times when I was in prison, and before that he and Marie were the silent twins with sad eyes who'd seen most everything there was to see at the house on Longfellow Avenue but been a part of almost nothing.

I don't know what we talked about that last visit before Michael went off to the war, but it wasn't Adriana or any other woman except maybe Marie.

I don't know for that matter how the twins got along between 1953 and the middle '60s when the both of them went off and never came back again. I imagine they carried on pretty much the way the rest of us had when we were growing up—getting into scrapes, playing hide-and-seek with the truant officer, sometimes not eating or wearing enough, often wishing we were something other than LaVoies. Except that I've often thought it must have been worse for the twins, because so many of us took off on them—Jack and Bernard and me in 1953, Mother two years later, Janine eight years after that. (Ronnie was gone already, of course, and while she said she looked in on the twins as often as she could, she was trying to live her own life with her own kids and her own problems, and could not have been very helpful to anyone at that time.) We weren't much maybe, but we were probably better than nothing, better anyway than Eugene and the Old Man, who, according to Eugene, believed the twins were born not quite right and were not much more than a pair of lookalike statues. The Old Man, Eugene once told me, called them "sawed-off cigar store Indians."

Both Michael and Marie left home as soon as they were able. Michael lied about his age and enlisted in the Army when he was sixteen. Marie, I learned, left about the same time—on the back of a Harley Davidson piloted by a forty-five-year-old employee of Rossy Grant's father.

Marie didn't have the looks of either Ronnie or Janine—she was wan and bony and not very healthy—but she was apparently every bit as man-crazy because the middle-aged biker she finally rode off with was hardly the first man she'd known. At first it occurred to me and Ronnie separately (Ronnie told me this later) that the twins ran off together, that Marie would somehow find a way to live close to wherever Michael was stationed (there would always be plenty of men around an Army base), because neither Ronnie nor I could envision the two of them living apart. Even in my dreams, I've never seen one without the other. In fact, they'd likely gone off in different directions, and no one knows if they ever saw each other again.

Michael came back occasionally and stayed for a while with a buddy in Columbia Heights, but by that time he was a career soldier moving from one posting to another. Marie was gone for good as far as I knew. Ronnie and I got Christmas cards from her for a while, but there was never any information, only her scribbled name at the bottom. The cards were postmarked from places in Washington State and California, but there was never a return address and she never said where or how she was living. Meslow told me he'd seen her working in a strip joint in San Francisco along about 1965, but she was using another name and refused to talk to him or acknowledge her hometown. He said she was coughing a lot and hadn't looked well. There were other sightings too—one by a cop friend of Meslow's who'd been with him the first time, this second time at a movie studio near San Francisco where people were making stag films—but there was nothing definite or substantial and never anything from Marie herself.

In November 1965, the Army informed the family that Michael was missing in action and presumed dead after the third day of the battle of Ia Drang Valley, Vietnam. It was a few years later that we more or less accepted the fact that Marie was dead too, if for no other reason than it was impossible to think of one existing very long without the other.

Why Adriana appeared with her own twins at the Longfellow house one Sunday afternoon in 1974, when I was staying there with Eugene, I can't remember. She was living in Texas by that time and I think she had remarried, her twin boy and girl about seven or eight years old. She was shy and dark and beautiful in a distinctly Latina way, and she hadn't gotten fat yet either, so I remember thinking that Michael had at least for a brief while enjoyed a little luck. I suppose she was calling on Michael's family out of courtesy, like she's doing today, and it must be hard because there was not much for her to say or do except smile that huge smile a person smiles at strangers. Who knows what she made of her dead husband's surviving brothers, one a religious fanatic and the other a crippled murderer, in that little cracker box of a house? Could she picture Michael growing up there with a drunken father and a crazy mother, with criminal brothers and slutty sisters, everybody coming and going and then disappearing for good?

Who knows what she makes of the motley crew assembled in front of her and her kids today, seventeen years later? She will remember me because of the wheelchair if nothing else, and maybe Eugene on account of his creepy smile. The rest of the group, Ronnie excepted, she's never laid eyes on, I'd guess, so maybe she's amazed that after all the coming and going and disappearances there are so many LaVoies still around.

She accepts Ronnie's outstretched hands and with the huge smile frozen on her face steps into the living room and lets Gervais help her out of her heavy coat.

Michael and Adriana's kids are named Richard and Annabel, Ronnie announces, dragging them into the living room as well.

"*Isabel*," Adriana says softly, and Ronnie, who's a little drunk, looks like she doesn't understand, and Adriana says, "My daughter's name is Isabel."

Ronnie looks at Adriana, then hugs the girl, and says with that famous laugh of hers, "Oh, sure, honey. I knew that. *Isabel*."

Adriana seems willing to come to the table where everybody except me has politely pushed back their chairs and gotten up to greet the new arrivals, but the kids hang back, still wearing their jackets and not looking at all happy to be part of Aunt Ronnie's "reunion." I have the sudden sense that despite their departed father's sweetness, the family curse lurks in his kids.

As Adriana settles in at the table, I can't help but notice that both Richard and Isabel are staring at me, apparently finding me, if no one else, of passing interest. I wonder if they remember the uncle in the wheelchair from that visit seventeen years ago and what if anything their mother has told them. Do they know what happened in 1953, when their father was only ten or eleven, when the family blew apart and their father said or did nothing, just stood there with his twin sister and watched? The way they look at me, with what seems to be a mixture of curiosity and some foggy knowledge, tells me that they've been told *something*, though who knows what. I wonder what Michael might have told Adriana, what others might have told Adriana about Michael's family, and what Adriana might have passed along to her kids. Michael never saw his kids, who were born after he'd left for Vietnam, let alone had a chance to tell them anything about anyone, so whatever they know would no doubt have come through Adriana.

I feel an unexpected stab of happiness amid the forced conversation and the pouring of weak coffee and the passing around of Ronnie's pumpkin pie, and I believe it has to do with Michael's kids. It was happiness I felt a while ago when I caught Joe's girl Heather looking at me that way. I know I shouldn't give a good goddamn about the curiosity or wonder or whatever it is that a couple of kids seem to have heard about me and my brothers—but obviously I do. I must want it or even crave it the way I must have wanted and craved Meslow's attention and thus allowed our current arrangement.

I know this contradicts what I said earlier about people forgetting and their forgetting being fine with me. The truth is, I want *someone* to know and to remember no matter what, afraid that the only thing worse than reliving what went on back then is denying it happened, which would be denying that we ever existed.

Adriana says she and her kids have come from dinner at her sister's place in Lakeville, and judging by the way she slurs a word here and there she may be tipsy herself. Her kids keep their distance, frowning at her references to them and avoiding her eyes when she looks at them. They are interested in me, however, and their interest picks me up. Richard reminds me of Jack—the expression, the attitude, the swagger—and Isabel has Janine's dark smolder. If I drink enough, if I let myself go, I can believe in ghosts.

Meslow, at least until recently, often talked about ghosts. On bad days the old cop would get as liquored up as I was and talk about the ghost of Dick Walsh, the Minneapolis police chief in 1953, who died several years ago in an Arizona nursing home believing he was Clementine Churchill, and the ghost of Meslow's partner, Marty Sutherland, who supposedly died of a heart attack in his sleep but in fact swallowed a bottle of sleeping pills after his wife of thirty years walked out on him. (Sometimes, for the hell of it, I'd mention the ghost of Jimmy Finnegan, who was the actual killer and crippler of the LaVoie gang, but Meslow pretended he didn't hear me.) The living and the dead, but especially the dead, have visited Meslow over the past almost four decades as often or nearly as often as they've visited me. How the sorry son-of-a-bitch would love to be here today!

That thought and my giddiness brought on by Michael's kids bring me to laugh. I take a swallow of my beer and hope that no one's seen me, and no one with the possible exception of young Richard has. He sort of smiles or smirks in my direction—and reminds me even more of Jack. Richard strikes me as a killer at heart if not in deed, which is exactly what Jack was until that September evening in 1953.

Thinking the way I am now, I wonder: Would Meslow pick up on that? A sadder but wiser man than he'd been in the fall of 1953, would Meslow spot the killer before he killed?

Suppose he did. Suppose, wandering among this ragtag Thanksgiving gathering, or sitting, say, where Gervais is sitting, soberer maybe than the rest of us, soberer than I am and soberer than Gervais is in any case, the old detective, the highly praised and heavily decorated super sleuth of the Minneapolis Police Department circa 1953, saw in young Richard Cruz LaVoie (or whatever the hell his last name is now) the seeds of a policeman's brutal, unprovoked death, the seeds of the brutal, unprovoked death of an innocent farmer, and the brutal but *not* unprovoked deaths of his fellow gang member and himself, not to mention the crippling of yet another pathetic gangster the exact degree of whose guilt may still be debated.

Then what would he do? Would he take the boy aside and warn him about his future? Would he pass the knowledge on to his colleagues, to the department to which he gave the best years of his professional life? Or would he content himself by merely keeping an eye on the kid, knowing that keeping an eye on somebody meant nothing, meant doing nothing, except afterward being able to say he'd seen it coming yet there hadn't been a goddamn thing he could do about it?

Meslow had *not* seen it coming—the brutal, unprovoked murder of Patrolman William Fredriksen. How could he, not knowing Jack, or at least not knowing the extent of the trouble Jack was capable of causing? Meslow, like most Minneapolis cops at the time, knew or had reason to know or hear about the LaVoie family. But whatever no good the Old Man and his sons had been up to till that time—even armed robbery and the occasional assault—didn't add up to murder. Why Meslow sees ghosts is the farmer, Thomas O'Leary, a father of seven himself, who was dragged out of his car and taken hostage at gunpoint, then shot point-blank between the eyes by the man who by this time, thirty-four days after the police officer's murder, should have been identified, tracked down, and taken into custody where neither he nor his brothers could hurt another soul again.

I believe Meslow on this day would do nothing. Maybe he wouldn't notice the smirk on Richard's face, or if he saw it wouldn't think of Jack LaVoie and the ghost of either Bill Fredriksen or Tom O'Leary. Like me, Meslow's an old man, dying and soon dead, a ghost any day now himself. His failure to identify and apprehend a cop-killer and two accomplices who were operating right under his nose and thereby save the life of an innocent man has in an odd way maybe kept him going longer than he might have gone on otherwise. Now I figure he's finally run out of gas. Meslow has less going for him than I do, and I don't have much, though I do have what Meslow wants and will never get, which is the certain and complete knowledge of causes and effects.

Stone sober, Meslow might say he'd do nothing differently if he had the chance to do it again, but of course he would—would try to anyway. The ghosts that keep him wide-eyed and awake at night would make him.

But then again, he can't. No one gets a second chance.

Poor Meslow. He was shocked when I told him that he'd been wrong all along about where we were going and what we were up to the day Fredriksen was murdered. But I could also say that nobody was more shocked than Bernard and me and maybe even Jack himself by the way things turned out.

We were robbers. We were a gang that robbed drugstores and liquor stores and once in a while a filling station like the Pure Oil on Lake Street that got my brothers rolling in the first place. Between July 14th, when I first got involved, and the end of August when Jack decided to kill Buddy Follmer, we pulled a total of seven jobs, one a week on average—two Southside drugstores, a drugstore in Robbins-dale, a liquor store in the Frogtown neighborhood of St. Paul, a liquor store on Central Avenue Northeast, a Phillips 66 on Penn Avenue in Richfield, and a Cities Service on Tenth Street downtown. On each job we used a stolen car with stolen plates, four different cars in all. On each job we followed more or less the same modus operandi—two of us going in while the other kept lookout from behind the wheel of the car. On all but one of the jobs I went inside with Jack while Bernard stayed in the car. I don't know why. We were just following Jack's orders.

We were remarkably lucky—not only were we never identified, we were never forced to shoot our way out of a situation, we were never pursued or even confronted by either the police or an armed citizen—and we confused being lucky with being invincible.

It was after the third job, the Cities Service station on Tenth Street, that the Minneapolis papers began describing us as gangsters. Our flashy outfits were reported in some detail, thanks especially to the description the kid on duty gave the cops.

The kid's name was Curtis Cousins, and he was eighteen years old and though he wore the thickest pair of glasses I'd ever seen on a human being, he described the hats and jackets and shirts and ties Jack and I wore that night in so much detail you'd have sworn he'd taken a photo. Fortunately for us, he couldn't remember much of anything about anything else—our faces, our heights and builds, the kind of guns we were carrying, the make or year or color of our car.

Most of what he recalled (and was reported in the papers) was wrong and therefore helpful to us, offsetting the description of the clothes. He said that one of us was about thirty years old while the other one was over six feet tall, that the older one talked with a Southern drawl, and that the car had either orange or yellow plates and seemed to be carrying four men when it sped away from the station. The papers, quoting Detective Inspector Harold V. Meslow of the Minneapolis Police Department (the first time I saw his name in print), then said authorities were tracking "a fast-moving quartet of nattily attired gangsters, possibly from the South or the southwestern United States, and believed to be driving a dark blue or black four-door sedan, possibly a Buick, with either Wisconsin, Nebraska, or Texas license plates."

The car was actually a green Oldsmobile with black-and-white Minnesota plates, and there were only the three of us inside it when we left.

But of all the newspaper accounts about our robberies that summer, that was the one that interested us the most. Bernard was beside himself, he was so tickled by the attention given to our outfits. Bernard, by that time, had begun to show the wear and tear caused by his marital troubles. I would find him locked up in the shop cursing and weeping and sometimes making noises about "ending it all." Since his marriage went bust, he was living for our jobs every week or so, and it annoyed him that either the cops, the papers, or both in some sort of gentlemen's agreement were being so stingy with the details. Curtis Cousins's account sent him over the moon.

"Nattily attired!" Bernard crowed, waving that evening's *Star* in my face. "Jojo, you and me and Jack, we're a 'fast-moving quartet of nattily attired gangsters'! Can you fucking feature that?"

Then he started to dance around the room.

Of course, Bernard would never have carried on like that in front of Jack. Jack hated the reported details about the clothing and was having, I'm sure, serious second thoughts about the wisdom of wearing such distinctive outfits in the first place. As a matter of fact, if he'd thought Bernard deserved the sole credit (or blame) for the hats and ties, I think at that point things would have gotten dicey between the two of them. As it was, Jack seemed to believe that the duds were more or less *his* idea, so he had mostly himself to blame. Bernard, mean-while, speculated that Curtis Cousins was so scared of us gangsters coming back to kill him that after giving the cops that description of our clothes, he deliberately led them astray about our height and age and accent and car, and would never testify against us if we were ever arrested.

Bernard said, "That four-eyed goof, after he blabbed about the hats and dark shirts, thought, *Oh my God, what have I done, going on like that about the clothes*, and started lying to save his hide. I'll lay you three-to-one odds that he *admires* us, the clothes and all, and craves our respect. Maybe he'd want to join us if we gave him the chance."

Well, Bernard made the mistake of saying that in front of Jack, who slapped him upside the head with the newspaper he'd rolled up like he was going to throw it on someone's front step, and said, "You stupid son-of-a-bitch! The motherfucker told them everything he saw, and he told it to them right. This is all a fuckin' cop trick to make us think we're free and clear!"

Whether Jack believed what he said I'll never know, but it sure as hell dropped a wet blanket on our celebration. Thinking we were invincible didn't mean we were careless. Jack was our leader, and Jack was the most careful person I ever knew. He would never throw caution to the wind, no matter how successful we might be, and we trusted him completely. If Jack said "Jump," we'd say "How high?" If Jack said the Curtis Cousins report was a cop trick, we'd agree with him, even though deep down we didn't believe it was a trick. Anyway, Bernard shut up and never said another word about Curtis Cousins or that Cities Service job or the sudden notoriety of our clothes, at least not in front of Jack.

I know for a fact, however, that a couple days after that job, Bernard's curiosity got the best of him and he called Curtis Cousins on the phone. (The papers provided the addresses of crime victims in those days, so all Bernard had to do was look him up in the city phonebook.) When Cousins said hello, Bernard asked him if he knew who it was, but before Cousins could answer, Bernard, apparently not knowing what he would say next and thinking he wouldn't be believed if he identified himself as one of the robbers, slammed down the phone. I had a feeling he'd try something along those lines, and once, when we were hiding out after Fredriksen's murder and Jack was out of earshot, I confronted him and he admitted as much.

"I still think he was one of us," he muttered a moment later, and that was the last either one of us said about it.

I had and still have my own hunch about that particular event, and that is that it also marked the point when Jack started thinking about doing something besides robbing stores and gas stations. We pulled another four jobs before we were through, but I believe the idea of another kind of crime had hatched and was growing inside Jack while we were doing them.

Jack had always been moody, given to long stretches of silence and long, unblinking stares that could scare the hell out of the people who saw him.

Mother couldn't bear those stares and silences, which Eugene once said began when Jack was a baby. Eugene said that Jack never cried, even when he tumbled down the basement stairs or burned himself playing with matches. Eugene said that one time, when Jack was three or four, Mother was so spooked by his steely eyed silences that she pulled down his pants and beat him with a yardstick until he started to bleed—but though *she* was sobbing like a madwoman, Eugene said, Jack didn't make a sound. The Old Man used to brag about Jack to his cronies—the "toughest little son-of-a-bitch on the block," he used to call him, again according to Eugene. The Old Man, however, was careful about how he handled Jack, the Old Man being as discombobulated as Mother by the stares and silence. Eventually, the Old Man had good reason to fear Jack from a physical stand-point—more than once Jack threatened to kill him and at least once, at that birthday party I told you about, actually knocked him on his ass.

Teachers, neighbors, friends of Mother's from the Tabernacle, even Ronnie's girlfriends who thought he was the handsomest boy in the neighborhood were, sooner or later, afraid of Jack. Supposedly, one of the teachers at Folwell Junior High, a shop teacher of some kind I believe he was, told another teacher about Jack LaVoie's cold stare. "It's like looking down a goddamn well," he was supposed to have said.

In the papers after he was killed, police and truant officers and social workers babbled on and on about Jack's temper, his "antisocial tendencies," his "hatred of authority." Nobody said anything in the paper about the silences or the stares, but that's what his family remembered more than the rest of it.

What might have made him that way was another matter. Mother blamed demons that came to the house disguised as feral dogs. Eugene blamed the Old Man's influence and example. Ronnie said it had to do with the hand-me-downs we wore to school and the Tabernacle, where other kids would recognize a patched shirt or pair of darned trousers their mothers had tossed in a giveaway bin, or the worn-out, multicolored bowling shoes that someone scavenged from the trash behind the Stardust Lanes. Bernard and I more or less agreed that Jack's moods had a lot to do with his clubfoot, which none of us ever talked about but was impossible to ignore.

As the summer of 1953 wore on, Jack seemed moodier than ever. Between Jack and Bernard, I sometimes thought I was going to drown in either anger or self-pity. I remember thinking that neither one of them could see beyond the walls of their own narrow lives, that the Army and the nearly three years in Europe and the experience of having a foreign girlfriend and an older pal had given me wider horizons than my older brothers would ever look out on, none of which made it any easier, but helped me keep things in perspective.

Jack would go days without saying a word to me or apparently anyone else. Even the day after one of our jobs, when I would still be high as a kite with the thrill of it, with the sights and sounds and smells of a store Jack and I had taken over for a moment were still bouncing around in my head and giving me goosebumps, I'd pass Jack on the stairs and he wouldn't so much as nod or say hello. Even Bernard, while slowly sinking in his personal swamp, complained about Jack's moods.

Jack was "taking the fuckin' fun out of the stickup business," he said, which made us both laugh out loud.

Bernard, though, was spooked by what happened on our sixth job (the sixth job that I had a hand in), which took place during the last week of August.

We'd borrowed Wade Adams's Studebaker again and driven up to New Brighton, about ten miles north of the Twin Cities, where Jack had stashed another stolen car with another set of stolen plates. We changed as usual into our gangster duds and drove back into Minneapolis in the stolen Chevy. By the time we'd hit town it was raining and almost dark, and Bernard was fretting about what the rain would do to our imitation silk neckties. Jack, who hadn't said a word since we'd driven out of Minneapolis almost an hour earlier, said, "Forget about the fuckin' clothes for once, Bernard. Tonight, you're coming inside with me."

Why Jack decided that Bernard would go in with him that night I never found out, but I remember feeling a little hurt, like I had done something stupid the last time, though Jack hadn't told me what or that he was dissatisfied with the way I was handling my assignments. Bernard, meanwhile, stopped talking. He was visibly nervous, obviously not thinking about our outfits anymore and probably wondering what *he* had done or not done to make Jack change partners after the previous several jobs.

We were heading south on Central Avenue when Jack told Bernard, who was behind the wheel, to take a right at Twenty-second Street and go around the block. I'd noticed a liquor store on the corner of Central and Twenty-second when we turned, and, sure enough, we turned again when we came around to Twenty-second and parked near an alley on the side.

Jack got out and Bernard followed, jogging to catch up and holding the brim of his hat as he ran. I climbed into the front seat and situated myself behind the wheel, pulling the automatic out of my jacket pocket and setting it in my lap and craning my neck to watch

them step inside the store through an entrance built into the corner of
the building.

I glanced at my watch. It was five minutes to nine, which must
have been the store's closing time, and at that moment there was a
terrific crash of thunder and the rain started coming down so hard
I could hardly see the door my brothers had passed through a second
earlier. The rain hammered the Chevy's roof like a rockslide, and
sheets of water ran down the windows making it impossible to see
anything. I thought, *Jesus Christ, I won't be able to see or hear if a half-
dozen fucking squad cars pull up with their sirens blaring and red lights
flashing, and I won't be able to see or hear my brothers shouting for help.*
I leaned over and rolled down the front passenger-side window enough
to see outside. The rain was coming down hard and heavy, but there
weren't any cops or anyone else around, at least not between the store
and our car.

I wondered how long Jack and Bernard would stay inside. I
wondered if they would wait a few seconds like people ducking in
someplace on their way someplace else, or if they'd come out quick and
efficient the way Jack and I had done on the earlier jobs.

The rain was steady now, maybe slightly lighter than it had been a
moment earlier, but nothing seemed to be happening. I glanced at my
watch again. Two or three minutes had passed, which wasn't much, but
which was beginning to seem like a lifetime. I wondered what Bernard
thought about when he was sitting behind the wheel waiting for Jack
and me to come out, and I wondered how long I should be prepared to
wait for Jack and Bernard now.

I knew, or thought I knew, what I'd do if another car pulled up
behind the Chevy and someone dashed into the store for a six-pack
of beer or something. I'd grab my automatic and jump out of the car
and follow the son-of-a-bitch inside, and as soon as he'd see Jack with
his forty-five stuck in the proprietor's face, I'd stick the muzzle of my
piece against the back of *his* head and tell him to not move a fucking
muscle or it'd be the last thing he'd ever do. If it was a cop who pulled

up behind me and headed inside, I told myself, *I swear to God I'll jump out and open fire and drop him before he reaches the store's door.*

I realized I was more excited than I'd ever been going inside with Jack. When I went in with Jack everything seemed to happen very slow, in an exact and orderly fashion, Jack telling everybody what they had to do and me adding a command or two if necessary, and everything taking place like we were in a play or a movie, with everybody and everything following the script. I could see the people and the layout of the store, and I could watch the door where there was always the possibility of trouble, knowing in my bones that the advantage would be mine, that whoever stepped into the store would be surprised and under my gun.

Out in the car, with the goddamn rain and thunder, I had no idea what was happening. I couldn't see the faces or hear Jack's commands or scan the back ways in and out. What if Bernard lost control of his emotions, saw a woman who reminded him of Judy and his blues got the best of him and he started shooting for the hell of it, the way you read about crazy people giving into whatever's tormenting them? I remember thinking, like a lightning bolt out of the night sky, how bad I wanted to sleep with Judy and what my life with her might be like if Bernard wasn't there. But the thought passed almost as quickly as it appeared, and I felt like a son-of-a-bitch and swore once again that I'd gladly kill anybody who got in my brothers' way.

I checked my watch—five minutes had gone by. Jack and I had never been inside more than five minutes—in all but the Cities Service job we'd been out within about three.

Sweat was running into my eyes, though it wasn't a very warm night. I had to pee really bad, I realized just then, but I wasn't sure I could move in any direction I was so wound up and scared. I wondered if during that last big thunder clap guns had gone off inside, the proprietor's coming out from under the counter and exploding in Jack's face, Bernard wheeling, opening up on the proprietor, two, three, four more explosions, glass and booze and blood flying in all directions.

I thought, *Christ, I'm going to piss in my pants*—when all of sudden there were the two of them coming out the door, Jack first and Bernard right behind him, Jack lurching through the rain with a bag in his right hand and his left hand gripping the gun in his pocket, Bernard stumbling along almost on top of Jack, almost but not quite pushing Jack toward the car, the two of them getting drenched charging through the wall of water. I felt the tears coursing down my cheeks and for a second thought the warm flow spreading between my legs was part of myself crying. The passenger doors flew open, that side of the Chevy dipped under the weight of my brothers piling in, and the car almost without my managing to slip the transmission into gear jumped away from the curb.

Jack, sitting beside me, gave zigzag directions that would take us back up north past the city limits. The fact that he didn't say anything about the piss stink in the car or complain about the downpour told me something had happened in the store that he hadn't counted on and hadn't happened before. I didn't say a word. I wanted to say how scared I was they weren't coming back, how glad I was to see them and to be driving away from that place in the rain, but of course I wouldn't have said those things no matter what Jack's mood was, no matter what might have taken place in that store, because as afraid as I'd been back there, I was more afraid that my brothers would get the wrong idea.

It wasn't until the next morning that I found out what had happened at that store on Central. I didn't bother asking Jack, which is another way of saying I didn't have the guts to bring it up or even knock on his door that next day. I'm not sure Bernard would have told me if I hadn't pressed him, but I was curious and embarrassed about not being able to control myself in the car. I'd grabbed a morning paper out of the box in front of Cianciolo's and thumbed through it in the alley behind the store, but there was nothing about the robbery. The storm had knocked out power and phone lines around town and apparently caused a lot of problems for both the paper and the police.

Walking to Bernard's shop, I had to jump over large puddles and tree branches that had come down during the night.

At first Bernard—who by that time was sleeping in the shop—didn't want to talk about the job.

"C'mon," I said, "I want to know what you guys were doing in there," but he just shook his head and pretended to be looking for something in a carton full of dials and knobs. I said, "Jesus Christ, Bernard, you had me so worried out there I pissed in my fucking pants!"

He laughed at that and shook his head and, half laughing and maybe half about to cry too, said, "You're not the only one, brother. Good thing I had to run through that rain."

Though it wasn't even ten in the morning Bernard and I cracked a couple of bottles of warm beer and started drinking. Bernard finally told me that Jack had gotten rough with the guy behind the counter. The guy, who must have been about the Old Man's age, was half-blind judging by his glasses—which were as thick as Curtis Cousins's, Bernard said—and crippled enough to need steel braces on his legs. He just stood there and stared when Jack told him to open the drawer.

"When Jack told him again," Bernard went on, "the asshole said, 'You don't scare me, you little turd. Whaddya think you can do to me that ain't been done already?' So Jack shot out his hand, the one without the gun, and whacked the guy in the face, sending those Coke-bottle glasses flying.

"Well, the guy stumbles around on his gimpy legs, then says, 'Okay, punk, now you're gonna get it!' and from out of nowhere, his back pocket maybe, he pulls this little silver automatic, points it at Jack, and pulls the trigger. But nothing happens—the gun just goes click. I'm about ten feet away, between the counter and a door that leads into a storeroom, and I'm thinking, *Oh Jesus, I'm going to have to shoot that motherfucker*, when Jack reaches out again and grabs the guy by the black bow tie he's wearing and jerks him half over the counter. Then he slams the guy's head down sideways on the countertop and jams the barrel of his gun in the guy's ear, the ear facing up, and says, 'You stupid cocksucker, I'm gonna count to five, then blow your fucking brains into the basement!'

"His face is beet red, Jack's is, I've never seen him so mad. He starts to count—one, two—but stops at three and says to me, 'C'mere, goddamn it. First we're gonna cut the fucker's balls off!' and with the hand that doesn't have the gun jammed in the guy's ear he grabs a fifth of Four Roses sitting next to the cash register and smashes it against the counter so all that's left is the bottle's neck and an inch or two of jagged glass."

Bernard stopped and took a long pull on his beer, which was shaking in his hand, and cleared his throat.

"Honest to God, Jojo, I thought he was going to do it," he whispered, clearing his throat again, his throat thick with something.

"He pulled the gun out of the old guy's ear and jerked him all the way up on the counter so he's laying there like it's an operating table, then twists his head sideways again and jams the gun back in his ear, which by this time is torn and bleeding. Jack looks at me again and shouts, 'Pull the fucker's pants down, will ya!' and I come up to the counter, but I'm saying, 'Jesus, Jack, let's just take the money and get the fuck out of here!' and, honest to Christ, I'm so fucking scared I've not only peed in my pants, I got all I can do to not start crying like a baby. Then I thought, *Fuck! Did I just call Jack by his name?*—in which case I thought we'd *have* to kill the guy. But I must have imagined that because Jack didn't say another word, he just shied what was left of the broken bottle against the wall and with his free hand jerked the guy off the top of the counter so he fell on his face in the broken glass and booze on the floor, then put his bad foot on the guy's neck.

"'Open it,' he said to me pointing to the cash register, and I did."

"Jesus," I said, thinking of myself sitting out there in the car unaware of all that's going on in the store, and Bernard said, "I went behind the counter and opened the cash drawer and took out whatever it was we split up last night—seventy-five, seventy-eight dollars, who cares?" He glanced at me, then away.

"Jack said nothing. His face was real tight, all the blood had drained out of it, there was just his eyes, it seemed like, and I thought, *He would've done it if I wasn't there. He might still kill the guy if we don't get our asses out of there.* So I grabbed the money and came around the counter and said, 'I got it, let's go,' and he lifted his foot off the guy's throat, stared down at him for a second, then kicked him in the balls with his good foot, hard like he was kicking a football or a dog, and the two of us went out, him in front, me right behind, almost pushing him, the guy curled up back there in the broken glass and Four Roses, making this high-pitched sound like a wounded animal. I swear to God, Joe, I'd never seen or heard anything like it, and I sure as hell don't want to see or hear it again."

The two of us sat there for a long time, neither of us saying anything, and drank a couple of bottles of beer apiece. I wondered why Jack hadn't shot the guy when the guy whipped out his own automatic, why he hadn't fired when the guy's gun didn't fire. Had he been so surprised to see that other gun that he froze? Had his nerve failed him at last? I don't know if I thought it at the time, but I've thought it since and I'm thinking it now—that his nerve failed and he was so angry he hadn't been able to pull the trigger that he was ready to cut the guy's balls off and blow his brains into the basement. In light of what happened later, I'm reasonably sure that's exactly what took place.

The following afternoon the *Star* had a story about the Central Avenue job. It ran on the bottom of the front page, but it didn't say much more than that the store had been robbed of an undisclosed amount of cash and the proprietor, Morris A. Wellman, age sixty-three, had been beaten by one of the gunmen. There was nothing about Jack jamming the gun into the guy's ear or threatening to castrate him or kicking him in the balls. It didn't say anything about the robbers' natty outfits or an additional gangster in the car or the car itself, for that matter, the downpour probably ruling out the possibility of eyewitness accounts. There was no mention of the earlier jobs.

"We're damn lucky," I said to Bernard the next time I saw him, probably the following morning.

He shook his head and said, "Well, I'm beginning to think our luck is running out."

I said, "Yeah, maybe it is"—the two of us knowing all the while that it was Jack who'd decide what we did next, and that one of the things Jack didn't put much stock in was luck—good, bad, or gone.

I don't think I've mentioned that I started looking for a job sometime in August. I hadn't said anything to either Jack or Bernard, I'm not sure why not, but started dropping in at an employment agency on West Lake Street and occasionally went off on a job interview. Whether Jack ever saw me coming or going in a white shirt, tie, and sport jacket I borrowed from Wade Adams I'd never know. He didn't say anything if he had, but I could imagine him snorting and saying something about how I should be careful I don't get my fancy outfits mixed up.

Anyway, with the names and addresses I got from that agency I took the streetcar downtown a couple of times and once went over to the Midway in St. Paul, interviewing for jobs. My honorable discharge was about all I had going for me, and in 1953 that wasn't much. There were a lot of guys home from the service, and more would be coming now that the war in Korea was over, and some of them had high school and even college degrees. The available jobs were pretty basic—driving a truck for a linen-supply company, working the loading dock at a downtown department store, custodial duties at a private hospital— but I didn't get a second look. I did get some temporary work at the big Fresh-Taste commercial bakery on Portland Avenue, but that didn't amount to more than sweeping and hosing down the floors once or twice a week and lasted only until the regular employees came back from vacation.

My goal was to have my own apartment away from the madhouse on Longfellow and away from Bernard too. I fantasized about having a place no one in the family knew about, where I could take Judy and we could go to bed whenever she could get free and no one, including Bernard, would be the wiser.

During the past couple of weeks, I'd phoned Judy at her parents' house, pretending to be looking for Bernard. The first time she hung up as soon as she heard my voice, but the second time we talked for a couple of minutes. She wasn't especially friendly, but she wasn't hostile either, and I got the distinct feeling that she wouldn't mind if I called again. *Why not?* I thought. She was lonely and depressed, probably going crazy back home with her parents and hungry for male attention. I didn't think she was going out with anyone at the time, not with the baby, and whatever she might have felt toward Bernard, I didn't think she felt that way about all men or even about me. I told her, during the second conversation, that I was done writing to Monika, that I couldn't maintain a relationship with only a pen and a piece of paper, and let her draw her own conclusions about my availability if that was an issue to her. I thought about telling her that the real reason I wasn't writing to Monika anymore was because I was thinking about someone else, someone much closer to home, but either the opportunity didn't present itself or I didn't have the nerve to say it.

There was some cash from the jobs my brothers and I were pulling, but split three ways it didn't amount to much, not more than fifty or sixty bucks apiece on the best nights, and it wouldn't be enough to pay for an apartment month after month. I'd have to eat too, and maybe buy some new clothes and eventually get a used car, and I wouldn't be getting any help from either the Tabernacle or the county.

Anyway, after three or four of those interviews, I'd all but given up the idea of both a regular job and an apartment of my own. I didn't give up the idea of Judy, though she remained as remote a possibility as the others.

I knew we weren't going to be doing many more jobs, not the way we'd been doing them up to then. The Central Avenue fiasco scared the hell out of at least two of us, and whatever Jack might have been thinking, Bernard and I were sure the next time or the time after that someone was going to get killed.

Money never had much to do with the robberies. Jack and I bought some new clothes for Janine and the twins, though the Tabernacle and the county still provided most of their meager wardrobes, while Bernard tried to keep his little family above water, but the stolen money didn't make anybody's life easier. The fact is, we were robbing those stores and gas stations for the thrill of it, for the way it made us feel before, during, and afterward, and because it seemed the only thing the LaVoie men knew how to do. For Bernard and me, it was also a matter of following Jack, who we loved and feared in nearly equal amounts, who we found both beautiful and ugly, who we felt sorry for and envied at the same time.

In all the time I've had to think about the three of us over the past many years, I haven't been able to come up with a satisfactory explanation for the way we felt about Jack and for why we went with him the way we did. Meslow has probably tried as hard as I have, but he hasn't come up with a good answer either, despite his reputation (in the papers anyway) as an astute observer of human behavior.

"Jack was the pied piper of Hamelin, and you were the rats," he said once.

"Maybe," I said, deciding to humor him for a moment. "But why? What was the draw?"

"Your father was a no-account drunk, and your mother was insane. Eugene was either in jail or in the clouds, and all Ronnie cared about was having a fresh man between her legs. That left you with Jack."

"We never thought about it that way."

"Nevertheless—"

"Fuck you, Meslow," I said. "You don't know what you're talking about."

I didn't disagree with him, I just didn't want to go into it again. It was true that Jack was our leader, but I'd never say that Bernard and I wouldn't have gotten into trouble if left to our own devices. Jack was the LaVoie man in his purest form, with the boozing and the lying and the desperation to be a big shot squeezed out, Jack alone with the anger and the hatred and the clear, clean, cruel intelligence uncolored by all the rest of it. Jack was the direct descendant of the Upper Peninsula LaVoies the Old Man sometimes talked about, the uncles and great-uncles who fought the Spaniards in Cuba and the Kaiser's Germans in France, and made names for themselves because they were tough and ferocious.

On most matters, the Old Man could not be trusted, but I believed him when he talked about those earlier LaVoies, because I could feel a little of that in myself and saw a lot of it, all of it, in Jack. I listened to the stories and looked at Jack, and I saw (without knowing or understanding what I was seeing at the time) everything the LaVoies were before the Old Man came along and before my mother's lunacy was added to our blood, and before growing up poor and crazed on Longfellow Avenue made the rest of us what we were or turned out to be. So maybe robbing those stores and gas stations made Jack feel more like himself, more like the LaVoies who lived inside him like the demons Mother said came to the house in the bodies of dogs, and it made us, Bernard and me, more like Jack.

We both knew what was eating at Jack—or thought we did anyway. Since that morning after the Brennan job in the middle of July, when I told him about Janine coming home from Buddy Follmer's house, I knew that Jack wouldn't let the situation with Janine go on forever. I don't know what if anything might have gone on between Jack and Janine. I do know how the sight of her could make *me* feel that summer I came home from Europe, and I have to believe it made Jack feel the same way. In any case, by that time, he had taken on the role of her protector, her guardian angel if that's what you want to call it, maybe because no one else had or maybe for another reason. I never heard him telling her where she could go and where she couldn't, who she could go with and who she couldn't. According to Bernard, two or three times before I returned home Jack had beat the hell out of guys he caught with Janine. He hadn't caught them in the act either, Bernard said, but maybe only sitting in the guy's car in front of the house or leaning against a tree at Powderhorn Park.

One time during the previous winter, Bernard said, he and Jack were waiting for a light to change on Cedar Avenue when they saw a car cross in front of them on Thirty-fifth Street. It was a tan Nash sedan and it was driven by a middle-aged guy they didn't recognize, and there in the front seat with him was Janine. Jack told Bernard to turn on Thirty-fifth and follow the Nash, which Bernard did, pulling up close and staying on the guy's bumper for a block or so, at which point the guy noticed he was being tailed and stepped on the gas. Jack told Bernard to stay close to the son-of-a-bitch, even though it could get dangerous what with snow coming down and the streets already slick.

The way Bernard told the story they rode the Nash's tail about half a mile east, almost to Hiawatha Avenue, when the Nash abruptly turned into a vacant lot and skidded against a utility pole and stopped. Jack and Bernard jumped out of Bernard's car, and Jack pulled the driver out from behind the wheel of the Nash and punched him in the face. Bernard said it was an older man, a guy about fifty, and he was wearing a nice topcoat and felt hat, and when Jack pulled him up off the ground, Bernard recognized him, despite the blood streaming from his nose, as a history teacher at South. Before Bernard could say anything, Jack punched the guy again, and the guy, whose name, Bernard said, was Klipstein or Kaplan, "some Jew name like that," buckled at the knees, flopped on the ground, and lay there in a moaning heap.

Bernard said he looked inside the Nash and saw Janine sitting on the passenger side of the front seat staring out the windshield. He said he told her to get the hell out of that car and wait for them in his car, and that's what she did without so much as a glance at Jack or the battered teacher.

Jack, meanwhile, had pulled the guy back up and slammed him against the driver side door of the Nash and asked him where he was taking his sister. Kaplan or Klipstein or whatever his name was said he was driving her home, that she'd stayed after school to wash the blackboard for him, and because of the foul weather he offered her a ride. Jack said that was bullshit because he was headed away from her home, and the teacher said that was because we had chased him.

"He said he didn't know who we were," Bernard told me, "and he didn't know what we wanted." Bernard said the guy was having a hard time talking because there was blood in his mouth and he was missing some teeth.

According to Bernard, Jack asked him if he'd touched Janine or tried to kiss her, and when the man said, "No, please, I never laid a hand on her," Jack hit him a third time, this time in the stomach, and promised to kill him if he ever saw him with Janine again. Then Jack and Bernard got back in Bernard's car, and the three of them, Janine sitting silent as a statue in the back seat, drove away, leaving the teacher lying beside his car—actually half under it, the guy having tried to crawl to safety. Neither Jack nor Janine said a word all the way home.

I asked Bernard if he thought the teacher had done anything with Janine. Bernard shrugged and said he probably had. "He never sicced the cops on Jack, which tells me he didn't want to answer their questions about Janine either."

I said, "Well, what if he hadn't?" and Bernard, who was talking like Jack would have talked if asked the same question, said, "Well, then he'll know better than to try anything in the future."

As you might expect, word got around not only about Janine, but about her brother Jack, so most guys contented themselves with longing gazes and, if they couldn't be easily identified, long, obnoxious wolf whistles.

At school, Janine was known as the "Sweater Girl" and drew admirers wherever she went. In the neighborhood when the weather was nice she was the constant object of long- distance attention, whether she was sunbathing in the yard or walking down the street or hanging around at the beach with the twins. If he didn't know better, a boy who might have seen her at South or the Tabernacle came to the house and asked for her, God help him if either Mother or Jack answered the door. Mother would lecture the boy with a rising voice and a shower of tears. Jack would promise to kick the shit out of the kid if he showed his mug at their door again. As active as she was, I don't think Janine had an honest-to-God boyfriend until she met Eddie Devitt, whose father owned a Chevrolet dealership on Lake Street, a year or two after Jack died.

Buddy Follmer was something else again, the one person Jack wouldn't dare slam up against a car or threaten or even stare at very long. I'm not saying that Jack was afraid of Buddy. It was more a case, Bernard and I agreed, of Buddy having the advantage of being older and a cop and on the attack.

Buddy had been jerking Jack around during the past year or two, pulling up in his unmarked squad car and asking Jack, who'd be walking along Thirty-eighth Street, minding his business, what the hell he was up to, where he had been, and where was he going—what today is called harassment and can get a cop in trouble. While Buddy called the rest of us "jitterbugs," he called Jack "Hopalong" or "Twinkletoes" or "Bojangles," for the obvious reason. Once he gunned the car while Jack and Bernard were crossing the street in front of him, causing the two of them to hurry out of the way, Jack dragging his bad foot and stumbling over the curb. Then Buddy rolled down his window and hollered at Jack, "Guess you're not the fancy dancer in the family, are ya, gimp?"

If Buddy bumped into Jack on the sidewalk or over at Cianciolo's, he'd use his bulk to block Jack's path, sometimes not saying a thing and pretending not to notice him, making it clear to everyone who saw them that whatever Jack might be to the rest of the neighborhood, he was nothing to Buddy Follmer.

I thought it was strange, Follmer badgering Jack, because, like I said, Buddy didn't bother much with the rest of us, even though one or more of us was often in trouble. I told you earlier that Buddy did a pretty good job sucking up to me when I was younger, and that I went along with it for a while, enjoying the attention and the close-up look at the two-way radio in the unmarked Plymouth. A couple of times, when he was alone, he opened the passenger side of the car and told me to climb in and he would drive around Powderhorn Park while the police radio squawked and buzzed practically between my knees. Once, he reached around behind him and pulled out a pair of handcuffs that he let me hold for a while, and even though I felt guilty riding with him, I remember thinking he really didn't seem so bad for a cop and that if it wasn't for the car and the handcuffs, he wouldn't seem like a cop at all.

Even then, Buddy was overweight and seemed to sweat all the time. He smelled so strong of Lucky Tiger hair oil it made my eyes smart. I couldn't imagine him chasing a thief or climbing over a fence to get the drop on a gangster or doing anything else that you'd imagine a police officer doing.

I couldn't have been paying too close attention because it took a while before I realized that all Buddy wanted to talk about was Ronnie.

"Tell me something, jitterbug," he'd say. "That pretty sister of yours, Rhonda—she run around the house in that skimpy bathing suit?" Or, "I imagine you've walked in on your sister in the bathtub once or twice—that right, jitterbug?"

I'm pretty sure I didn't answer him, at least not directly, but maybe he wasn't really looking for answers from a stupid little brother, maybe he just wanted someone to talk to. My mother used to talk to herself, and she was nuts. Maybe Follmer had to talk to someone so he could tell himself he was sane. Buddy was a married man, a father, a cop, about thirty at the time. Ronnie wasn't even in high school yet. Besides yourself, who would you talk to about an underage girl if you were Buddy? I think he liked to hear his lustful words out loud and knew that I wouldn't understand what was going on and do anything about it.

I came to know, the way kids sometimes know things, that Follmer was an outcast, a guy people didn't like, even hated, and made fun of behind his back. I don't think it had anything to do with his being a cop, except (I would learn later) that other cops hated him as much as if not more than the rest of the population. Sometimes, such a person tries too hard to be liked, and that makes the situation worse.

Meslow told me that Follmer grew up in Iowa, in Sioux City or Fort Dodge or somewhere like that, had walked a beat up here, Duluth, I think it was, then came to the Twin Cities to work for the MPD when he was still in his early twenties.

Meslow said Buddy had gone into police work because it was the only way he could think of to get respect from people, had stayed in police work to avoid the war, and had finally been sacked because he'd found it an easy way to make more money than he was paid as a cop. I don't know about all that, though it sounds about right. What I do know is that by the time Buddy had been living on Longfellow Avenue for a while he was someone people avoided on the street. I remember Donald Harrison and Rossy Grant making pig noises from behind the Harrisons' hedge when Buddy and his homely wife were out in the yard. I remember Wade Adams, on a dare from Donald and his cousins, pissing against the side of the Follmers' house, then taking a shit in one of their window wells. Wade said he'd take a shit in Buddy's gas tank too, if the car didn't belong to the city and shitting in it would be a criminal offense.

Once, Rossy said to Bernard, "You know why Follmer's always giving Jack a bad time, don't you? It's because he's too fucking fat and lazy to chase after the rest of us. Jack's the one guy the asshole can catch up to."

Bernard thought that made sense and told Jack what Rossy said. Jack told Bernard that Rossy as usual was full of shit, that Follmer picked on him because Follmer was afraid of him. "He wants to get me before I get him," Jack said, according to Bernard.

How Buddy managed to be intimate with my sisters was never clear, and while it was something we obviously took seriously, it wasn't something we wanted to talk about in so many words.

Watching Ronnie sunbathe in the front yard and then talking about her in the privacy of his car was not enough, at any rate, to keep him happy—he obviously decided that he had to have more. At some point, he or his wife hired Ronnie to babysit for them, and that's probably when things got physical. All I know for sure is that one day I was sitting on the ratty couch in the living room looking at someone's comic books when Ronnie and a friend from school came home and sat down on the front steps. Ronnie, by this time, must have been fifteen. I knew she was smoking cigarettes and sipping liquor out of pint bottles her boyfriends would hide in their letter jackets and had been sexually active with at least Donald and Rossy and maybe Wade and a few others too. That afternoon, Ronnie and her friend sat outside the screen door out front laughing and giggling and talking mostly low enough so they couldn't be heard.

I wasn't interested to begin with, but every once in a while something the girls said made my ears perk up. Then, no doubt assuming that no one was around, Ronnie started talking in a more or less normal voice, and I heard almost everything whether I wanted to or not.

She used the word "seduced," which I'd heard for the first time only a day or two earlier and wasn't sure I knew the meaning of, only that it had something to do with sex. She talked about "going down" on someone, which I thought I knew the meaning of, and then said something about handcuffs. When she said all she had on was his handcuffs, I realized that the man she'd seduced or had seduced her and who she'd gone down on or who'd gone down on her and whose handcuffs she was wearing when she wasn't wearing anything else was Buddy Follmer!

I remembered Buddy asking those questions while I sat in his car, and though it had been a year or maybe more since the last time that happened, everything more or less came together in my head. I knew that I should have been angry, that I should have done something or told someone, but I wasn't and I didn't. Ronnie with a man was not a novelty to me by that time—it was a fact of life, like the Old Man in the workhouse and Mother talking to herself—and that this time it was Buddy instead of Rossy or one of the others didn't seem to make things a great deal different. It just seemed strange, is all, the picture in my mind of the two of them together.

How and when Jack found out about them I don't know. When I told Bernard what I'd heard, *he* already seemed to know, which means that Jack must have known also. Jack might have been either on his way to or on his way back from detention down in Red Wing at that time, or maybe Buddy was still too much for him to deal with. In any case, I can't recall Jack saying or doing anything directly on account of the information.

Time went by, and Ronnie was spending so much time with so many different men that I don't think anyone, even Ronnie herself, could keep track of them all. Buddy, in other words, was one of at least a half-dozen and surely not the only married one with kids and maybe not even the only cop. I didn't have much contact with him by that time. He didn't need me anymore, and I was old enough to know better than risk being seen in the company of a cop, particularly a cop who everybody in the neighborhood, with the possible exception of his own wife, knew was fucking my sister. Sometimes when he saw me on the street, he'd give his horn a toot, but I'd pretend I didn't see him. I never told anyone about riding in his car, though the way things seemed to go on the avenue, I was afraid some people knew.

When I came home from the Army, Ronnie had gotten married, lost her husband, then gotten married again, never moving very far from the neighborhood or at least from some of the neighbors— her first three husbands had all grown up on or near Longfellow Avenue—but apparently having little if anything to do with Follmer. Buddy, meanwhile, had turned his attention to Janine. Exactly when he started up with her no one seemed to know. He'd undoubtedly noticed her early, when she was thirteen or fourteen and already stopping traffic on the street—how could he not have? Maybe they'd had sex for some time before I became aware of it that night of the Brennan drugstore job.

Bernard was, by that time, married and out of the house with troubles enough of his own. If Jack knew, he didn't say anything to me, though he didn't seem surprised so much as angry when I told him about her coming back from the Follmers' house that night. Maybe he'd managed to stop her from seeing Buddy and then she was seeing him again, or maybe not. Maybe that night was the first time, though I doubt it.

Again, it was different with Janine. Janine seemed younger and more vulnerable than Ronnie, and Jack and I were older by that time too. If I'm honest with myself, I have to say that by that time I'd been with a girl at least as young as Janine and that because I knew what it was like for Buddy, I might have felt guilty along with everything else.

One day, when I'd had too much of Meslow's booze and talked more than I should have about a lot of things, Meslow said, "Both you and Follmer committed statutory rape—you know that, don't you? You were no better than he was, even though your piece of jailbait was a kraut." I thought about Monika, about the wine and cigarette smoke, the clothing and condom wrappers scattered around her girlfriend's little second-floor bedroom, and told myself there was never a girl in the world who wanted it as bad as Monika and then thought, yes, there was, there was Janine. Meslow was correct, of course—a fifteen- or sixteen-year-old girl hungry to fuck is not equal to a twenty- or thirty-year-old man fucking her, not equal in the eyes of the law or in the eyes of anyone who knows what's right and what's wrong.

"Maybe you thought you were fooling around with Janine when you were fooling around with the kraut," Meslow continued, pushing his luck, and maybe he was right about that too, though I was never conscious of the possibility at the time I was with Monika and I don't think it occurred to me until I was home and feeling what I was feeling when I saw Janine walking barefoot down the street, and even then I wasn't sure that what was passing through my mind was anything more than bullshit. To this day I don't know if what he said was true.

Jack said nothing about what was going on in his mind at that time, and even when he told Bernard and me we were going to kill Follmer, he didn't let on what he was feeling. He said we were going to kill the son-of-a-bitch because of what he was "doing to the family," and while we understood only the broad outline of what he was talking about, we figured we'd know the rest of it, or as much as we needed to know, when the time came.

At Ronnie's house the group gathered around the dinner table is breaking up—or maybe I'm snapping out of my reverie and only now noticing something that's been happening for a while.

I look around and, instead of ghosts, I see Elaine and Heather stacking dirty pie plates and collecting the silverware, leaving only half-empty coffee cups and tumblers of flat beer and the saucers that some of us have been using for ashtrays. At one end of the table, Ronnie, who the booze and cigarettes and the long day that began before we drove up to the graves have finally made to look her age, is asking Adriana about her family. Gervais has padded into the living room with B.J. and settled into the big recliner in front of the television set. Eugene stands halfway between the table and the TV, looking like he can't make up his mind where he should be and what he ought to be doing. The day has taken a toll on him too, and he didn't seem to be in very good shape to begin with.

I wheel myself in the direction of Michael's kids or where they were standing a minute ago, but the boy, Richard, has gone off somewhere, to the john maybe or outside to the car, and now there's only the girl who sees me coming too late to get away.

"Do you remember me from the last time?" I ask her. I don't know why, except I'm as drunk and worn out by the long day as the rest of them, plus for some reason I'd really like to know.

Isabel looks at me with her mother's eyes black and shiny as marbles and says, "I remember the wheelchair." She says it after a little pause when she was wondering, I suppose, whether telling the truth was going to hurt my feelings.

"You must have been seven or eight then," I say.

She shrugs and says, "I guess."

She sniffs and wipes her nose with her fingers—brown fingers with three or four silver rings, the flimsy, woven kind that make me think of sideshows and carnivals, nothing that looks like something serious she'd been given by a man. Up close, I can see the makeup, the marks left by chicken pox or acne underneath, a chipped front tooth, a scar the shape of a fingernail under one eye. Isabel has been around the block once or twice since the last time I saw her.

"You remind me of my sister," I tell her. This is a lie that slides out of my mouth before I realize I'm saying it, though as lies go, I've told a lot worse.

She sniffs again and glances at Ronnie sitting with her mother in the dining room. I say, "No, not Ronnie, a different one—one that died."

"Marie?" she says.

"Janine."

She sniffs again and nods. "Oh, yeah," she says. "I've heard of her."

I smile and almost say, "Oh, yeah? How much have you heard?" But that wouldn't sound right, and what would be the point? Whatever the girl might have heard about Janine would have come from her mother, who got it from Michael or maybe someone even farther removed from the Janine I watched walking barefoot down the warm summer sidewalk. Instead I say, "She had dark hair and eyes like yours, though maybe not quite as dark. She was pretty too."

Now I sound like a dirty old man as well as a drunk and tired one, and Isabel forces a smile and instead of looking at me, looks over my shoulder toward her mother, whose voice I can hear mingling with Ronnie's and the noise of the football game coming from the other direction. Then she looks around, no doubt wondering where the hell her brother is when she needs him.

"Your dad was a soldier," I babble on, changing the subject so she won't think the wrong thing and go off and leave me there alone or available to Eugene, sounding stupid then instead of dirty. Of course she knew her father was a soldier because if he hadn't been a soldier, he'd likely be with her today, or maybe the four of them—father, mother, brother, and sister—wouldn't be wasting their holiday at this house full of drunks and whores and murderers. Her father might have known enough having left in the first place to stay away and not come back even on a holiday. "I mean," I add before she can say something, "he was a career soldier, not someone who just enlisted for a couple of years like me or got drafted."

She glances down at me and sniffs. "I didn't know you were in the war, Uncle Joe," she says.

I'm flattered she remembers my name and our relationship. But war? I think. Who ever said anything about me being in a war? Then it dawns on me that maybe she didn't know why I was in the chair, that she assumed my condition was because of a car accident or something that happened on the job, or that now, with the mention of her warrior father, she figured I'd lost the use of my legs and whatever else might not be working in the same war that killed her father. Could it be that she's never heard of the LaVoie gang?

I grin my yellow, boozy grin while my head spins with the possibility, however remote, and say, "I wasn't in the war. I was talking about your dad."

She gives me a funny look, like I'm speaking in a foreign tongue—which, it occurs to me, is entirely possible—and I say, "I was in the Army, but it was *between* wars, I guess you could say."

"Oh," she says and wipes her nose again with her fingers.

She's uncomfortable, I'm uncomfortable. But because Michael connects us, neither one of us can easily turn away.

"Where'd your brother go?" I ask her. I can't think of anything else to say.

"I don't know," she says. "Out, I guess. Maybe to smoke."

"He can smoke in here," I say. "Everybody else is."

Isabel laughs. "He's not smoking what you're smoking."

She laughs again, and I do too. Why not? The LaVoies are what the experts call "substance abusers." The old ones have abused the bottle, the young ones something else, the abusing maybe having skipped Michael, though, if so, Michael would be the only one. I picture Richard outside in the driveway, firing up a joint, cupping his hand around the flame, sucking in the grassy smoke, holding it, letting it out, coughing a little, but feeling better, more relaxed, not so bored.

In Germany my friend Jake MacDill used to come around with little cubes of hashish, I never asked from where. There was marijuana sometimes too, but Jake preferred the hash, which he broke up and smoked in an old pipe listening to jazz on Armed Forces Radio. Jake would take a deep drag, hold it in for what seemed a supernaturally long time, and, while he was holding it in, pass the pipe to the next guy, which every now and then was me. I preferred alcohol— German beer and various European liqueurs were awfully good after the war, even when everything else wasn't—but the idea of smoking hash with Jake and his friends was something different, something I knew I'd probably never do again after my discharge. (Shorty Gorman didn't like blacks, so I was usually the only white guy in the room.) The hash helped relieve the boredom, but it also gave me a scratchy throat, so after a half-dozen times I told Jake thanks but no thanks, I'd stick with the booze.

Now I picture Richard and me back at my place in Meslow's building, sharing a joint the way Jake and I shared that hash pipe. Maybe Isabel is there too, but she's not in the picture, only Richard and myself, passing the skinny cigarette back and forth. I tell Richard he's the spitting image of his Uncle Jack, and Richard says, "Yeah," like maybe he's heard that before. "Jack killed the cop—right?"

He asks the question casually, the way he might have asked if Jack was the second oldest of the brothers, but it takes me by surprise.

"Yeah," I say, and then, before he can say anything else, I ask, "What about you? Who are you?"

"Me?" he says, shrugging, "Well, I done some things I ain't proud of, but I never killed nobody. That's something I could never do."

I look at him through the haze of sweet smoke and say, "Yeah, well, neither could Jack until the moment he did."

I blink then, catching myself as I seem to doze off, and hear Isabel saying something sharp I can't make out, probably not to me, to her mother and Ronnie. Then Gervais is getting up, a big, dark, slow-moving shadow to my right, and B.J., moving faster, is stepping past him, and behind me young Joe's voice and either Ronnie or Elaine is saying, "What's he doing?" and Isabel, now standing above me, says, "I think he passed out."

Who the fuck are they talking about? I ask myself, knowing it's me, and then there are Ronnie's warm hands on my face and someone, probably Joe, takes my chair by the handles and turns it so people can help me.

I'm drunk, I tell myself, *not dying, not yet*, and I might have said it out loud because someone laughs. Someone else says, "He's okay, just tired, the long ride and the big meal," and someone else says, "He hardly touched his food," and then someone wheels the chair away from the group and pushes me into the bedroom. I'm aware of water running in the bathroom and either Joe or B.J. lifting me out of the chair and laying me down on Ronnie's bed, and then whoever was running the water—it's either Ronnie or Elaine—spreads a cold, damp wash rag over my eyes and forehead.

Passing out or falling asleep or maybe doing a little dying—that's one way to get out of an awkward conversation, I tell myself.

I lie on my right side, my dead legs bent like I'm still sitting in the chair, the room smelling like Ronnie, like Ronnie's perfume and cigarettes and the reek of what I imagine is sex mixed together. And though I can't see anything with the wash rag over my eyes, I'm aware of someone remaining with me in the room—a couple of people maybe, someone bending over me, someone spreading an afghan and saying something, though not to me, and then moving away, out of the room, first the one and then the other.

And then the door closes, and I'm alone.

I'm asleep, I'm awake. Maybe only a minute or two at a time either way. I think of those fat little cartoon books we used to look at when we were kids, the kind you flipped through so the moving pages made it look like Popeye or Bugs Bunny or the Lone Ranger was moving.

One day when I was a kid I found an old-fashioned movie projector in a dusty box in the basement. I must have been down there while Mother or Ronnie was doing the laundry because I'd never go down there by myself, not after I learned what happened to Yvonne, and I must have been in the other room where the big furnace with its thick octopus arms was because that's where there were boxes that must have belonged to the people who lived in the house before we did.

In one of the boxes I found a tin contraption about the size and shape of a toaster. It had a cord and plug and fell open at a hinge in the middle—one half had a couple of lenses, the other half contained a spool and crank and a place to screw in a light bulb. There was a paper bag with the contraption, and in the bag were a dozen or so rolled-up scrolls of thin paper that were actually little movies—*The Adventures of Tom Sawyer*, *Little Women*, *Nicholas Nickleby*, and a couple featuring Hopalong Cassidy and Tom Mix. We didn't have any books at home (except the Bible), and I hadn't gotten very far in school by that point, but somehow I knew the names of some of the stories and was excited to find them on those scrolls. I went looking for Bernard and Jack, but found only Eugene, who came down the basement with me and looked through the stuff that I'd found.

Eugene said that sometimes in the movies girls do a striptease—I didn't know what a striptease was, only that it was dirty—and I could tell that he was interested.

For the next several days, Eugene, Ronnie, and Bernard came

downstairs and looked at the projector and the movie scrolls. For a while, everybody was excited by what I'd found and talked about making our own movie theater in the basement. There wasn't much room under the fat arms of the furnace, but it was dark because there were only a couple of small windows covered with yellowed newspaper pages and spiderwebs, and it was cooler than the rest of the house on hot days.

Eugene took charge of our private theater. He had not yet heard Billy Graham preach at the fairgrounds so was not yet the born-again Christian he became, and he still had a terrible temper and swore ferociously when he couldn't get the projector to work. Several of the paper scrolls were torn or so brittle or otherwise damaged that they fell apart when Eugene unrolled them. A couple of them got jammed and ripped when he tried to crank them through the projector. Only one, *The Adventures of Tom Sawyer*, actually worked the way it was supposed to, but for the time being that was enough.

Eugene took a light bulb from the laundry room and screwed it into the projector. Then he grabbed a bed sheet from one of the beds upstairs and fixed it to a rafter with thumbtacks. After he plugged the projector into the wall, we all sat quiet on the cold, cracked concrete floor and watched the sheet come alive with blurry, blown-up comic book pictures while Eugene slowly cranked the spool through the box. Once he got the hang of it, he would crank with one hand and with the other jiggle the shutter up and down in front of the lenses making the characters move in stiff, jerky motion. In this particular episode— it lasted only a minute or two—Injun Joe either killed someone in a graveyard by hitting him with a shovel or got killed the same way, and the action scared the hell out of me. I'd only watch it when everyone else was down there watching it too.

Then, just like that, our little theater adventure ended. I suppose a kid can watch the same minute movie only so many times before he gets tired of it, which is probably what happened. One day, Ronnie and I were the only ones in the basement, and though we were both scared of Injun Joe, we were determined to watch and tried to get the projector to work without Eugene and the others. I don't know if the light bulb had burned out or if there was something wrong with the plug or what, but we couldn't turn the projector on, and after a while I got frustrated and tore the scroll when I tried to remove the bulb.

"Goddamn it," I hollered—"goddamn this goddamn piece of shit!"—remembering what I'd heard Eugene say, and the next thing I knew Ronnie was running up the stairs and Mother had me by my collar and dragged me into the laundry room where she bent me over the hard edge of the tub and rubbed a bar of lye soap across my bared teeth.

"Thou shalt not take the name of the Lord thy God in vain!" she screamed in my ear, and for a minute I was afraid I was going to drown down there like Yvonne.

That was the last time I went down the basement to watch a movie or do anything else in a long while. Then one day, Bernard told me that Mother had thrown the projector and the movies in the trash, calling movies the "devil's playthings." Bernard said she'd have never let us watch the movies in the first place if she'd known what we were doing down there.

"Mother's loony, you know," Bernard said, which seemed to explain some things, but not others.

I haven't thought about our short-lived basement cinema for decades. It's one of the few happy memories I took with me from the house on Longfellow. It goes back to a time, I guess, when things were beginning to go bad, but I was too young to know it or to imagine how bad things would get. I suppose that since I wasn't literally starving and usually had enough to wear, even if the food was skimpy and the clothes were hand-me-downs, all the other stuff was pretty much removed from my everyday thoughts or was stuff I could understand and deal with in my childish way.

Ronnie was still there, and so were the others, including Eugene, at least some of the time. I was too young then to fully understand right from wrong, sane from crazy. There were only moments when I was happy and moments when I was not, and after all the years those moments have come together like bricks in a wall and formed something solid and all of a piece, and now it's impossible to separate one brick from another.

Why do those days in the basement come back to me now, curled up on Ronnie's bed such a long way in both time and distance from Longfellow Avenue? Maybe it's the booze and the tiredness, maybe it's the sight of Michael's kids and the thought of being young.

Maybe it's because the basement—now that I think of it—was where Jack first told us we were going to kill Buddy Follmer. Yes, at least a dozen years after we squatted on the basement floor watching Injun Joe kill someone in a graveyard with a shovel, the three of us first talked about killing Buddy Follmer. With a gun.

It was the last of August or first of September, I'm reasonably sure of that, the hot summer starting to give way to a wet, cool fall, and Jack was tired of robbing stores and gas stations. He didn't say that in so many words, but it was something we sensed—even Bernard, who was so scared of what he imagined happening on the next job and so down in the dumps because of his wife walking out on him that I think he was having trouble making sure his socks matched in the morning. I was, by that time, caught up in thoughts about Judy, thoughts I shared with no one, but I sensed the coming change in plans, though I was as surprised as Bernard when Jack finally announced what he had in mind. Maybe we'd gone downstairs to look for something, something big enough for the three of us to have to carry up the steps, or maybe Jack had gone down there to think or to find something he needed for his own private purposes and Bernard and I followed. That wouldn't have been unusual.

Anyway, it was in the basement that Jack, out of the blue, said, "What we're going to do, we're going to kill Buddy Follmer."

Neither Bernard or I asked why or when or where or with what. We just looked at each other and then back at Jack, who might have been standing in the shadow cast by a forty-watt bulb, and maybe asked him to come again since we might not have been sure we'd heard him right. But we'd heard him fine, and maybe for that matter we knew enough of what was happening not to have to ask him just then why we'd want to kill Buddy Follmer, knowing that after the why, the when and where and with what were secondary considerations. Anyway, before either Bernard or I could say a word, Jack said, "The son-of-a-bitch has shamed the family long enough."

And that was that for the time being. The three of us went back upstairs, and the next thing we did together was pull our last job of the summer, which was the Phillips 66 station in Richfield. That happened the following night, and I remember it very well because, among other things, I went inside with Jack again and instead of just a pump jockey closing up like there'd been on the previous filling station stickups, this time there was a young guy and his girlfriend, who reminded me of Monika.

We'd gone back to the garage in Robbinsdale that we'd used a couple of times already, including the Brennan drugstore job, and we changed our clothes in the dark and then climbed into a stolen blue Mercury with stolen Minnesota plates, and Bernard drove the three of us south on what was then called the Beltline to Normandale Boulevard to Sixty-sixth Street and then east on Sixty-sixth to Penn.

Bernard turned on the radio and found the dance music he liked, and for once Jack didn't tell him to turn it off. Because Jack was quieter than usual, I began to worry that maybe what almost happened at that Columbia Heights liquor store might happen wherever we were going tonight. Bernard must have been thinking the same thing because he seemed even more interested in the music than usual, humming and singing along and slapping his free hand on the dashboard along with the beat of the music, Jack not once saying a word or reaching out to grab Bernard's hand or turning off the radio himself. It was drizzling, and the Merc fishtailed on the slick pavement, but even then Jack didn't say anything or glance over his shoulder to see if there was a cop on our tail. I did, and there wasn't.

As usual, Jack had timed the job so we'd pull up and walk in and walk out again when whoever was working was about to close up for the night and the odds of an establishment full of customers were slim to none. A yellow Cadillac convertible was pulling out when we pulled in. There was an older man wearing a straw hat and a much younger-looking woman sitting up tight beside him, the two of them laughing about something. I remember thinking, *That old bastard is going to get his ashes hauled before the night's over.* The girl might have put me in mind of Monika—she sure as hell looked young enough—because when I walked in the station door behind Jack I almost dropped my pistol, the skinny blonde inside bore such a striking resemblance to my German girl.

The girl was sitting on a metal stool chewing gum and figuring something on a pad of paper, the smoke of a cigarette rising lazily from an ashtray on the counter. The toilet flushed behind the men's room door.

"We're closed," the girl said without looking up, but then a young guy stepped out of the john zipping up his fly and saw us and realized right away what was happening, and it didn't matter if they were closed or not.

"Open the drawer, shithead, or we'll kill you both," Jack said to the kid.

When the girl looked up, she didn't look as much like Monika as she did when we came in the door, but she looked enough like her that between her and the girl in the yellow Cadillac, I knew that it would be Monika, not Judy, that I'd be thinking about the rest of the night. The girl had climbed off the stool and stepped back to make room for the guy to get at the cash register. The guy wore a greasy white shirt with an orange and brown Phillips 66 patch above the pocket and fiddled with a bunch of keys hanging from his belt.

Jack told the girl to get the hell out of the way, so she took a couple of steps away from the register and stood against the back wall, and while Jack kept his automatic on the boy, I held my gun on her. I told her to keep her mouth shut even though she wasn't saying anything and wasn't going to make a sound judging by the fear in her big green eyes, and then I suppose because she reminded me of someone I thought I loved, I told her she didn't have to worry because no one was going to get hurt. Jack, waiting for the kid to open the register, gave me a quick glance that told me to shut the fuck up, so that was the last thing I said. When we left with a zippered canvas sack full of cash, I felt at least as relieved as I'd felt the other times and something else too, something like regret for having to leave so soon and without there being more between me and the girl.

On our way back to Robbinsdale Jack sat on the floor in front and I lay on the floor in back so if the cops spotted us they would see a car with only one man in it, not two or three as would have been reported, and when I stopped thinking about the girl for a minute it occurred to me that the three of us had just pulled our last job together. Though he'd given indications, Jack had not said that in so many words, but I knew it all the same and I remember wondering what we'd do instead. I forgot for the moment what Jack had said the day before and let my mind wander back to the girls I'd seen that night, but the thought of them made me sad, like I was walking away from that too.

Maybe we were all feeling the same thing—like three guys leaving the field after playing their last football game together—because Jack and Bernard were quieter than usual. For once Jack seemed more sad than angry, like he was grieving after something instead trying to get even for whatever it was that he was or had happened to him, and Bernard looked at least as sorry as Jack.

No one said a word all the way back to the garage, where we changed out of our fancy clothes back into our T-shirts and jeans and climbed into Wade's Studebaker and drove home. The fact that we went directly back to the garage after the job and didn't split up before making our way home seemed proof that we weren't going to do any more of them, like we were in a hurry to put all that behind us. I don't think Jack intended it to happen that way—it's just that he didn't exercise his leadership the way he'd exercised it in the past, and everyone ended up doing the same thing without making a conscious decision to do it that way.

Sitting in the Studebaker behind our house, Jack unzipped the canvas bag we'd taken at the Phillips station, pulled out and counted a handful of bills, then gave us each our share.

I folded my share and stuffed it in my jeans without counting it.

The next few days passed much as most of the summer had, the heat giving way, however, to rain and chilly evenings, like the weather could read the calendar.

Jack was holed up, as usual, in his room upstairs. Passing his door (I was sleeping in Eugene's tiny room next door at the time), I would hear either the television—usually turned to one of the game shows he liked—or dead silence, which meant he was reading or sleeping or maybe lying on his bed staring at the water-stained ceiling and thinking black thoughts. I didn't stop to knock or put my ear to the door, afraid, I suppose, of what I might hear over the TV or the silence.

Bernard, meanwhile, had been told by old man Oleski to vacate the repair shop where he had been living since his breakup with Judy. He told me later that Oleski had walked in the door the morning after the Phillips 66 job, looked around with tears in his eyes, and said, "Get the hell out of here, you worthless prick. You've made a fucking mess of everything."

"He looked pathetic standing there in the dust, holding on to those aluminum canes he used on account of the arthritis," Bernard told me. "So I thought whatever Judy had told him about the two of us, the old bastard was pissed because of the pain in his knees. But the way he told me to get my ass out of there—that I'd turned the place into a pigsty—I knew right away that what really pained him was the sight of his fucking shop gone to hell, the fucking money-grubber."

Luckily, Bernard didn't have anything except a few clothes and some toiletries, so it wasn't hard moving out of the shop, the only question being where he would go now. He spent the next few days, I learned, with Ronnie, who was then living with Wade Adams in a basement apartment near Minnehaha Falls.

I wasn't doing much of anything at the time. I'd more or less given up looking for honest work and taken to wandering up and down Lake Street and sometimes took the streetcar downtown and sat in bars drinking beer by my lonesome on the proceeds of our last job. I tried to keep an eye out for Janine, at least going home from school, which started again the day after Labor Day, but she seemed to have restricted her after-school activities—so much in fact, I was afraid she might be pregnant. I couldn't ask her and wasn't about to snoop around in the bathroom wastebasket for signs of her period, so one day I mentioned it to Ronnie, who'd stopped by the house to look in on Mother. Ronnie laughed that sunny laugh of hers and said it was sweet of me to worry.

"Janine knows how to take care of herself," she said. "If she was going to get pregnant, it would've happened by now."

Ronnie told me that Bernard was sleeping on her couch for a while. Then, almost as an afterthought, she told me that *she* was pregnant, presumably by Wade.

"You're worried about the wrong sister," she said with a little giggle that made me think of the days when she used to lie in the sun in the front yard enjoying the whistles and wolf calls.

"Maybe so," I told her. Maybe so.

Later the same day, I stepped out of the Sailor Tap at Forty-second and Cedar and saw Judy walk into Haslett's Pharmacy next door. It was another cool day, so she was wearing a sweater and a scarf tied under her chin. I'd been doing a lot of thinking about Monika and even thought about writing her again. In fact, I'd been sitting in the Sailor daydreaming about her, about pulling together what money I could get my hands on—maybe pulling another job or two, with or without my brothers—and going back to Germany. I was thinking so much and so hard about Monika I'd more or less blotted out Judy, and then, out of the blue, there she was, by herself on the street in front of me.

I wasn't so drunk or so caught up in thoughts about Monika that the sight of Judy in a tight sweater didn't have an instant effect. I remember thinking that all the time we were kids on Longfellow Avenue, Judy Oleski didn't mean anything to me. She was just another older girl with a nice figure and no match for Ronnie or Janine, who was just starting to blossom. Judy was not that pretty, had no special talents I ever heard about, and wasn't especially popular. Even when Bernard wrote to tell me that he and Judy were engaged—he said he'd met her at a dance and one thing led to another, which is the way things generally worked—I didn't think about her with any strong feelings, no more, I guess, than I'd have thinking about any other girl Bernard might marry.

Then that summer I came home from Germany, and there she was, and I started looking at her in a whole new light, like she's Jane Russell or something. And while she was now part of the family, she really wasn't—she wasn't blood, only someone who married into it, like Rossy or Wade. There were days in all the summer heat and boredom when I'd think of hardly anyone or anything else.

I decided to follow her inside the store, immediately feeling conspicuous because Haslett's was one of the drugstores Bernard and I had talked about robbing. We never did because Jack never picked it, probably because it was too close to our house and even if we wore masks, which we never did, somebody might have recognized one or all of us. Once we'd started robbing stores, I couldn't help but feel like I stood out somehow, even in ordinary circumstances, that I looked suspicious, shifty-eyed and dangerous, even when all I was doing was buying a pack of cigarettes or a bottle of Aqua Velva. That day I almost lost sight of Judy, who'd walked all the way to the back of the store, where a pharmacist stood behind an elevated counter. I went over to the magazine stand and flipped through an *Argosy*, taking a peek over my shoulder every couple of seconds, feeling I was being watched. Finally, while Judy was apparently waiting for a prescription, I bought the *Argosy* and a pack of Black Jack gum, and decided I'd wait for her outside.

I crossed the street and leaned against the wall of Mel's Grocery and pretended to be looking at the magazine. Anyone seeing me would suppose that I was waiting for the Thirty-fourth Avenue streetcar, which ran south on Cedar before turning east at Forty-second. If Judy spotted me, she would probably wonder where I was going on the Thirty-fourth Avenue car and why I was catching it half-a-mile from my house, but I figured there was no place else I could go if I wanted to see her when she walked out of the store.

Standing there half-drunk and not having had a woman for an entire summer, I wanted Judy so bad I would've forced it if the opportunity presented itself. Good thing for both of us it didn't, at least not in actual fact. What happened was this. Judy came out of the store and turned the corner and ducked into the dry-cleaners next door. If she saw me, she didn't let on, but I don't think she did. Maybe she was in a hurry to get home to the baby. I stood there long enough to see her come out of the dry cleaners with something on a hanger, a dress or a coat, wrapped in brown paper and then walk east on Forty-second.

I pictured myself crossing Cedar against the light and walking after her. I could've caught up with her before she reached Nineteenth, but then what would I have said or done? If I'd had Wade's car, I might have pulled up at the curb and asked her to climb in. Assuming she did, tossing the coat or whatever it was into the back seat, I'm not sure what I would've done next. Maybe driven south on Cedar, past the city limits, through Richfield and Bloomington, then into the country. There were gravel roads crossing the highway, and one of them would have led into a stand of trees, where no one could see us. I'd offer her a drink out of a pint of Canadian Club I found in the glove compartment and light a cigarette for her, and after a couple of swallows of the whiskey I'd work up the nerve to kiss her.

And when I was kissing her, I'd run my hands under her sweater and unhook her brassiere.

I'm not proud to admit, even to myself, that the only thing preventing me from forcing myself on my brother's wife—she was still my brother's wife—was the absence of a borrowed car. In my own defense, I did none of that in fact, only in my mind, though I should also confess that right up until the day that slug from Jimmy Finnegan's thirty-thirty ended once and for all what had passed for my sex life, I gave taking Judy by force very serious thought.

Once or twice when we were on the run, I considered telling Bernard about that daydream. There would be times then, trying to sleep in the car or on the floor of an abandoned hunter's shack, when thinking about fucking Judy would not be enough and my curiosity would grow almost stronger than my desire and I'd be desperate to hear my brother talk about what it had been like with her. I wanted to know what she looked like naked. I wanted to know how she smelled and what she said during sex. I wanted to know how she felt when he was inside her.

Once or twice toward the end, when we'd be away from Jack, we did talk about "our" women, but we never got down to what I really wanted to know, and what Bernard did tell me I figured was at least as much bullshit as what I told him. Bernard, remember, was a terrible liar. So, I've learned, are most men, including me, when they're talking to other men about sex.

On the day I was describing, Judy disappeared around the corner at Nineteenth, and I caught a northbound streetcar on Cedar. In the weeks after the shootout, I saw her picture in the paper, but I never saw her in the flesh again. I surely thought and dreamt and made up vivid fantasies about her from time to time—even later, when doctors told me that physical arousal was impossible for a man in my damaged condition.

Coming back to the house that afternoon, or maybe it was the next day, I discovered that Eugene and Jack had been at it again.

It had been a while. The two of them had stayed out of each other's way probably by accident as much as either one's decision. But their warfare had gone on, in fits and starts, since they were kids and could flare up without warning, even after Eugene had accepted Jesus Christ as his Personal Savior.

I don't know how it started this time, who attacked who, but there was a J.C. Higgins baseball bat involved and the leg of one our mismatched dining-room chairs, and Eugene evidently got the worst of it. There was fresh blood on the living-room floor and two new dents in the plaster beside the sofa, and the closet door in the hallway had been splintered. The bat lay under the dining-room table, the chair leg in the kitchen, and in the bathroom, Eugene sat on the edge of the tub, pressing a bloody towel against his face.

It was a Thursday, I'm pretty sure, and Mother might have been at the Tabernacle and had the twins with her, and if Janine had been home when the fight started, she wasn't there now. I stood in the bathroom door and looked at Eugene. He'd taken his shirt off, and the blood looked like fresh paint against the pasty flesh of his face and shoulders. I noticed that he was starting to develop a paunch.

"Where's Jack?" I asked him. I wasn't looking to start a conversation, but there was always a chance that, one of these days, Jack would kill Eugene or vice versa.

Eugene looked at me over the top of the blood-soaked towel.

"Out, I guess," he said in the flat, uninterested way he had of saying most everything in those days.

"He okay?" I asked.

"No worse than me, goddammit," he said. Adding, in the same flat voice, "Sorry"—for swearing, I guess.

Maybe it was the beer, or maybe it was something else, anyway what I said was, "Jack has a gun, you know."

Eugene shrugged. "What the hell do I care?" he said at last, adding, again, a soft, "Sorry."

It was hard to imagine Eugene going after anyone with a bat or a chair leg, the way he was sitting there with that fucking towel, the way he looked so washed out and flabby, the way he just *was*. I could imagine, however, a lot of people, including myself at that moment, going after him with a blunt object of some kind. So more as a hopeful promise than a brotherly warning, I said, "One of these days, he's going to put a bullet in your head." But Eugene didn't even look up, he just dabbed at his face with the towel and said, "No, he won't. He's chickenshit." And this time he didn't bother to apologize for his language.

I went upstairs, but found no one, so I followed a spotty trail of blood out the back door and down the alley in the direction of Thirty-eighth Street. The blood petered out after a couple of houses, but, by that time, I figured Jack had gone looking for Bernard. Bernard was bunking at Ronnie and Wade's apartment, and I wondered if Jack was going to walk or hitch a ride to the Falls. Walking was more likely because I doubted that anyone would pick him up in his condition. I wasn't up to walking that far so I took a left on Thirty-eighth and headed east toward Hiawatha, where I figured I'd thumb a ride as far as the Parkway. Maybe I'd get there before he did, assuming that's where he was going. I had nothing better to do, did I?

Well, I hadn't walked more than a block before I saw Jack leaning over the curb and spitting into the gutter. There was a lot to spit, I noticed right away, and as I got closer I could see that a lot of what he was spitting was blood.

I asked him if he was okay, and he said, "Never better" and spit some more. He finally stood up and looked at me and grinned, the blood filling the gaps between his teeth like grout. "The motherfucker looks a lot worse than me, don't he?" he said in his tough-guy voice.

He laid a finger alongside his nose and snorted out more blood along with the snot. And it was true. Whatever Eugene had done to Jack's insides to make him spit blood like that, he hadn't done all that much to anything that showed. Jack's left eye was swollen shut, and there was a shiny bruise along the left side of his head, but that was about all in the way of visible damage.

I wondered why he hadn't used his gun on Eugene. *I would have*, I thought at that moment, considering the amount of blood he was spitting into the street. At the same time, I was mightily relieved that he hadn't, and even more than that I was glad to see that he seemed to be all right.

"Where you going?" I asked.

He snorted again and said, "Crazy. Wanna come along?"

I grinned and said sure. I loved Jack more than anyone or anything else in my life—more than the booze I couldn't seem to get enough of at the time and more than the girls I thought about more insanely every day.

I'd go wherever he led me, even to hell.

FIVE

"Joe?"

Silence.

"Jojo? Are you all right?"

I open my eyes, but can't see a thing. A cold finger runs down my back, and for a moment I'm thinking I've drunk myself blind. Then my eyes are filled with light, not bright light but light, a blurry vision, and I remember the wash rag that someone laid across my face and that someone has now taken away.

I'm aware that I'm shivering like a freezing dog under the afghan, and when I touch my skin where my shirt opens at the collar the skin is clammy. My right arm, which I'm lying on, is asleep, which means that what little of me there is left with some feeling is not feeling so good.

"Jojo! You okay, honey?"

The voice, of course, is Ronnie's, and it strikes me that she doesn't sound as drunk as she did the last time I heard her, though who knows how long ago that was. For all I know, it's tomorrow morning.

"What time is it?" I ask her, not really caring, but curious.

"Almost a quarter past five," she says. She's smoking a cigarette, I can tell by the way she says it. "Are you okay, hon?"

I tell her I don't know, and that's the truth. I'm hurting much more than I'm willing to let on, and I would love a drink of anything, even water. I also feel, I don't know, like something's changed, that something's not right about the situation I'm in, like I just woke up and someone's rearranged the furniture. Disoriented, Meslow might say.

"You don't look so good, hon," I hear Ronnie saying, like she was reading my mind, answering my unasked question as to how, at that moment, do I look? "You're awfully pale. White as a ghost. You aren't on some medication we don't know about, are you? Extra pain pills or something?"

I can't help but laugh.

"You don't feel no pain, you don't need no pain pills," I tell her, misleadingly. Ronnie laughs a little too. We both know I've taken enough aspirin over the years to kill a horse or at least tear up my stomach.

"What can I get you? Armand's got some Bromo-Seltzer, if you want it."

I'm okay, I think I tell her. Now I feel like I'm floating, like I'm in some halfway situation where I'm not sure what exactly is going on. I think I'm talking to her, for instance, but I wouldn't bet the ranch on it.

"I'm okay," I say, louder, and this time I'm pretty sure I really said it.

"Adriana and her kids had to go," Ronnie says. "They wanted to say goodbye, but they didn't think they should wake you. They said how glad they were to have the chance to see you."

"I'll bet," I think I say.

"Oh no, hon," she says. "They meant it. You're someone people are happy to see."

I laugh again—I'm pretty sure I do. I'm someone people are *surprised* to see. Then I feel a stab of sadness that I didn't get to see the twins again, Richard and Isabel. They're LaVoies, all right. They're LaVoies a hell of a lot more than they're whoever else they are, Cruzes, and whoever else might have had a hand in shaping them, and that means the odds of their living a good, long, everyday kind of life are slight. I sure as hell won't see them again, either one of them—that I *would* bet the ranch on.

"Eugene's leaving pretty soon," Ronnie says. There's a breathless way she talks when she's smoking. "I told him to stay for leftovers, but he thinks he's got to go for some reason." In a lower voice she adds, "I'll bet he hasn't said a dozen words since dinner. He just sits there like a worn-out piece of furniture, looking sad and tired even when he smiles. He's like a ghost. You can almost see right through him."

Eugene is a son-of-a-bitch, I try to say. But I'm not sure it comes out.

"You want him to say goodbye before he goes?" she says, and I wonder if that's why she's here—to see if I would say goodbye to Eugene. This was a family reunion after all, wasn't it?

Well, I'm sorry, Sis, but the reunion wasn't my idea. I've seen and heard enough of Eugene for a lifetime. The motherfucker isn't the only reason I've been lying here like this for thirty-eight fucking years, but he's one of them, one of the only ones left. I let my eyes slide shut and pretend that I'm too drunk or tired or something to have heard her, and figure that's something she can tell the others, Eugene included. She can tell him I'm dead, as far as that goes.

I hear her sigh and clear her throat. I sense her standing there beside the bed, no doubt wondering what she should do. Then she bends down again and tugs the afghan up around my shoulders. She pats me on my cheek and whispers, "Okay, Jojo, lie there and rest." Then I hear (or think I hear) footsteps on the carpet and the door closing softly behind her.

At Ronnie and Wade Adams's apartment that night at the end of August 1953, Ronnie was there for a while, then left, and it was just the three of us brothers and Wade, who Ronnie was now married to, asleep in front of the portable television in the couple's bedroom.

Ronnie didn't say where she was going. I just remember her foot-steps on the carpet, Ronnie carrying her shoes so she wouldn't wake

Wade, who'd worked a double shift at the Ford plant across the river and had fallen asleep with his boots off and a plate of macaroni and cheese going cold in his lap.

Ronnie was, by that time, a couple of months pregnant, apparently by Wade, but that didn't keep her from stepping out when she got bored, since she wasn't showing anything to speak of yet and even if she was it wasn't likely to stop either her or the men she was seeing at that time, including old pals like Rossy Grant. I'd have felt sorrier for Wade, who was a good guy and another Longfellow neighbor, if Wade himself hadn't been one of the several men who slept with Ronnie when she was married to Donald Harrison. Ronnie and Wade were both what you'd now call consenting adults. What's fair is fair.

Anyway, Ronnie took off—just like she's left me now, shoes off for a silent escape—and Jack and Bernard and I were sitting around the wobbly little kitchen table that came with the crummy three-room apartment, eating the warmed-up macaroni and white-bread Spam-and-mayo sandwiches that Ronnie put in front of us and drinking the Grain Belt that Wade picked up on his way home from work. Bernard, who'd been sleeping on the living-room sofa that also came with the place, found some dance music on Ronnie's portable radio. He kept the sound low so it wouldn't wake Wade in the other room, but the fact that he had it on at all made me think he was feeling better about life than he had been of late.

He did a snazzy little dance step with an imaginary partner when he went to the ice box for the beer, the kind of thing I hadn't seen him do for weeks.

Jack was done hawking up blood, at least for the time being, and I interpreted his not eating much of Ronnie's supper only as a sign he wasn't hungry. Jack was never a big eater. As a matter of fact, none of us LaVoies ever had much of an appetite, at least compared with chow-hounds like Donald and Rossy and even Wade, which more than one person has blamed on how little we got used to eating when we were kids. You never fill it up, the stomach shrinks, I've heard people say, which seems as good an explanation as any, I guess. Some people have said we were undernourished as kids, and that's what kept us small, though that, I think, is horseshit since the Old Man's people have always been small (or so he said) and since, except for Jack's clubfoot, we were normally developed—in Ronnie's and Janine's case spectacularly developed—and since there was never anything wrong with us that wasn't caused by a baseball bat or the leg snapped off a dining-room chair or a slug from a cop's thirty-thirty.

If we were undernourished as kids, maybe it made us mean, maybe it made us a lot of things, but that's something we're never going to know, so I figure what's the point of going on about it.

So the fact that Jack didn't eat a lot of Ronnie's macaroni wasn't unusual, and the fact that he may have been quieter than usual made me think he had something on his mind, which, after the boredom and frustration of the past several days, would be worth listening to, if and when he decided to let us in on it.

I was trying not to think about Judy, especially now that I was sitting next to Bernard, but seeing Bernard in a dancing mood made it all the harder. There were actually moments when I was pretty sure I was capable of doing something rash. Thinking about Ronnie going off to fuck somebody tonight didn't help matters either, though there was something kind of comical about that too, Ronnie watching out the window for a car, then tiptoeing out the door while Wade sawed logs with the macaroni and cheese in his lap now cold as a corpse in the other room. All things considered, it was probably good timing that Jack spoke up when he did, even if what he said was going to seal our fate.

After not saying anything for five or ten minutes, Jack said, "Here's how we're going to kill Follmer."

I remember Bernard and I both turning our heads from whatever it was we'd been looking at to look at Jack. Aside from the swollen eye and the shiny welt on the side of his head, I didn't think he looked any different than usual, or any different, at any rate, than when he told us about killing Eugene or getting even with Donald Harrison's cousins. A little more intense maybe, but that's it.

Bernard started to say something, but before he could say it Jack said, "Turn down the fuckin' radio, will ya, Bernard? Better yet, turn it off."

If Jack was concerned about Wade hearing us from the other room, he didn't show it. Truth be told, it didn't cross my mind, Wade listening in, since Wade was too damn tired to finish his supper, much less stop his woman from stepping out on him, and since Wade was an old friend and now at least legally part of the family. Bernard turned down the radio—we could still hear it, the Dorseys, Benny Goodman—but the music seemed a long way off.

I finished the last of my sandwich and shook a cigarette out of Wade's pack of Old Golds, which he'd left on the table.

"We're going to watch him for a couple of days," Jack said, "then decide on the best place to hit him. It might be in his driveway, some night when the motherfucker pulls in there by himself. It might be over on Twenty-seventh and Lake, where he gets his hair cut. Maybe we follow him and see where he eats lunch. Nail the fat fuck when he comes out the door."

Nobody said a word for a minute, then Bernard asked if we'd do it out in the open, where people could see us.

Jack said, "It don't matter if anyone sees us. Everybody's surprised, everybody's scared out of their shoes, nobody but us and Follmer are going to have guns, and he ain't going to be able to use his. Who knows if they even let him carry one anymore."

"Jack, people are *going* to see us," Bernard said. "They're going to look at mugshots and sit down with one of those police artists who'll draw pictures of us that they'll run in the paper. People are going to know it was us from the pictures."

I was thinking the same thing, but didn't dare say so. I was surprised that Bernard was as direct as he was.

"No one but the Old Man and Eugene got mugshots taken of

them," Jack said. "And if there's a witness who can help the cops draw a picture, it ain't going to matter because we ain't going to be around by that time."

The thought of Judy flashed in my mind again, and I heard myself say, "We're leaving town?"

Jack slowly slid his stare from Bernard to me.

"You in love with this burg, Jojo?" he said. "The good ol' City of Lakes is dear to you?"

I shook my head. The truth is, it was and it wasn't.

"I don't know yet where we're going to go, but we're going," Jack said to both of us. "Mexico maybe, or up through Canada to the Northwest Territories and Alaska."

I didn't dare glance at Bernard, knowing the look I'd see on his face, the look that showed how worried he was about never seeing his wife and baby again, even though he wasn't likely to see much of them no matter what he did or where he lived. Going to Mexico or Alaska was the same, I'm sure he thought, as going to the moon. I have to admit I felt the same sort of sadness when Jack said what he said, the kind of sadness you felt in the pit of your stomach when the bottom of your world has fallen out. There I'd been, not more than a couple of days ago, thinking about working my way back to Europe on a steamer, going back to Monika and settling down and becoming a good German, and never coming back. That hadn't bothered me at all, but maybe that's because I knew it was never going to happen.

Jack must have seen the looks on our faces because, after another few seconds, he said, "I don't know about that yet. Maybe we'll just go up north for a while."

The idea of killing Buddy Follmer must have been wriggling around in our heads since that day in the basement because neither Bernard or I was shocked or even very surprised when Jack brought it up in Ronnie's kitchen. It was something both of us knew was coming once Jack had announced it in the first place, and that each of us had done some thinking about in his own way, and without ever saying it in so many words to ourselves or to each other, it was something each of us wanted to do.

I doubt if we'd have ever thought of it if Jack hadn't brought it up. I don't think I would have realized how much I hated Buddy Follmer for doing what he was doing or had done with Janine. But when Jack told us what we were going to do and why, we knew we were going to do it and that it was what we wanted to do. So when Jack laid out his plan, it was only some of the details that bothered us, not the idea itself.

We sat there talking for another ten or fifteen minutes, not just about killing Follmer, but about other things too, Eugene and the Old Man and other people or events that crossed our minds, and then Wade came in from the bedroom holding his dinner plate in one hand and looking sour and mean the way a guy looks when he wakes up after falling asleep in a chair.

He looked at us and said maybe we could leave him a beer or two if we didn't mind, a sarcastic edge to his voice that we weren't used to hearing. Wade, like I say, was basically a sweetheart, a quiet, hard-working, no-bullshit kind of guy, who always seemed to do right by his friends. It was Wade's Studebaker that we'd borrowed all summer, Wade never asking where it went or what we used it for, Wade asking only that it have enough gas when we returned it to get him over to the Ford plant and back, which it usually, but not always, did.

Wade was a small, wiry guy, no bigger than us LaVoies, with black, curly hair, a lot of black hair on the arms and legs, and a five o'clock shadow that he'd been shaving since seventh grade. We'd known Wade as long as we could remember, since the Adamses, who had only the one child, lived two doors the other side of the Harrisons. Wade may not have been the first boy to have sex with Ronnie, but he was no worse than second or third, his blue jaws and curly hair making him a worthy early rival of Donald and Rossy and the others that she put out for.

Bernard once told me that Jack had broken Wade's jaw in a fight when they were in junior high. I found that hard to believe because Wade would've given Jack no more reason to break his jaw than Donald or Rossy did, the younger boys treating Jack with respect or staying out of his way entirely, and, like I said, a boy fooling around with Ronnie was never the cause, so far as I knew, of Jack going after the boy. Wade, what's more, might have been Ronnie's favorite. She might have even loved him. There were disagreements, of course—boys will be boys and all that—but Wade was not the kind of guy to either give or get a beating from anyone. He was a sweetheart right up until the day he walked out on Ronnie and the baby and was never heard from again. I considered the story about Jack busting Wade's jaw just another one of Bernard's inventions.

But that night Wade woke up from his nap definitely out of sorts. He dropped his half-eaten dinner into the sink, grabbed a Grain Belt out of the ice box, and snapped the cap off on the edge of the counter. I knew what he was thinking. He was thinking, *That goddamned Ronnie, who I'm supposed to be married to, is giving it good to some guy over at the Falls Motel or maybe on top of a goddamned picnic table in the Deer Pen, and here sits her lowlife brothers, not one of them with a job or even the thought of one, eating the food and drinking the beer that I bust my ass welding joints on pickup trucks paying for.* Wade was not the kind of guy who had thoughts like that very often, but that night was one of the nights he did—I could tell from the expression on his face and the way he wouldn't look at us when he was talking. He would never say as much in so many words because he was still Wade, still a sweetheart, and because, like everybody else, he was afraid of Jack and who knows, when Bernard and I were with Jack, maybe afraid of the two of us as well.

If I'd had any doubt about that, the doubt was erased when Jack pushed himself away from the table and without a word, with only a long, cold stare in Wade's direction, stood up and dragged his bad foot toward the door. Wade looked like he'd been slapped across the face. He put his bottle on the counter and followed after him, saying, "No, it's all right, Jack. I didn't mean for you to leave and not drink the beer, I just had a horseshit day at the plant and came home with a bitch of a headache."

But there was no way Jack would turn back. Wade knew that as well as we did, so Wade turned to us when we stood up and started walking after Jack and said the same thing to us. I felt sorry for him and started to say that everything was okay, but Bernard, who liked to act like Jack in that kind of situation, shook his head like he was too disgusted for words, and the three of us stumbled out of the apartment and into the cool night air, Wade in his stocking feet a few steps behind us.

Out of the corner of my eye I saw Jack, who was standing outside the door, come up fast and grab Wade by the front of his blue work shirt and slam him against the wall. Wade's face above the five o'clock shadow went white so fast you'd have thought Jack had yanked a plug and the color ran out the bottom. Holding Wade by the shirt, Jack slammed him against the wall again and hissed in Wade's face, "I swear to Christ, if you so much as lift a finger against Ronnie, I'll come back and put a bullet between your fuckin' eyes." I doubt if Wade had ever hit or even threatened Ronnie, but that didn't seem to matter.

Then Jack told Bernard to go inside and fetch his things and come back to the house because the three of us had more important fish to fry.

One of the things Meslow was especially curious about after I let him in on the hitherto unknown fact that we'd been out to kill Buddy Follmer the day we killed Fredriksen, was why Jack told us the murder plan when he'd never told us where we were going before we robbed a drugstore or gas station.

"Know what I think?" Meslow said.

"No," I said. "Don't give a damn either."

"I think your brother was chickenshit. Killing Follmer was something he was afraid to think about doing by himself. He needed his little brothers in on this from the beginning, maybe so he wouldn't back out. Or maybe he wanted the two of you to talk him out of it, or warn Follmer so he wouldn't have to make the attempt. Jackie boy had all the balls in the world when it came to sticking a pistol in the face of an unarmed pump jockey, but he was chickenshit when it came to going after a cop—even a fat, lazy motherfucker of a cop who was chickenshit himself."

I didn't answer him right away. Finally, I said, "No, he thought this was a family matter, not just another drugstore or filling station, and it was important we all be involved."

Meslow laughed at that. I'm not sure what it was he thought was funny—what I said or the way I said it—not that it mattered one way or the other.

"Besides," I went on, "Jack needed help setting it up. He wanted to do it right, and he wanted us to get away. He figured it would take more information than he could gather on his own. He was in a hurry."

"Oh, Christ," Meslow muttered, waving his hand dismissively. But he might have believed what I'd told him because he didn't say anything for a while after that. He might have believed it because he knew that the LaVoies had at least a passing familiarity with the ways and means of assassination and premeditated murder on account of the Old Man's employment by Bunny Augustine. During the '30s and '40s, Bunny was allegedly responsible for the killings of a news-paperman, at least two cops, and a handful of others—shady types the papers referred to as "police characters"—and each was done, or so people were led to believe, after careful planning and calculation.

I remembered a day, when I was about twelve, standing in front of Cable's drugstore on Thirty-eighth Street with Bernard, looking at the morning paper in the pay box. On the front page was a big photo of a fat guy in a suit lying on his side in a gutter. His hat lay bottom up a few feet from his head, and in between the hat and the body there was a shiny trickle of dark liquid, dirty gutter water or blood.

Bernard said the guy was an accountant, whatever that was, who worked for Bunny Augustine. He pointed to a small, dark spot on the back of the guy's head where his hair ended and his neck began and said that was where the bullet entered. I squinted at the spot and thought it looked like a mole, but Bernard said that shooting a guy in the lower right side of the brain was the best way to kill him and was Bunny's trademark. I didn't know what "trademark" meant either, but, sure enough, on the bottom half of that front page there was a smaller photo of a smiling Bunny Augustine and a headline that said that he'd been questioned and released. The paper said that Bunny told the police that he'd been getting a haircut at the time the man was gunned down.

It's possible then that Meslow, once he found out about Jack's plan to kill Follmer, thought that we'd been playing gangster, that we'd heard enough about Bunny Augustine and his goons from the Old Man, to want to imitate him ourselves. But that would be wrong too. I don't remember Jack once mentioning Bunny Augustine (or any other gangster) when we were getting ourselves ready to kill Follmer. I don't think Jack ever had romantic ideas about Bunny and those "police characters" who were turning up in the papers every so often. Bernard did, that's for sure. Before he got married, Bernard liked to dance, as I believe I've mentioned, at Bunny's North Side Club, and, of course, it was Bernard who got us wearing the hats and ties that were supposed to make us look like big-time hoods. Jack never idolized Bunny that way. By the time we were adults, I'm pretty sure he would've thought that Bunny was a chump for employing stumblebums like the Old Man.

The truth is I don't know why Jack got us into the plot the way he did. I never asked, and he never told us, which was generally the way we'd operated from the beginning.

The only thing I remember bothering me about the course our life was now taking was our relationship with Wade Adams. It wasn't right the way we'd treated Wade that night at his and Ronnie's apartment, and I felt guilty about it for a couple of days. Wade was a friend (even then I had trouble thinking of him as my brother-in-law), someone we could count on in a pinch, and I didn't see the point of Jack getting rough with him. What had Wade done except get pissed about his wife sneaking out on him and the three of us drinking his beer? But then the guilt passed too, because roughing up Wade like that had been Jack's decision, and even if it didn't make a lot of sense, I was Jack's brother, not Wade's.

Besides, there was work to do. We knew the lay of the land around Buddy's house and we knew the Lake Street barbershop where Buddy got his ears lowered every other Saturday morning. His comings and goings downtown were something else again, so the three of us spent a few days watching for him outside the Courthouse, where the police department headquarters was located, and following him back and forth between the Courthouse and a place called the Mayflower Grill on Fourth Street, a block-and-a-half away.

Buddy was as dumb and lazy as everybody said he was. He would step out of the Courthouse at 11:45 and walk up Fourth Street with the newspaper under his arm and his eyes on the sidewalk except when a good-looking young woman—the younger, the better— crossed his path. Then he'd look up and follow her a ways down the street. Though the weather was cooler now, he always seemed to be sweating, his red, round face slick below the brim of his fedora, and after walking a little more than a city block he'd be mopping his face with his handkerchief.

The Mayflower Grill was a greasy spoon off the lobby of a small hotel that stood across the street from the Telephone Building, and the days we tailed him the place was so crowded that Buddy had to wait for an empty stool. While waiting, he read the paper. He never said a word to another person, nor did anyone say anything to him. It was almost impossible to imagine him with Ronnie and Janine, not only because he was fat and ugly, but because he always seemed so alone.

One afternoon, after we'd watched him downtown, the three of us sat in a booth in the rear of the Sailor Tap on Cedar Avenue. We'd taken the Thirty-fourth Avenue streetcar back to the neighborhood and, at my suggestion, rode on past our stop and got off in front of the Sailor. We had a couple of bucks between us and decided to drink some beer. There were a few people in the bar, but they sat up near the front while we sat in the back and kept our voices down and talked about killing Buddy Follmer.

Bernard, eager to talk like a gangster, said, "Me, I'd just stroll up nice and easy behind the fucker, stick the barrel of my piece up close behind his right ear, and, *pop! pop! pop!* let him have it right there on the street. He'd go down like a sack of potatoes, and some broad would scream, and I'd smooth as silk step into the car that you guys would pull up to the curb."

Jack snorted. "So you're the guy that's gonna do it, huh, Bernard?" It didn't sound mean, the way he said it, but it didn't sound as though he could envision the picture Bernard had painted.

Bernard shrugged. "Sure," he said. "Why not?"

Jack glanced at me and smiled. "I dunno," he said. "I just have this vision of you missing the fucker and shooting some other poor bastard in the face."

Bernard didn't say anything back, and Jack, who seemed to be feeling pretty good that afternoon, asked how I'd do the job.

I lit one of Bernard's Lucky Strikes and took a deep drag and, feeling pretty good myself at the moment, said, "I see you and me waiting around for Buddy to go into the men's room at the restaurant, and one of us waits outside the door so no one else goes in while the other one follows him inside and, when he steps up to the wall to piss, moves up close and, *pop! pop! pop!* like Bernard says, puts three bullets in his brain. Then, nice and easy, the shooter walks out, nods to the one keeping watch, and then we both walk outside, where Bernard is waiting with the car."

Jack squinted at me through the cigarette smoke. It was dark in the back of the bar, and the smoke made it darker.

"What if there's someone else in the can?"

I thought about that for a minute. "It depends," I said. "If some guy's sitting in the stall with the door closed, no problem, we leave him be. If he's standing there alongside Buddy, then I guess we gotta plug him too."

Jack said, "You'd have the balls to do that, Jojo? Shoot a guy because he happened to choose that moment to take a piss?"

I thought about that too, then said, "No, but you do."

Jack grinned at me through the smoke.

The three of us went on like that for the better part of an hour, inventing new possibilities and elaborating on what someone said before.

It was exciting to sit in that smoky bar, talking about the plan, partly because Jack was treating us like we were a gang where everyone had his say and partly because each of us could picture killing Buddy Follmer without having to actually do it. I think we each felt a little like Bunny Augustine and his hoods sitting in Bunny's office behind the dance floor at the North Side Club talking about rubbing out this or that muckraking newspaperman or this or that crooked cop. Jack, of course, was Bunny, smoking one cigarette after another while patiently listening to his lieutenants put in their two cents' worth, but he would eventually decide on the where, when, and how of the hit. It didn't matter who Bernard and I were so long as we were sitting there with the boss and were in on the decision.

I thought about the Old Man and how he never would have had the chance to sit with Bunny in the back room of the North Side Club and decide who lived and who died, and how, even on his best days, he was lucky if he got to fetch one of Bunny's cars or pick up the dry cleaning for one of Bunny's lieutenants.

The Old Man was, if anything, one of those poor bastards who could wind up on the receiving end of a Bunny Augustine murder plan. Because he drank too much and didn't have the sense or the discipline not to talk when he drank, he could very well end up, I thought, lying face down in the gutter like that guy on the front page of the paper. Then again, I knew the Old Man wasn't important enough for that to happen. Bunny probably couldn't remember the Old Man's name, the Old Man being just another no-account rummy who hung around and cadged a drink and a pastrami sandwich now and then, and ran an errand when Bunny and his cronies snapped their manicured fingers.

Eventually, the three of us ran out of beer money and went home. Nothing had been decided—or, at any rate, Jack hadn't announced anything if it had—and walking north on Cedar, my mind slipped back to thoughts about Judy. As excited as I'd been about killing Buddy, I was not what you'd call obsessed with the idea, and, in fact, if I'd had my druthers, I would've chosen to fuck Judy over killing Buddy any day of the week.

I'm not sure how much of our plotting and reconnaissance I told Meslow about, once I told him we'd been out to kill Follmer. It couldn't have been too much because there was a lot I had forgotten or buried in my subconscious after we killed Fredriksen instead. I never said a word about Follmer when the cops interrogated me in the hospital and when Twyman, the county prosecutor, asked me questions during the trials, letting them think we were out to rob that drugstore at Twenty-seventh and Lake when Fredriksen had the bad luck to cross our path. I knew from the beginning, from the moment that Meslow walked into Hiawatha General's emergency room and asked if I was a Catholic, that the cops and the lawyers would never get the story straight if I didn't want them to. And since the idea of killing Follmer was a family matter, it wasn't something I wanted them to know.

Besides, by that time, so much had happened, and everything had changed so much I wasn't sure if I hadn't dreamed up the Follmer part in the first place. The few pieces that did seem real I quickly forgot, or thought I had.

I can't tell you how much time passed between that night at Ronnie's apartment and the day Jack said we were going to do it—we were going to put on our hats and gangster outfits and pop a couple of bullets behind Buddy Follmer's ear.

Other things were going on at home and in the neighborhood, and I had all I could do to keep my mind off Judy. As a matter of fact, I'd more or less reached the point where I decided it was useless to try to forget Judy and began planning a way to get close to her and maybe slip away with her (I refused to think about the baby). More than once, I called her on the phone only to hang up, embarrassed and ashamed and maybe afraid too, before I ever said a word or she knew who was calling.

In my mind, she was not Bernard's wife anymore or the Judy Oleski she was before she married him. She was a fantasy, like Marilyn Monroe and Jane Russell were to a lot of guys, someone who existed in the flesh somewhere and for some lucky men, but who, as far as you were concerned, lived only in your mind. Maybe that was enough. Maybe it was all to the good. But it was a mysterious process that I never figured out, how Judy once existed in my life and then, without dying or moving out of town, stopped living there and became more make-believe than real. I even thought for a while that I was in love with her. I reminded myself that I'd been in love with Monika too, and all I was doing was confusing desire with love. When I cared to admit it to myself, all I wanted to do was fuck Judy, not marry her, though I wanted to fuck Judy for the rest of my life, or, anyway, that's what I thought at the time.

Sometimes I wonder what Judy would think if she knew this today. Maybe she knew it all the while, maybe she knew it when she talked to me on the phone that once after she and Bernard split up, maybe she knew it before that, when I'd come around the apartment after I first got home from the service, maybe she knew it before I did myself. But I doubt it. I'm pretty sure Judy didn't give me much thought if she thought about me at all, and that, when the shit hit the fan in the fall of 1953, I was just one of the three LaVoie brothers who killed the policeman and the farmer and thereby damaged the good name and reputation of everyone connected with them. But that realization came later. In those few days leading up to our attack on Buddy

Follmer, that was about all I could think about, the fantasy that Judy had become.

Meanwhile, the situation at the house was going from bad to worse.

One day after school, Marie was bit on the wrist by the Harrisons' dog, a usually harmless mongrel that probably thought he was playing with her. Marie wasn't hurt bad, but the dog had to be watched for rabies, and neither Marie nor Michael would set foot outside for days. (Turned out Skipper wasn't rabid, but the twins would run in the house whenever they saw him.)

The Old Man was worried about the Jews again, having said or done something to put him, he believed, on the outs with Bunny Augustine's crowd. He would sit at the dining-room table with his back to wall, then jump up and peek out the front windows whenever he'd hear a car door slam. He was no more willing to go outside than the twins were, and in the evening, he'd send me or Bernard over to Cianciolo's for cigarettes and beer.

One night during that period, I found myself sitting at the table with the Old Man, finishing some leftovers from the ice box. He and I were the only ones at the table, and all of a sudden, as though he just noticed I was there, he said, "Well, young fella, what the hell you gonna do with yourself—get married, get a job, get outta this madhouse?"

It had been several days since he spoke to me. I was surprised he remembered who I was, let alone show an interest in my future. I shrugged and said, "Get a job, I guess."

The Old Man lit a cigarette and, speaking with one eye squeezed shut against the smoke, said, "What kinda job would that be? You go out and get an education when the rest of us wasn't looking?"

Again, I was surprised that he was taking an interest, then remembered the letter he had written me when I was in Europe. "I did some typing in the Army," I said.

The Old Man squinted and grinned like he'd learned something either interesting or funny. "You know how to typewrite, do you?"

"I do okay."

"You don't say," the Old Man said.

"I do say," I said, pushing myself away from the table.

I glanced at him sitting there staring at me through the haze. He seemed to have something on his mind, like, after all these years, there was something he wanted to make sure I understood about the world that had maybe taken him some time and hard knocks to find out for himself. Thinking about his unlikely letter, I thought maybe I should give him the benefit of the doubt. Judy was on my mind again that night, and I thought about strolling past the Oleskis' house once it got dark, to see if there was anything to see through a bedroom window. But I waited for a moment to see what words of wisdom the Old Man might have.

He reached out and grabbed my wrist and pulled me toward him across the table. I was surprised again, this time by how much strength the little weasel still had in him.

"You want some advice you can take to the bank?" he said, the cigarette bobbing up and down between his lips as he spoke.

"Sure," I said with a shrug. "Why not?"

"I never went to school past the seventh grade," he said, "but I learned a thing or two for myself over the years."

"I'm listening."

"Information's good as gold."

"So tell me."

He cleared his throat and said, "Never work for a goddamned Jew."

I looked at him, then yanked my arm out of his grip. My back was beginning to ache, leaning across the table like that.

"That's it?" I said. I'd have laughed if I'd been in a better mood, but I wasn't so I didn't, I just pulled myself away from the old fool. I said, "If you hadn't worked for that goddamned Jew, you wouldn't have worked at all."

My father leaned back and shook his head.

"I woulda worked for myself," he said in a grand manner. "I woulda been a *on-trop-a-noor*," making it sound, whatever he was talking about, like something French and important.

Now I did laugh, sour mood or not. I wished Jack and Bernard had been around to hear what he'd said.

"What the hell would you have done on your own?" I asked him.

"What Bunny did," he said, like I was a moron to ask such a foolish question. "I woulda cut deals with the Southside Irish, shown them what I was made of, then start taking those micks out one at a time until I owned both sides of town. Also, I woulda opened a club."

I quit laughing and shook my head.

"Like hell," I said, feeling angry again that I had such a buffoon for a father. It would have been bad enough if the guy was just a drunk and a tin-pot bully. On top of that he was stupid as a pile of rocks. He was a coward too, for not standing up to Bunny or whoever it was in Bunny's gang who made life tough for him, as though he was anything more than a broken-down piece of shit who couldn't have done Bunny or his pals any harm if he tried. The worst thing was, whatever made the Old Man what he was, was also inside his sons and there wasn't a thing we could do about it. Times like that I could've killed him on the spot, or wouldn't have felt bad if someone else did.

The next day, Mother wandered away by herself, and for a while we thought she might have fallen in the river. We didn't live that far away. It would have been easy for her to take the Thirty-eighth Street car to the River Road, but odds were she walked.

It must sound preposterous when I describe these things one after another, but that's the way things happened at our house—like the salt people say, "When it rains, it pours." And I'm telling only a small part of what actually went on, my memory not so good when it comes to what I once might have known and no help at all with the rest of it. God only knows everything that went on when I wasn't around and that I never heard about or that I heard about from Bernard, which wasn't always something I put a lot of stock in. Mother wandering off just a day or two before we tried to kill Follmer and killed Fredriksen instead was one of those things I knew about firsthand because I was there and saw what there was to see.

At that time in her life, Mother was spending most of her days in the back bedroom, where she would read the Bible and pray, or sit with her head in her hands and weep.

It was getting so bad that even the Old Man, who hadn't paid any genuine attention to his wife for years, would occasionally stand up and slam his hand down on the table and ask nobody in particular, "What in the name of Christ is that woman doin' in there?" Not that the Old Man, who was rarely home anyway, would go in and see for himself—he was as spooked by Mother as the rest of us, and he may have realized that his sudden bellowing presence would likely make things worse.

When Mother did come out of the bedroom, she looked like a ghost, her skin so pale it seemed transparent, her once-brown hair not going gray so much now as losing its color entirely. Her gray eyes bulged out of her skeletal face like an insect's, though I don't think it was a case of the eyes really bulging so much as the face shrinking around them. As little as the rest of us ate, she ate even less.

She'd gotten so bad in the few months since I came home that the ladies from the Tabernacle weren't coming around much anymore. I guess I couldn't blame them, thinking what it must have been like stepping up to our door in those days, never knowing if the Old Man was going to curse them off the front steps or Jack was going to give them one of his death stares.

I do remember, about the time we were beginning the robberies, coming home one afternoon and finding three of those old biddies sitting with Mother in the living room with their Bibles open on their knobby knees. I don't think I'd seen the three of them for several years, but they looked the same as I remembered them, with their pinched, rouged faces and silly little hats and polka dot dresses. Two or maybe all three were sisters.

Mother looked up when I came in and said, "Oh, ladies, you know my son Joseph, don't you? He has returned to us, praise Jesus, from the war."

But the others glanced up like I was another one of the demons who lived in that awful house and then quickly looked back at their Bibles. I passed on through as fast as I could and was halfway up the stairs before they started to sing. All of a sudden, I remembered when we were little, five or six or so, and how we'd have to stand in front of those Tabernacle ladies and recite Bible verses and listen to the "testimony" of whoever had one or dared to make one up. The verses and the testimonies were bad enough, but the singing was even worse. The sound of those women singing "The Old Rugged Cross" was so awful I couldn't even laugh about it afterward. The singing made my skin crawl. It was sad and hideous and inescapable, and I hated Mother for singing like that, even when she wasn't singing at all, when I only thought about her doing it.

By the fall of 1953 though, it was rare to have those ladies in the house reading their Bibles and singing their awful songs. If Mother saw her friends at all anymore, it was when Eugene took her to Sunday services at the Tabernacle, which he did every once in a while, or the few times when she wandered over there on her own. Once in a while, she would answer the door in order to chase off a man looking for Janine or go down the basement to wash clothes only to forget what she had gone down there for and come back upstairs wringing her hands and muttering about "the baby."

No one knows where Mother was actually headed the day she disappeared. Bernard said maybe she was walking to Ronnie's apartment near the Falls, but that didn't seem right because she'd never tried that before and never let it be known that she was interested in going there and wouldn't know how to get there if she were. I think she started walking and didn't care where she was going—she was just going to go as far as she could and then stop. Maybe she thought she was walking with Jesus, or walking *to* Him, wherever she thought He might be that afternoon. She had her hat and her one decent dress on, and she carried a purse with about twenty cents and a couple of streetcar tokens inside.

She was gone all that afternoon and night and most of the following morning, and when the cops brought her home just before noon she couldn't or wouldn't tell anybody where she'd been. One of the cops—they were a pair of uniformed officers driving a black-and-white Ford—said a woman who lived on the River Road had called to report a person sitting in a lawn chair in her front yard. The woman in the chair wouldn't tell her who she was or what she was doing there, so the homeowner called the police. The cops tried to get her to talk too, but she didn't say a word, so they took her downtown.

And guess who it was downtown that identified her?

None other than Sergeant Ernest Follmer.

"Good thing you got a neighbor who recognized her," one of the uniform cops, a big, red-faced guy named Holcomb, said to me. "She woulda been sitting down there till who the hell knows when, and you mighta been lookin' around thinkin' she was dead."

"Yeah, good thing," I said, thinking not so much about Mother right then as about Buddy Follmer and the funny way things work.

We never did figure out where she was going or what she had done all night except sit in that woman's lawn chair. Luckily, it was a mild, dry night. I told Jack and Bernard, who had been out looking for her, about Follmer, and we all laughed—two of us thinking that maybe Buddy had just saved or at least prolonged his life by identifying that lost soul who was our mother, but the third, the one that counted, not thinking any such thing, thinking it was only a coincidence. To Jack's way of thinking, Mother wandering off like that was another reason to do what he was determined to do and then get the hell out of that loony bin as fast as we could.

Jack was at the breaking point—that much was obvious to both Bernard and me. Every day he seemed to be wound a little tighter, like the propeller on one of those airplanes I'd see kids playing with at Powderhorn Park, the kind where you twisted a thick rubber band until it was wound so tight a guy risked losing a finger if he let go and didn't get his hand out of the way of the propeller fast enough.

Except for going out to follow Follmer around or to look for Mother, Jack never left his room. Even to Bernard and me, he was saying less and less, and there hadn't been all that much conversation to start with. He seemed distracted—not like Janine, listening to her private music—but like somebody adding up everything bad that had happened to him in his life. The ugly bruise on the side of his head had turned a dirty yellow-green, and the skin on his face seemed to grow tighter and tighter, making his eyes seem to bug out like Mother's. Jack didn't look like he was fading away though. He looked like there was something burning behind his eyes, and the heat was making his skin go yellow and tight. His eyes, which you always noticed on account of that stare, now seemed ready to jump out of his skull.

I don't know how much longer Jack could've gone on like that—probably not another day, at least not another day like the ones we'd been having for a while—so I was relieved when the day the cops brought Mother home from her mysterious adventure, Jack said that today is the day we're going to kill Buddy Follmer.

One day, after I had been at the Cloud for about a year, a guy named A.M. Gilchrist sent me a letter saying he was interested in writing an article for one of the big national magazines, *Life* or *Look* or *Saturday Evening Post* (I don't remember which), about the killing of Patrolman Fredriksen. Gilchrist said that while he could never condone what we did or try to make the officer's murder seem less heinous than it was, he could sympathize with our "lot in life"—that's what he called it—and would like to give me an opportunity to tell my "side of the story."

I had to laugh. Like I was sitting there in my wheelchair, staring out at the yard, waiting for some asshole to come along and give me the opportunity to tell my "side of the story," like what I'd been involved in was some fucking argument between neighbors or a family spat. I also had to laugh because the guy said he wanted to "reconstruct" the day of the Fredriksen shooting, reassembling every moment, every sight, sound, and impression he possibly could, so the reader of the article he was writing would know what it was like to be "inside the head" of a murderer at the time he murdered. Only I'm pretty sure he didn't say "murderer," I believe he said "actor," like I was James Dean or Montgomery Clift, someone who was playing a part in a movie. I tore up Gilchrist's letter and tossed the pieces in the toilet. What did he think I was going to tell him—*Well, lemme see, first of all that morning I ate a bowl of Wheaties*?

That morning, I probably didn't eat much of anything—maybe a piece of burnt toast if someone left one sitting on the table—but whatever it was or wasn't, I wouldn't have been able to remember it the next day, let alone a year-and-a-half later.

There was nothing special to remember about that day, at least not until the cops brought Mother home from downtown and Jack said today's the day we're going to kill Buddy Follmer. People were coming and going, same as always, the weather was cool, but mostly sunny for a change—nothing out of the ordinary at all, no matter what finally happened. The day, I'm trying to say, was no more special going into it than the three of us were anything out of the ordinary when we woke up that morning. We weren't killers until we killed the patrolman. We weren't infamous or notorious or anything else except a trio of sawed-off schmos—and the day wasn't anything more or less different than we were, at least until everything changed.

It was a Saturday, brighter than it had been for a while, and it wasn't long into the afternoon when Jack said today was the day. We were standing behind the house, on the edge of the alley—Bernard was burning trash in the lopsided burner that sat back there, that burner hit so many times by so many cars racing up and down the alley that it didn't have a shape any longer, it was just a blackened tangle of rusty wire. Mother was back in her bedroom, sound asleep, Eugene and Janine and the twins had walked to Cianciolo's for groceries, and God knows where the Old Man had gone. Jack, with those eyes bulging the way I described them and that stretched-tight look about him, stared at Bernard and me, and said, "Well, you up to it?"

I glanced at Bernard, who was looking at me, and then one of us, I don't remember which, said, "Sure, Jack," and the other one nodded.

Because it was Saturday afternoon, I wondered where Jack had decided to do the killing. At that time, Buddy usually worked a few hours on Saturday morning, then every other week stopped at the barbershop on East Lake on his way home. As far as I knew, Buddy was by that time in the day sitting in his living-room three doors down from where I was standing, sipping a cold Hamm's or Grain Belt and watching a ballgame on television, or maybe out in his driveway, washing the car. I figured that Jack had changed his plans, had decided he couldn't wait a single day longer before we did it, all the stalking and planning not important anymore, the only thing that mattered was doing it. The thought of walking down the block and shooting Follmer right there in broad daylight made my blood run cold, but if that's what Jack had decided, I knew I'd go along and Bernard would too.

But Jack must have had the same reservations because he told us to get our hats and jackets and ties out of his room (where we'd taken to stashing them), put the outfits and some extra underwear and socks in the duffel bag I'd brought home from the Army, then wait for him in the alley behind the Tabernacle, where he'd come by and pick us up in a car.

Wade Adams's car? Bernard asked, knowing better. Jack said no, he had "reserved" a different one. He'd meet us behind the Tabernacle at 3:30, and we'd go from there. Bernard started to say go where, but Jack cut him off, saying, "Don't worry, there ain't anybody there on Saturday afternoon"—meaning at the Tabernacle. That still didn't tell us where we were going to kill Follmer, much less how we were going to do it and where we were going afterward, but it was enough to get us moving and to understand that, one way or another, we were finally going to do it.

Jack disappeared down the alley in the direction of Thirty-seventh Street while Bernard and I went back inside the house. We walked past Mother's door and went upstairs to Jack's room. We had a little more than an hour to kill before we had to meet Jack, but neither Bernard or I had anything to do, so we closed Jack's door behind us and stood in his room and wondered what was next.

Bernard said, "Better take a good look around, Jojo."

"Why's that?" I said, knowing why.

"Because this might be the last time you see the place."

I shrugged and said, "I left here once and came back."

"This will be different," Bernard said, and, for a minute, I thought he was going to cry.

I tried not to look at him so neither one of us would be embarrassed. I shrugged again and said, "It ain't that great a place, is it, so I don't think we're going to miss it all that much."

Without turning to look him in the face, I sensed his head turn and his eyes point in my direction, and then I heard him sigh. Still without looking back at him, I went down on my knees and pulled the duffel bag out from under Jack's bed. I swiped at the dust that covered it with my hand, stood up again, and tossed it on the bed, its top open and facing us like a wide, gaping mouth.

"Let's get our shit together," I said.

The duffel bag made me think of getting ready to come home from Germany, the way I threw it on the bed and its mouth flopped open like that. Shorty Gorman was watching me the way Bernard was watching me now, only Shorty was trying to make me mad, was trying to goad me into a fight, and I was confused and angry and not quite sure about what I was going to do. "The minute you get on that train to Frankfurt," Shorty was saying, "Monika's gonna be free to do what she pleases—you know that, doncha?" I didn't say anything. I was thinking about what Monika and I had said to each other the night before, the last time we were together, the last time we'd *ever* be together, angry and then not angry, promising and then telling each other that promises didn't matter between people who lived so far apart, Monika finally crying and running off while I just stood there and thought, *Well, that's that, isn't it?* I told Shorty to shut the fuck up, I didn't know anything, and neither did he. The duffel bag had my name, LA VOIE, JOSEPH A., and serial number stenciled in black ink along the side, and all it ever held was everything I owned.

Now I told Bernard to stick his shit inside the bag too. I felt much the same as I'd felt the last time I'd filled it up before going somewhere.

Bernard and I didn't say anything for a while, even after we'd finished packing the bag. Afternoon sunlight streamed in the dusty little window that faced south, and we could hear somebody, probably old man Harrison, mowing his lawn. I wondered what Jack had put his stuff in because his hat and jacket and tie were not in his closet, and his underwear and sock drawer was cleaned out. He would have taken his money with him, but I wondered how much that could be—a couple of weeks having passed since our last job. The guns were gone, which was no surprise, and I figured he had somehow gotten all his stuff out of the house earlier in the day because I didn't see him with anything when he was giving us our marching orders in the alley.

I could tell, glancing at Bernard, that some of the same thoughts were going through his head too, I could tell the way he was looking around, thinking. And then our eyes met and, for reasons I can't explain, the two of us started laughing.

"You ever think you'd be a desperado?" Bernard said, with a grin I hadn't seen for a long time.

"Is that what we are?" I said, grinning back. "Desperadoes?"

"That's what we're gonna be soon enough," he said, and, who knows why, we started laughing again.

I looked at him and thought for a minute and then said, "I guess that's what we've been for most of the summer, ain't it?"

And he said, "Not like the desperadoes we're *gonna* be," and laughed. Then just like that he stopped and said, "Jesus Christ, Jojo, what the fuck's that crazy Jack got us into?" and, no longer laughing either, I said, "I don't know, Bernard. But here we fuckin' go."

At ten minutes after three, the two of us decided we couldn't sit there any longer. Bernard grabbed the duffel bag, and we left Jack's room.

At the bottom of the stairs, Bernard stopped abruptly and asked me in a sudden whisper, "Think we ought to say goodbye to Ma?" I glanced at the closed door of her room—the door, like all the other wood in the house, scratched and scraped and dented from everything that had gone on—and shook my head.

I said, "She's probably asleep."

I doubted that, but I wanted to get away from her door all the same, wanted to get out of the house and away from Longfellow Avenue as fast as I could. On the one hand, I would've liked to say something to Janine and the twins, not that they would understand what was about to happen any more than Mother would, but, on the other, I wanted to go. I felt wound up as tight as Jack had seemed the past few days— tight enough so it showed. Besides, who, when they're going off to kill someone, stops to tell people they're going? Whoever it was they told would say, "Going where?" and what would you say, "I'm going to kill the cop that lives down the block"? And when the other person says, "Oh, yeah, and then what?" what do you say, "I don't know, Mexico or maybe Alaska"?

Bernard must have been thinking the same thing because I saw him hesitating, looking around, maybe considering leaving someone a note—something to mark his passage. I'm sure he was wondering, like I was, why Eugene and Janine and the twins hadn't come home yet from Cianciolo's, figuring then, like I was, that Janine walked over to the park where there'd be guys throwing a football around, and that Eugene, having the day off and the twins underfoot, decided to trail along after her. Anyway, we realized that there was nobody in the house except Mother, who might have been asleep, and so there was nothing to do but leave, which we did, walking out the back door and then walking down the alley to where it connected with the east-west alley that ran parallel to Thirty-eighth Street, and then walking up that alley toward the Tabernacle.

The Tabernacle was deserted and silent. The blue-haired organist, Elda Tannenbaum, must have finished practicing for Sunday morning, and Pastor J.A. Hawley's DeSoto was not sitting alongside the alley door, where he usually parked it. We could smell the burnt coffee wafting up from the open basement windows, but that smell was always there—I remembered it from the day a long time ago when Jack and I kicked the shit out of Donald Harrison's cousins in that alley.

Bernard lit a Lucky Strike, glanced at his watch, and spit some loose tobacco off his tongue. "Three-thirty on the nose," he said. "So where the fuck is he?"

I glanced at my own watch and realized that I was sweating heavily. It was, like I said, a pleasant day, and I hadn't been the one carrying the duffel bag, so I must have been more nervous or excited or scared than I figured I'd be—than Bernard seemed to be, for that matter.

To take my mind off Jack, I thought about that fight with the Harrison cousins, about guys cursing and sweating and swinging on each other with their sport jackets flying open and their neckties flung over their shoulders and blood bubbling out of their noses, their white shirts speckled with red. The thought of it, the thought of a bunch of guys mixing it up behind a church in their Sunday finest made me smile. Then the thought of Jack pulling out the sap and really getting down to business made me laugh, and I laughed so loud that Bernard turned and looked at me and pointed out that I was sweating like a pig.

"Don't say *you* ain't nervous," I said.

"I ain't *that* nervous," he said, and his saying that, or maybe just the way he said it, made me laugh again.

"Fuck you," I said.

"Fuck you and the horse you rode in on," he said back. And we both laughed.

Jack pulled into the alley five minutes later. He was behind the wheel of a cream-colored '49 Oldsmobile we hadn't seen before, and he was already wearing his dark shirt and white tie and snap-brim straw hat.

"How come you ain't dressed yet?" he said, peering up at us from the open window of the Olds, his left arm in the sport jacket bent at the elbow and resting on the window frame. Bernard started to answer him, but Jack gunned the Olds' big Rocket V8 engine and told us to get our asses and the duffel bag in back, slide down below window-level, and put our outfits on so we'd look ready for business.

Jack was as excited as I ever saw him, but now it was an excitement he seemed to be more or less in control of—he was riding it the way you'd ride a wild horse. His voice was different, not as cold as it had been earlier in the week when we were stalking Buddy, and sure as hell not as frantic as it would be in the days ahead, when we'd be running and dodging and hiding to save our lives. It was loud and excited and almost happy-sounding, at least as happy- sounding as we'd ever heard that voice.

Jack talked almost the entire time he drove while Bernard and I scrambled around on the floor of the back seat getting out of our regular clothes and struggling, sweaty as we were, into our gangster outfits. After about ten minutes on the street, Jack pulled the Olds into an empty parking lot behind a small brick building off Marshall Avenue. We'd crossed the river into St. Paul. It's odd, I guess, but I can't remember much of anything he said all that time, but then I couldn't remember what he'd said as soon as he stopped talking. Maybe I was so caught up in the sound of his voice, or so confounded by the fact that he was talking the way he was, nonstop and with that tone and pitch no one up to then had ever heard from him, the words themselves slipped past unnoticed. Maybe I was as excited as he was, as excited as I was nervous, thinking about where we might be going and what we were going to do, thinking that wherever we were going, Buddy Follmer was going to be there and we were going to kill him.

I didn't know what we were doing behind that building, and when

I looked at Bernard, I could tell he didn't know either, which meant that, whatever Jack had been talking about on the way over, it either didn't have anything to do with where we were now or Bernard hadn't heard any more than I had. I remember how the whole idea and all the different possibilities made me smile. I also remember thinking that I'd probably smiled and laughed more that afternoon than I had since Shorty and I used to horse around in Germany. Bernard would've said the same thing if he'd had the chance—Bernard, who'd been one of the saddest, sorriest, down-in-the-dumps son-of-a-bitches on the face of the earth for the previous two months—and he wouldn't have been able to say why exactly either.

Then everything was quiet. Jack had quit talking, and I wondered if we were supposed to be listening for something, though I couldn't imagine what. I thought maybe Jack was trying to think of something more to say, but there was probably nothing he hadn't said already. Then Jack said real soft and steady, "Follmer is visiting his mother across the street. She lives in the apartment above that bakery, and Buddy comes to see her every other Saturday afternoon. He parks along the side there, gets the old lady something from the bakery, and goes upstairs to visit her. He's usually up there for an hour."

I glanced at Bernard. He was obviously thinking what I was thinking. "How come we didn't know that?" he said. "How come we didn't follow him over here?"

Jack said, "Because the last time he came over here was two weeks ago. We weren't following him then."

"So how did you know he came over here?" Bernard said.

"Dumb luck," Jack said. "I heard his wife talking to Cianciolo at the store. She was bitchin' about how no matter what she might want to do or where she might want to go, every other Saturday afternoon Buddy sees his mother in St. Paul. He visits the old lady for an hour, then leaves. She mentioned the name of the bakery like it was a landmark Cianciolo would know, so I looked it up in a St. Paul phonebook and got the address. When I looked up Follmer, the old lady's address was the same as the bakery only with an apartment number after it."

Resting my chin on the front-seat back and gazing through the windshield, I could see the Gustafson Bakery sign between the buildings on our side of the street. From my angle, I couldn't see the windows above the sign, and I couldn't see where Buddy's car was parked on the side of the bakery. I thought about Buddy sitting up there with his mother, the two of them eating doughnuts or caramel rolls from downstairs, the two of them fat and getting fatter while we waited across the street, and I wondered if his mother might be anything like ours. I doubted it. Maybe she was crazy, but if she was, I figured she'd be crazy in a different way, not having so much to do with religion and having more to do instead with food or living by herself or having a son who couldn't keep his hands off underage girls.

"We're gonna kill the son-of-a-bitch when he comes down from upstairs," Jack said. "He'll come down from upstairs, step out the door next to the bakery door, then walk around to the side of the building, where his car's parked. That's where we're gonna get him."

He started the Olds' engine. While keeping the car in park, he reached down and pulled a canvas bag up from between his legs, set it on the seat beside him, and with his right hand carefully opened it up. Bernard and I leaned forward, looked over the back of the front seat, and saw the two forty-five-caliber automatics, one blue-black and the other one nickel-plated, and saw Jack take the blue-black automatic and stick it in his belt. In the soft, steady, careful voice he was using, he said, "Joe, take the other gun. Bernard, come up here and drive."

I reached over the back of the front seat and grabbed the nickel-plated forty-five. It looked smaller than the blue-black military-style pistol that Jack had stuck in his pants and seemed lighter than the forty-fives I'd held in the past. I didn't see the wild horse or any other insignia on the grip, so I figured it was foreign-made and probably fucked with this way or that to make it difficult to identify. Like the car, the gun was stolen, and asking Jack about it would've been more trouble than it was worth. Anyway, Jack was sliding over to the passenger side of the front seat while Bernard jumped out, ran around the back to the driver's side, and slid in behind the wheel. He knocked his hat cockeyed getting in, cursed, and set it right again. I sat back behind Jack, the automatic in my left hand and down between my knees where no one passing by could see it, and saw Jack point to the alley between the two buildings in front of us on our side of the street and fell back against the seat when Bernard stepped on the gas and the Olds jerked forward.

"Jesus Christ!" Jack said to Bernard. "Can you drive this thing or not?"

Bernard giggled nervously and said, "I'm okay, I'm okay. Fuckin' transmission sticks."

Jack leaned forward and peered through the windshield. He said, "Go out here, take a right, then take a left at the corner and go through the alley behind the bakery. You want to come out over there, on the side street, behind Follmer's car."

I leaned forward and dug my chin into the back of the front seat again and saw Follmer's unmarked black Ford parked near the corner of the bakery block, facing Marshall Avenue. (The MPD had switched from Plymouths to Fords after the war.) Bernard jerked the Olds forward, but not as sudden this time, then eased it out onto Marshall and drove like Jack said to the corner, where he hung a left, then hung another left at the alley and drove behind the bakery and the other little businesses on the block, then came out at the far end on the side street, where Buddy's car sat.

Bernard stopped at the end of the alley, and Jack said, "Park over there," pointing to a stretch of empty curb under a large elm tree a couple of car lengths behind the Ford.

Bernard crept out of the alley, turned left, and pulled up along the curb where Jack had pointed.

"Cut the engine," Jack said, and Bernard shut the Olds down.

In a flat, even voice Jack said, "Start it up again when he comes around the corner. When he crosses the street and walks toward his car, we pull alongside before he can get inside. I get out, step up, and put two bullets behind his ear. If he turns around before I shoot and tries to run for it—Joe, you let him have it. When he's down, we go. Take a right onto Marshall, Bernard. I'll tell you where to go from there."

I tried to say something but couldn't. There was something rising out of my chest and filling my throat like a fist. Another fist was beginning to pound against my ribs. *Holy Christ!* I thought, *we're gonna do it. After all the talk and the stalking and the daydreams, we're finally gonna do it!*

I looked past Bernard's head, his jug ears a fiery red below his hat brim, and waited for Buddy to come walking around the corner. What if he stayed for dinner? I imagined his mother pulling out a board and a coffee can full of marbles and the two of them playing Chinese checkers at the kitchen table. Maybe there was roast beef in the oven, maybe a couple of pork chops. Maybe Follmer had brought the old lady a cherry pie, and after eating the roast or the pork chops, the two of them would eat the pie with a scoop of vanilla ice cream on top. I had never in my life spent a lot of time thinking about food—there was seldom enough to eat at home so I taught myself not to think about it—and now, seconds away from killing a man, all I could think about was what the guy might be eating. His last supper.

I took a deep breath, then heard Jack and Bernard take deep breaths, and I wondered if they were thinking about food the way I was. Who knew what was going on in Bernard's mind? Jack, I guessed, would be thinking about Janine—he'd use her to keep his anger hot, her image the spur that drives him to pull the trigger. I tried to think about Janine, but couldn't. All I could see, honest to God, was Buddy and his mom eating cherry pie over a Chinese checkerboard.

Then Buddy stepped around the corner. He was wearing a brown fedora pushed back on his head and a lightweight plaid jacket that zipped up the front, and as he walked toward his car he was holding something in front of his face with both hands.

"The cocksucker's eating a bismarck!" Bernard said out loud.

"Last one ever," Jack muttered.

"Christ, look at the size of it!" Bernard shouted.

The windows were rolled up, so it's not like Buddy would've heard Bernard, but Jack told him to shut the fuck up anyway and start the engine. "Wait now," Jack said. "We want to shoot the fucker, not run him over."

Sitting in back, I heard the Olds rumble to life and saw Buddy glance in our direction, and out of the corner of my eye I saw Jack's window going down. I thought, *What if Buddy sees us and whips out his gun?*—then thought, *Buddy doesn't know our car and can't see our faces behind the windshield. He's too busy stuffing that fucking bismarck in his yap to notice anything anyway. And he wouldn't take his gun to visit to his mother, would he?*

I reached over and tried to lower my window with my free hand, but the window stuck. I pictured myself coming out the door if Buddy tried to get away from Jack and opening fire on Buddy's fat back as he moved away from me.

Buddy was almost at his car. Then he stopped a few feet before he got to it, probably wondering how he was going to fish the keys out of his pocket with his hands full of pastry filling, and I thought maybe we *should* run the fucker down, him standing in the middle of the street preoccupied with a bismarck.

Jack hissed, "Move your ass, motherfucker!" but Buddy stood still with Bernard half out our parking space, his foot on the brake so not going anywhere either.

If Buddy had noticed us sitting there, then creeping away from the curb, he didn't seem to care, because he stood there blocking our path for a good five seconds before finally taking a couple of steps toward his car and moving his fat ass out of our way. Standing only a foot or two from the Ford, he held what was left of the bismarck between his teeth while he pulled a handkerchief out of his back pocket and started wiping his fingers.

"Don't stop till I tell you," Jack said in a whisper, then "Go!" he said louder, and Bernard, lifting his foot off the brake, let the Olds lurch forward.

The fist in my chest felt like it was going to pound through my rib cage, and I couldn't tell you if I was breathing or not. I wasn't thinking about food or mothers or anything in the world except putting a bullet behind Buddy Follmer's ear.

Coming off the back seat, leaning forward so my knees practically rested on the floor, I looked over Jack's shoulder and saw Buddy in the middle of our windshield, moving to our right, then slipping off the windshield's angled edge and appearing in the corner of Jack's window. Then he was filling Jack's window, his fat back and ass.

Bernard, per Jack's orders, didn't stop. The Olds kept rolling, and I thought, *Open your door, for chrissake, open your door!* But Jack hadn't made a move, hadn't opened his door, hadn't even stuck the big automatic out his open window, and now we rolled past Buddy's car.

I jerked around in the back seat, not understanding what had happened—what was happening—and saw Buddy stepping away from the Ford, brushing at something on the front of his jacket, then giving something a quick little kick. The fucker had dropped the bismarck in the street.

"Jack!" I heard myself squeak, forcing the name up and out past the fist jammed in my throat, but, before I could say anything else, Jack said, "Go, goddamn it, go! Turn right at the corner!"

Behind the wheel, Bernard let his breath out in an explosive burst. I saw his right hand rise and push the hat up off his forehead and run the hand across his eyes. "Jack," he started to say, but that was all he got out before Jack said, *"Drive!"* I couldn't have said anything if I'd wanted to, which I didn't. I realized I had to piss.

I let myself fall back against the back seat, pushing my hat up off my forehead the way Bernard had. When I ran my hand across my face, it was cold and wet—clammy, you'd call it, and, when I took stock of the situation, I realized the word applied to my whole body—I was soaked in cold sweat.

I thought, *If this is what it's like not killing a man, what's it like actually killing one?*

For the next ten minutes, nobody said a word except Jack telling Bernard where to turn. At one point—we were still on the St. Paul side of the river—we stopped along a double set of railroad tracks, and the three of us got out and peed into some discarded tires leaning against the wall of a building that was apparently closed for the weekend. While we were standing there, I glanced at Bernard, who glanced back at me, but neither one of us said anything to each other or to Jack, who wasn't looking anywhere but at where his piss was disappearing inside an old tire.

It was still light, though the sun was starting to drop down behind the Foshay Tower in downtown Minneapolis, which we could see, the tallest buildings anyway, from where we'd stopped the car, and it was already cool enough so standing there wet beneath my clothes I felt myself shiver. Jack might have been shivering too, though I didn't want to look and make sure. I didn't want to make eye contact with Jack, didn't want him to see me looking. I had no idea what was going to happen next—I wasn't sure what had happened during the past half-hour—but I knew that it'd be up to Jack to decide and it wasn't going to be good for anyone.

What *had* happened outside that bakery? Why hadn't Jack told Bernard to stop the car? Why hadn't Jack jumped out of the car like he said he was going to? Why hadn't he stepped up behind Follmer when Buddy was standing there, wiping off his sticky fingers, and done what he had planned to do?

Why didn't I jerk *my* door open, jump out, and do the job myself?

I didn't know, and I didn't want to know. All I wanted was to go somewhere nobody would pay me any attention and get out of my sweaty outfit and forget that whatever happened ever happened. I didn't care whether Buddy Follmer lived or died, I just never wanted to see the motherfucker again. As events transpired, I never did.

We got back in the car and drove along the railroad tracks for a while, then Jack told Bernard to go back across the river. I noticed a street sign and realized we were on University Avenue—I'd been there on one of my job interviews—and then Jack told Bernard to cross the Franklin Avenue Bridge and follow the West River Road back to Lake Street.

Nobody said a word, only Jack every once in a while telling Bernard where to go. The Olds reeked of sweat and cigarette smoke, so we rolled down the windows to let the stink out. The early evening air was golden, the setting sun reflecting off the buildings, but chilly now too, so the windows went back up again after a minute, and we rode along in silence.

How long that cop had been following us I couldn't say. He probably picked us up on the River Road before we got to Lake Street. In any case, he was behind us when we turned right onto Lake, and we hadn't gone another block or two before he flashed his light and siren.

He must have switched it on and off real quick because I wasn't sure it was even a siren I heard, it was more of a sudden moan, but Bernard said he was watching the squad car in the rearview mirror and saw the red light mounted above the windshield go on and off.

"He just flipped it on and then off again," Bernard told me later. "Like he didn't want to make a big show of it or anything."

Bernard, looking in the mirror, said, "What should I do?"

Jack was silent for a moment, then said, "Stop the car."

Bernard said, "I think I can outrun the fucker," but Jack said, "Stop the damn car."

Bernard glided to the curb and eased to a stop. He sat perfectly still, his ears beet-red again under the hat brim, and stared into the rearview mirror. I twisted in my seat and watched the black-and-white Ford stop ten or fifteen yards behind us. Because of the low-slanting sunlight bouncing off the squad car's windshield, I couldn't see the cop or cops sitting behind it, but I pictured whoever was there glancing at a clipboard with stolen cars and license-plate numbers on it and then lifting the two-way radio phone from under the dashboard and calling headquarters. For the second time in less than an hour, something shot up into my throat, and something else began pounding against my ribs. Then I remembered the automatic in my waistband.

"What should I do with my gun?" I asked Jack.

Jack said, "Stick it under the seat. You too, Bernard."

I pulled the gun out of my pants and, glancing back at the squad car again, leaned forward and slid it under the front seat. Something sharp, the tip of a spring from the seat or something, jabbed me under my fingernail—I pulled my hand away and cursed.

I looked back and saw a cop climbing out of the driver's side of the squad car, a young guy with a baby face slicking his brown hair back before putting on his peaked cap. I looked at the other side of the car, but no one else was getting out. I felt high as a kite then because the baby-faced cop was alone, and he had not seen the Olds or the license number on a clipboard list of stolen cars and plates, and he was not going to arrest us for anything. I thought, with a rush of relief and excitement that felt as good as a long, hard piss, *We haven't done a goddamn thing! We haven't killed anybody!*

The cop bent down to look through the rear-door window on the driver's side of our car, then stepped forward and rapped on Bernard's window with his knuckle. Bernard rolled down the window, but didn't say anything, even when the cop bent down again and filled the window with his face. The cop looked at each of us in turn—Bernard, then Jack, then me, then Bernard again. I felt conspicuous in our gangster getup and hoped it didn't signify anything to the cop except we were three dressed-up little shitbirds cruising Lake Street, looking for girls.

Bernard said, "I wasn't speeding, officer," and the cop, with his hands on his knees now, said, "Relax, pal. I didn't say you were."

Bernard glanced at Jack, who was not looking at either Bernard or the cop, but was staring straight out through the windshield, like he was looking at something coming toward us, and the cop said to Bernard, "Your right taillight is either burnt-out or defective. You aware of that?"

Bernard shook his head. "News to me, officer," he said.

The cop said, "I'm not going to write you a citation, but you get that light fixed first thing Monday, understand?"

Bernard sighed and said, "Sure thing, officer. I'll take care of it soon as they're open."

The cop looked at each of us again and stood up. I had a sudden, sickening feeling that he thought Bernard was wising off to him, but then, without another word, he turned and headed back toward his car.

"Jesus H. Christ," I said letting out the breath I hadn't realized I'd been holding, "if that wasn't—"

Before I could finish the sentence, I saw Jack's door fly open and Jack lunging out of the car and lurching past my window toward the rear of the car, and, as I twisted in my seat, I saw Jack behind the car now, between the trunk of the Olds and the front of the Ford, and he was thrusting the big blue-black automatic out at arm's length and making the gun jump in his hand. There were one-two-three bursts of flame from the pistol, one-two-three explosions overlapping the flame, and the babyfaced cop, who had turned toward Jack, who was beginning to form a frown beneath the bill of his cap, was staggering diagonally away from the explosions. Then I couldn't see the cop at all. Then Jack was moving again, another couple of steps in the direction the cop had gone, and then, though I couldn't see the flame this time, I heard three more explosions, one-two-three on top of each other like the first ones, Jack jerking his arm down toward the street, in the direction of the cop.

Then Jack was lurching back around the rear of the Olds. I realized with a shock that I had opened my door and started to get out—I couldn't remember doing it, but I was halfway out the door, one foot in the street—and Jack, coming around from the rear of the car, said, "Get back in!" so I did, just ahead of him. But diving in, I knocked my hat against the top of the open door, and the hat fell off and rolled out of sight.

I might have said something or might not have, I don't know, but all that mattered was that Jack was back inside the Olds and that Bernard had the car in gear and was roaring away from the curb.

I looked through the rear window and saw the cop—whose name we'd learn was William Francis Fredriksen, who was three days shy of his twenty-seventh birthday, who left five children at home and number six on the way—I saw the cop stretched out on his back in the middle of East Lake Street, his arms flung wide like he'd fallen from a great height.

I *didn't* see either his hat or mine in what was left of the evening's golden light.

SIX

When Ronnie comes for me this time, I can't see or speak. I mean I can't see her or anything around me in the bedroom where I'm lying, and I can't form words with my mouth or force enough wind up through my voice box to make myself heard. But that's okay. There's nothing in this room I need to see and nothing more I want to say to Ronnie or anyone else. Inside my head, the words march forward like the infantry of a battered army, thick columns of worn-out soldiers who tramp along one rank after another, where they started only a dim memory and their ending only a wish.

I can hear all right, which is how I know that Ronnie's in the room, and what I hear is her whispering to someone, Elaine and one or the other of her boys, but it's the kind of whisper you don't mind if everyone hears. Without seeing anything, I can feel the weight of someone kneeling on the edge of the bed, and I can smell the cigarettes and the beer people have been enjoying all afternoon—people are standing around, bending over the bed, looking at me. *Get lost*, I think but don't say, *I'm with my brothers now, we've killed a police officer, and we're on the ride of our lives. The cop is down, my hat has disappeared, and that cream-colored Oldsmobile is roaring into the sunset.*

I hear Ronnie say, "Honey, go get Armand, will ya?" and then there's one less person in the room, one less shadow falling over me.

I hear someone, probably Ronnie, lighting a cigarette, then exhaling with a couple of small, dry coughs, then the phone ringing somewhere a long way off, in another part of the house, though I remember seeing a yellow extension phone on the table next to the bed. Then a young man's voice is saying something I can't make out, then there's the shuffling arrival of Gervais, who, even though he's been drinking the same beer and smoking the same cigarettes, has his own smell that might have something to do with his being old and black.

It must have been good, whatever they told him, because this time of day I'm pretty sure it takes a lot to get Gervais out of his recliner. I'm touched that he made the effort.

Ronnie says, "He doesn't seem able to see or talk. I'm not sure he can hear us either."

Gervais's big, pungent shadow slides across me, and I can almost feel his concern. "Oh, shit," I hear him say, "you don't think he's had an em-byool-ism, do you?"

"You mean a stroke?" Ronnie says.

"Well, stroke or em-byool-ism or some damn thing—I ain't a doctor," Gervais says.

Maybe he's scared, or maybe he's pissed he had to vacate his chair for his crippled ex-con brother-in-law, who might be dying in his bed. He doesn't seem as caring as he did a minute ago.

A third voice, I think it's Elaine's, says, "Maybe we should call 9-1-1, just in case." If it was ever time to say something out loud, it's now, but I can't.

Nobody says anything for another few seconds, then Ronnie, moving around the bed, says, "No, he's okay. He gets this way, exhausted—you know, like there's nothing left inside him after he's been out all day. He gets so tired he can't even talk."

I don't know if I've ever been like this—can't see, can't talk, can hardly move—but I'm glad she said what she said. I don't think I could stand to have anybody touching me right now, not anybody who wasn't family, at any rate. In my mind's eye, I'm seeing that front-page photo of the cops hauling me out of that game farm on October 3, 1953, me on one of those simple canvas stretchers they used back then, the cops—all but one of them in plain clothes—dressed for a deer hunt in cold, wet weather, the one in a deputy sheriff's uniform grinning at someone out of the picture, the asshole, me flat on my back with my eyes shut held up at shoulder level, like I was some kind of trophy or something. I don't remember the actual scene at all—I was unconscious or in shock from the bullet that dropped me or maybe from the knowledge that my brothers were dead, or maybe I was just exhausted from everything that had happened in the last month. The photo was in among the clippings Jerome Briscoe collected at the Cloud. I've since that day been helped along or pushed on wheels, but I've never been carried like that anywhere, not when I've been conscious and aware of it. The thought makes my skin crawl.

Ronnie has her own reasons for not wanting a rescue squad barging in here and hauling me away, and I doubt it has anything to do with paramedics tracking mud over her shag carpets, but more to do with her idea of her "family reunion" ending with one of us being taken away from her again. She'd never say it, but what she's thinking, I'm pretty sure, is that *if Jojo dies, he dies right here*—enough of everybody going off and never coming back again. I'm thinking, *That's right, Sis! Stick to your guns this time. Don't let 'em take me away!*

No matter what she says, I'm going. But I'm leaving the premises in my own way, if not on my own terms. I'm sliding down into the hole I've found inside myself—my own black, bloody hole—which goes down and back and around in circles and ends in what I imagine is death.

I can't say for sure where we went right after killing Patrolman Fredriksen, only that I remember our flight being very quiet and strangely peaceful, like we were traveling in a dream or underwater.

For a long time, no one, not even Bernard, said a word. Jack didn't tell Bernard where to go. Bernard for once seemed to know or be able to guess, or maybe he was driving any which way, finally getting lucky and ending up clear of the Saturday evening traffic, the noise and the lights of the city, in a field where there didn't seem to be anything growing, in the silent dark under the stars.

We sat in that field with our lights off and the Oldsmobile's engine ticking. I figured we were somewhere north of the city, maybe up past New Brighton, where we'd gone before the Central Avenue liquor-store job, but I couldn't narrow our location down any further than that. I knew that no one was going to say anything about the cop—was going to speculate about his condition, for instance—because there was no doubt in any of our minds that the cop was dead. I knew because I'd seen the cap coming off his head that he was dead before he hit the ground and that Jack knew it too, and that Jack had other reasons that made him put the extra bullets in the guy lying in the street. It sounds funny, I know, but I felt bad for Jack for thinking he had to do that, had to kill a guy that was already dead. To me, it was another sign of how far gone Jack was and maybe had always been. And the cop? *Well,* I thought, *by that time it sure as hell couldn't matter to him.*

This will sound funny too, but it felt like everything had been clarified, straightened out. There was nothing else we had to worry about in our lives except this one single thing, which I couldn't or wouldn't put in its own words just yet. Bernard didn't have to fret about Judy and the baby and the radio-repair business anymore. I didn't need to wonder about Judy either, or about Monika, or my sisters, and I didn't need to think about looking for a job or finding my own apartment. Jack could forget about Buddy Follmer, forget about Janine, for that matter, though knowing Jack, I knew he wouldn't forget about either one of them until he was dead.

I thought we had finally done something so big, so important, that nothing we had done before and nothing we would do in the future could make any difference, because soon we were going to die too.

The three of us sat there in the dark car, in the middle of that dark field, smoking cigarettes, all of us, even Jack, I think, feeling this incredible sense of calm. There was nothing to worry or even think about anymore. The three of us were dead men.

Finally, Jack said, "Let's get out of these clothes and go home."

Bernard said, "Go home? How can we go home?"

Jack said, "We drive home, that's how. We stash this car, boost another one, then drive home. One of us rides in the trunk because they're looking for three of us."

Jack might have been talking about strolling over to Cianciolo's for a pack of Luckies, his voice was so calm. I could hardly remember the anger and excitement that had been there earlier in the day, that's how calm and collected he was now. I felt as calm as he sounded, and didn't want to break the spell, and knew that Bernard would say what I had on my mind anyway.

Bernard asked Jack if he didn't think someone might see us, and Jack said so what if they did—unless they saw us with that cop on Lake Street, what difference would it make?

"They don't know it was us, Bernard," he explained in the voice he was using now. "Nobody's saying, 'Oh, it must have been those LaVoie boys from over on Longfellow,' because there's no reason for anyone to say that."

"Unless someone who knows us saw us there on Lake Street," Bernard said, his voice not so calm anymore, certainly not as calm as Jack's.

"But nobody did, nobody that knew us," Jack said.

Without turning his head to look at me he said, "What about it, Jojo? Did you see anybody you knew back there, anybody who would rat on us to the cops?" And I, of course, my voice maybe not as calm as Jack's at that moment but calmer than Bernard's, said, "No, Jack. I didn't."

So, without further discussion, we stripped out of our jackets and ties and black shirts, and put on the white T-shirts and blue jeans we'd been wearing before we hooked up at the Tabernacle. Jack told me to take the gangster outfits and climb into the trunk with them, and then told Bernard they would switch places in the front seat, and we drove out of that field, though in which direction I couldn't say because I couldn't see anything. There was a ratty blanket in the trunk that I wrapped around myself because I was cold.

Twenty minutes or so later, the car stopped, and, after another couple of minutes, Jack came around back and opened the trunk and motioned for me to bring the clothes and follow Bernard around the side of a long row of connected garages that sat behind a cluster of two-story apartment buildings.

In the pitch-black yard behind one of the buildings, I squatted down beside Bernard while Jack stowed the Olds in one of the garages. Jack was a genius at finding out-of-the-way places—"sneak spots," we called them. Bernard said Jack did a lot of scouting, sniffing out hide-aways like this and spotting cars he could boost if and when he needed them, garages that nobody was using and cars that people left unlocked and unwatched. Bernard said Jack once told him, "There's nothing easier than stealing a car. You don't need special tools, you don't even need to bust a window because people don't like to lock their cars. All you need is the balls to get in, fuck a little with the wiring if the keys aren't already in the ignition, and drive away." All I knew was that Jack stole cars like some people drink water—it came so natural that I don't think he ever had any doubts about what he was doing.

In another five minutes, we heard Jack give a short whistle, and Bernard and I ran through the dark backyards to the alley and climbed in the maroon Pontiac coupe Jack had removed from a garage down the street. At Jack's command, I handed the bundle of dress-up clothes to Bernard, who crawled into the Pontiac's trunk, and I climbed into the front seat and sat calm and mostly silent while Jack drove the three of us home.

The neighborhood was quiet. Even crossing Lake Street at Lyndale, I saw nothing out of the ordinary—maybe a squad car or two more than you might normally see, but it was now almost eleven o'clock on a Saturday night and who knows what else might have been going on?

It was like the calm after a storm, I remember thinking, though I had no way of knowing how much of a storm there had been during the previous several hours, the city seeming quieter than usual. Later, I figured that the city was in shock—something so terrible had happened, something so sudden and unexpected, like a tremendous lighting strike, that everybody was stunned still and silent. It wasn't, I thought later, like the city was home in bed. It was more like everybody just wanted to stay down and out of sight like we were. Anyway, the few people who were out and about wouldn't be interested in a couple of guys driving home from a bar or the movies and keeping to the speed limit and were goddamn sure both taillights were in working order.

The Pontiac didn't have a radio, so if there were any bulletins about a cop-killing that night, we weren't going to hear them until we got home.

It seemed like a week had passed since we'd left Longfellow Avenue that afternoon. I had something like the feeling I felt when I first got home from the Army, when everything seemed to have undergone an important change, but still looked and felt and smelled pretty much the same as I remembered it.

When we passed the Follmers' house, I noticed that Buddy's car wasn't parked where it usually was that time of night, and I felt a little shiver run down my spine, thinking that every cop in town, even desk jockeys like Buddy, were out looking for the killer of one of their own. I saw Jack glance at Buddy's house too. I knew the same idea was running through his mind, and I wouldn't have been surprised if he felt a shiver himself.

Nobody was up when we got home, and nobody stirred when the three of us sat down at the dining-room table with a loaf of white bread and a jar of mayonnaise and drank beer and ate mayonnaise sandwiches until the beer and the bread and the mayonnaise were gone. Afterward, we climbed the stairs and went to bed and each of us fell asleep (we agreed the next day) before our heads hit the pillow.

* * *

The next morning, the headline that ran across the top of the *Tribune*'s front page was large and black—*DRAGNET FOR CITY COP-KILLERS*. Below the headline there was another one in slightly smaller type: *Officer, Father of 5, Gunned Down on E. Lake St.*, and still another one reading, *5-Year MPD Veteran First Killed in Line of Duty since 1939.*

In the middle of the page there were two photos. One showed the dead cop's squad car parked where he left it near the curb and, a few feet from the front left fender, the dead cop's cap lying upside down with a circle drawn around it in chalk on the pavement. The second was a studio photo of the cop, identified below as Patrolman William F. Fredriksen, with his wife, Georgeanne. The photo must have been taken several years earlier, because it took me a few seconds before the guy in the picture really looked to me like the guy we'd seen in the flesh.

The *Sunday Tribune* was the one paper the Old Man occasionally brought home from Cianciolo's, and now Bernard and I sat on the faded sofa in the living room looking at that front page. Apart from the headlines and photos, there wasn't much information, mainly, I suppose, because neither the cops nor the reporters had time to collect a lot of facts.

What information there was, we both realized with relief, was wildly off base on several of the points that were important to us. It reminded me of the story they ran the day after we robbed the Cities Service station on Tenth Street, where Curtis Cousins got everything wrong except the fancy outfits. I remembered Jack saying that was a cop trick, that Curtis Cousins had in fact told them everything in as much detail and with as much accuracy as he told them about the clothes, and that we shouldn't take for granted who knew what. I didn't believe it was a cop trick myself (Bernard didn't either), but I couldn't say for sure that it wasn't, and now, looking at that morning's front page, the thought of cop tricks crossed my mind again.

The paper said that a Minneapolis police officer had been shot down in cold blood by a car full of gunmen after a short automobile chase two blocks west of the Lake Street Bridge. Witnesses said the officer was shot by at least two men firing pistols after the officer approached their car, a light-colored, late-model Buick or Packard. A third man reportedly jumped out of the car and coolly fired several additional bullets into the officer's body. The light-colored car contained four to six men, who might have been either Negroes or Indians, according to witnesses, and was believed to have proceeded west on Lake before turning south at Minnehaha.   "Police Chief Richard Walsh called the murder 'brutal and unprovoked, a senseless crime that will outrage the entire state of Minnesota.' The Minneapolis Police Department, Walsh vowed, 'will not rest until Patrolman Fredriksen's craven killers are apprehended.'

"Detective Inspector Harold V. Meslow said that roadblocks had been set up on all major thoroughfares out of the city and that police departments in the five-state region would be looking for the gunmen and their vehicle. Meslow said that anybody who might have witnessed the crime, seen the car, or noticed anything suspicious in the area of the murder should contact the MPD immediately."

I was relieved to see no mention of my hat, and wondered what the hell happened to it. Could it possibly have been overlooked at the scene? If so, was it possible the hat was still there, underneath a parked car or maybe flattened by a passing truck and lying unnoticed, just another piece of garbage in the gutter? Maybe it had been overlooked by the cops in their rage and their hurry and picked up by a gawker, one of the so-called witnesses to the shooting, or by someone passing by. It was, if it hadn't been flattened by the traffic, a good five-dollar snap-brim fedora, and even an eyewitness might not have associated it with the crime, especially if had sailed or rolled or skidded some distance from the dead cop in the street. How far, I wondered, could a hat go?

I didn't mention the hat to either Jack or Bernard (not until later), but as I sat there reading the paper, the hat was what I was thinking about, and I wondered if I should go over to Lake Street and see if, by some chance or miracle, I could find the damn thing myself. I was angry at my brother for coming up with the fucking hats in the first place, and I was angry with myself for getting out of the car when there was no good reason to, and I was angry with the cop for setting off the whole damn chain of events because of a busted taillight.

The Old Man wandered in from the back bedroom about that time, his hair going every which way and his yellow face covered with a derelict's gray stubble and a cigarette burning in the corner of his mouth. He looked underfed and pathetic, like a sick man, in his soiled undershirt, stained boxers, and sagging socks. He yanked the A Section of the paper out of Bernard's hands, held it out at arm's length, and squinted at the screaming headlines on the front page.

"Holy Jesus Mother of Christ!" he hollered. "A car fulla tough guys gunned down a fuckin' cop! Right over there on Lake Street! Can you feature that, for chrissake?"

Bernard and I exchanged glances. Then Bernard, who couldn't help himself, looked up at the Old Man and said like a dummy, "You don't suppose it was Bunny and his boys, do you, Pop?"

The Old Man stared at the paper, moving his lips to show that he was reading, the cigarette moving around in the crack of his mouth, the smoke curling up into his eyes making him squint especially on the one side so he looked like Popeye the Sailor Man. He said, "Oh, hell no. What the fuck would Bunny wanna do that for, a young cop like that?"

"I dunno," Bernard said, pressing his luck. "He did it before, didn't he? The last time a city cop was killed, back there, like the paper says, in 1939?"

"That don't count," the Old Man said, still staring through the smoke at the headlines and pictures. "That was Vincey Oudekerk, who was on Bunny's payroll. Vincey got too big for his britches and thought he could squeeze more cash out of Bunny, so one day Bunny said, 'Fuck that, you double-crossin' Dutch flatfoot,' and plugged him. He personally turned Vincey around, shoved him down on his knees, and put a slug behind his ear. *Bingo!* That ain't the same as this here. This is a goddamn assassination, that's what this is."

Bernard glanced at me again. I could see that he had all he could do not to laugh, the dumb bastard. I knew what he was thinking. All this time he'd been fancying himself a tough guy, a gangster, a fancy dresser with a gun. Now, according to his father, he was a fucking assassin! *Assassin!* That was a word that had never entered Bernard's feverish mind, at least not in connection with his criminal activities, but that's exactly what he was, what he'd become. Just ask the Old Man!

Me, I kept thinking about that goddamn hat. I couldn't get the hat out of my mind, no matter what the Old Man said and no matter what Bernard was thinking. I wanted to talk to Jack. I wanted to tell him what had happened (if he didn't know already), I wanted to apologize for being careless, I wanted to warn him that he'd possibly been compromised by my losing that goddamn hat. While the Old Man stared at the paper, I pictured Jack lying on his back on his bed upstairs, a cigarette in the corner of his mouth too, but silent, squinting up through the blue smoke at the ceiling, at the bare bulb hanging above the bed, thinking also about the hat. *Jojo*, he was thinking, *because of your carelessness, you've let down your brothers, you've given aid to the police. They know who we are on account of you.* Jack didn't talk like that, but I pictured him thinking that, thinking that the next thing he had to do was put a bullet behind *my* ear. I pictured us in the alley, behind the Harrisons' garage, Jack turning me around, pushing me down on my knees, then firing a forty-five slug into the back of my head. *Bingo.*

But, of course, that's not what happened. Five minutes later, Jack appeared in the flesh, dressed and shaved and looking as though he'd had a good night's sleep after an uneventful Saturday night. He glanced at the paper the Old Man was holding, frowned, and looked at us. He looked at the Old Man again and said, "The radio says there was a shootout on Lake Street. Some cop tried to arrest a car full of Indians."

"Assassins!" Bernard said with a wink, but Jack ignored him.

I looked at Jack, trying to figure out if he might be harboring thoughts about me and my hat, but he didn't seem to have a care in the world.

"Fuckin' Injuns," he said.

He looked again in our direction and jerked his head as a signal for us to follow.

Bernard got up and I was right behind him, and the two of us left the Old Man to his paper and followed Jack through the kitchen and out of the house.

Outside, in the alley, Jack said, "Well, boys, we're the most wanted sons-of-bitches in the Upper Midwest. Every cop, sheriff, state trooper, and G-man between here and Chicago is looking for us."

Bernard, still buzzed about being an assassin, said, "They're looking for a bunch of Indians, the way it sounds."

"Or niggers," I said, trying to get my mind off the hat.

"Horseshit," Jack said. "The cops know there ain't no carload of Indians or niggers in the entire country that'd have the balls to gun down a cop in broad daylight."

I thought again about Curtis Cousins and the wild-ass description of the gangsters who robbed his filling station that night two months ago. Maybe Jack was right. Maybe the cops *were* playing games with us. Then again, if they'd been playing games the first time, it sure as hell hadn't done them much good. No one had laid a finger on us, and now one of their guys was dead.

Bernard seemed less pleased with the situation than he'd been a minute ago. He looked first one way and then the other, like, all of a sudden, the three of us might be in jeopardy standing there in our alley.

"What are we going to do, Jack?" he said in a tight whisper that sounded an awful lot like someone on the verge of tears.

Jack took a quick look around himself and said, "We're gonna go up north and find a hunter's shack to hang out in for a while. If things cool down after a couple days, maybe we come back. If they don't, we keep goin' north, up to Canada."

It sounded easy enough, and, as far as I was concerned, the sooner we got going, the better. I thought of the miles rolling away behind our car, rolling away between me and that hat. "When are we leaving?" I said.

Jack said, "Right away. We got everything we need"—I pictured the duffel bag in the trunk of the Oldsmobile, wherever the hell we left it—"so all we got to do is ditch the Pontiac and hit the road."

Bernard took another look around. I remembered what he said the day before about seeing this place for the last time. That seemed a year or two ago, and now it seemed a lot more likely than it had then. I thought about the Old Man excitedly reading and rereading the paper in the house, Mother sitting on the edge of her bed listening to some yammering evangelist on the radio, Janine and the twins still in bed, still sleeping, or maybe awake now, startled by the Old Man hollering about a car full of cop-killers. I didn't know whether Eugene was home or not—I guessed not, figuring that if he was, we would've seen him by now.

Then I wondered what Buddy Follmer was doing down the block. I wondered if he was sleeping, or maybe fucking his wife, or maybe sitting at the kitchen table, filling his fat face with bacon and eggs while reading about his dead comrade in the paper. Then I thought, *No, he's not home. Like every other cop in this part of the country, he's out looking for his comrade's killers.*

I said, "What if they've set up roadblocks?"

"They probably have," Jack said. "But they can't watch every fuckin' road out of town, can they?"

Maybe they can, I thought, but didn't say it.

Bernard said, "What if—" but once again Jack cut him off.

"Listen," Jack said, lowering his voice, "they know it wasn't Indians or niggers that shot that cop, but that doesn't mean they know who did. If they knew, if they had any real dope on the killers, they'd have been here already."

He looked hard at Bernard, then smacked him upside the head with an open hand. "You with me or not, Bernard?" he said, and Bernard, his eyes wide and watery, the side of his face already red from the blow, said, "Sure, Jack, I just—"

Jack hit him again, harder this time, staggering him. "This ain't no time for pussies, Bernard," he hissed. "Joe and me, we're ready to roll, and we don't want no pussies slowin' us down. Right, Jojo?"

I didn't look at either Jack or Bernard, I was looking somewhere down the alley, but I told Jack he was right.

Jack gave us an address in Brooklyn Center and told us to take the Lyndale Avenue streetcar up there and meet him at a drugstore near the address at noon. He'd ditch the Pontiac over by the fairgrounds and get to Brooklyn Center on his own. He looked hard at Bernard and said, "Don't talk to nobody and don't wet your pants if you see a cop. We're fine if nobody panics."

It was already a quarter to eleven. Jack got in the Pontiac and drove up the alley toward Thirty-seventh Street. Bernard and I went inside to wash up and grab something to eat. The Old Man was sitting on the sofa, still looking at the paper, and Janine was in the kitchen toasting bread on the stove for the twins.

I looked at her for a minute before remembering that she was in a roundabout way the cause of what had happened, that before the burned-out taillight and that cop on Lake Street there was Buddy Follmer coming out of his mother's place in St. Paul, and before that there was Janine walking home one night with her blouse unbuttoned and her sandals in her hand.

Her thick, dark hair was up off her neck, gathered in a careless Sunday-morning way and done up with bobby pins, and she was wearing a pink bathrobe that used to be Ronnie's and before that belonged to someone from the Tabernacle, and her pretty feet were bare on the worn-out linoleum. I thought about those hot afternoons at Lake Nokomis and her lying on a towel in the front yard and, once more, pictured her the night she strolled home after doing whatever she'd been doing with Buddy Follmer.

I wanted to say something to her, something about everything that had happened, not for her sake or even mine and Bernard's so much as for Jack's. I wanted to tell her that Jack had done something terrible for her or because of her, and that I wasn't blaming her for anything that happened or was going to happen in the next few days if it went that long, I just wanted her to know for Jack's sake. I knew, even while I was thinking that, there was no way she would've understood what I was talking about, that even if I told her exactly what had happened and what was going to happen probably sooner than later, she would have looked at me without understanding a thing, and maybe when I was finished she would ask me what any of that had to do with her. I looked at her one more time, and then I turned away. She hadn't even been aware I was there.

I heard Eugene coming in the front door and the Old Man hollering again about the assassination of a cop on Lake Street and Eugene saying he knew all about it—the killers were escapees from St. Cloud.

Bernard came down from upstairs, and, without a word to anybody, the two of us went out the back door and set off up the alley. I tried to put the house and everybody in it out of my mind and thought again about my hat.

Meslow found it hard to believe that we'd spent the night after Fredriksen's murder sleeping in our own beds, only a few blocks from the crime scene. I'm sure he didn't want to believe it because that would have been embarrassing for the cops and embarrassing for him especially, because, from the very beginning, he was the cop they'd put in charge of finding Fredriksen's killers.

One day, after we'd been drinking for a couple of hours, Meslow admitted that they were looking for a carload of Indians the night of the murder and a good part of the following day.

There had been some kind of disturbance after a birthday party at a Chippewa reservation in Wisconsin the night before the killing, some white people had been roughed up, and on Saturday cops on both sides of the border were on the lookout for more trouble. Some of the Indians were wearing hats, it seems, and when one of the Lake Street witnesses mentioned young men wearing hats, it wasn't difficult to jump to the conclusion that maybe the Indians that had roughed up the people in Wisconsin killed Fredriksen.

"You gotta go with what you got," Meslow said. "For three hours after the killing and all the next day, we had officers knocking on doors between Hiawatha Avenue and the river, asking if anyone had seen anything unusual. We were on the radio and TV, begging for help."

But Meslow's "dragnet," as the papers called it, turned up only three so-called witnesses that Saturday night and Sunday.

One was a woman named Hilda Wycroft, who was walking her dog on the south side of Lake Street, half a block from the spot where Fredriksen stopped us. One was a nineteen-year-old kid who was pumping gas at the Pure Oil station about half-a-block in the other direction—the same Pure Oil Station, though probably not the same attendant, that Jack and Bernard held up six months earlier, when they were just getting started. The third was a middle-aged guy by the name of Cedarstrom, who was the conductor of an out-of-service Selby-Lake streetcar that passed us on its way to the car barn on Nicollet. A few days later, a fourth and fifth witness notified Meslow via long distance from a Chicago suburb. They were a married couple named Shindeldecker who said they had driven past the site in the opposite direction as the Selby-Lake car. They'd been visiting their daughter in Minneapolis and were leaving town to return to Illinois, and said they hadn't realized what they'd seen until they talked to their daughter on the following Monday.

Meslow didn't have to tell me about those people though, because each of them testified at my first trial.

I can't say I remember the specifics of their testimony after all these years, but the important thing is that none of them could say much that tied us to the crime. Each could identify, at least by the time of the trial, photos of a '49 Oldsmobile like the one we'd been driving, and each could place the Olds at the scene at the time of the killing. The streetcar conductor, who got closest to the spot when he passed it as Fredriksen was approaching the Olds, thought the men in the car were wearing hats, though he also said that, from his angle, he couldn't see any more than the bottom of the faces on the driver's side of the car. Homer Cedarstrom's main value to the prosecution was his sworn testimony that Fredriksen had approached the Oldsmobile with his service revolver still in its holster, which added to the county attorney's claim that the patrolman's murder was, as he put it a dozen times, "cold-blooded, senseless, and unprovoked."

Meslow told me it was the old lady with the dog, Hilda Wycroft, who said the man who she saw outside the Oldsmobile had dark skin.

"She said she couldn't tell for sure from where she was standing, but she thought he was either a Negro or an Indian," Meslow said. We'd been drinking for a while, and his words had begun to slur. He gave out a dry little laugh and added, "Actually, the first thing she said, she asked if there were still gypsies in the city, because she thought the man looked like a gypsy."

Though both the old lady and the Pure Oil kid heard several closely spaced gunshots that sounded like automobile backfires, neither one saw the shooting. A panel truck partially blocked the kid's view, and that Selby-Lake streetcar ran directly between the Olds and the old lady just as the gunfire began. When the streetcar had passed, the cop was out of sight and the man in the hat was running around to the far side of his car. She saw the cop lying on his back in the street only when she took a few steps closer. When, a second later, the killer's car came roaring past the spot where she'd been standing, she'd already turned in fright and started dragging the dog back the way they'd come. She never got a good look at the car's occupants.

Faintly interested again, I said to Meslow, "The Sunday paper said that witnesses were talking about two men firing simultaneously from a late-model Buick or Packard, then a third man jumped out and shot the cop after he was down. Someone also said they saw us turning south on Minnehaha. I know where the idea of the dark skin came from, but what about all the rest of it?"

Meslow took another swallow of his Canadian Club and flashed a long-toothed grin.

"I don't remember," he said. "Maybe we made it up."

So they didn't know who killed Patrolman Fredriksen that Saturday night or the following Sunday or for a long time afterward, and, while Meslow could make a lame joke about it twenty-some years later, the truth is the cops made a mess of the investigation and embarrassed themselves. To me, it still seems preposterous—three guys gun down a cop in broad daylight on a busy street in the killers' own neighborhood, and, for the better part of a month the investigators don't have a clue as to the killers' identity.

It made me think more than once during the time we were on the lam about Jack's comment earlier that summer—how robbing drugstores and filling stations was like taking candy from a baby. That's the way it seemed the first few days after Fredriksen's murder. I couldn't believe we had gotten away with it. I guess I never believed we'd get away with it forever, but, for those first couple of days, it seemed possible and impossible at the same time. My mood and therefore what I believed or didn't believe was swinging back and forth all the while, like a treetop in a windstorm.

Deep inside, whenever I thought to look there, I knew that everything had been settled, that nothing we did from that point forward could change what we'd done already or could make events come out any different, that, sooner than later, the three of us would be dead as dogs. But nothing made me look deep inside. I found, to my surprise, that I could go for a long time—several hours, sometimes even a day and a night or two—without thinking any such thoughts and that I could live the life I was living with no more fear than I'd lived it up till then.

Bernard had settled down as well, so when the two of us left the house that Sunday morning, I don't suppose we appeared any jumpier or more suspicious than we did ordinarily. We were a couple of guys out on a Sunday morning, wearing light jackets with the collars turned up and Bernard wearing shades against the bright September sunshine, looking no more like a pair of renegade Indians or murderous blacks than Abbott and Costello. Our shortness didn't make us feel conspicuous either, since the papers had said nothing about anybody's height, and neither one of us was wearing a hat and neither one of us would ever wear a hat again. The guns were stashed with our fancy outfits in the Oldsmobile's trunk, wherever the Olds was hidden that morning.

We caught the Thirty-fourth Avenue streetcar on Cedar. The car was about three-quarters full of mostly older women going to or coming home from church and two or three couples in casual clothes heading downtown, I guessed, for a movie matinee. Nobody gave us a second glance, not even the girls I looked at while they held hands with their boyfriends, though I don't think I imagined the frightened, uneasy expressions on the older riders' faces. The faces told me that something terrible had happened, something people didn't understand and could hardly imagine, like a nightmare come true. A couple of the old ladies wore defiant looks on their faces, like the devil had appeared in their midst, but, by God, they weren't going to turn and run. A couple of the others looked like they were on the verge of tears.

Nobody said a word, not even the boys and girls holding hands, and I tried to remember if that's the way it usually worked on a streetcar—everybody staring straight ahead, looking scared or sad, nobody saying boo. I thought that maybe I should say something to Bernard, something innocent and dumb, something about the weather or one of the cards above the windows advertising Juicy Fruit gum and Pepsodent toothpaste or some good-looking girl we might pass on the street, but nothing came to mind. Nothing occurred to Bernard either, because he didn't open his mouth until we reached the corner of Twenty-fourth and Chicago, where the streetcar turned right and pointed north toward downtown and we got off and started to walk west along Twenty-fourth Street to Lyndale.

"Those people on that car," Bernard said when we were on the sidewalk. "I think they were scared of us."

"They were scared of something," I said, hoping it wasn't us.

Walking west on Twenty-fourth Street, I thought about a lot of things that had nothing to do with what we had done or where we were going or what was going to happen to us. I thought, for instance, about getting jumped by a gang of the Phillips neighborhood toughs we used to know and sometimes mix it up with at South or Powderhorn. Phillips was a neighborhood of rundown houses and tenements and boarded-up storefronts between our house and downtown, where we believed everybody was poor and mean. It wasn't mostly black and Indian the way it is today, but we always more or less took for granted that even the white people who lived there then were all on relief, crazy, drunk, and dangerous. Why the LaVoies, of all people, would think people in Phillips were any different from them, I couldn't say, except that most everybody in *our* immediate neighborhood seemed to have a job and a halfway decent place to live, and it was unusual for someone on Longfellow, present company excluded, to get in serious trouble with the law. As a matter of fact, we were the only ones we knew who were on relief, crazy, drunk, and dangerous, but then you never look at yourself the same way you look at others.

At any rate, the thought occurred to me, walking along Twenty-fourth between Chicago and Lyndale, that maybe it wasn't the cops we ought to be worried about right then, it was guys who were a lot like us.

We didn't see any cops. I figured that if they were looking for Indians or Negroes, they'd be focusing their attention farther north, around Franklin Avenue, or south, along Fourth. In those days, like I said, Phillips didn't have a lot of either, it mostly belonged to white trash like ourselves. But what we saw of the locals that bright Sunday noon wasn't very threatening—older people in twos or threes on their way home from church, a few kids riding up and down along the sidewalk on bikes with playing cards clothespinned to the spokes, a fellow in a shapeless sweater dragging a rake though the litter in the narrow yard between two houses.

Between Portland and Park, a couple of guys about our age were throwing a football back and forth in front of a shabby fourplex. I thought I recognized one of the guys, a short Irish-looking kid with a face full of freckles and a head of wild red hair, and he must have thought he recognized me too because he shouted, "Hey, Archie!"

Bernard and I looked at each other as we walked past, and the guy shouted, "Archie, you asshole! Suck my dick, why doncha!" I was tempted to break stride just long enough to push his ugly Irish mug in, but I knew that once we got into it, there's no way we'd get out again, so I kept walking.

"Archie, you dumb Swede son-of-a-bitch—kiss my ass!" the guy hollered after us, giving me the finger with both hands, but that, thank God, was the end of it. Crossing Portland, I mentally added the prick to the list of guys that already included Donald Harrison's cousins who I'd come back and kill if I had the chance, now that I was a killer.

The Lyndale streetcar took us into and out of a mostly deserted downtown and then up through the North Side, where there were plenty of cops on the street. Where Lyndale crosses Plymouth, I saw three cops hauling a skinny black guy toward a squad car. The guy's hands were cuffed behind his back, and he was dragging the toes of his shoes on the pavement as the cops, holding him under his armpits and by the front of his torn shirt, hauled him past three other skinny Negroes, who were laughing at their out-of-luck buddy. All of them seemed to be drunk—and two of them, I noticed with a stab of excitement, were wearing fedoras. Bernard noticed the hats too.

"That's those cheap ones niggers buy," he whispered. I thought the hats looked a lot like ours.

The few people sitting on our side of the car all watched the cops and the Negroes, and no one paid the slightest attention to the two of us. We might have been ghosts passing invisibly among them.

I saw at least three more squad cars in the next two blocks, and then we didn't see any at all. I thought, *There aren't many people who I'm glad I'm not, but a Negro is one of them.* I thought about Jake MacDill, who got out of the Army about the same time I did. Jake always said he was going back to Kansas City when he was discharged, so I pictured him and his pals sitting around at night smoking dope and drinking cheap wine, and thought that, while Jake wasn't a bad guy at all, I'd bet my summer's robbery income that he and his pals are either in jail or on their way by this time. Black people seemed to attract bad luck and trouble like magnets.

A few minutes later, Bernard jabbed an elbow in my ribs and nodded toward a squat brick building with a fake stone front and no windows and a turned-off neon sign over its red double doors that said NORTH SIDE CLUB. It was Bunny Augustine's joint on West Broadway. I thought about the Old Man going in and out the back door with Bunny's other goons and recalled Bernard's cock-and-bull story about one of Bunny's girls going down on him in the men's room. *What a bunch of goddamn losers we are, us LaVoies,* I thought. At that moment, I hated the Old Man, and I hated Bernard, and I hated myself for being part of those sorry lives.

I noticed there weren't any cops in front of Bunny's place and remembered the Old Man's words about Bunny never stooping to kill a cop who wasn't trying to screw him. No, it hadn't been Bunny Augustine who killed Patrolman Fredriksen. It had been a gang of wild-ass assassins.

The streetcar seemed to take forever to get up to Brooklyn Center, and by the time we hopped off and found our way to that drugstore, it was twenty after twelve. We looked around the all-but-empty soda fountain and went back outside and saw Jack behind the wheel of the Olds in an alley, waiting.

When we climbed in, he stared straight ahead out the windshield and asked if we'd stopped for lunch and a couple of beers or something. Bernard said we'd almost gotten in a fight walking through Phillips, and Jack said it was a good thing we hadn't. By that time, my head was starting to hurt, and I didn't feel so calm anymore, so I didn't bother to qualify Bernard's exaggerated account. It occurred to me to ask about the bum taillight, and Jack said he'd taken care of it. Without going into detail, he said he'd replaced the defective bulb.

I was already thinking I wanted to get the hell out of the city and find some place dark and quiet where none of us had ever been and where no one would ever think to look for us.

Jack drove across a double set of railroad tracks behind a bank of white grain elevators and pulled into an empty shed, where the only light was the dust-speckled streaks of sunshine slanting through cracks in the rotting lumber walls.

Jack got out and removed a pair of stolen plates from the trunk, replaced the plates that were already on the car, and tossed the old plates in the trunk. He also pulled out four or five heavy-looking gun belts, the kind you strapped across your chest and shoulders, each bristling with forty-five-caliber bullets, and laid them on the floor of the back seat. He didn't say where he'd acquired the belts, which made me think of Mexican banditos in the movies, and said we'd put them on only if we got in a shootout with the cops. *We may be short of food and money*, I thought, *but we'll never run out of ammo.*

When Bernard asked when we were going to head north, Jack said we were heading north already, we were just lying low until it got dark enough to go the rest of the way.

"We can't paint the car here—it would take too long," Jack said. "That means we got to travel after dark until we can do it tomorrow."

I thought about Jack's plan and wondered if it was a good idea to drive the Olds at all. I knew the eyewitness accounts mentioned a Buick and a Packard, but I would have felt better driving something other than the Olds, which could, after all, be mistaken for a Buick or a Packard. On the other hand, the Olds was large and comfortable, with plenty of room in the back seat and a reasonably clean trunk for sleeping and hiding out. With new plates and a paint job, I supposed Jack was right—it would probably be as safe as anything else we could beg, borrow, or steal during the next several days.

Little by little, my calm returned, and I stretched out and dozed in the back seat until it was my turn to sit on the front bumper with a pistol in my lap in the unlikely event anyone made the mistake of bothering us in that shed.

"You were so fucking lucky," Meslow told me twenty years later. "Not half-a-mile west along those same damn tracks a pair of sheriff's deputies jumped a couple of shitheads sleeping on potato sacks in a boxcar. They'd gone AWOL from Camp Ripley and hitched rides down to the city that Saturday morning, looking for some excitement. Well, they found it. When those deputies discovered a military forty-five on one of the stooges, they kicked the guy in the balls and worked him over with their sticks and then beat up his buddy.

"'These are the guys! Fuckin' cop-killers!' one of the deputies kept hollering. 'Let's kill the motherfuckers right here!' He probably would've too, if it wasn't for his slightly more disciplined partner and the other squads that quickly arrived on the scene. Seems the first deputy had been in the MPs with Bill Fredriksen—they'd been roommates and friends."

I'd heard about the AWOL guardsmen before, but this was the one part of the story I didn't mind thinking about again, partly, I suppose, because it made the cops look bad and partly because it was as good as it was going to get for the three of us.

I lit another one of Meslow's Pall Malls, poured myself three inches of his Canadian Club, and waited for him to continue.

"Some kid riding through that rail yard on his bike had seen the guys in the boxcar," he said, talking to himself as much as to me. "They were sleeping off a bad drunk, the AWOLs were, and one of them had smashed up his hand, though he couldn't remember how, and the two of them weren't hiding in that boxcar so much as trying to stay out of the daylight. Their big mistake was having the stolen automatic on them. Every cop between here and Manitoba knew by that time that it was a forty-five automatic that killed Fredriksen."

By the time Meslow saw the two guardsmen an hour later in the Hiawatha County jail, they were in pretty bad shape. The deputy who'd known Fredriksen had apparently cooled down enough to let his partner and a couple of Brooklyn Center cops get the cuffs on the guys, but then the first deputy went crazy again and started working them over with his billy club and flashlight. This time the other cops let it go, maybe figuring there was no stopping the crazy deputy, and when the deputy finally ran out of gas, the suspects had maybe a half-dozen teeth between them and one had lost an eye. That story never made the papers, but there was eventually a couple of lawsuits against the county. Meslow couldn't remember how the lawsuits came out.

The guardsmen, Meslow told me, were only two of about twenty guys the cops had pulled in from various locations around the Twin Cities and southern Minnesota by Sunday night. There was a stolen Packard with four young black guys in it that ran a red light and collided with a squad car at Thirty-eighth and Bryant late Saturday night. There was a Buick stolen in Richfield by a couple of thirteen-year-old delinquents and their twelve-year-old girlfriends, who were picked up early Sunday after having car trouble a few miles north of Mankato. There was a character named Horowitz who pulled a starter's pistol out of his jacket in a St. Paul greasy spoon Sunday afternoon and bragged about killing a Minneapolis policeman. According to Meslow, by 8 p.m. Sunday, there were suspects in half-a-dozen jails or hospitals.

I said, "That just goes to show you how many innocent people the cops can haul in once they put their minds to it."

Meslow either didn't hear me or didn't have an answer to that one.

The guardsmen were the most promising suspects, Meslow said, because of that forty-five in their possession. They were transferred to a city lockup, both of them by that time bloody, babbling wrecks, and Meslow, who'd hurried downtown from a roadblock near the Minnesota River when he heard about the gun, admitted that he thought they had the killers.

"I never believed it was Negroes or Indians," he said, staring out the apartment's fly-specked windows at God knows what. "I thought from the moment I saw Fredriksen lying there in the street that this was done by a couple of knuckleheads looking for kicks. I'd run into a few colored boys who'd take a shot at a cop if they were cornered, but not one who'd shoot a cop off his feet, then go back and put a couple more slugs in the dead man's head. That's something a certain kind of demented white guy would do.

"The guardsmen's names were Furia and Kovics, and they'd previously lived on the same Nordeast block, and, though neither one had done hard time, both were lifelong fuckups. They had dropped out of Edison High School in the tenth grade, hadn't held a decent job for more than a month, and looked for fights in those Polack joints up there on the weekends. After one of the fights, a judge who happened to be from the neighborhood told them to find a uniform to get into or he'd send them to St. Cloud, so they joined the Guard. They'd been in the Guard for less than six months, and already they were about to get the boot for insubordination. The uniform hadn't built any character at all.

"I walked in, and the more I heard, the more I thought, 'Goddamn! This is it. We got the- sons-of-bitches!'" Meslow went on.

"Then I thought the assholes might bleed to death before I got a confession, so I had them hauled over to Hiawatha General and started questioning them on the way. I might have smacked them a couple of times en route, but I'm not sure they would have noticed. Both of them were bawling like a couple of spanked babies and finally one of them—the curly headed one, Furia—he pulls a piece of paper out of his pocket and blubbers, 'Please, sir, call this number. These are the girls we were with last night.'

"I might've smacked him again and called him a lying piece of shit, but now I wasn't so sure. I still thought they were the type all right—maybe the other guy, the big one, Kovics, more than Furia—the two of them together, at any rate, something ugly waiting to happen. But if they'd been hanging around Saturday afternoon and night, drinking rotgut and fucking chippies, then no matter what kind of garbage they were, they weren't the garbage we wanted. And that's the way it turned out. The girl who answered that number was Furia's second cousin twice removed or some damn thing, and she and her friend—the both of them married to other guys, by the way—had indeed spent the better part of the weekend, including Saturday evening, in the sack with our heroes. The girls' husbands, who were fishing in Wisconsin at the time, were pals of the boys back in the neighborhood.

"Furia and Kovics were a couple of dirtbags, but they didn't kill Fredriksen."

The other dozen-and-a-half suspects taken in during those first couple of days were eliminated almost as quick, Meslow said.

"The niggers were dope-heads, buzzed on airplane glue and paint thinner. They'd just botched the stickup of a crap game in the back room of a Fourth Avenue barbershop when they broadsided the squad car on Bryant. Damn near had another dead patrolman that night—two of them. Luckily, the niggers weren't going very fast. The officers in the squad car walked out of the hospital the next day with only a few bruised ribs and a broken arm between them, and the niggers weren't much worse. We ended up charging them with armed robbery, possession of stolen merchandise, illegal possession of weapons, auto theft, driving while under the influence, et cetera—everything you could think of except homicide. They were driving a light-colored Packard, and they were about as dark as you could get without black paint, but they all had chickenshit twenty-twos, none of which had been fired in weeks.

"I knew it the moment I walked into the holding cell at Hiawatha General and saw the four of them waiting to get their faces stitched up and some broken bones set. They were a couple of brothers and a brother-in-law and a fifteen-year-old cousin from Omaha, and, though even the kid had a record as long as your arm, none of them had ever apparently killed a man, least of all a cop."

Meslow paused to light another cigarette.

"That guy Horowitz, in St. Paul, was a crazy Jew who claimed to have masterminded the Puerto Rican attack on Truman in 1950. Now he said he was on his way to assassinate Hubert Humphrey when Fredriksen tried to stop him. Obviously a lunatic with a fertile imagination.

"The kids picked up near Mankato were runaways—a druggist's son and his buddy and a couple of girls they'd been fucking around with in junior high. They were on their way to Mexico, the druggist's son told the Highway Patrol, where they were going to search for gold like Bogie in *Treasure of the Sierra Madre*. Their luggage consisted of a couple changes of clothes apiece and about sixty bucks, a box of rubbers, and a rusty German Luger—all stolen from the druggist. When the Highway Patrol told me the Luger was missing its firing pin, I decided I didn't have to pursue that lead any farther."

Thinking of Bernard talking to the Old Man that long-ago Sunday morning, I asked Meslow if he ever thought Bunny Augustine might have had his hand in the murder.

"No," the old cop said abruptly. "This was nothing like that Oudekerk hit back in the '30s. Oudekerk was a scumbag. Everybody knew he was on Bunny's pad, which is why nobody but the papers paid much attention when Bunny killed him. Fredriksen was clean as a hound's tooth. Bunny wouldn't have touched him with a ten-foot pole. What for? He had no reason."

I was thinking about what Meslow had said earlier, about us being lucky. I guess he was right—that kid on the bike could have spotted our Oldsmobile going into that shed, and that crazy sheriff's deputy could have beaten one of us so bad we would've lost an eye. Then again, I knew it couldn't have happened that way. Those deputies wouldn't have snuck up on a couple of hungover drunks in our case, they would've walked into a deadly ambush, the three of us with our pistols and gun belts waiting till they opened the shed door to see what the kid had seen and then letting them have it with everything we had. If it came down to hand-to-hand combat, I had visions of the ass-kicking we gave Donald Harrison's cousins behind the Tabernacle. Either way, they wouldn't have taken us, not like they took those idiot guardsmen in the boxcar.

Nobody, I knew then, would've taken us straight on, not that day, not for the first couple of weeks, when we were fresh and strong and full of ourselves. Jack, I believed then and, to some extent, still believed all those years later, was invincible that Sunday and probably was for many days to come. I knew there was no future beyond those days— what was done was done—but until then, for the short time we had left, nobody would get the best of the LaVoies.

It had been us and no one else, after all, who killed the cop.

It was good and dark by about eight o'clock that Sunday night when we pulled the Olds out of the shed and drove with the headlights off for a while along the railroad tracks and then, in an open area away from any houses or buildings, we turned the lights on, crossed the Mississippi going east, and hooked up with Highway 47, heading north. Before 47 branched off in a northwesterly direction, we drove east a couple of miles on a dirt road and picked up Highway 65 north and stayed on 65 for the next hour.

I remember all our twists and turns during those first few days because Jack appointed me the gang's navigator, and I unfolded and then folded up our Conoco road map so often you could see through the creases.

Neither Bernard nor I had been around the state very much. Bernard joked that he had at least been as far north as St. Cloud, where the prison was, and at least as far south as the Red Wing school for boys, but the scenery looked different when you were staring at it through the screened window of a police van. Thanks to Uncle Sam, I had seen Kansas, New Jersey, and, eventually, western Europe, but I hadn't seen much of anything in between and had never been anywhere before or since.

In my ignorance I believed that Minnesota was divided cleanly into north and south halves, with Minneapolis and St. Paul more or less in the middle. North of the cities was all lakes and pine forests, south all barns and cows and cornfields. I never said that to Bernard, who liked to pretend he was a man of the world and would've made a joke of some kind, or to Jack, who somehow seemed to know his way around and might have wondered if I knew any goddamn thing at all. But that is what I thought, and, that Sunday night, I was glad to be heading into the woods where it would be harder to find us than in an open field.

Just north of Soderville, we passed a police car heading south, in the opposite direction we were going. Jack was driving and I was sitting beside him with the map on my knees and Bernard was on the floor in back. Jack and I had our guns on the seat between us, and when we realized the oncoming car was a cop, we both reached over and put our hands on the weapons. When the squad car passed, I twisted in my seat and watched its taillights getting smaller, and I saw Jack watching in the rearview mirror, and neither one of us was breathing.

Bernard, who hadn't seen the car from where he was sitting, must have sensed the tension because right away he said, "What? What's the matter?" Jack said, "Stay down, Bernard," and I said, "It's okay, we're past him," and Jack and I began breathing again, feeling, at least I did, that we'd passed our first test.

Though it was dark, you could tell that the land was flat on both sides of the road, with small stands of trees and a billboard and a short parade of red Burma Shave signs appearing every now and again as we flashed past. Jack was keeping to a steady sixty to sixty-five miles an hour so as not to attract attention, and we both knew, looking at the countryside in the dark, that we could leave the road and hide ourselves in the trees if we had to. There wasn't much traffic. What few cars we saw were mostly heading south, toward the cities, their occupants returning home, I guessed, from a weekend at their cabin up north.

I thought about what I imagined to be those cabins, picturing them made of logs and having a gauzy horsetail of smoke rising from the chimney like on the maple syrup cans, and I envisioned the three of us spending cold nights in soft beds beneath woolly blankets, listening to the owls and loons or whatever the hell it was you listened to when you were in the woods. It was a nice thought in one sense, yet in another it made me uneasy. I didn't like spiders and bats and snakes and wolves, and figured the woods were full of them. I'd heard people talk about poison ivy, though I don't think I'd ever seen it, and I remembered hearing about wood ticks and bloodsuckers, which I wouldn't want to deal with either. We were familiar with mosquitoes and wasps and little basement spiders, but not all the other serious bugs and creatures.

The only person we knew who'd actually spent any time in the woods was Rossy Grant. He used to tell us about staying at his uncle's cabin on Lake Mille Lacs. I don't remember too much of what he said about those trips, except that Mille Lacs was so big you couldn't see the other side and that there were pretty Chippewa girls who were wilder and more eager to please than any girl you'd ever find in the city. I got the idea, though, that Rossy didn't really like going up north. Maybe it was having to spend extra time with his old man, or maybe it was having to shit in an outdoor toilet. Or maybe he lied about the Chippewa girls and, in fact, there was no one wilder or more eager to please than the LaVoie sisters on Longfellow Avenue. In any case, what little I knew about going up north I got from Rossy, and a lot of what he said I eventually wrote off as bullshit.

The thought of Ronnie and Janine made me homesick. I figured Bernard was having similar thoughts and was mooning over Judy, who I was thinking about too. I figured I'd spend the rest of my life wondering what it was like to fuck Judy, and I'd think about Bernard actually knowing and that, before we died, I would have to beg that he tell me.

There was no way of knowing or even imagining what Jack was thinking about, but I would've bet it wasn't Judy or even Ronnie and Janine any longer.

When I looked over at him as he drove, his face was lit by the dim green light from the dashboard, and he reminded me of a wild animal himself. He didn't look angry or scared or happy or sad—there didn't seem to be any emotion at all behind the faintly glowing face.

I imagined Jack not thinking at all, or at least not thinking the way I was thinking, one thing leading to another like the cabin led to Rossy who led to my sisters who led to Judy and so on. I imagined him instead operating purely on instinct, like an animal, responding to the police car when it appeared and then responding to whatever might come along next, but blank and untroubled and ready for anything in between. That's the way I believed an animal—a porcupine or a wolf— operated in the wild, working purely on instinct, which was better than thought because it meant the animal wouldn't be distracted by other thoughts and was always ready. Looking at Jack like that took the homesickness away, it made me feel confident and strong. It made me sad too, because I knew that Jack would be the first of us to die.

I must have been staring because Jack all of a sudden turned toward me and asked me where exactly I thought we were. I don't think he really needed to ask—he did it to get my eyes off his face. I unfolded that Conoco map again and guessed that we were between the towns of Isanti and Cambridge, and no sooner had I told him that than we passed a sign that said *CAMBRIDGE Pop. 2,430* and, after another few seconds, we were passing houses and a church and a two-story brick building that looked like a school.

Jack slowed the car to about twenty-five miles per hour, and we drove down the main drag of the town, past stores that sold tractors and farm machinery and a couple of small cafes with unlit 7-Up and Coca-Cola signs in their dark windows and a tidy brick-front bank, everything closed because it was Sunday and looking small and sad in the weak yellow light of the occasional street lamp. Where Highway 65 crossed Highway 95, Jack stopped, looked up and down the crossing road for a second, then turned right onto 95, heading east. When an old man leaning on a cane at the corner bent down to look at us, Jack speeded up, and, though the old man was the only living thing we'd seen so far, I figured Jack was as anxious as I was to get the hell out of there, away from the light. Jack had said, when we were headed out of the cities, that we don't want to stay on any road more than an hour in case somebody was tracking us, and it had been about an hour since we'd gotten on 65, so it was time we got on something else.

All of us were hungry by that time, and the sight of those cafes made me think of pancakes and waffles and roast-beef sandwiches. My head had been aching for a long time, so long I'd stopped thinking about it until now, when hunger was undoubtedly making it worse, and I thought that maybe the headache would make me sick and I wouldn't be able to eat anything even if I had the chance. I knew Bernard was as hungry as I was because he'd gone as long as I had without a bite, and now he was moving around in the back seat, and then he straight out asked Jack when we were going to eat.

"Soon," Jack said, and I felt a little better.

About a mile outside Cambridge, when there was no sign of a car in either direction and no house lights except one in the far distance, Jack slowed down and spotted a dirt road and turned off the highway. He followed the dirt road far enough, maybe a quarter-of-a-mile, so we couldn't be seen from the highway, and, under a huge tree, killed the engine.

Jack got out and walked around to the trunk, and Bernard and I, stretching our arms and legs like we'd just risen from a long winter's nap, followed him. Jack opened the trunk and pulled out a paper sack I hadn't noticed before and from the sack pulled out a loaf of Wonder

Bread and a jar of Welch's grape jelly. Then he dug around in the trunk some more and came out with a military canteen wrapped in canvas and topped with a thick black cap attached to the canteen with a little chain.

"It's all the water we've got till morning," Jack said, handing the canteen to Bernard.

The three of us sat on the rear bumper of the Olds and ate our jelly sandwiches. Jack said he'd lifted the bread and jelly out of somebody's kitchen near the fairgrounds after he'd ditched the Pontiac. He said he was walking down an alley and there was a house with no garage backed up to the alley—a house like ours, he said—and sitting on a table right inside the screen window was the bread and jelly, so he slit the screen with his pocketknife, reached inside, and grabbed both the loaf of bread and the jelly jar in one fell swoop. A fat man in an undershirt and suspenders was standing at the stove with his back to the window listening to the radio and, according to Jack, had no idea someone was cadging his lunch.

Jack grinned and made a couple of quick strokes in the air with his hand and said, "Zip, zip! Just like that!"

If Bernard had been telling the story, there's no way I'd have believed it, but that was Jack talking, so it had to be true. Then I remembered the stories from when I was a kid about tramps walking through the neighborhood, stealing things out of people's yards and back porches. The stories, wherever and from whoever I heard them, had frightened me when I was little and even now, for some reason, made me uneasy.

Jack stopped grinning and said, "We got, I figure, about a 130 bucks between us. We're going to have to buy food and gas and maybe some extra socks. So in order to make that money go as far as we can, we'll have to steal things when the opportunity presents itself. We don't take unnecessary risks, we don't do nothing reckless or just for the hell of it, but if something's there and we need it, we're going to take it."

"Like candy from a fuckin' baby," Bernard said, his old cocky self again, and, if I wasn't as pumped up by Jack and his story, it was because I was tired and my head was hurting bad. Anyway, for one reason or another, the idea of stealing things again, even if it wasn't at gunpoint, depressed me, and I thought about those tramps taking things from houses back on Longfellow and didn't like the idea that I was going to be one of them. I'd had nightmares about tramps when I was a kid—I hadn't thought about them for years—and now I was going to give other kids the same bad dreams. That made me sad.

I would've liked to climb back into the Olds and stretch out and sleep after we had eaten, but Jack, like some crazy magician yanking rabbits out of a hat, kept pulling surprises out of the car's trunk. From under a couple of blankets, he produced three gallons of metal paint and a pair of heavy-duty brushes, and said we'd better get going if we were going to have a new car by daybreak. Bernard, squinting at the labels in the faint glow of the car's dome light, asked him what color the paint was, and Jack said maroon like that Pontiac coupe, but, when we opened the cans with a church key that Jack pulled from his pocket, it looked more like an ugly blackish brown.

Jack cursed. Bernard asked where he got it, and when Jack didn't answer, I thought about the tramps again, this time slipping into an open garage or tool shed and slipping out again with a couple of cans of paint. But why the fuck would tramps want paint? None of this was making sense.

Jack said he'd bought the paint a month ago at a hardware store in Richfield. It was on special, he said, a buck and a quarter a gallon. "I figured a guy never knows when he's going to need to change the color of his horse," he said when he was done swearing. "Whatever color this shit is, that's the color of our horse when the sun comes up tomorrow morning."

We started on the top, two of us working with the brushes at a time, one on each side, and slowly but surely, and quicker than I expected, the Olds' pale skin disappeared underneath the dark paint.

I had the feeling we were making it disappear there in the thick country darkness, and I thought maybe we should cover ourselves while we're at it.

The fresh-painted Olds looked like hell. It would've looked like shit if the paint had dried as brown as it appeared in the dark, but when it started to get light again in the morning, it proved to be more red than brown. The car's original cream color and the layer of dust we'd picked up on the road and been in too much of a hurry to remove obviously had a lot to do with the way our paint job turned out. If we'd had the time, we would have primed it first, or, at the very least, hosed it down before applying any paint. Since we didn't, we just went ahead and did the best we could and tried not to slop any more on the chrome and windows than we had time to scrape off before we hit the road again.

By the time the sun was up, we were heading north on Highway 61 in an Olds sedan the color of a dirty brick. The label on the can said the paint would take at least twenty-four hours to dry. Jack figured, however, that driving on a dry, cool day would speed up the drying time considerably, and, every now and then, he would roll down his window and touch the outside of the door with a fingertip to see how it was coming. I hoped it wouldn't rain.

In 1953, U.S. 61 was the most direct route between the Twin Cities and Duluth, so we figured we couldn't stay on it more than an hour lest we attract someone's attention. At the same time, we were concerned that we would be conspicuous on the back roads, and that the dirt and gravel on a lot of those roads would make the drying paint look even worse than it did already. We were close enough to the Wisconsin border to pop over the line from time to time, thinking that maybe people over there might not be as alert to killers from Minneapolis as Minnesotans would be. We had not yet seen a Monday paper, but were afraid to stop while we were still inside a hundred miles of the Twin Cities. The longer we kept going, we figured, the faster the paint would dry and the less likely it would be for someone to connect us with the killing.

Though we had no idea what exactly the police were looking for at that point, one or sometimes two of us were always out of sight on the floor of the back seat. We changed drivers on the fly, climbing over the seat or sliding under one another, and if we had to piss, we used one of the empty paint cans, then slowed down enough to empty the can on the fly. Wherever we were and whatever we were doing, our guns were in easy reach on the seat beside us or on the floor between our feet.

Outside of a spot on the map I'd never heard of called Solon Springs, heading east now on a county highway, we stopped long enough for Bernard to climb into the trunk and then drove into town and pulled into a one-pump Shell station to gas up. Jack and I went inside before the kid who worked there could come out, and Jack asked if we could pump our own. The kid, who'd been looking at a girly magazine, shrugged and said he didn't care, though he'd have to check the amount when we finished. That was fine, Jack said, and, in the meantime, the kid could show us on the big wall map behind the counter the best way to get to the Twin Cities. We were Canadians, Jack told him, down from Winnipeg, Manitoba, but we'd taken a side trip into Duluth and had somehow ended up in Wisconsin.

The kid glanced at Jack with a funny expression and then looked outside at the car. Before he could say anything, Jack said, "We bought that piece of shit in International Falls, where we crossed the border. The guy said for another five bucks he'd put a permanent wax job on it, but whatever he used ruined the finish."

The kid looked at the car through the window, whistled, and said, "Jeez, it looks like he used a Hershey bar." Then he showed Jack the best way to the Twin Cities while I filled the car with gas.

When I came back in the house, the kid went out and looked at the numbers on the pump. When he returned, Jack said "Say, pal, we heard on the radio that someone shot a cop in Minneapolis. You hear that too?"

The kid said we owed him $3.35. "Yeah," he said. "They think it was either Indians or niggers."

Jack said, "You don't have this morning's Minneapolis paper, do you?" and the kid said that all the papers were at Bill Butler's store around the corner. Jack shook his head and said, "Maybe Minneapolis is the wrong place to be going to right now, Indians on the warpath and all," and the kid laughed.

We left the Shell station and headed in the direction we'd come from to make the kid think we were going to hook up with U.S. 53 going south as he recommended, but then doubled back below the town and proceeded farther into Wisconsin. Jack didn't want to stop twice in the same place, especially when the place was as small as Solon Springs, so we never did get the Minneapolis paper.

A few miles out of town, Bernard said what the three of us had surely all been thinking, when he wondered aloud why we didn't pull our guns and hold up that Shell station while we were at it.

"We're assassins now, not robbers," Jack said matter-of-factly. "Besides, that $3.35 of ours was probably all the honyocker had in his till this morning. Not worth having the local sheriff coming after us." Nothing more was said on the subject after that.

We tried the radio every few minutes, but even when we picked up the scrap of a newscast from somewhere in the area, we didn't hear anything about a cop-killing. Was this another police trick, I wondered, or had I dreamt the whole thing, or was I dreaming now as I dozed off curled up on the Oldsmobile's wide back seat? Bernard was content to pick up some band music every once in a while, and Jack didn't seem to care one way or another so long as we kept moving, and, by the end of the day, we were somewhere in the middle of the Chequamegon Forest, convinced there was not a soul in the world who knew where we were. The brick-colored paint still wasn't dry, but it was tacky now and there wasn't a cloud in the sky.

That night, parked a few hundred yards off the road in a thick stand of tall trees, we finished the last of the bread and jelly and completed our first full day on the run. Except for the two hours before sunup when it was my turn to stand guard, I lay curled on the back seat and slept like a baby.

The next morning, while Bernard and I washed up in the trickle of an ice-cold stream about a hundred yards from where we'd spent the night, Jack drove into the town of Cable, which we'd passed on the way into the forest the day before, for groceries and a Twin Cities paper if they had one.

Wiping my face on the blanket I'd spent the night wrapped in, I looked at Bernard and saw him shivering in his undershirt and his hair going every which way like the Old Man's on Sunday morning, and I figured I didn't look any more ferocious than he did, though the two us both had the grips of our pistols sticking out of our jeans like a pair of tough guys in the movies.

Bernard glanced up and saw me looking at him and read my mind, because he laughed and said, "Public Enemas Number One and Two—that's us, Jojo."

"Who's Number One?"

"Me," Bernard said. "'Cause I'm so fuckin' graceful on my feet." And he did a fancy little dance step right there beside the stream.

"Not so fast, Fred Ass-taire," I said. "I'm an Army veteran. I made the world safe so you could dance and rob drugstores."

Bernard laughed. "Not so fast yourself, G.I. Jerkoff. The war was ancient history by the time you got there. All you did was drink and fuck, fuck and drink, while I was dancin' and robbin' drugstores."

I was going to make a crack about Judy, but I didn't have the nerve so instead I said, "What about Jack?"

"What *about* Jack?"

"Public Enema Number *Three*?" I asked. "He's not going to like that."

"Fuck 'im. If he bitches about it, we'll tell him that high number wins."

"He won't buy that."

"Then fuck 'im again. Fuck Jack and the funny-colored horse he rode in on."

At that, the two of us bent over and put our hands on our knees and laughed harder than we'd laughed for who knows how long— maybe all summer. The silly talk made us both feel better. We were both feeling a little more chipper because it was morning, because whatever might have been coming after us had not caught up to us while we slept. But we knew the good feeling would wear away during the day, and that it wouldn't take long before our hunger and fear and tiredness would make things look dark again. Without Jack for a few minutes, we were like a pair of kids—foolish and helpless and lost in the woods, but happy to be out from under his thumb.

Jack was back within an hour. He had twelve dollars' worth of groceries in two boxes in the trunk and a *Minneapolis Star* beside him on the seat covering his automatic. Hungry as we were, we were more interested in the paper.

"It's from yesterday," Jack said, climbing out of the car, "but it's the best those huckleberries could do. There wasn't nothing but static on the radio either. Jesus, what a fuckin' wasteland this is."

He spread the *Star*'s front page across the ticking hood of the Olds, the reddish-brown paint still tacky, but not sticky enough to make a mess of the paper. The headline, in big black letters, screamed *CITY'S BIGGEST MANHUNT CONTINUES.* Smaller headlines below the big one read *Police Ask Public's Help in Search for Cop-Killers* and *Chief Hints at Fresh Clues, New Witnesses.*

The second of the smaller headlines made my stomach flip, but the stories underneath the headlines didn't give much fresh information. There was no mention of Indians or Negroes, but the stories said that several suspects had been detained and questioned in the Twin Cities and as far away as Rochester, and that because the murder weapon was believed to be a forty-five caliber automatic, detectives were speculating the gunman might be or have been a soldier. The number of persons in the suspects' car was now believed to be three, and police were looking for a late-model yellow or white Packard, Buick, or Oldsmobile sedan with Minnesota license plates. I read the stories twice, and, to my great relief, I didn't see a word about a hat.

Jack said, "Well, they know there's three of us," and Bernard said, "They know we're driving an Olds too," and Jack said, "They're saying that because people think those three makes look alike."

"It doesn't sound like they're looking for Indians anymore," I said, and Jack said, "I told you, they never were. Niggers or Indians—they were never looking for either one."

Bernard lifted the paper off the hood of the car and began reading out loud. "Minneapolis police chief Richard Walsh," he read, "Monday described William Fredriksen's killers as 'the most despicable, craven, cold-blooded criminals' he'd encountered in nearly three decades in law enforcement. 'These vile men,' a visibly furious Walsh said during a press conference at his Courthouse office said, 'are the scum of the earth. It's not even right to refer to them as men,' he added. 'They're animals, no better than wild beasts, with no more sense of fair play and decency than a feral dog.' Walsh is personally heading the investigation, which he said was already the most extensive in city history and possibly in the history of the state."

Bernard looked up to see if we were listening. We were.

" 'The bereaved family of Patrolman Fredriksen and the entire city of Minneapolis can rest assured,' the chief said, 'that I am committed not only to solving this horrible crime, but to insuring the conviction and punishment of its perpetrators.' "

Bernard wadded up the paper, tossed it on the ground, and spit on it. "Who does that motherfucker think he is, calling us dogs?" he said.

"What does 'craven' mean?" I asked, but neither Bernard or Jack answered me.

"We shot the wrong fuckin' cop, you ask me," Bernard said, giving the balled-up paper a swift kick. I thought about Buddy Follmer, about creeping past him on the street outside the bakery, but that's not who Bernard meant.

Jack said, "Enough already, Bernard. The son-of-a-bitch is talking for the papers. The people on the street are screaming for action. 'How come you can't catch these guys—they shot that cop in broad daylight?' and because he's the chief, he's got to say something."

Bernard said, "I heard the fucker's on Bunny's payroll," but Jack snorted and said, "Who told you that, the Old Man?" and Bernard said, "I dunno, I just heard it." Then Jack sighed, tired of the conversation, and said, "Walsh is a dumb motherfucker like all those other motherfuckin' cops. If they catch us it'll be by accident."

I didn't say anything at the time, but there was one cop who scared me, and that was Detective Inspector Harold V. Meslow, who was also mentioned in the paper. Both Walsh and Meslow were pictured, but while Walsh looked stupid and confused, Meslow looked smart and determined, with that long wolf's jaw and sad dark eyes that made him seem like someone who didn't need to sleep or rest and who wouldn't let something go until he was done with it. Even his name, Harold V. Meslow, for some reason made me nervous. I imagined him a modern-day Sherlock Holmes, who could see through lies and disguises and phony evidence, and who somehow knew it wasn't four or six Indians or Negroes in a Packard or a Buick, but from the beginning that it was the three of us in a cream-colored Olds.

I didn't agree with Jack that all cops were dumb and that the only way they could catch us was by accident. I thought, *Detective Inspector Harold V. Meslow is going to figure out it was us and run us down and kill us.*

Of course, I've never told Meslow that and never will. Why should I give him the satisfaction, if that's what it would give him, especially since, strictly speaking, that's not the way it happened—that, strictly speaking, Jack was right, when the cops finally caught up to us, it was by accident and on account of our own fatigue and mistakes, and because of a Judas in the family, and that it wasn't even Meslow who did the shooting once they'd stumbled on to us, that all Meslow did when the shooting started was hold a fucking umbrella?

I've never told Meslow much at all about those nearly four weeks on the lam because, truth be told, I can't remember much about it. After the first couple of days, the specifics of where we went and what we did on the way and then when we got there seemed to blur and run together like the details of a watercolor painting when you brush on too much water.

We'd spend two or three days in one place, like the Chequamegon Forest, then move on. We drove farther east for a while, all the way into Upper Michigan, hid out in the Porcupine Mountains (which I'd never heard of and weren't the kind of mountains you see in movie westerns) then doubled back through northern Wisconsin sometimes following the shore of Lake Superior, which was gray and grim and angry-looking the way I imagined the Atlantic Ocean to be, and sometimes cutting inland and stopping for groceries and gas. We'd spend a day or two in an out-of-the-way hunter's shack, but, more often than not, we lived in the car, which, before we crossed back into Minnesota, we painted again, this time a thick Navy blue, using three cans of paint we stole out of a farmer's equipment shed.

One night after we crossed the state line south of Duluth, we came upon a '48 Chrysler in a ditch beside a county highway. It was pitch-dark, and whoever had driven the Chrysler off the road had walked away, maybe to get help or maybe to get lost, and Jack removed its plates and stashed them in our trunk in case we needed them later. There was half a carton of Chesterfields and a nearly full quart of Johnnie Walker scotch whisky in the back seat, and we took that as well and spent most of the night on the road, thinking that maybe our luck had taken a turn for the better.

Actually, the way I remembered it, our luck had been pretty good, all things considered, the first couple of weeks of our run. We'd gotten out of town unknown and untouched to begin with, then managed to remain anonymous—almost invisible, or so it seemed—while moving back and forth across the three states. If people noticed us at all, they didn't pay us more than passing attention. The back roads and woods of those areas were practically empty. It was part of our good luck to be up there in the middle of September, between the summer fishing season and most of the fall bird- and deer-hunting. It seemed we had the woods to ourselves.

On the other hand, we were cold and hungry much of the time. We relied on small fires and the Olds' heater until it quit, and walked around wrapped in blankets like we were in fact a gang of Indians. The nights were especially cold, one night chillier than the one before, or so it seemed, and maybe because of the way we were dressed, and maybe because we were eating even worse than usual, the cold was harder to take than I ever remembered it, especially when it rained most of every day at the end of our second week in hiding. Worse than all that, though, was the boredom and weariness that set in about midway through that second week. Every day was like the day before it, every night the same too. It didn't matter where we were—in the so-called mountains of Michigan, or passing through some tank town in Wisconsin, or hunkering down in the woods south of Duluth—one day was no different from any other.

It was like the boredom I used to feel in the Army, at least until I met Shorty and Monika. Because of the routine, because there was so much you couldn't do, Wednesday was like Tuesday, which was like Monday, and so on. I'm pretty sure that boredom tires a guy out a lot more than breaking rocks, I don't know why. We were turning into zombies, Bernard said after the three of us had spent a couple of hours sitting in the car, watching a steady rain fall through the tree-tops where we were parked. I had never heard the word before. Bernard said that zombies was what you called people who were still walking around after they'd died.

The boredom and fatigue made our situation more dangerous than ever because we ran the risk of getting caught in the open. If we could trust the occasional Twin Cities or Duluth paper we managed to pick up, we still had not been identified as Fredriksen's killers, and there was no reason to think that the killers might be driving around northern Minnesota and Wisconsin. We rarely, for that matter, saw a police car or any other sign that Detective Inspector Meslow and his men were closing in. At the same time, it was getting harder and harder to close our eyes, to rest and relax, no matter how sleepy we were on our feet. With every passing day, with every cold, wet morning following a cold, wet night, we all had the feeling that time was running out. It got to the point during the third week where all three of us kept our eyes open all night, even when we weren't moving, staring into the dark, dripping woods where we'd parked, imagining men with flashlights and shotguns and high-powered rifles creeping toward us.

I found myself dreaming with my eyes wide open—"zombie dreams," you could call them—and the Old Man or Bunny Augustine or Buddy Follmer or Detective Inspector Meslow were out there in the dripping trees. Sometimes, especially early on, I dreamed about Monika and Ronnie and Janine and Judy, and I'd wake up hard and hot and sometimes ashamed, but then it seemed to be only the men, and then only Meslow and his cops, and they came at all hours, and it didn't matter whether I was awake or asleep.

Sometimes, one of us would start talking and would talk nonstop for a couple of hours or more on end.

Bernard would tell me stories about Jack when Jack was on a grocery run, or about himself and his dancing and his fucking around with Bunny Augustine's girls while I was in the Army. Jack would talk about Eugene, and how Eugene hated him from as far back as he could remember, and how Eugene tried to drown him when he was little. I would talk about the Army, about Shorty and Jake MacDill and, to a lesser extent, Monika, and about some of the places I'd visited when I was in Europe, careful not to make it sound like I was bragging about experiences they would never have. We talked about the jobs we'd

pulled that summer, but those stickups seemed so small and insignifi-
cant and long ago now, after all that had happened, that they weren't
very interesting anymore.

We didn't talk at all about Fredriksen, who, by our third week
on the run, was only a name and photo in the paper. I can't remember
dreaming about Fredriksen either.

One night, toward the end of that third week, Jack, in the middle of
talking about something else, said, "Follmer knew about the holdups."

We were sitting in the car, Bernard behind the wheel, Jack beside
him in the front seat, me stretched out in back. I sat up straight and
saw Bernard swing his head in Jack's direction and heard Bernard say,
"What?" Maybe we were hearing someone talk in a dream.

Jack, staring straight ahead through the windshield, said, "I went
up to him one night outside his house and told him to keep his fuckin'
hands off Janine, and he grabbed hold of my shirt and said, 'Listen,
Hopalong, I got news for you.' He said, 'I know about the Pure Oil and
Cities Service jobs. I know about Brennan's drugstore. I know about
that strong-arm shit you got into at that liquor store up on Central. I
know about the fancy-ass clothes and the guns and the stolen cars with
the stolen plates. I been protecting your sorry ass, and it ain't because
we're neighbors. The only reason you and your worthless brothers are
walking free today is because of my feelings for your sister.'"

I looked at Bernard, who looked back at me, and then the three of
us all stared straight ahead into the dark.

The idea of Buddy Follmer protecting us made some dim sense. I
remembered the days, so long ago now they seemed like I might have
read about them in a book, when Follmer and I rode around in his
unmarked car, Follmer asking questions about the girls. In my current
zombie state of mind, I couldn't decide if that was good or bad, if
Buddy had been an okay guy then or an asshole, and then I figured it
must have been bad and that's why we decided to kill him. The question, of course, was why we didn't, why we killed someone who didn't
have anything to do with any of that instead.

"Then Follmer knows we killed Fredriksen," I said. I thought, *If they found the hat, he sure as hell knows*, but didn't say it.

Jack said, "It don't matter if he does. He ain't gonna tell because then everybody's gonna know about him fooling around with Janine. His wife would throw him out of the house, and he'd be arrested for statutory rape."

Maybe I dreamed all that, but I doubt it. To this day, it seems to make some sense, though it still doesn't explain why it was Fredriksen who died and not Follmer.

Those were the last words I remember being said about either Follmer or Fredriksen, or the reasons, right or wrong, why all of this happened.

The next morning, we drove out of the woods and, for the first time in many days, we pointed the car south toward Minneapolis, knowing what lay ahead. Though nobody came out and said it, one way or another, we were finally going home.

We were zigzagging actually, cutting back and forth across the Wisconsin border and occasionally heading as far west as Mora, Minnesota.

It was somewhere a few miles east of Taylors Falls, on the Wisconsin side of the St. Croix River, when we first heard our names on the news. Bernard was driving. He had turned on the radio to find some music but, since it was right on the hour, all there was was news—and the news was about us. A man said, "Minneapolis police chief Richard Walsh said today that an all-points bulletin had been issued for three members of a south Minneapolis crime family in the fatal shooting of Patrolman William Fredriksen earlier this month. Walsh identified the men as John Michael LaVoie, twenty-eight, and his brothers Bernard and Joseph, both in their early twenties. Walsh said that all three LaVoies have extensive criminal records and should be presumed to be armed and dangerous."

"Jesus Christ!" Bernard shouted. "Did you hear that?"

He was so excited he swerved onto the gravel shoulder.

Jack was dozing in the back seat. He sat up and screamed at Bernard to keep the car on the fuckin' road.

Sitting beside Bernard up front, I thought, *They found my hat!* I figured that Follmer told on us, and then remembered what Jack had said about Buddy. Then I thought, I'm not sure why, *No, it was Eugene.* Eugene had seen our hats and the rest of it, and now he was getting even for everything that had gone on, everything that Jack and the rest of us, the rest of the world maybe, had done to ruin his life.

A few minutes later, we crossed the border at Taylors Falls and, in the little burg of Lindstrom, a few minutes after that, Jack went into a drugstore and bought that morning's *Minneapolis Tribune.* Our names were in the paper now too, along with a lot of incorrect information about our ages and heights and criminal records. Our photos, I was relieved to see, were yearbook photos from junior high and high school. Nobody, I figured, who didn't know us when we were kids would be able to identify us from those pictures.

Jack handed me the paper to read out loud, which I did on the floor in the back seat. I found it so hard to believe that the characters I was reading about were us, I had to stop every few sentences to look at our names again to make sure.

Jack, like I said at the beginning, was pissed at all the mistakes they made, while Bernard seemed barely able to keep the car on the road he was so excited about having finally made a name for himself. I thought, *Well, now Meslow has our names, our addresses, our records, even our family members' names—so now it will be only a matter of hours, maybe even minutes, before they spot our car, stop it, and kill us.* I'd been thinking as much since the night we sat in that empty field after killing Fredriksen, but now I could hear the clock ticking. *The next sound I hear,* I thought, *will be the roar of their guns.*

As it happened, it was still a matter of days before the end, and that meant more driving and more nights parked under the dripping trees. The boredom was gone now, however, broken by the sound of our names on the radio and once, in a well-equipped lake cabin we broke into looking for food, on a fuzzy television screen, along with the faces of our teenaged selves. Bernard could hardly contain his excitement when we were mentioned in the same breath as Bunny Augustine and described like members of the old-time James Gang, while Jack screamed about everything they had wrong about almost everything.

"Who the fuck they talking about anyway?" he hollered. Then he'd be pissed when he couldn't get the latest update on the case because the Minnesota-Michigan State football game was hogging the airwaves.

Then, just like that, it was over. Like some incredibly long trip that covered the same territory so many times everything had lost its shape and color and blurred into one endless stretch of waterlogged landscape, it was all at once at its end.

We ran out of gas.

SEVEN

The day before—it was a Friday, the first day in about ten it didn't rain—we parked behind a ramshackle barn on an abandoned farm off a gravel road somewhere, I think, in Isanti County. The sun was shining, and the sky was perfectly blue, and if we hadn't been so tired and hungry, we might have actually enjoyed ourselves a little.

We'd reached the point in our running where we believed we couldn't afford to be seen up close. We couldn't go into a store for groceries, we couldn't stop for cigarettes and a paper. We still had a couple of dollars left, but we felt there were too many people even out here in the boondocks who knew about us now, who'd be keeping an eye out for three short white guys, who might be able to match our haggard, red-eyed faces with the teenaged faces in the news. True, we'd been slowly edging closer to home, closer to Detective Inspector Meslow, closer to the end, but while each of us was ready to give in to whatever was waiting, there was something that pushed back against our giving up.

For the past few days, we'd stolen what little food and gas we needed to keep going. We'd park somewhere out of the way, and one of us would go off to a nearby farm or cabin or trailer home, and, if the coast was clear, break in and take what we could carry. We didn't bother with money even if it was sitting on the table—all we cared about now was enough to eat to keep us going another day or two. In the evening, if our gas was low, we'd pull up alongside a car parked a little ways from a house and use some rubber tubing Jack had come up with somewhere and fill the Olds' tank from the other. Our luck continued to hold, and no one confronted us. I'm not sure what we would've done if someone had—opened fire and run away? That no longer seemed very likely, but I wouldn't have ruled it out.

That Friday morning it was my turn to do the scavenging, so from that abandoned farm where we'd parked I walked across a cornfield that was now all mud and stubble and through a patch of trees to a small white house we'd seen on our way through. The house sat at the end of a long dirt track, sharing the property with a couple of smaller buildings, a garage and a shed and what looked like a chicken coop, behind a line of evergreens that was supposed to work, I guessed, as a windbreak. There wasn't a barn so I figured it wasn't a farm, but there was a yard and a pair of lawn chairs under a big oak tree and a long swing hanging from one of its branches, which told me that a family lived there and the breadwinner worked somewhere else.

I was too hungry to scout the place out any better than that and walked right in the front door. The house was even smaller inside than it looked from the road and was filled with old but neatly arranged furniture and family pictures. From the kitchen in back came the smell of baking bread that almost made me faint it smelled so good. I didn't know where the house's owners were and didn't care. I wanted that bread and whatever else I could carry out of there so bad that I'd have ripped it out of their mouths if I'd had to.

But there was no one in the living room and no one in the kitchen—just two big loaves of bread cooling on the table. I looked around and grabbed a dish towel that was hanging on the sink and wrapped the bread and a jar of jam and three large apples that were sitting on the table in the towel.

I looked down and saw the mud I'd tracked in and thought again about the tramps from when I was a kid. Then, looking up and glancing out the kitchen window, I saw a yellow-haired woman in the yard behind the house. She was young, about my age, I figured, and wore a man's maroon sweater over a blue-and-white checked dress, and she was hanging sheets on a clothes line. Playing with a stick a few feet from the woman was a little girl with yellow hair like her mother's. The breeze was twisting the skirt of the lady's dress around her pretty legs and puffing up the big white sheets like the sails of a ship, and with the sunshine and deep blue sky and everything shiny from the rain that'd just ended, I thought maybe I'd already died and gone to heaven.

The bread was warm in the large bundle I was holding against my chest, but for several minutes I couldn't move. I stood and watched the woman while she bent down and pulled sheets and pillow cases out of the large basket at her feet, then straightened up and hung the sheets on the sagging line using clothes pins she pulled out of a pocket of the sweater, the fresh laundry opening and swelling in the breeze.

I often thought about that woman and wondered what might have happened if I had stayed a while instead of running off with the warm bread in the dish towel, leaving my muddy footprints and the smell of my fear and excitement in her kitchen. I had a gun after all. I could have made her do whatever I wanted—could've made her go with me into the bedroom, or do something right there against the kitchen table, and then have her make me a big meal afterward. I could have taken her back through those muddy cornfields, to fuck and cook for all of us, to be a hostage that we could use as a bargaining chip if we had to. I could have shot her between the eyes and carried off her little girl who'd make sure the cops never got close enough to take us.

Or I could have laid my pistol on the table and told her how much I wanted this to end and begged her to call the sheriff, or I could've sat down and, with the picture of the woman bending and standing and the sails billowing in the wind the last thing I'd ever see, blow my brains out. What I did though was take the bread and run out the front door and run back through that cornfield and leave her to see the footprints and believe that there'd been a tramp in her home.

For a long time afterward, I wondered if she ever looked at my picture in the paper and thought that maybe it hadn't been a tramp after all, it had been me.

The next day, Saturday, October 3rd, the weather turned gray and cold and wet again, and on a gravel road not far from some houses west of the town of Forest Lake, we realized there was nothing left in the tank. It was almost three o'clock in the afternoon, and we'd been driving for about an hour, keeping to the back roads, but going nowhere in particular. Bernard was behind the wheel, and suddenly he began saying, "Oh no, oh no," and I heard the engine coughing and sputtering above the dance music on the radio.

Bernard guided the dying car onto the shoulder, and, simple as that, our travels were over.

The Olds' gas gauge had stopped working about the time the heater conked out, but we thought we had a pretty good idea of when we were running low. Maybe it was another sign of how weary we'd become, how we'd turned into sleepwalkers or zombies, the living dead. I'd been sitting on the floor in back and now got up on the seat. Jack, sitting beside Bernard up front, smacked the dashboard with the heel of his hand, but he was too dragged out to smack it again.

For a long time, the three of us just sat there wrapped in our foul blankets, listening to the Dorsey band on the fading radio. After a while, there was an on-and-off ticking noise on the roof and windows, and it dawned on me that it was starting to sleet—in my mind's eye I saw the car buried in snowdrifts up to its roof like the cars in those photos of the Armistice Day Blizzard when I was a kid. Everything we owned including our gangster outfits, everything that had kept us alive and going for the past three weeks, was there in that car, but now I wanted to get away from it, to leave the goddamn ugly piece of dark blue shit where it finally quit on us.

Jack must have had the same thought because, after a long, tired sigh, he shoved open his door and said, "Let's get the fuck out of here before we freeze to death." We left everything except our guns and gun belts. We stuck the guns in our waistbands under our jackets and slung the belts over our shoulders and left the Olds like a dead beast of burden on the side of the road.

There was a row of three or four houses on one side of the road about fifty yards behind where we stopped, so we started walking in the opposite direction—toward the east or northeast, if I'm not mistaken. A cold mist laced with tiny ice pellets that came at us sideways in a brisk wind and stung our eyes and foreheads was everywhere in the air. About a quarter mile later, a green Chevy sedan came roaring down the road toward us. When it was a short distance past us, the driver slammed on the brakes, rolled down the window, and hollered something. I never did find out who that guy was or what he wanted, but his presence was enough to make the three of us jog off the road and head across another muddy field.

Tired as we were, we jogged another quarter mile or so—Jack dragging his foot, lagging behind us a few yards—to a thick stand of trees, where we stood for several minutes struggling to catch our breath. Though there didn't seem to be anyone coming in any direction, Jack said we couldn't stay where we were and we couldn't run much farther, so we had to get ourselves another car.

On the other side of the trees, another dirt road cut through the field, running at an angle to the road we'd been on. Another car—it turned out to be a beat-up '39 Ford coupe—was coming in our direction, its headlights glowing pale yellow in the shimmering mist.

"Come when I call you," Jack said, lifting his heavy ammo belt off his shoulders and handing it to me.

Then he hobbled out of the trees, down and then up again through a boggy ditch, and onto the road. With his wild hair, filthy clothes, and face rough with stubble and grime, he looked like something a dog might have dragged out of the woods, but, when he straightened up in the middle of the road and waved his arms over his head, the Ford skidded to a stop.

Bernard and I watched Jack hop around to the driver's window and yank the forty-five out from under his jacket, and then, not waiting for his call, we came running out of the woods to join him.

When we came up out of the ditch, splashing through about a foot of cold water and onto the road, I saw that the Ford's driver was a middle-aged man with glasses and thinning hair. Jack had already jerked open the driver's-side door and was shouting at the guy to slide over, and then Jack was sliding in behind the wheel with the forty-five in the guy's face and hollering at Bernard to get in on the other side and for me to crawl in the back.

My heart was pounding in my chest, and not just on account of the exertion. I looked at Bernard, who held his pistol up to the side of the guy's head, as Jack put the car in gear and saw that Bernard's eyes were gleaming.

"Know who we are?" he hissed in the guy's ear.

Jack, still trying to catch his breath, said, "Shut the fuck up, Bernard!"

But the guy, sounding more confused than afraid, said, "You're the St. Croix brothers, ain't you?"—like he was taking a guess.

Bernard cocked his pistol alongside the guy's head and said, "We're the *LaVoies*, asshole." The guy, flinching, bumped against Jack, who again told Bernard to shut the fuck up.

Then Jack asked the guy where that road was taking us, and the guy said, "Forest Lake. It comes out on Highway 6, west of town."

On both sides of us there was so far nothing but empty fields and knee-high brush and an occasional clump of trees, everything looking wet and forlorn in the rain and sleet. Inside the car, the four of us, pressed together and breathing hard, were steaming up the windows.

Jack said, "What happens if we go south?" and the guy said, "A mile or two you hit the game farm."

At the next opportunity, about half-a-mile farther on, Jack turned the Ford sharply off the road to Forest Lake and headed south on what was little more than a set of tire tracks through the brush. Looking past Jack's shoulder, I watched the speedometer needle jiggle up to fifty, then sixty, the car jerking and bouncing along the dirt road like a runaway carnival ride.

Wedged between Jack and Bernard, Bernard holding a pistol to his head, the guy was sitting up stiff and straight. At the same time, he was shaking, like he was outside in the rain, in the wet brush and trees that were rushing past the car's windows. Bernard asked him what his name was, and he said O'Leary, Tom O'Leary. He was wearing a faded denim jacket over a flannel shirt, and the back of his leathery neck was burnt a deep red that looked permanent, so I figured he was a farmer. I imagined he was on his way to town, minding his business and maybe thinking about what his wife was cooking for supper, maybe with nothing more on his mind than picking up a couple of gallons of paint or a sack of roofing nails at the hardware store, maybe thinking about going to church the next morning—then running into the LaVoies.

I thought, *Farmer O'Leary is one unlucky son-of-a-bitch.*

The guy knew it himself because the next thing he said was that he was a married man and the father of seven kids, that his family was waiting for him at home. Bernard, sitting beside him, snorted and said, "Tough shit, I have a family too," and then, in a softer voice said, "We ain't going to hurt you, we're gonna let you go as soon as the coast is clear."

O'Leary nodded, but continued to shake.

Jack told Bernard to shut up.

Then ahead of us in the mist there was another set of headlights coming toward us, and, at the last minute, Jack jerked the Ford off the track, and the car coming toward us swerved to the other side of the track, and, as it flew past, we saw the white door and the siren and lights on its roof. I spun around in the back seat and squinted out the rear window and saw the squad car maneuvering around in the brush and making a U-turn, then bouncing back up on the track and coming after us, its headlights yellow points in the misty distance.

Jack gave the Ford more gas and the car began to fishtail in the wet dirt and grass, and O'Leary said, "Oh please Jesus!" and Bernard told him, "Shut your mouth—Jesus ain't on board."

Jack, looking in the rearview mirror, said, "Smash the back window, Joe, and fire when you can see their faces."

I discovered to my surprise that the pistol was already in my hand. I slammed the butt against the glass, but it didn't break. It took me three or four blows before it cracked and broke, and then I had to pry pieces off a couple at a time, trying not to cut myself as the car swerved and skidded and once spun off the slick track entirely. When I'd made a hole large enough to fire through, I saw the cops about a hundred yards behind us, their roof light a tiny cherry dot.

A few seconds later, Jack braked hard and made a sharp skidding right turn that took us off the track and into standing water. Then, after some frantic spinning of the wheels, we lurched back onto the road, only now, judging by the sudden racket under the car and in the wheel wells, we were on gravel.

As I bounced around in the back seat, banging my head against one of the coupe's side windows, Jack stepped on the gas and roared off. O'Leary was saying "Oh Jesus! Oh Jesus!" over and over again, and Bernard was shouting at him to shut up, and I thought the next thing I'd hear was Bernard beating him with his pistol. Kneeling on the back seat, I stared through the hole in the broken rear window and saw, after another couple of seconds, the tiny spot of red slowing down and then turning and then coming again in our direction.

Then, over the roar of the engine and the clatter of gravel under the car, I heard, or thought I heard, sirens in the distance, first coming from one direction and then another. I also thought I heard the drone of an airplane overhead, but figured I was imagining things. But then Bernard, leaning forward to rub away the steam on the windshield with his fist, said, "I think they got a fuckin' airplane!"

"Goddamn it!" Jack shouted a few moments after that, and I twisted around in my seat, and, up ahead of us about fifty yards, I saw a dark-red state trooper's car turned sideways across the road. Looking out over the hood was a man in a trooper's hat with a rifle or a shotgun in his hands. As Jack began to brake, Bernard grabbed O'Leary by the collar of his jacket and shoved him forward, practically into the windshield, where the trooper could see him. Jack leaned on the Ford's horn, yanked the car to the shoulder of the road, and maneuvered it, fishtailing and throwing up gravel, around the trooper's car. As we passed, Jack hollered, "Hostage!" at the trooper, who looked back at us over the top of his shotgun (I could see now it was a shotgun), but he didn't fire.

"Fuck you!" Bernard screamed at the trooper as we swerved past, missing the squad car by inches, and jerked O'Leary back into his seat.

Another fifty yards past the squad car, Jack wrestled the Ford back into the middle of the road. But he must have cut back too sharp because, all of a sudden, we were off the road again and skidding along the shoulder and then, with a sickening bump that threw me on the floor, we were stopped cold, tipped almost sideways in a ditch. Struggling to get up where I could see, I heard Jack gunning the car, jerking it into first gear, then reverse, the transmission screaming and the wheels spinning in a horrific, hot-smelling whine underneath.

"Get out, goddamn it!" Jack hollered, giving up on the gas. The three of us dragging and shoving O'Leary, scrambled out of the car, which was lying at nearly a forty-five-degree angle in the ditch.

"Where do we go?" Bernard shouted.

The four of us were standing in the middle of the gravel road, three of us with pistols, the fourth stumbling around and shaking like an epileptic. The two squad cars we'd passed were back at the roadblock, maybe a hundred yards behind us, three men in hats and tan uniforms and slickers with long guns standing beside the cars, and all around us, though we couldn't see any of them yet, were the overlapping sirens of approaching squad cars. It seems funny to say it, but all I could think of at that moment was a bunch of howling cats climbing over each other, one on top of the other, making enough noise to scare the fucking devil.

Jack reached out and grabbed O'Leary's jacket and jerked him around so the farmer was standing in front of him.

"Hey, motherfuckers!" he shouted at the troopers, standing down the road. "We got a hostage here, and we'll kill him if you come any closer!"

The troopers didn't shout back, so I wondered if they'd heard Jack what with all the sirens. Then Jack pointed with his forty-five toward a cluster of trees about thirty yards off the road to our right, and the three of us with Jack and Bernard dragging O'Leary along between them slogged through the soggy brush in that direction.

We scuttled along, the four of us bent at the waist, myself and I'm sure the others expecting to hear the troopers' shotguns explode behind us and then feel a swarm of hot buckshot tearing through our clothes and flesh, but we made it to the trees without the troopers doing a thing. Once behind the protection of the outer ring of yellow trees, we all dropped down, Jack and Bernard yanking O'Leary down with them, the cold wetness of the brush and ground in the stand of trees soaking through what wasn't soaked through already.

Gasping for breath, Bernard said, "Maybe we can make a deal."

Struggling for breath himself, Jack said, "There won't be no deal. They're gonna kill us."

O'Leary started to pray again, and this time *I* told him to shut up.

I said, "They're gonna surround us," and turned to see if what I said might already be true, but there was nothing but brush and scrub, as far as I could tell, on the other side of the trees. The sirens, however, were getting louder, one on top of another, coming, it seemed, from all directions. And now, to our left, I could see a column of cars, like a military parade, streaming into sight along the road that ran in front of us, their lights blazing. Another racket was coming from overhead, and, when I looked up, I saw the plane we'd heard in the car—a silver Piper Cub, I guessed it was, with black and red markings on the wings, coming in low above the trees, then rising and turning sharply on its way back up. I assumed that whoever was in the plane was a cop, a state trooper probably, and wondered if they would drop grenades or tear gas to flush us into the open. I'd thought that planes couldn't fly in this kind of weather, but I guess I'd been wrong about that too.

Then I realized that everything had changed. The hunger and tiredness that had weighted us down like our wet blankets an hour earlier had disappeared. Our hearts were pumping, and there was electricity in our blood. But I knew at the same time that our hearts wouldn't be pumping for much longer, and that before long, hostage or no hostage, our blood was going to be splashed all over the cold, wet ground.

Some of the sirens had quit now, suddenly, one shutting off and then another, and in place of their howl was the sound of car doors opening and slamming shut and men talking to each other in urgent voices, several men exchanging information, a few of them giving orders to the others in voices loud enough for us to catch every few words where we were squatting in the trees. There must have been a dozen, maybe a dozen-and-a-half squad cars strung out along the gravel road, with maybe twice as many men running low and crouching behind the cars, most of them carrying rifles or shotguns. The cops, I figured, must have had a pretty good idea of our whereabouts—we were not much more than three-quarters of an hour from the cities at that point—because they were on us in a hurry.

I duckwalked to my left a few yards, keeping low myself, and saw for the first time another road that evidently intersected with the road in front of us about a hundred yards away. There were more cars crawling along *that* road, their red lights barely visible in the mist, and I noticed that, among the mostly dark-colored cars, were a couple of long, white ambulances that looked like ghosts in the gloom.

"Hey!" I heard Bernard say excitedly. "Ain't that Walsh, the police chief?"

"Where?" I said, turning from the approaching ambulances.

"The guy in the gray raincoat," Bernard said, pointing. "That's the guy in the papers, the fat asshole."

I wasn't sure I was looking in the right spot or if I could make out Walsh from his picture in the papers. Who I did see—I was sure of it—was Detective Inspector Harold V. Meslow, and the sight of him sent a shiver through my body. He was walking along the road to our left, a tall, lanky, long-faced man wearing a gray fedora and a tan raincoat, a white shirt and dark necktie peeking out from between the flaps of the coat. Beside him was a shorter, younger-looking man, also in a hat and raincoat, the shorter man carrying something—a deer-hunting rifle, it looked like, with a scope.

Unlike the other cops moving up and down the road, though, Meslow and the guy with the rifle were walking fast, but weren't running or crouching behind the cars. Meslow, or so it seemed, wasn't even carrying a gun—he was holding an umbrella! Both men were looking across the scrub toward the trees where we were hunkered down.

It was like a bad dream turning into flesh and blood in front of me. The guy I'd been having nightmares about for the past two weeks, the relentless sad-faced hunter who'd been coming out of the woods to get me all this time, had finally arrived as an actual fact. For some reason, I was almost glad to see him.

Several minutes passed without anything happening. I figured the cops would start hollering for us to throw down our guns and come out with our hands in the air, but they didn't say a word to us all that time, so I figured they were waiting, the chickenshit cowards, for more cops, more guns, more cars and ambulances to join them.

The three of us—and probably O'Leary too—knew it was only a matter of time, minutes or even seconds, before they gave us their ultimatum, and then only another few minutes before we'd have to do what we were going to do. In all the time we'd been on the run, we never discussed how we would respond when it came down to this. We didn't have to. We knew what we were going to do and what was going to happen when we did. We knew it the night we killed Fredriksen, and maybe before that.

* * *

Meslow took another swallow of booze and said, "When we found the hat on Lake Street, I knew it was you."

"The hell you did," I said.

"Not your names, not yet, but I knew it was the fancy little assholes who did the drugstores and gas stations that summer."

"Like hell. You thought it was a couple of AWOL National Guardsmen or some hopped-up coloreds or a group of thirteen-year-old kids."

"The guardsmen, yeah. But that was before we had the hat."

Turned out that my snap-brim fedora had rolled under a parked car that, for the life of me, I couldn't remember being there on Lake Street that Saturday night, a Mercury coupe belonging to some guy visiting his girlfriend in an apartment above the storefronts where Fredriksen pulled us over.

The funny thing was, when the cops asked the kid to move his car so they could sweep the street for shell casings, one of the cops, a rookie who didn't know his ass from his elbow yet, I figured, picked up the hat and sent it flying, not suspecting it had anything to do with the killing. Two days later, the guy who ran the movie theater down the block spotted the hat in the weeds between the theater and another building. He picked it up and called the Fifth Precinct on the odd chance, he said at my first trial, that they might be interested. The theater owner, amazingly enough, was a brother-in-law of the guy Jack slapped around at that liquor store up on Central, and the theater owner, because of what his brother-in-law had told him, had the picture of bad guys wearing hats in the back of his mind.

Anyway, to hear Meslow tell it twenty years after the fact, the cops, meaning then Detective Inspector Meslow, knew the moment the hat came in that it wasn't any Negroes or Indians or joy-riding adolescents who murdered Fredriksen. It was, as Meslow put it all those years later, "three sawed-off fancy-pants punks" who'd graduated from small-time boosts to cold-blooded murder.

"The problem was, because it was nothing I could prove, Walsh insisted we check every fucking lead that came in, no matter how farfetched or how far out of our territory it happened to be," Meslow said. "We were getting calls from as far away as Denver and Memphis. People were calling with stories about a car full of gun-toting niggers sideswiping someone on the highway, a car full of Indians with Army-issue carbines shooting up a roadhouse, a couple of drunks bragging to a couple of whores about gunning down a cop somewhere though they couldn't remember exactly where.

"And Walsh wanted every call checked out. Every one of us detectives was running around town, around the state, around the fucking country, chasing down leads we knew weren't going to get us anywhere. Walsh didn't want it to end. He was in the papers every day, and on the radio and TV. I held your hat up in front of his face and said, 'One of the gunmen was wearing this hat. These are local punks—young, white, make-believe gangsters—and I'll stake my career that they're still in the vicinity,' but Walsh said, 'Niggers wear hats too.' Then he said, 'I don't think the people of Minneapolis are willing to believe that local boys, even local niggers, would shoot down an officer in cold blood, and I agree with the people.'

"The dumb, egomaniacal son-of-a-bitch. We would've had you punks inside a week if he hadn't sent us running all over hell, looking for you where you weren't."

"You would've gone up north?" I said, knowing what he'd say.

"We *did* go up north. I would've sent everybody up there, stopped anything that moved between Fargo and Sault Sainte Marie. Minneapolis boys always run north when they're in the soup. They think they can hide out forever in the woods like they were Eagle Scouts. Most of you don't know anything else, you've never been anywhere or done anything. You think palm trees start growing the other side of the Iowa line."

"You never would've got us if we hadn't been on our way home," I said.

So he opened a road map of the state of Minnesota, slapped a spotted yellow hand down on top of it, and said, "Show me! Show me your tracks!"

"Fuck you," I said, thinking of my days as Jack's navigator with that worn-out Conoco map in my lap. "I couldn't if I wanted to, which I don't."

"Why not?"

We were both shouting now.

"Because most of the time I didn't know where we were."

Calming down, Meslow said, "Where were you when you stole the bread out of that woman's kitchen?"

I looked at him, surprised. I hadn't thought about the yellow-haired lady hanging sheets on the line for a long time. It seemed to be a dream more than something that actually happened, and I was surprised that anybody else would know about it. I shook my head and said I had no idea.

"Bullshit," he said.

But I shook my head and said, "That's the truth," not saying but thinking that the episode might have taken place on Mars for all I knew or could remember. And now the thought of it—of the blue sky and the white sheets filling out like sails in the breeze, the breeze twisting the lady's skirt around her legs—made me sad, like it was another thing I might have had and then lost.

I was getting tired of the interrogation—tired period. I wanted it to end like the real interrogation had ended. I said, "That was Finnegan with the deer rifle, walking along the road with you that afternoon, wasn't it? You were carrying his umbrella."

"Joe?"

I can't see her. I'm not even sure I hear her. I'm not sure I'm not dreaming this, maybe dreaming everything, but I sense Ronnie's presence nearby. I believe I'm still on her bed, her and Gervais's bed, though it's not Gervais I feel nearby, it's only Ronnie. Rhonda Irene

LaVoie Harrison Adams Grant Gervais. Like the Old Man said, you'd have thought she was trying to marry all the Presidents, at least until she married Gervais.

"Jojo," I think she's saying. "It's me, hon."

I feel the bed dipping on one side. I can't be sure, but I think Ronnie is now lying down beside me. I'm not sure if I'm lying on my back or my side, whether I'm dressed or not, whether I'm still covered with something, an afghan or a quilt. I'm not cold, but I'm not warm either. The only thing I can be sure of are the words in my head, and now Ronnie's. Maybe we've gone, and all there is left is our words.

"It's late, Jojo, almost midnight," I believe she is saying. "Everybody's gone, and Armand's asleep on the couch. No need to get up. I'll just lie here and wait with you."

Wait with me?

Wait for what?

What happened happened—it happened a long time ago. Now there's nothing left.

Maybe there's someone else named Jojo she's talking to.

But, wait—there *is* something left. There's the grand finale, though again, strictly speaking, it was neither grand or even the finale except for Jack and Bernard. And for the farmer, O'Leary.

The rest of us were left to die our own deaths, each in his or her own way. To say that Jack and Bernard and even O'Leary were the fortunate ones—sent swiftly from this vale of tears to meet their maker in a better place—would be sentimental horseshit, the kind of slop you'd expect to hear at the Tabernacle or from my brother Eugene. All you can say and still be telling the truth or something reasonably close to it is that Jack and Bernard and O'Leary died quickly, each of them dead before hitting the ground, which had at least the advantage of sparing them worry about what happens next.

I don't know how much time went by before the cops decided there might be enough of them to come get us if they had to. I knew they weren't going to open up and fill the air with rifle fire and bird-shot, not with the hostage in the trees with us, but I figured they'd try lobbing in tear gas or drop a smoke bomb from the airplane, which every few minutes I could hear but not see circling around above us. But for what seemed like an awfully long time—fifteen, maybe twenty minutes—there was nothing, not even sirens, not even much in the way of information-sharing and order-giving among the army of cops gathered on the road.

There must have been a hundred people out there, in all kinds of uniforms and suits and getup, some in orange hunting jackets and caps, some in hip boots and ammunition vests, some in military fatigues, some looking like they just got up from dinner and threw on a hat and coat to go see what the excitement was about. I recalled, out of the blue, a party that Ronnie talked about when she was in high school. She called it a come-as-you-are party and said the girls showed up wearing curlers and bathrobes and one guy, it might have been Rossy Grant, walking in with shaving cream on his face and a bath towel pinned around his middle. Funny what crosses your mind when you're huddling under the shadow of death.

It was amazing to think about—all those people descending on a godforsaken game farm in the rain and sleet, most of them not expecting to be there any more than poor O'Leary had, though there were surely a couple of them, Detective Inspector Meslow for one, who'd thought about that moment as hard and often as we had.

Then they decided it was time.

There was a godawful shriek that made me jump, then a metallic voice coming from someone speaking through a bullhorn behind one of the cars on the road.

"This is Chief Richard Walsh of the Minneapolis Police Department," the voice said. The sound of it reminded me of the public-address announcer's voice at a South High football game when we were kids. "I want you to stand up, throw out your weapons, then come out of those trees one at a time with your hands straight up over your heads."

There was a pause, and then Jack shouted, "Fuck you, Walsh! We got a hostage here, and we're gonna blow his brains all over this swamp if you take one fuckin' step toward us." His voice sounded raw and shrill after the metallic voice of the bullhorn.

There was another pause, then Walsh, on the bullhorn, said, "Mr. O'Malley has done you boys no wrong. Send him out here unharmed, and that will be to your credit."

Jack snorted. "They don't even have your name right, farmer," he said to O'Leary. "How does that make you feel?"

O'Leary, the poor bastard, said something that I couldn't make out. I'm pretty sure he was crying.

My heart was pounding against my ribs. The cold and the wet and now the sound of that bullhorn set my teeth chattering, and I had to piss in the worst way. I remembered that half-witted kid at Brennan's drugstore who wet his pants while I held a gun on him and thought, *Oh, shit, that's what's going to happen to me.* It was bad enough that they were going to riddle me with bullets, but afterward those motherfuckers will look down at my body and howl because I wet my fucking pants. Well, fuck them, it wasn't going to happen that way, I decided, and, kneeling down in the weeds and scrub in that dripping clump of trees, I unzipped my fly, pulled out my cock, and took what turned out to be the last piss I'd ever enjoy.

Bernard turned when he heard the racket and laughed out loud. He said, "Hey, Jack! Get a load of Jojo." Then he said, "I can see the fuckin' headline already. DESPERADO DIES WITH BOOTS ON AND DICK OUT!" Bernard laughed again, and I grinned at him, loving him so much it brought tears to my eyes, desperately hoping to remember what he looked like laughing that way, knowing I wouldn't see that sight again.

Then Bernard duckwalked a few feet closer to me and whispered, "I called home yesterday, Joe. That last cabin we broke into—there was a phone in the kitchen, and I called the house when you and Jack were outside. I talked to Janine for a couple seconds, told her we were still alive and close to home. I might have told her Isanti County. She said, 'Okay' and hung up."

Before I could say anything, Jack, who was squatting ten, fifteen yards away and apparently didn't hear him, shouted, "Fuck this! We ain't sittin' in this fuckin' swamp another second. See that shack over there?"

He was pointing with his forty-five at a shed about fifty yards across open country to our right, something I hadn't noticed until that moment.

"That's where we're gonna to go."

Before Bernard or I or Walsh with his bullhorn could get another word out of our mouths, Jack was on his feet jerking O'Leary up by his jacket collar, and when the both of them were standing Jack pushed O'Leary away and, as O'Leary took one and then a second stiff-legged step backward, with his hands coming up from his sides like they were jerked up on strings, Jack swung the automatic up and shot the farmer in the face.

In my mind's eye, I saw O'Leary falling backward into the brush, his arms flapping up and away from his body like he was trying to fly the hell out of there, but in fact the three of us were stumbling out from behind those trees by the time he hit the ground.

My ears were roaring from the explosion of Jack's pistol, but now I heard loud popping noises and realized that both Jack and Bernard, running forward, were firing in the direction of the police cars. There was a shout from the road, a sudden squawk from Walsh's bullhorn, and I fired my gun too, not looking where it was pointed. A few steps ahead of me, Bernard was plodding forward in the wet, uneven brush, and, a step or two in front of him, Jack was moving jerkily on his bum foot, looking like a guy dragging a sack full of rocks. They looked like they were running in a dream, in slow motion, all that effort but going nowhere, and I suppose I did too.

There was a sharp crack from the direction of the road, and, ten feet ahead of me, Jack's head exploded in a pink cloud of blood and brains, and he pitched forward and sideways, his arms flung out like he too was trying to fly. I turned my face toward the road and saw Meslow holding the black umbrella and the other guy, his elbows braced on the hood of a maroon car, firing the scoped rifle from under the cover of the umbrella. There was a second crack, and, as I looked back at my brothers, I saw Bernard, who'd also turned to look toward the road, going up on his toes, bringing his hands up in front of his chest, the high-powered slug twisting his body around so it faced the way it had come, then heaving it down on the ground. Bernard's eyes were wide open, and his mouth made a perfect *O* as he flopped backward, but if he saw anything it was only the low gray sky, and if he made a sound, I didn't hear it.

I might have shouted something, Bernard's name or a curse, and I might have taken one or two more steps across the uneven ground, I don't know.

There was a third crack, and something went zinging past my ear, and, right on top of that, a fourth. Something punched me hard in the back just above my belt, and my wind and what I imagined was my life flew out of me in a bloody arc and rainbowed over the lifeless bodies of my brothers, and that was the end for me.

"Four shots, three hits. Two kills and a crippling knockdown."

That's the way that late afternoon's action was summed up by a Hiawatha County sheriff's deputy in a magazine article written by the journalist A.M. Gilchrist, who I'd ignored when he asked me to help him write about the Fredriksen murder, but who wrote his article anyway— wrote a couple of them actually, published in *Argosy* or *True* or one of the other men's magazines back in the '50s. The deputy, whose name escapes me, was one of the dozens of cops and troopers and deputies who'd rushed to that game farm, and, according to Gilchrist, was one of the half-dozen men who hauled me on their shoulders to an ambulance. Maybe he was the asshole who was laughing in the newspaper photo.

The shooter, I learned a few weeks after the fact, was Jimmy

Finnegan, the St. Paul Police Department's designated marksman. (The Minneapolis sharpshooter was home in bed, according to Gilchrist, nursing a bad case of shingles.) I was surprised at the time, and then later when I was steady enough to think about it that there hadn't been a solid barrage of rifle fire and scattershot the moment the three of us charged out of the trees. O'Leary was down—the cops would've heard Jack's forty-five and seen only the three of us busting into the open—so there was no reason for them to hold back.

When I asked about it the first time, one of the cops who was guarding me in the hospital's critical-injury ward said, "You little turds weren't worth the cost of the bullets."

"Yeah," his partner said, sidling over to my bed to join in the fun, "we were pissed that Finnegan wasted a shot. Four slugs were more than you deserved."

Twenty years later, however, Meslow told me that Walsh wanted us, as he put it, "dead but not destroyed." Meslow said, "Walsh had some cockamamie idea about revealing the inner workings of a homicidal mind in an autopsy, so his orders were, once we got you in the open, to kill as cleanly as possible." I thought about Gilchrist's intention of getting inside the head of a cop-killer and wondered if Walsh had given him the idea. As far as our own shots were concerned, Meslow repeated what I already knew—that my brothers and I hadn't come close to hitting any of the cops on the road.

"Your brother could only hit things that were close up and unsuspecting," Meslow said.

After that, or from the moment I took that hit in the spine until sometime the following afternoon or even later, there wasn't much I could remember. And what things have come back to me are probably not in the right order and might be, as far as that goes, only dreams or pictures caused by the shock and the confusion and the gas the doctors used to put me under for my surgeries.

I have only the dimmest recollection of the cops hauling me out of that field, the ambulance ride down Highway 65 to Hiawatha General, being rolled on a cart into the hospital and then to the operating room, where they took me first.

I remember, it had to be sometime later, opening my eyes in a cubicle with drab green walls and a big round lamp above me, thinking, for some reason, I was back in the Army and that I was being questioned about passing secrets to the Russians. My head was swimming, and I remember thinking my body had been frozen below my chest. There were the mingled odors, I remember, of SenSen and rubbing alcohol and Spic 'n' Span. There were hoses running in and out of my body, where exactly they went in and what they carried and were connected to I couldn't tell and didn't care.

I don't think Meslow's was the first voice I heard in that room. That voice asked if I was a Catholic, and I remember thinking that whoever they were after, they'd got the wrong guy, because, whatever I was, I wasn't a fucking Catholic. I was more tired than I'd ever been in my life, more tired than I would've thought possible, and all I wanted was to sleep or die.

I must have known that my brothers were dead, but it didn't seem to matter. If I'd passed secrets to the Russians—well, I was sorry, but there was nothing I could do about it now.

It wasn't until the end of November, more than six weeks later, that I read my so-called deathbed confession. It was typed up on a couple of sheets of paper my court-appointed attorney, an oily little shyster named Clement Bonsell, handed me before the start of the first trial. It looked like the script of a play we performed at the Cloud, the questions and answers between Meslow and me going back and forth with our initials after the first mention of our names. The date, 10/4/53, and military-style time, 0847, were typed at the top of the first page. It read, best I can remember, like this:

HAROLD V. MESLOW: Can you hear me, Joe? Can you hear what I'm saying?
JOSEPH A. LAVOIE: Yeah, I know.

HVM: Tell me your name, Joe. Tell me your full name.

JAL: No answer. Shakes head.

HVM: Is your full name Joseph Alvin LaVoie?

JAL: Shakes head.

HVM: That's your name, isn't it, Joe?

JAL: No response.

HVM: You're Joe LaVoie. I've got that much right, haven't I?

JAL: Yeah. I know.

HVM: And your brothers, Joe, their names are John LaVoie and Bernard LaVoie.

JAL: Yeah. Jack.

HVM: You called John Jack. Have I got that right, Joe?

JAL: Yeah, yeah. I know that. Jack.

HVM: What?

JAL: Jack is dead. I know.

HVM: Bernard is dead also, Joe. Did you know that?

JAL: Yeah. Jack too.

HVM: Listen carefully, Joe.

JAL: Yeah.

HVM: You and Jack and Bernard shot and killed that police officer on East Lake Street in September, didn't you?

JAL: Shakes head.

HVM: You didn't shoot Officer Fredriksen?

JAL: Yeah. Jack.

HVM: Jack shot Officer Fredriksen?

JAL: Yeah, I know.

HVM: You were with Jack when he shot him, right? Shot Officer Fredriksen.

JAL: Shakes head. I didn't shoot . . . Inaudible.

HVM: What? Didn't shoot? Didn't shoot who?

JAL: No response.

HVM: You and Bernard were in the car when Jack shot that cop on East Lake Street. Isn't that right, Joe?

JAL: I didn't shoot nobody. Just . . . Inaudible.

HVM: Just what? Just what, Joe? Answer me.

JAL: No response.

HVM: Joe. Look at this, will you? Look, Joe. Is this your hat?

JAL: What?

HVM: Your hat, Joe. Is this your hat?

JAL: Yeah, I know.

When I finished reading, I turned the pages over to see if there was more. "Is this it?" I asked Bonsell, who I'd never seen before and hadn't asked for, who showed up one day in my hospital room wearing a yellow bow tie and carrying a beat-up leather briefcase with his initials stamped on the side. He had a pencil mustache and smelled like whiskey and cigars, and, though he was younger and better groomed, he reminded me of the Old Man. I wondered if he'd done any work for Bunny Augustine.

Bonsell said, "That's all they gave me, Joe. Can you vouch for its accuracy?"

"They got my middle name wrong. It's Alvah, not Alvin."

"Okay," Bonsell said. "But the rest of it? Is that the way you remember it?"

"I don't remember any of it," I said. That was a lie. I remembered the hat and a lot of the other things too.

Of course, there was no question about my confession. When I finally came out of the fog, maybe two or three days after that "deathbed interview," I told Meslow and whoever else asked that Jack shot both Fredriksen and O'Leary and that Bernard and I were with him at the time and that the three of us had robbed a half-dozen or more drugstores, liquor stores, and filling stations during the summer. I told him and the others everything they wanted to know, except why we'd killed the cop and how we'd managed to avoid their dragnet for as long as we had, which I couldn't grasp myself at the time, the answer to either question.

I didn't want or plan to answer anything Meslow or anybody else might ask me. But then Meslow leaned down low over my bed, his long, sad face stopping only a foot or so from my own, and said, "Your brothers are dead, Joe, and you're going to spend the rest of your life in a wheelchair. Why don't you make it easier on yourself and what's left of your family by cooperating?"

Then he stood up and stepped back, and I saw Ronnie standing in the door. She came in and bent over my bed and kissed me on the mouth and left the side of my face slick with her tears. She said, "Oh, my God, Jojo, what have you done?" and, when I said I hadn't done anything, she said, "Jojo, please tell them the truth. That's all we have left."

I wasn't sure what the hell she meant by that—"all we have left"— but I was thinking about what Meslow had said, and it dawned on me that he was saying I would never walk again, that what Finnegan's deer slug had taken away from me in that swamp I was never going to get back, no matter how much longer I'd be unlucky enough to live. I looked at Ronnie and said I hadn't done a goddamn thing and then watched her walk out of the room. When she was gone, I told Meslow most of what he wanted to know at the time.

From that point forward, I cooperated fully, or almost fully, with the prosecutor and the grand jury and the lawyer Bonsell, who I figured was excited by Ronnie, though she was obviously pregnant, and even more by Janine, once he'd met them, and tried to do a good job looking out for my interests, I figured, as a means of getting one or both of them into bed.

For the first month after my shooting, I was confined to a private room on a restricted floor of Hiawatha General, where a uniformed cop was always present and where the only people I saw on a regular basis were my doctors, two or three nurses, Meslow, prosecutor Ferdinand Twyman, and a couple of Twyman's stooges, who I called Flattop and B.B. Eyes after the characters in the Dick Tracy comic strip. After that, apparently with the doctors' okay, I was moved to the little hospital wing of the Hiawatha County jail up in one of the Courthouse towers, where I spent part of the day getting used to my wheelchair and was always under the eyes of a guard. They obviously didn't think I was going to run away, but they were afraid I'd try to kill myself before they could convict me of murder.

The day I arrived, one of the guards, after he wheeled me into my cell, jerked my head back by my hair and whispered in my ear, "I'd kill you myself, cocksucker, if Twyman wouldn't have my ass." Once they knew I wasn't going to squeal on them, they'd yank my hair or twist my ears or clip me upside the head with an elbow whenever they got the chance and felt like it. I'm pretty sure they spit in my food before they handed it to me. But I never complained or made any noise or did anything to get people any angrier with me than they already were. It wasn't that I was afraid or sorry or anything else that some folks might have thought. The truth was, I didn't give a damn. What else could the fuckers do to me?

Ronnie came around one day looking very pregnant (which she was, with Mickey Adams), and Janine not saying anything, but drawing all eyes away from me and the others, and once Mother holding onto Eugene and not seeming to know where she was or who she was visiting. When I asked about the Old Man, Ronnie said he refused to believe it was me who was in jail for Fredriksen's shooting, claiming that I was off somewhere in the Navy. She said that Wade and Rossy would've come along if visiting rights weren't restricted to immediate family. I'm pretty sure she was lying about Wade, but probably not about Rossy, who I think would've wanted to see me if he'd been allowed.

But I found the family's visits hard to take, so I asked them not to come until I was feeling better. I'd see them at the trial, I said to Ronnie, and for the first time I really thought about suicide. It wasn't the wheelchair, or the way the guards were treating me, or even the fact that Jack and Bernard were gone. It was knowing that this was the way my life was going to be from now on, that it will never be better than this.

I guess, when I thought about it, I always knew there wasn't going to be big improvements in my life, that I wasn't going to strike it rich somehow, or end up marrying a beautiful woman, or have my own private place to live a long way from Longfellow Avenue. Now, though, sitting in that fucking chair and staring at the winter sky through a small, square window that had a wire grille across it, I knew there would never be a real job or a night in bed with a woman like Judy or Monika or a place I could leave if and when I wanted to. What there was right now there would always be, so long as I lived, and there was nothing worse to think about than that.

But there was no way to commit suicide in the county jail, not while I was confined to a bed and a chair and not allowed a wristwatch or a shoelace or anything else that could be choked on or wrapped around my neck, and there was always someone watching. More than once, I thought about frail little Mahatma Gandhi starving himself until the British gave him what he wanted, but I was always too hungry not to eat what they gave me, even when it'd been salted with someone else's spit.

Killing myself was only one of the many impossible things I would think about, and finally it was no more interesting than anything else that crossed my mind in those first few months that followed my knockdown.

On the Friday following the game-farm shootout, Jack and Bernard were buried side-by-side on that slope at Crystal Lake cemetery in north Minneapolis.

I didn't attend either the private service in the Crystal Lake chapel or the burial itself. I didn't *know* about the event, much less about any of the details, until a couple of days later. I lay in my narrow bed at Hiawatha General, dimly thinking that they were going to have to put the two of them in the ground sooner or later.

During a five-minute visit the following Monday, Ronnie said that she and Janine, assisted by Freddie Halvorson, the undertaker on

Twenty-third Avenue, had picked out the spot and that Eugene, with help from Rossy Grant, had paid for flowers. Their pine-box coffins were county-issue. The "simple service," as Ronnie described it, was officiated by a friend of Rossy's family—a defrocked Episcopalian priest, Rossy told me later—and the coffins were buried under two small markers that were eventually removed because of what vandals were doing to them.

Mother was too weak and confused to come out of her room, and the Old Man was off someplace no one knew where, so it was just the other five surviving kids plus Wade and Rossy and, for some reason, Meslow and Ferdinand Twyman in attendance. There were reporters too, but Twyman had a half-dozen uniformed cops keep them and about a hundred-odd thrill-seekers, or whatever the hell you'd call them, outside the chapel and away from the freshly dug graves.

Both of my brothers had died instantly, as neatly and cleanly as Chief Walsh had specified, though there wasn't enough of Jack's shattered brain for the scientific probing Walsh, according to Meslow, had in mind. Bernard, whose bullet punctured his left breast at the nipple and ripped through a portion of his heart, would have thus made the better subject, though he was not the homicidal maniac in the family, he was only a fancy dancer and a born and incurable liar. Both Jack and Bernard were opened up and examined as part of the required autopsy process, but after that there was nothing else to do with the bodies except bury them.

Lying in my hospital bed after I learned about the funerals, I closed my eyes and imagined myself a corpse ready for burial. I tried to picture Jack on one side of me with his eyes closed and his hair combed and wearing a clean white shirt someone from the Tabernacle had donated, and Bernard similarly tidied up and stretched out on the other side, the three of us looking not all that different from the way we looked when we were alive, though maybe appearing an inch or two shorter if we weren't wearing shoes.

It was strange and peaceful to picture it like that, and, because the three of us were together, it wasn't—at least for the few moments I was able to keep the image steady in my head—nearly as sad as you might expect.

For that matter, it didn't seem any more real or unreal, any better or worse, than what had brought us all to that point and now was carrying at least one of us forward, whether he wanted to go that way or not.

"Joe?"

What?

"Can you hear me?"

No. Yes.

"You're cold. Aren't you, hon?"

I'm always cold.

"Maybe the afghan's not enough. Let me get a blanket from the other room."

The bed dips, then rises, then bounces on its springs. The scent of her—perfume, cigarettes, plus something maybe from a long time ago—goes away as the bed steadies, then returns almost at once, or so it seems, along with the suddenly dipping bed and the soft, hoarse sound of her voice.

"Here I am, Jojo. See if this makes it better."

Ronnie is a sad, almost old woman whose kids have grown up and moved out, whose fourth husband is probably dreaming of younger, riper sex, and whose crippled, cop-killing brother is dying in her bed.

She stands up again and kicks off her shoes or whatever she's wearing on her feet and then lies back down on top of the bed again, lifting the afghan and blanket at the same time, and coming in close, her body pressing tight against me, her arms coming around, closing, clutching, clasping me to her breasts. She is crying too, her tears a tickle of my neck, her smoky breath warm and wet.

"Joe?"

Yes.

"Jojo?"

What?

"Oh, God, Joe, I'm sorry. I'm so, so sorry."

My first trial, for the murder of Patrolman William Francis Fredriksen, was one of the quickest murder trials in the history of the Hiawatha County District Court, or so anyway said the Twin Cities papers. The jury was selected the first morning, a week before Christmas. After lunch, Ferdinand Twyman called eight witnesses to the stand. They were three of the five persons who'd been near the crime scene on Lake Street that evening, the first policeman on the scene after the shooting, the movie-house proprietor who found my hat, the county medical examiner, Fredriksen's widow, and Detective Inspector Harold V. Meslow.

Their testimony, which took less than four hours altogether, was, as you might expect, damning.

A brave young police officer, who was also a loving husband and father of five (with the sixth on the way), was murdered in cold blood after stopping three heavily armed members of a Southside crime family to alert them to a defective taillight on their car.

The officer was attacked while returning to his squad car—shot three times at close range and then three times more while lying mortally wounded in the street, his own pistol still in its holster.

John Michael—"Jack"—LaVoie, now himself dead, was identified by eyewitnesses as the shooter. He was the ringleader of a gang of three brothers who'd robbed and terrorized at least a half-dozen Twin Cities businesses during the past year.

A hat belonging to another one of the brothers, the defendant Joseph Alvah LaVoie, was found at the murder scene. The defendant not only admitted to owning the hat, but to losing it at the site immediately after Jack LaVoie gunned down the officer. A pair of similar hats, as well as three dark dress shirts, three light-colored neckties, and three dark sport coats, used during the brothers' crime spree, were found in the trunk of a 1949 Oldsmobile that had been discovered on an Ottoson County road by a sheriff's deputy about an hour-and-a-half before the game-farm confrontation.

After a short break, my lawyer, who hadn't uttered a peep all afternoon, called his one and only witness to the stand. I'd been taken off whatever pain medication they'd been giving me, so I was reasonably clearheaded. Wheeled to the stand by a bailiff (my arms worked, but I was still weak), I felt okay from my chest up, nothing, or nearly nothing, below. I think I was amused to see the jurors and spectators staring at the red-and-green plaid blanket somebody had protectively draped over my dead legs, like my lower half was part of the crime scene.

Clement Bonsell asked about my mother and father, my education and religious training, and my military service between July 1950 and June 1953.

He asked about our summer crime spree.

He asked about that Saturday evening in September, and I told the court almost everything I remembered.

He asked if, on the evening in question, we'd planned to shoot a police officer in general and Patrolman William Fredriksen in particular, and I told the court no, which was half the truth.

He asked about the hat that was found at the scene and, holding the battered and soiled fedora in my hand for the first time since that September evening, I admitted that it looked a lot like mine.

Finally, he asked if I had shot and killed Officer Fredriksen. I said no. He asked who had, and I said my brother. He asked which brother, and I said Jack.

When he asked if I was sorry about what had happened, I said that yes, I was. I said none of what happened had been planned or intended. I said I felt especially sorry for Fredriksen's widow and children. I said I could imagine how tough it would be for them without their husband and father. Yes, I was very sorry. It was by that time, however, almost five-thirty in the afternoon, and Fredriksen's widow had left the courtroom and didn't hear my expression of regret and remorse. I hoped she read it in the next day's paper, though I have no idea if she did.

When, the next morning, it was time for his summation, Bonsell said I was the "product of my environment," that I was no different from a dog you beat and deprive of food and affection and then let loose on the neighborhood.

"Tragic as it was, what other result could you expect?" he said, reading from a few pages of scribbled notes in his hand. "At any rate, it had been Jack who'd been in charge not only that tragic September evening, but throughout the past year, and it had been Jack who'd fired the fatal shots into Patrolman Fredriksen after their East Lake Street encounter." The law was the law, he said, so Joseph LaVoie was legally as guilty as his brother. But surely the jury could distinguish between their respective actions and intent. Joseph LaVoie was "heartily sorry" for his crime, was, in fact, already "serving a life sentence with no chance of parole from the cruel appliance on which he'll depend until he dies," and posed no further threat to society. He was guilty of murder, but not in the first degree.

Summing up for the state, Twyman said that, yes, under Minnesota law, I was as guilty of murder as my brother. He also said the crime was premeditated in the sense that we were "heavily armed, sociopathic career criminals prepared and eager that particular evening for a violent confrontation—mayhem and even murder just waiting for an excuse to happen," he said. The three LaVoie brothers, he concluded, had "viciously and cravenly struck as one" against "the heart and soul of civilized society, not only robbing a family of its head and provider, but depriving the community of a stalwart guardian." If Minnesota still had the death penalty, Joseph LaVoie would join his brothers in "their well-deserved hell." Since it doesn't—"regrettably, the death penalty was abolished here forty-two years ago"—the punishment that should be provided is life in prison with no chance for parole.

At four o'clock that afternoon, Judge J. Bryant Hopwood asked the jury if it had reached a decision, and the jury foreman, a tall, middle-aged hardware-store owner whose name escapes me but reminded me of Donald Harrison's old man, said it had and that the verdict was guilty in the second degree. The judge immediately sentenced me to life in prison, with parole a possibility, assuming the prisoner's good behavior, in seventeen years. He then wished everybody a Merry Christmas.

The second trial, which took place the following March in Forest Lake, lasted only slightly longer.

I was accused of first-degree murder in the killing of Thomas Jerome O'Leary at the Carlton Emery Game Farm in Ottoson County. On Clement Bonsell's instruction, I again pleaded not guilty to the first-degree charge in the hope of a second-degree conviction, and once again that's how the jury decided. The judge—this time, one Chester T. Marvey—sentenced me, also on the spot, to a second life term that would run concurrently with the first one. He called me an "animal" who had lived by the "law of the jungle" and said my "dissolute, debauched, and degenerate life" was over.

He asked if I had anything to say.

I shook my head no.

I'd already become an inmate at the adult reformatory at St. Cloud, confined to the hospital ward with a handful of other cripples and defectives, so the second sentence did not at the time seem to make much difference. I told Bonsell that I wasn't going to go anywhere anyway, that I didn't have any plans for the next thirty-five years, so what did it matter?

Bonsell seemed to feel bad when that second trial was over. Neither conviction would be appealed, so he would no longer represent me on the county's tab. With tears in his eyes, Bonsell said he'd done his best and hoped I didn't bear him a grudge. I said there wasn't much more he could've done, thanked him for his trouble, and wished him a better defendant next time.

We shook hands, and that was the end of it. I never saw or heard from him again.

The entire six-month period between the shootout and the end of my second trial seemed a distant blur, even immediately afterward. I might as well have passed through it in a state of shock or as a sleepwalker for as much as I could recall during the next several years.

I remember reading about the trials in Jerry Briscoe's clippings and thinking about the defendant like he was the character in a book. He was inevitably described as a small, boyish man who, in his disabled condition, appeared even smaller and younger than he was, who never smiled, laughed, or showed the slightest emotion, yet maybe, because of the stylish woolen sweaters reportedly provided by his sisters, never seemed to be a pathetic figure either.

Reading the clips, I would sometimes wonder who the prosecution was talking about. Neither that little guy in the handsome sweater nor yours truly all those years later seemed to have been large or important enough to have taken part in the horrible events the prosecutors and their witnesses described. I remember trying to picture the half-pint in that gangster's snap-brim fedora, and, in my mind's eye, I saw it falling down over the kid's eyes and resting on his ears. Same thing with the guns—not only the murder weapon, but the entire LaVoie arsenal that was displayed at both trials. Who could imagine that little shit wielding one of those lethal weapons?

I was surprised by some of the things people who supposedly knew us told reporters before, during, and between the trials. Donald Harrison's parents, for instance, said our family had a long history of mental illness. They brought up our criminal records, which I thought was fair enough, but then made comments about Ronnie and Janine showing themselves off around the neighborhood and the Old Man coming home at all hours in limousines full of gangsters and Mother screaming at the neighbor boys who came to the door selling Christmas wreaths. A couple of Ronnie's girlfriends said they were afraid to step inside our house because the way Jack looked at them gave them the chills.

Even that old biddy, Mrs. Wannstedt, found something nasty to say, recalling how Jack and Bernard and I used to hang around outside Cianciolo's and holler "unchristian" language at her and her friends on their way to the Tabernacle. "It was on account of those boys," she was quoted as saying, "that poor Marguerite began seeing demons. Those boys drove her out of her mind."

Oddly, no reporter thought to speak to Buddy Follmer, who, as a Minneapolis cop and a Longfellow Avenue neighbor, might have provided some insight. But there was neither a quote or a mention of Follmer in any of the clips I read.

I read all that stuff and the things said by my family with the strange sensation of squinting through the wrong end of a telescope. Mother had, since the beginning of the first trial, refused to come out of her bedroom and was often described as suffering from "neurasthenia," which I figured was the official term for nervous breakdowns. The Old Man was referred to as a no-account and small-time hood and, after scuttling what little credibility he might have had when he insisted I was in the Navy at the time of the Fredriksen shooting, usually ignored. The older girls were photographed coming into or leaving court, but they either refused to answer reporters' questions or their answers weren't very interesting because they weren't quoted often. The twins were overlooked entirely, which was one thing I was happy about, and which left, for all intents and purposes, Eugene and the in-laws past, present, and future to reveal whatever remained of the LaVoie family secrets.

Eugene was interviewed three or four times before and between the trials, saying virtually the same thing each time, which wasn't much. He said, for instance, he knew nothing about his brothers' criminal activities, that in fact, though he and Jack and Joe lived under the same roof, he hardly ever saw the others, owing to his job and to his church activities and to all the attention he had to give to his mother.

He said that while he wasn't shocked to learn that the boys had gotten into trouble again, he never dreamed they were capable of murder, and said that he felt far worse about the killing of Fredriksen and O'Leary than he did about the deaths of Jack and Bernard, that, hard as it was to say, his brothers "got what they had coming." He said his main concern now was holding what was left of the family together, protecting his mother and his little brother and sister from the anonymous callers and letter-writers who "threatened to burn down the house and hang its occupants from the street lamp." He prayed every day, he said, for "those who were so full of hate they were blind to the fact that the dead policeman and farmer weren't the only victims of the LaVoie gang."

Eugene said nothing about betraying his brothers, but then I hadn't expected him to and wasn't surprised or angry that he didn't. I hated him only when it occurred to me to hate him. Otherwise, he didn't exist.

Wade Adams was interviewed just once, before the start of the first trial, and said he'd been afraid of Jack and had warned Ronnie that Jack was capable of getting in "big trouble." He was vague about why he said that and then went on to say a couple of nice things about Bernard and me.

Sometime between the first and second trials Wade disappeared. Ronnie said in a note to me at the Cloud that she thought Wade had gone to work on a construction job in either Alaska or New Mexico, that the "pressures" had gotten to be too much for him, and that she wasn't surprised he was gone. Rossy Grant, she made it clear, was looking after her.

Rossy was telling whoever asked that the LaVoies were "not half as bad as they were made out to be," that they were "poor and often desperate and cursed with bad luck," and that they were friends and neighbors, and that he would do what he could on their behalf. What he didn't say, but what I knew—what I could see and smell and even feel when I was given the chance—was that Rossy, though he had long been sharing Ronnie's bed, was crazy in love with Janine.

Actually, the only really damning report from inside the family circle came from Judy Oleski (though not yet divorced from Bernard, she used only her maiden name in an interview a week after the game-farm shootings). She told the *Tribune* that Bernard had trouble telling the truth and had a jealous streak that caused trouble between the two of them, but that basically he was a quiet, humorous, and gentle human being. It was only when his brothers were around that he drank too much, ranted and raved, and played the tough guy. "It was bad enough," Judy told the reporter, "when Jack would come by and the two of them would go somewhere and Bernard would come back either drunk or wanting to fight about something. When Joe came home from the Army, the three of them would go out, or maybe Joe would come over and hang around the apartment. I was scared then, when the brothers were together, scared of what the three of them might do.

"When I tried to tell Bernard how I felt, he got mad and threw things around and hollered about how when the chips were down, the only people he could count on were his brothers. He said, 'Then blood is all that matters.'"

Of all the stories the papers printed about the LaVoies, Judy's interview was the only one that got under my skin. Maybe her old man put her up to it, maybe she was jealous of my sisters and wanted some attention, I didn't know. I thought about that long-ago afternoon when I'd thought about snatching her on the street, taking her away, doing what I'd fantasized so often about doing with her. I wished then that I had done it, that I had made it tough on her, that I had hurt her, even killed her. There was nothing attractive about her anymore. She was just one more person who decided to spit on my brothers' graves. But then that anger passed, and all I felt was bad for the way she felt about us. About *me*, I guess I'd have to say.

I asked the nurse who took care of me for a piece of paper and an envelope, and I wrote Judy a note, saying that I'd never intended to come between her and Bernard, that I'd just been a guy home from the

Army with nothing better to do than hang around with my brothers, that all I really cared about in the world was my family. If I had caused her pain and worry and not just something she felt for the sake of the papers, I was sincerely sorry. I told her I hoped the bad things wouldn't be all she'd remember about Bernard and his family.

I double-checked the address in the phonebook and sent the note care of the Oleskis. But if Judy ever received it, I don't suppose I'll ever know. I never heard from her, and often wished I could kick myself for having said to her what I said.

Fuck her, I thought.

Fuck all of them except my brothers and my sisters, Mother and the Old Man, and Rossy Grant.

None of the others deserved the time of day.

Somewhere now between heaven and hell Detective Inspector Harold V. Meslow comes calling.

This will be his last shot at me, maybe the last shot he'll take at anybody, so ripe is his cancer that its color has eaten its way through his skin, like rust through the paint of a jalopy. Meslow comes shuffling round-shouldered on lead feet, his drooping eyelids and gray jowls reminding me of the old detective on the *Barney Miller* TV show. Fish, the old cop's name is.

I don't know where we are this time. Maybe only inside my head. Meslow produces once again a quart of Canadian Club, though he's down to its last couple inches, and shakes a Pall Mall out of a crumpled pack, then, with a trembling hand, strikes a match and lights the cigarette for me. I wonder if this might be my last mouthful of whiskey and tobacco smoke. An hour ago, it wouldn't have mattered. Now it might.

"I got nothing more to tell you," I say to him. I don't mean that as unfriendly as it sounds.

"Yeah, well . . .," he says. He sounds like he's trying to make up his mind. "I have something to tell you."

"You better hurry," I say.

He clears the sludge from the back of his throat and says, "It wasn't Eugene."

What?

"It wasn't Eugene who told us who we should be looking for and then where to look. It was Ronnie."

Ronnie?

"Ronnie said that Wade Adams overheard you boys sitting in their kitchen plotting to kill Buddy Follmer. She said Jack beat up Wade that night, but Wade didn't say anything until a week or two after Fredriksen's murder. Then when he and Ronnie were fighting about something, Wade said the three of you were the ones who killed the cop.

"She told us she slapped Adams's face, but knew he was telling the truth. She said she'd dreamed about the cop's murder for several nights afterward and that you and your brothers were always in the dream."

I don't believe you, motherfucker! Why are you telling me this?

I'm screaming, but I make no sound.

Meslow, hearing nothing, takes another drink and continues.

"Ronnie told Follmer, who she said she was seeing again, that she was afraid you had killed Fredriksen. She did not, she said, tell him that *he* was the original target. Nobody, I'm sure—certainly not Follmer himself—knew that until you told me all those years later. To this day, wherever he is, assuming the son-of-a-bitch is still sucking air, Follmer doesn't know that he was the one who was supposed to be shot dead in the street."

No!

Meslow says, "For some reason, Follmer didn't tell anybody at the time. But then, when Bernard called home from Isanti County, Janine told Ronnie and Ronnie told Follmer and Follmer, lying about how he found out, called me. He said he'd overheard Janine at the Italian's grocery store on Thirty-eighth Street. He said he heard Janine telling the girl who worked there that her brothers had killed the cop and that they were hiding out just north of the city.

"I knew it was you as soon as we found the hat," Meslow says. "I didn't know your names, but I knew you were the punks from the drugstore and filling-station jobs. When I finally talked to your sister and got your descriptions, checked your records, and heard more about your comings and goings during the past several months, everything came together. All we had to do was find you."

Unable to make myself heard, I refuse to listen anymore. Meslow is talking to himself now, just another old fool abandoned and forgotten, looking backward, over his shoulder, so he won't see what's standing in front of him.

I have no idea why he's saying what he's saying. Maybe all he wants is to have the final word. Now at last, when there's nobody left to contradict him or steal his thunder, with Chief Walsh an Alzheimer's patient and Jimmy Finnegan dead of plugged arteries, Detective Inspector Harold Victor Meslow can take the stand and tell what really happened in the fall of 1953, when he tracked down and ran to ground the infamous LaVoie gang in the greatest moment of his life.

Maybe he believes he's repaying me for what I've told him—and for what I haven't told him—during the past twenty years. I lied plenty during our many conversations, but I also told the truth and figured he was smart enough to separate the one from the other.

If that's what he's been doing tonight, fine. No one says I have to believe what he's been telling me.

My name is Joe LaVoie.

It's been a long day followed by a long night, and now there's nothing left to see or tell of except the two human forms lying on their sides one against the other like spoons on that sad suburban bed. My sister Ronnie, who I loved till the end, is sobbing like a little girl, refusing to let go, refusing to get up, refusing to face the truth and forget.

"I'm sorry, Jojo—I'm so, so sorry," she whispers again and again. The words come herky-jerky, clogged with bitter tears.

I won't—I can't—answer.

In the living room Armand Gervais mutters something unintelligible, rolls over, and goes back to sleep.

CITY COP-KILLER J.A. LAVOIE DIES IN HIS SLEEP

MINNEAPOLIS, MINN. (UPI) — Joseph Alvin LaVoie, the pint-sized cop-killer who survived the sharpshooter's rifle fire that felled two of his brothers, was buried beside them and other members of his large, troubled family Tuesday, 38 years after he was crippled during the spectacular climax of one of the state's most intensive criminal manhunts.

LaVoie, 59, died in his sleep early Friday at his sister's home in suburban Chaska. According to the sister, Rhonda Gervais, LaVoie succumbed to internal bleeding caused by an untreated stomach ulcer. "He was bleeding to death for a couple of months, but none of us knew it," Mrs. Gervais said, citing a preliminary Hiawatha County autopsy report.

LaVoie had been confined to a wheelchair since he was paralyzed from the waist down in the October 3, 1953 shootout with police in which brothers John and Bernard LaVoie both died. The trio had eluded police for nearly a month following the murder of Patrolman

William Fredriksen during a routine traffic stop on East Lake Street in Minneapolis.

In separate trials in late 1953 and early 1954, LaVoie was convicted of second-degree murder in the slayings of Fredriksen and Ottoson County potato grower Thomas O'Leary, whom the brothers had taken hostage as their pursuers closed in. LaVoie served almost 22 years of concurrent life sentences at St. Cloud State Penitentiary—one of the few paraplegic inmates in Minnesota's correctional system—before he was granted a parole in 1975.

Following his capture, LaVoie told investigators that he, John (known in the family as Jack), and Bernard had been responsible for a series of unsolved filling station, liquor store, and pharmacy holdups in the Twin Cities during the summer of 1953. He described the trio as a self-styled outlaw gang that adopted fedoras, dark shirts, and white ties as their gangster-style trademarks.

Since his parole, Joseph LaVoie lived quietly in various Twin Cities locations, according to his sister. He declined interview requests and was rarely seen in public. Today his name and history would mean little to most Twin Citians under the age of 50. For decades, however, the name LaVoie evoked vivid memories of the family's violent past.

In 1975, Minneapolis Tribune columnist Harry Hammaker noted that "of the nine LaVoie siblings, four died early deaths—one by drowning, one in an auto accident, and two by gunfire. Two others disappeared—one fighting in Vietnam and one amid the counterculture on the West Coast and are presumed dead. One, Joseph, lives out his life in a wheelchair.

"People blame poverty, lack of parental control, a failure of the criminal justice system, even the LaVoies' diminutive stature. I would add to that list some kind of curse—a dark star or black cloud—that shadowed them for decades. The LaVoies simply couldn't get anything right. They couldn't catch a break. They couldn't win for losing."

Besides his sister, Joseph LaVoie is survived by another brother, Eugene, and several nephews and nieces.

ACKNOWLEDGMENTS

L ike *The Secret Lives of Dentists*, this book draws its inspiration from
an actual crime—a series of crimes—that shook the Twin Cities and
much of the Midwest during my impressionable childhood.

During the summer of 1957, three young wannabe gangsters—
members of a large, poor, seriously troubled south Minneapolis family
named O'Kasick—stole cars and robbed drug stores and supermar-
kets. One night, they were chased down a Southside street by a pair of
Minneapolis patrolmen. During the ensuing firefight, one of the cops,
Robert Fossum, was killed and the other, Ward Canfield, was griev-
ously wounded. The three O'Kasicks escaped unhurt, but a month
later they were cornered by a posse on a game farm north of town.
Two of the brothers (and a hostage) were killed on the spot. The third
committed suicide in prison a year later.

For a lot of citizens at the time, at least one of whom grew up to
be a writer, the O'Kasick saga would forever remain a vivid memory—
like John Kennedy's assassination and, closer to home, the murder of
Jacob Wetterling, gruesome markers of our 20th-century experience. I
thought about writing a nonfiction book about the O'Kasicks the way
I'd written about the murders of Carol Thompson and Jim Sackett.
But I decided the story I wanted to tell about a tragically dysfunctional
family, their spectacular crimes, and their shadowed, midcentury

environment, though aroused by memories of the O'Kasicks, would be mostly my invention.

So the LaVoies are not the O'Kasicks, nor is the Longfellow Avenue in my book intended to replicate the mean Phillips neighborhood streets where the O'Kasicks struggled to stay above water. My characters are mine, and so are my locations. Granted, the LaVoie brothers are undersized and overamped like the O'Kasicks, and the fedoras and hoodlum getup the LaVoies adopt are similar to the natty duds worn by the O'Kasicks. But the LaVoies' nuclear and extended families as well as their sundry friends and neighbors, plus the cops, lawyers, and cellmates of their saga, are all creatures of my imagination.

I wish to thank Dan Mayer, my editor at Seventh Street Books, and the production and creative staff at its parent, Start Science Fiction; my wife, Libby Swanson, and many pals, including Dick Coffey and Jeff Thompson, for their encouragement and support.

ABOUT THE AUTHOR

Writing as W.A. Winter, Minneapolis journalist William Swanson is the author of *The Secret Lives of Dentists*, published by Seventh Street Books, and three suspense novels—*Handyman*, *See You / See Me*, and *Wolfie's Game*, available online from Kindle Books and Smashwords.com. Swanson is the author of *Dial M: The Murder of Carol Thompson*, *Black White Blue: The Assassination of James Sackett*, and *Stolen from the Garden: The Kidnapping of Virginia Piper*, all published by Borealis Books, an imprint of the Minnesota Historical Society Press.